EBURY

ALL COLOUR COLLECTION

365

SLIM &
HEALTHY
DISHES

ALL COLOUR COLLECTION

365

SLIM &
HEALTHY
DISHES

EBURY PRESS LONDON

First published by Ebury Press
an imprint of The Random Century Group
Random Century House
20 Vauxhall Bridge Road
London SWIV 2SA

A catalogue record for this book is available from the British Library

ISBN 0–09–175362–7

Photography by Sue Atkinson, Jan Baldwin, Martin Brigdale,
Laurie Evans, Ken Field, Melvin Grey, John Heseltine, Tim Hill,
James Jackson, David Johnson, Paul Kemp, Don Last,
James Murphy, Peter Myers, Alan Newnham, Grant Symon,
Rosemary Weller, Andrew Whittuck, Paul Williams

Typeset by Clive Dorman
Printed and bound in Italy by New Interlitho S.p.a., Milan

COOK'S NOTES

- Both metric and imperial measures are given in the recipes in this book. Follow one set of measures only as they are not interchangeable.
- All spoon measures are level unless otherwise stated.
- All ovens should be preheated to the specified temperature.
- Whenever possible, low-fat and high-fibre ingredients are used in the recipes. Use fats and oils which are high in polyunsaturated fatty acids, such as corn, soya, sunflower, safflower and olive, in preference to butter and animal fats. Use semi-skimmed milk and yogurt rather than full cream milk and cream. Wholemeal flour and raw brown sugar should be used in preference to their refined alternatives.

CONTENTS

BREAKFASTS

Start each day with a nutritious well-balanced breakfast and you will be less likely to succumb to unhealthy mid-morning snacks. Serve wholegrain cereals with semi-skimmed milk, or enjoy a refreshing fruit salad or vitality drink. For a more substantial start to the day, try one of the cooked breakfast suggestions.

DRIED FRUIT COMPOTE

SERVES 6

50 g (2 oz) dried apple rings	300 ml (½ pint) unsweetened orange juice
50 g (2 oz) dried apricots	25 g (1 oz) hazelnuts
50 g (2 oz) dried figs	

1 Cut the dried apples, apricots and figs into chunky pieces and put in a bowl.
2 Mix together the unsweetened orange juice and 300 ml (½ pint) water and pour over the fruit in the bowl. Cover and leave to macerate in the refrigerator overnight.
3 The next day, spread the hazelnuts out in a grill pan and toast under a low to moderate heat, shaking the pan frequently until the hazelnuts are browned evenly on all sides.
4 Tip the hazelnuts into a clean tea-towel and rub them while they are still hot to remove the skins.
5 Chop the hazelnuts roughly. Sprinkle them over the compote just before serving.

HONEY AND ORANGE APRICOTS

SERVES 8

100 ml (4 fl oz) fresh orange juice	8 ripe apricots, stoned and sliced
30 ml (2 tbsp) lemon juice	450 g (1 lb) blueberries, stalks removed
50 ml (2 fl oz) clear honey	

1 Mix together the orange and lemon juices. Add the honey and stir until it has dissolved. Add the apricots and blueberries.
2 Chill for at least 1 hour before serving.

COOK'S TIP

This is very easy and quick to prepare. It can be made the day before, and kept in a cool place.

APPLE AND DATE PORRIDGE

SERVES 6

100 g (4 oz) dried dates	25 g (1 oz) bran
1 large cooking apple	15 ml (1 tbsp) light raw cane sugar
25 g (1 oz) butter or polyunsaturated margarine	175 g (6 oz) porridge oats

1 Stone and roughly chop the dried dates. Roughly chop but do not peel the large cooking apple, discarding the core.
2 Melt the butter or margarine in a large saucepan, stir in the bran and sugar and cook stirring, for about 2 minutes.
3 Pour 1.1 litre (2 pints) water into the pan, then sprinkle in the porridge oats. Bring the mixture to the boil, stirring.
4 Add the dates and apple, and simmer, stirring, for 5 minutes or until of the desired consistency. Serve hot.

MUESLI

MAKES 14 SERVINGS

250 g (9 oz) porridge oats	175 g (6 oz) sultanas
75 g (3 oz) wholewheat flakes	175 g (6 oz) dried fruit, such as apricots, pears, figs or peaches, cut into small pieces
50 g (2 oz) bran buds	
75 g (3 oz) sunflower seeds	semi-skimmed milk, to serve

1 Mix together the porridge oats, wholewheat flakes, bran buds, sunflower seeds, sultanas and dried fruit.
2 The dry muesli will keep fresh for several weeks if stored in an airtight container.
3 Serve in individual bowls with milk. Accompany with low-fat yogurt, if liked.

COOK'S TIP

A Zurich clinic, founded at the beginning of the century by a Swiss doctor called Max Bircher-Benner, frequently served a fruit diet which became so popular that it gained world wide fame as Bircher Muesli, Swiss Muesli or just Muesli. The original muesli, which he prescribed to be eaten both at breakfast time and supper, was based on fresh fruit, with porridge oats (the German word muesli means gruel) added. In this recipe dried fruit is suggested but fresh fruit such as apple, often grated, pears and berries may be used instead.

BREAKFAST VITALITY DRINK

SERVES 1

2 pink grapefruit	10 ml (2 tsp) honey, or to taste
1 lemon	5 ml (1 tsp) wheatgerm
1 egg	

1 Squeeze the juice from the grapefruit and lemon, and pour into a blender or food processor.
2 Add the egg, honey and wheatgerm and blend until well combined. Taste for sweetness and add more honey if liked. Pour into a long glass and serve immediately.

VARIATIONS

Yogurt Vitality Drink
Blend 1 sliced banana with 10 ml (2 tsp) wheatgerm, the juice of 1 orange and 150 ml (¼ pint) low-fat natural yogurt until smooth. Serve as above.

Vegetable Vitality Drink
Soak 50 g (2 oz) shredded coconut in 300 ml (½ pint) boiling water for 30 minutes; strain. Blend 225 g (8 oz) grated carrots with the juice of ½ lemon until reduced to a pulp. Strain, then mix with the coconut milk. Add 5 ml (1 tsp) wheatgerm oil and whisk vigorously to combine. Serve as above.

BRAN MUFFINS

MAKES 4

75 g (3 oz) plain wholemeal flour	300 ml (½ pint) semi-skimmed milk
75 g (3 oz) bran	30 ml (2 tbsp) honey
7.5 ml (1½ tsp) baking powder	butter or polyunsaturated margarine, for spreading
1 egg, beaten	

1 Grease a 4-hole Yorkshire pudding tin. Sift the flour, bran and baking powder together into a bowl. Stir in the bran from the wholemeal flour left in the bottom of the sieve.
2 Make a well in the centre and add the egg. Stir well to mix, then add the milk and honey. Beat to a smooth batter. Divide the batter equally between the prepared tins.
3 Bake in the oven at 190°C (375°F) mark 5 for 25 minutes until risen. Turn out on to a wire rack and cool for 5 minutes. Serve split in half and spread with butter or margarine.

VARIATION

For a more substantial breakfast serve these muffins topped with scrambled egg.

DATE AND YOGURT SCONES

MAKES 10

50 g (2 oz) stoned dates, finely chopped	50 g (2 oz) polyunsaturated margarine
75 g (3 oz) plain white flour	50 g (2 oz) light muscovado sugar
150 g (5 oz) plain wholemeal flour	150 ml (¼ pint) low-fat natural yogurt
15 ml (1 tbsp) baking powder	semi-skimmed milk, to mix
pinch of grated nutmeg	

1 Coat the dates in 25 g (1 oz) of the white flour. Place the remaining white and wholemeal flour in a bowl with the baking powder and nutmeg. Mix well.
2 Rub in the margarine until the mixture resembles fine breadcrumbs. Stir in the sugar and dates, then make a well in the centre of the mixture.
3 Place the yogurt in a small bowl, add 30 ml (2 tbsp) milk and whisk lightly until smooth. Pour into the well and mix with a palette knife to a soft dough. Leave to stand for about 5 minutes to allow the bran in the flour time to absorb the liquid. Lightly knead the dough on a floured surface until just smooth.
4 Roll out until 2 cm (¾ inch) thick. Using a 5 cm (2 inch) round cutter, stamp out 8 scones, re-rolling the dough as necessary. Place on a baking sheet, then brush with a little milk.
5 Bake in the oven at 230°C (450°F) mark 8 for about 10 minutes or until well risen and golden brown.

SERVING SUGGESTION

These scones are at their best eaten really fresh. Serve them split and spread with a little low-fat soft cheese and sugar-reduced jam.

MUSHROOMS WITH BACON

SERVES 2

100 g (4 oz) oyster or flat black mushrooms, trimmed	pepper, to taste
30 ml (2 tbsp) Greek strained yogurt	2 rashers streaky bacon
5 ml (1 tsp) Worcestershire sauce	Ciabatta or French bread, warmed
	parsley, to garnish

1 Cook the mushrooms with the yogurt, Worcestershire sauce and pepper in a small saucepan until just tender.
2 Meanwhile, grill the bacon until crisp. Cool slightly and snip into small pieces.
3 Serve the mushrooms on slices of warmed bread, topped with the bacon and garnished with parsley.

SERVING SUGGESTION

If available, serve this savoury breakfast dish on slices of Ciabatta, an Italian bread made with olive oil. It is very light and has an interesting texture.

BREAKFAST PANCAKES

MAKES 4

25 g (1 oz) plain wholemeal flour	polyunsaturated margarine for frying
25 g (1 oz) medium oatmeal	100 g (4 oz) back bacon, grilled and chopped
salt and pepper	2 tomatoes, sliced and grilled
4 eggs, beaten	
250 ml (9 fl oz) semi-skimmed milk	

1 Put the flour, oatmeal, salt and 15 ml (1 tbsp) egg into a bowl. Gradually add 150 ml (¼ pint) milk to form a smooth batter.
2 Heat a little margarine in a 20 cm (8 inch) non-stick frying pan. When hot, pour in 45 ml (3 tbsp) of the batter, tilting the pan to cover the base. Cook until the pancake moves freely, turn over and cook until golden. Repeat to make 4 pancakes.
3 Beat together the remaining eggs, milk and salt and pepper. Scramble in a small saucepan over gentle heat, stirring until the egg starts to set.
4 Place spoonfuls of the egg into the pancakes, add the bacon and tomato slices. Fold the pancakes over. Serve warm as a snack or for breakfast.

SERVING SUGGESTION

There's no need to save pancakes for Shrove Tuesday. They are quick and easy to prepare, and good at any time of day. This breakfast recipe uses a mix of wholemeal flour and oatmeal and makes a welcome change from toast topped with grilled bacon, scrambled eggs and tomato slices.

GLAMORGAN SAUSAGES

MAKES 8

175 g (6 oz) fresh breadcrumbs	salt and pepper
100 g (4 oz) Caerphilly cheese, grated	2 eggs, separated
1 small leek, very finely chopped	about 60 ml (4 tbsp) semi-skimmed milk to mix
15 ml (1 tbsp) chopped parsley	plain flour for coating
large pinch of mustard powder	15 ml (1 tbsp) polyunsaturated oil
	15 g (½ oz) butter or polyunsaturated margarine

1 In a large bowl, mix together the breadcrumbs, cheese, leek, parsley and mustard. Season to taste. Add 1 whole egg and 1 egg yolk and mix thoroughly. Add enough milk to bind the mixture together.
2 Divide the mixture into 8 and shape into sausages.
3 Beat the remaining egg white on a plate with a fork until frothy. Dip the sausages into the egg white, then roll in the flour to coat.
4 Heat the oil and the butter or margarine in a non-stick frying pan and fry the sausages for 5-10 minutes until golden brown. Serve hot or cold.

COOK'S TIP

These were the poor man's meatless substitute for the real thing, and are today an interesting dish for vegetarians.

HERRINGS IN OATMEAL

SERVES 2

2 medium herrings, cleaned, heads and tails removed	15 ml (1 tbsp) polyunsaturated oil
salt and pepper	15 g (½ oz) butter or polyunsaturated margarine
50 g (2 oz) medium oatmeal	lemon wedges, to serve

1 To remove the backbone of the fish, put on a board, cut side down, and press lightly with the fingers down the middle of the back. Turn the fish over and ease the backbone up with the fingers. Fold the fish in half. Season well and coat with the oatmeal.
2 Heat the oil and butter or margarine in a large non-stick frying pan, and fry the herrings for about 5 minutes on each side. Drain well before serving hot, with lemon wedges.

COOK'S TIP

The oatmeal in this dish adds to its bulk and fibre as well as absorbing the rich oiliness of the herrings. Herrings are economical fare, in season all year and at their best from June to September. Ask your fishmonger to prepare them.

SMOKED FISH KEDGEREE

SERVES 4

175 g (6 oz) long grain brown rice	1 egg, hard-boiled and chopped
salt and pepper	30 ml (2 tbsp) chopped parsley
275 g (10 oz) smoked haddock	juice of ½ lemon
25 g (1 oz) butter or polyunsaturated margarine	

1 Put the rice in a large saucepan of boiling salted water and cook for about 35 minutes or according to packet instructions until tender.
2 Meanwhile place the haddock in a pan, cover with water and poach for about 15 minutes.
3 Drain the fish well, then flake the flesh, discarding the skin and bones.
4 Drain the rice well. Melt the butter or margarine in a frying pan, add the rice, haddock, egg and parsley and stir over moderate heat for a few minutes until warmed through. Add the lemon juice and pepper to taste, turn into a warmed serving dish and serve immediately.

SOUPS

Flavoursome homemade soups are nutritious and satisfying. For optimium flavour make your own stock – keep a supply in the freezer – or use one of the low-salt stock products now available. Here you will find plenty of ideas for light refreshing starters, as well as more sustaining soups which make tasty meals in themselves.

ICED TOMATO AND BASIL SOUP

SERVES 4

450 g (1 lb) tomatoes, chopped	600 ml (1 pint) chicken stock
1 small onion, chopped	salt and pepper
15 ml (1 tbsp) tomato purée	30 ml (2 tbsp) soured cream, or smetana to garnish (optional)
15 ml (1 tbsp) chopped basil	

1 Purée the tomatoes, onion, tomato purée and basil in a blender or food processor. Pass through a sieve into a medium saucepan, then stir in the stock and heat gently to remove froth. Season to taste.
2 Chill before serving, garnished with swirls of soured cream or smetana, if liked.

COOK'S TIP

A refreshing chilled soup, best made when tomatoes are at their cheapest and most flavoursome. The pungency of fresh basil adds a delicious herbiness.

CHILLED ASPARAGUS SOUP

SERVES 6

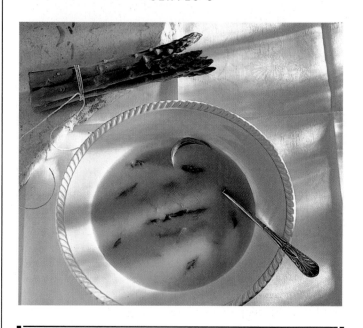

700 g (1½ lb) asparagus	1.4 litres (2½ pints) chicken stock
salt and pepper	150 ml (5 fl oz) low-fat natural yogurt
25 g (1 oz) butter or polyunsaturated margarine	grated lemon rind, to garnish
2 onions, chopped	

1 Cut the heads off the asparagus and simmer them very gently in salted water for 3-5 minutes, until just tender. Drain well and refresh with cold water.
2 Scrape the asparagus stalks with a potato peeler or knife and cut off the woody ends. Thinly slice the stalks.
3 Melt the butter or margarine in a large saucepan. Add the asparagus stalks and onions, cover and cook for 5-10 minutes, until beginning to soften.
4 Add the stock and season to taste. Bring to the boil cover and simmer for 30-40 minutes, until the asparagus and onions are tender.
5 Allow to cool slightly, then purée in a blender or food processor until smooth. Sieve to remove any stringy particles, then stir in the yogurt.
6 Chill in the refrigerator for 2-3 hours. Serve, garnished with the reserved asparagus tips and lemon rind.

ICED SWEET PEPPER SOUP

SERVES 4

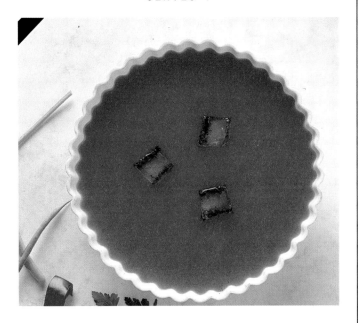

60 ml (4 tbsp) chopped coriander	900 ml (1½ pints) vegetable or chicken stock
225 g (8 oz) red peppers, seeded and sliced	150 ml (¼ pint) semi-skimmed milk
125 g (4 oz) onion, sliced	salt and pepper
225 g (8 oz) ripe tomatoes, sliced	

1 To make the coriander ice cubes, put the chopped coriander into an ice-cube tray, top up with water and freeze.
2 Place the peppers in a large saucepan with the onion, tomatoes and stock. Bring to the boil, then lower the heat, cover and simmer for about 15 minutes or until the vegetables are tender. Drain, reserving the liquid.
3 Sieve the vegetables, or purée them in a blender or food processor, then sieve the purée to remove the tomato seeds.
4 Combine the reserved liquid, vegetable purée and milk in a bowl with seasoning to taste. Cool for 30 minutes, then chill in the refrigerator for at least 2 hours before serving, with coriander ice cubes.

COOK'S TIP

Do not confuse the herb coriander with the spice of the same name. In this recipe, the fresh herb is used. Looking rather like frondy parsley, it is available at many supermarkets and also at continental and oriental specialist shops. Its flavour is highly aromatic, much stronger than parsley. The spice coriander is used extensively in Indian cookery; it is available as whole seeds and in ground form. The herb and the spice are not interchangeable in recipes.

ICED PEA AND MINT SOUP

SERVES 4

225 g (8 oz) green split peas	2 bay leaves
2 litres (3½ pints) unsalted vegetable stock or water	salt and pepper
1 cooking apple	90 ml (3 fl oz) low-fat natural yogurt, to serve
25 g (1 oz) mint leaves	mint sprigs, to garnish
juice of lemon	

1 Rinse the split peas well under cold running water. Put the peas in a large saucepan and add the stock or water.
2 Bring the liquid slowly to the boil, then skim off any scum with a slotted spoon.
3 Peel and core the cooking apple, then chop roughly. Add to the pan with half of the mint, the lemon juice and the bay leaves.
4 Half cover the pan with a lid and simmer gently for about 1 hour or until the peas are very tender.
5 Discard the bay leaves. Work the soup to a purée in a blender or food processor, then work through a sieve into a bowl, pressing with the back of a metal spoon. Add the remaining mint, with salt and pepper to taste. Leave until cold, then chill in the refrigerator for at least 4 hours, preferably overnight.
6 To serve, taste and adjust seasoning, then pour into individual bowls and swirl with yogurt. Garnish with mint sprigs. Serve chilled.

COOK'S TIP

Split peas are most often associated with warming winter soups like the famous split pea and ham soup from northern England. This recipe for iced split pea soup is cool and delicate, quite the opposite. You can buy two types of split pea, green and yellow; either can be used for this soup, but the green ones give a prettier colour. Both kinds have been split through the middle, as the name suggests, then skinned. This makes them easy to cook – and ideal for puréed soups.

CHILLED CUCUMBER SOUP

SERVES 4

1 medium cucumber, trimmed	30 ml (2 tbsp) chopped mint or snipped chives
300 ml (½ pint) low-fat natural yogurt	salt and pepper
1 small garlic clove, crushed	300 ml (½ pint) semi-skimmed milk
30 ml (2 tbsp) wine vinegar	mint sprigs, to garnish

1 Grate the unpeeled cucumber into a bowl, using the finest side of a conical or box grater.
2 Stir in the yogurt, crushed garlic, vinegar and mint or chives. Add seasoning to taste and chill in the refrigerator for 1 hour.
3 Just before serving, stir in the milk, then taste and adjust seasoning. Spoon into individual soup bowls and garnish with sprigs of mint.

SERVING SUGGESTION

This soup can be make in advance and is ideal served before the main course of a barbecue.

CREAM OF LEMON SOUP

SERVES 6

25 g (1 oz) butter or polyunsaturated margarine	1.1 litres (2 pints) chicken stock
2 onions, thinly sliced	2 bay leaves
75 g (3 oz) carrot, thinly sliced	salt and pepper
75 g (3 oz) celery, thinly sliced	150 ml (5 fl oz) single cream or smetana
2 lemons	spring onion tops or chives and lemon slices, to garnish

1 Melt the butter or margarine in a large saucepan and add the vegetables. Cover and cook gently for 10-15 minutes until the vegetables begin to soften.
2 Meanwhile, thinly pare the lemons using a potato peeler. Blanch the rinds in boiling water for 1 minute, then drain. Squeeze the juice from the lemons to give 75-90 ml (5-6 tbsp).
3 Add the lemon rind and juice, stock and bay leaves to the pan; season. Bring to the boil, cover and simmer for 40 minutes or until the carrots and celery are both very soft.
4 Cool the soup a little, remove the bay leaves, then purée the pan contents in a blender or food processor until quite smooth.
5 Return the soup to the clean pan, reheat gently, stirring in the cream or smetana. Do not boil. Adjust seasoning to taste. Serve hot or chilled, garnished with chopped spring onions or chives and lemon slices. Serve with pitta bread.

CLASSIC CONSOMME

SERVES 4

1.1 litres (2 pints) homemade cold beef stock	bouquet garni
100 g (4 oz) lean rump steak	1 egg white
1 carrot, quartered	salt, if necessary
1 small onion, quartered	10 ml (2 tsp) dry sherry (optional)

1 Remove any fat from the stock. Shred the meat finely and soak it in 150 ml (¼ pint) cold water for 15 minutes. Put the meat and water, vegetables, stock and bouquet garni into a deep saucepan; lastly, add the egg white.
2 Heat gently and whisk continuously until a thick froth starts to form. Stop whisking and bring to the boil. Lower the heat immediately, cover and simmer gently for 2 hours. If the liquid boils too rapidly, the froth will break and cloud the consommé.
3 Scald a clean cloth or jelly bag, then wring it out. Tie it to the legs of an upturned stool and place a bowl underneath. Pour the soup through, keeping the froth back at first with a spoon, then let it slide out on to the cloth. Repeat. The consommé should now be clear and sparkling.
4 Reheat the consommé, add salt if necessary, and a little sherry to enhance the flavour, if liked. Do not add anything that would make the liquid cloudy.
5 Consommé may be served hot or cold, plain or varied by the addition of a garnish. A good cold consommé should be lightly jellied.

VARIATION

Consommé Julienne
Cut small quantities of vegetables such as carrot, turnip and celery into strips and boil separately; rinse before adding to the consommé to prevent it from becoming cloudy.

GOLDEN VEGETABLE SOUP

SERVES 4

25 g (1 oz) butter or polyunsaturated margarine	225 g (8 oz) cauliflower, broken into florets
1 large carrot, cut into 4 cm (1½ inch) matchsticks	1 medium onion, sliced
2 celery sticks, cut into 4 cm (1½ inch) matchsticks	2.5 ml (½ tsp) ground turmeric
100 g (4 oz) swede, peeled and cut into 4 cm (1½ inch) matchsticks	1 litre (1¾ pints) vegetable stock
	salt and pepper
	snipped chives, to garnish

1 Melt the butter or margarine in a saucepan, add all the vegetables and cook for 2 minutes, stirring occasionally.
2 Add the turmeric and cook for 1 minute. Pour over the stock and adjust seasoning. Bring to the boil and simmer for 20 minutes. Garnish with snipped chives and serve with crusty brown bread.

VARIATIONS

Served in larger quantities this hearty soup can make a meal in itself. You can use any other orange or light coloured vegetables – such as potatoes, sweetcorn, yellow courgettes, pumpkins, turnips – that have a firm enough texture not to disintegrate during cooking. Be sparing with the turmeric; it is for colour only and too much will spoil the taste.

LETTUCE SOUP

SERVES 4

350 g (12 oz) lettuce leaves	150 ml (¼ pint) semi-skimmed milk
100 g (4 oz) spring onions, trimmed	salt and pepper
50 g (2 oz) butter or polyunsaturated margarine	shredded lettuce or 60 ml (4 tbsp) soured cream, to finish (optional)
15 ml (1 tbsp) plain flour	
600 ml (1 pint) vegetable or chicken stock	

1 Chop the lettuce leaves and spring onions roughly. Melt the butter or margarine in a deep saucepan, add the lettuce and spring onions and cook gently for about 10 minutes until both the lettuce and onions are very soft.
2 Stir in the flour and cook, stirring, for 1 minute, then add the stock. Bring to the boil, cover and simmer for 45 minutes to 1 hour.
3 Work the soup to a purée in a blender or food processor, or rub through a sieve. Return to the rinsed-out pan and add the milk with salt and pepper to taste. Reheat to serving temperature. Finish with a garnish of shredded lettuce or a swirl of soured cream, if liked.

SERVING SUGGESTION

This soup has a pretty colour and delicate flavour. It makes a lovely summer starter served with Melba toast.

SPINACH SOUP

SERVES 4

450 g (1 lb) fresh spinach	salt and pepper
900 ml (1½ pints) vegetable or chicken stock	450 ml (¾ pint) buttermilk
15 ml (1 tbsp) lemon juice	few drops of Tabasco sauce

1 Strip the spinach leaves from their stems and wash in several changes of water. Place the spinach, stock, lemon juice and seasoning in a pan. Simmer for 10 minutes.
2 Work the spinach through a sieve, or strain off most of the liquid and reserve, then purée the spinach in a blender or processor.
3 Reheat the spinach purée gently with the cooking liquid, 300 ml (½ pint) of the buttermilk and the Tabasco sauce. Swirl in the remaining buttermilk. Serve with warm wholemeal rolls.

BORSHCH

225 g (8 oz) chuck steak	225 g (8 oz) ripe tomatoes
1 carrot, sliced	30 ml (2 tbsp) tomato purée
1 onion, stuck with a few cloves	15 ml (1 tbsp) red wine vinegar
2 celery sticks, chopped	1 bay leaf
1 bouquet garni	5 ml (1 tsp) sugar, to taste
salt and pepper	90 ml (3 fl oz) soured cream or smetana, to serve
350 g (12 oz) raw beetroot	

1 Put the beef in a large saucepan with the carrot, onion and celery. Pour in 1.2 litres (2 pints) water and bring to the boil. Skim off any scum, add the bouquet garni and salt and pepper to taste. Lower the heat, cover the pan and simmer for 1 hour until the meat is just becoming tender.

2 Meanwhile, peel the beetroot and cut into thin matchstick strips with a very sharp knife.

3 To skin the tomatoes, spear on a fork and hold over a gas flame, turning the fork until the skin of the tomato blisters. Leave until cool enough to handle, then peel off the skin with your fingers. Alternatibely plunge into a bowl of boiling water for 30 seconds, then peel. Chop the tomato flesh roughly.

4 Remove the beef from the pan and slice into thin matchstick strips. Remove the vegetables and bouquet garni with a slotted spoon and discard.

5 Return the beef to the pan and add the beetroot, tomatoes, tomato purée, wine vinegar and bay leaf. Simmer for a further 50 minutes to 1 hour, until the beef and beetroot are really tender. Discard the bay leaf, then adjust seasoning, adding sugar to taste. Serve the borshch hot, with the soured cream or smetana handed separately.

SPICED LENTIL AND CARROT SOUP

60 ml (4 tbsp) polyunsaturated oil	50 g (2 oz) lentils
200 g (7 oz) carrots, peeled and grated	1.1 litres (2 pints) chicken stock
1 medium onion, finely sliced	salt and pepper
10 whole green cardamoms	parsley sprigs, to garnish

1 Heat the oil in a heavy-based saucepan, add the carrots and onion and cook gently for 4-5 minutes without browning.

2 Meanwhile split each cardamom and remove the black seeds. Crush the seeds with a pestle in a mortar, or use the end of a rolling pin on a wooden board.

3 Add the crushed cardamom seeds to the vegetables with the lentils. Cook, stirring, for a further 1-2 minutes.

4 Add the chicken stock and bring to the boil. Lower the heat, cover the pan with a lid and simmer gently for about 20 minutes, or until the lentils are just tender. Season to taste with salt and pepper. Serve hot, garnished with parsley sprigs.

WATERCRESS SOUP

SERVES 4

2 bunches watercress	750 ml (1¼ pints) vegetable stock
50 g (2 oz) butter or polyunsaturated margarine	300 ml (½ pint) semi-skimmed milk
1 medium onion, chopped	salt and pepper
50 g (2 oz) plain wholemeal flour	

1 Wash and trim the watercress, leaving some of the stem, then chop roughly.
2 Melt the butter or margarine in a saucepan, add the watercress and onion and cook gently for 10 minutes until soft but not coloured.
3 Add the flour and cook gently, stirring, for 1-2 minutes. Remove from the heat and gradually blend in the stock and milk. Bring to the boil, stirring constantly, then simmer for 3 minutes. Add salt and pepper to taste.
4 Sieve or purée the soup in a blender or food processor. Return to the rinsed-out pan and reheat gently, without boiling. Taste and adjust seasoning, if necessary. Serve hot.

SERVING SUGGESTION

Try serving this delicately flavoured soup with a swirl of Greek yogurt over the top of each bowl, adding only a few calories to each serving.

BRUSSELS SPROUTS SOUP

SERVES 4-6

225 g (8 oz) Brussels sprouts	salt and pepper
225 g (8 oz) potatoes, peeled	150 ml (¼ pint) semi-skimmed milk
25 g (1 oz) butter or polyunsaturated margarine	30 ml (2 tbsp) low-fat natural yogurt
900 ml (1½ pints) chicken stock	chopped walnuts, to garnish

1 Remove and discard the outer leaves of the sprouts. Wash the sprouts well and then chop roughly. Slice the potatoes. Melt the butter or margarine in a saucepan, add the sprouts and cook gently for 2 minutes, stirring.
2 Add the potatoes, stock and salt and pepper to taste. Bring to the boil, cover and simmer for 25 minutes or until the potatoes are tender.
3 Sieve or purée the soup in a blender or food processor. Return to the rinsed-out pan, stir in the milk and heat thoroughly.
4 Add the yogurt and heat through, without boiling. Taste and adjust seasoning. Serve hot, garnished with chopped walnuts.

FRENCH BEAN SOUP

SERVES 4-6

30 ml (2 tbsp) polyunsaturated oil	900 ml (1½ pints) chicken stock)
125 g (4 oz) onion, finely chopped	150 ml (¼ pint) semi-skimmed milk
450 g (1 lb) frozen whole French beans	45 ml (3 tbsp) low-fat natural yogurt (optional)
30 ml (2 tbsp) flour	salt and pepper
15 ml (1 tbsp) chopped parsley	snipped grilled bacon or garlic croûtons, to garnish

1 Heat the oil in a large saucepan and stir in the onion. Cook for 3-4 minutes until soft but not coloured. Mix in the beans, flour, parsley and stock. Bring to the boil, cover and simmer for 10-12 minutes, stirring occasionally or until the beans are quite tender.

2 Allow the soup to cool slightly, then purée in a blender or food processor. Return to the rinsed-out saucepan, add the milk and reheat gently.

3 Stir in the yogurt and adjust seasoning before serving. Garnish with snipped grilled bacon or croûtons.

COOK'S TIP

Instead of frying bread croûtons, make them from toasted slices of bread. Rub with a cut garlic clove and cut into dice.

CARROT AND ORANGE SOUP

SERVES 4-6

30 ml (2 tbsp) polyunsaturated oil	1 litre (1¾ pints) chicken stock
700 g (1½ lb) carrots, sliced	salt and pepper
2 medium onions, sliced	1 orange

1 Heat the oil in a saucepan, add the vegetables and cook gently for 10 minutes until softened.

2 Add the chicken stock, season with salt and pepper to taste and bring to the boil. Lower the heat, cover and simmer for about 40 minutes, or until the vegetables are tender.

3 Sieve the vegetables or purée with half of the stock in a blender or food processor. Add this mixture to the stock remaining in the pan.

4 Meanwhile pare half of the orange rind thinly, using a potato peeler, then cut it into shreds. Cook the shreds in gently boiling water until tender.

5 Finely grate the remaining orange rind into the soup. Stir well to combine with the ingredients.

6 Squeeze the juice of the orange into the pan, then reheat the soup gently. Drain the shreds of orange rind and use to garnish the soup before serving.

BEAN AND CORIANDER POTAGE

SERVES 4

small bunch of fresh coriander	400 g (14 oz) can chopped tomatoes
30 ml (2 tbsp) polyunsaturated oil	30 ml (2 tbsp) tomato purée
225 g (8 oz) onion, chopped	1 garlic clove, crushed
350 g (12 oz) fennel, trimmed and chopped	salt and pepper
10 ml (2 tsp) ground coriander	400 g (14 oz) can cannellini beans
1.4 litres (2½ pints) chicken or vegetable stock	coriander sprigs, to garnish

1   Tie the coriander stalks into a bundle; chop the leaves, cover and refrigerate.
2   Heat the oil in a saucepan. Add the onion and fennel and fry over a moderate heat until starting to brown.
3   Stir in the ground coriander and cook for 1 minute. Mix in the stock, tomatoes, tomato purée, garlic and seasoning. Add the coriander stalks and bring to the boil. Cover and simmer for 30 minutes.
4   Drain the beans then stir into the soup. Cover and simmer for about 10 minutes or until the vegetables are tender and the beans heated through.
5   Remove the coriander stalks. Stir about 45 ml (3 tbsp) chopped coriander leaves into the soup. Adjust seasoning and garnish with sprigs of coriander to serve.

WINTER LENTIL SOUP

SERVES 4

30 ml (2 tbsp) polyunsaturated oil	225 g (8 oz) red lentils
125 g (4 oz) bacon, rinded and chopped	1.7 litres (3 pints) vegetable stock
225 g (8 oz) carrots, cut into small chunks	15 ml (1 tbsp) tomato purée
225 g (8 oz) parsnips, cut into small chunks	salt and pepper
450 g (1 lb) leeks, sliced	juice of 1 large orange
	grated cheese, to serve (optional)

1   Heat the oil in a large saucepan. Add the bacon and cook until lightly browned, stirring occasionally.
2   Mix in the carrots, parsnips, leeks and lentils. Fry for 1-2 minutes, stirring occasionally.
3   Pour in the stock, adding the tomato purée and seasoning. Bring to the boil, cover and simmer for about 25 minutes or until the lentils and vegetables are tender.
4   Stir in the orange juice and adjust seasoning. If wished, top each portion with a sprinkling of grated cheese to serve.

LONDON PARTICULAR

SERVES 8

15 g (½ oz) butter or polyunsaturated margarine	450 g (1 lb) split dried peas
50 g (2 oz) bacon, rinded and chopped	2.3 litres (4 pints) chicken or ham stock
1 medium onion, roughly chopped	salt and pepper
1 medium carrot, diced	60 ml (4 tbsp) low-fat natural yogurt
1 celery stick, chopped	chopped grilled bacon and croûtons, to garnish

1 Melt the butter or margarine in a large saucepan. Add the bacon, onion, carrot and celery and cook for 5-10 minutes, until beginning to soften.
2 Add the peas and stock and bring to the boil, then cover and simmer for 1 hour, until the peas are soft.
3 Allow to cool slightly, then purée in a blender or food processor until smooth.
4 Return the soup to the pan. Season to taste, add the yogurt and reheat gently. Serve hot, garnished with chopped grilled bacon and croûtons.

COOK'S TIP

It's a long time since London was blanketed regularly in thick fogs known as 'pea soupers', but that's how this gloriously green soup got its delightful name! And it's still a dish that's perfectly designed to keep out the chill on a misty autumn evening.

CURRIED POTATO AND APPLE SOUP

SERVES 4

50 g (2 oz) butter or polyunsaturated margarine	1.2 litres (2 pints) vegetable stock or water
4 medium old potatoes, peeled and diced	salt and pepper
2 eating apples, peeled, cored and diced	150 ml (¼ pint) low-fat natural yogurt, at room temperature
10 ml (2 tsp) curry powder	

1 Melt the butter or margarine in a large saucepan. Add the potatoes and apples and fry gently for about 10 minutes until lightly coloured, shaking the pan and stirring frequently.
2 Add the curry powder and fry gently for 1-2 minutes, stirring. Pour in the stock or water and bring to the boil. Add salt and pepper to taste. Lower the heat, cover the pan and simmer for 20-25 minutes.
3 Sieve the soup or purée in a blender or food processor, then return to the rinsed-out pan.
4 Stir the yogurt until smooth, then pour half into the soup. Heat through, stirring constantly.
5 Pour the hot soup into warmed individual bowls and swirl in the remaining yogurt.

CONSOMME WITH EGG AND PARMESAN

SERVES 4

1 litre (1¾ pints) homemade chicken stock or two 450 ml (15 fl oz) cans chicken consommé	15 ml (1 tbsp) semolina
	pinch of freshly grated nutmeg
3 eggs	salt and pepper
45 ml (3 tbsp) freshly grated Parmesan cheese	

1 In a large saucepan, heat the chicken stock or consommé to barely simmering point.

2 In a separate bowl, beat the eggs, then add the Parmesan, semolina, nutmeg and seasoning. Add a cupful of the hot stock or consommé and stir until smooth.

3 Pour the mixture slowly into the pan of simmering stock, beating vigorously with a fork for 3-4 minutes.

4 Leave to stand for 2 minutes to set the egg strands completely. Serve hot, in warmed individual soup bowls.

VARIATION

Pasta in Brodo

Replace the eggs, Parmesan and semolina with 225 g (8 oz) pasta shells or bows. Cook in the consommé until tender. Serve sprinkled with freshly grated Parmesan.

LENTIL, BACON AND VEGETABLE SOUP

SERVES 4-6

30 ml (2 tbsp) polyunsaturated oil	75 g (3 oz) red lentils
15 g (½ oz) butter or polyunsaturated margarine	1 bacon knuckle
	10 ml (2 tsp) ground ginger
1 large onion, chopped	2.5 ml (½ tsp) ground cloves
3 celery sticks, roughly chopped	salt and pepper
3 medium carrots, thinly sliced	chopped parsley, to garnish

1 Heat the oil and butter or margarine in a large saucepan, add the onion, celery and carrots and fry gently, stirring, for 10 minutes until lightly coloured.

2 Add the lentils and 1.4 litres (2½ pints) water, then the bacon knuckle. Bring slowly to the boil and skim off any scum with a slotted spoon. Lower the heat, add the ginger, cloves and salt and pepper to taste, then half cover the pan and simmer for 1½ hours. Stir often, adding water if necessary.

3 Remove the knuckle from the pan and set aside to cool slightly. Work the vegetables and liquid to a purée in a blender or food processor, then return to the rinsed-out pan. Reheat, stirring, then taste and adjust seasoning. Thin to the required consistency with water, if necessary.

4 Strip the meat from the bacon knuckle and cut into bite-size pieces. Add to the pan and heat through. Serve very hot, sprinkled with chopped parsley.

SERVING SUGGESTION

This soup is thick and nourishing, just the food for an evening meal on a cold winter's day. Serve with crusty French bread or granary rolls and cheese, or with hot garlic or herb bread.

BROAD BEAN
AND BACON SOUP

SERVES 4

225 g (8 oz) shelled broad beans	300 ml (½ pint) vegetable stock
225 g (8 oz) shelled peas	salt and pepper
1 large onion, chopped	chopped grilled bacon and parsley sprigs, to garnish
450 ml (¾ pint) semi-skimmed milk	

1 In a large saucepan, simmer the broad beans, peas and onion in the milk and stock for 20 minutes, until the beans are tender.

2 Purée one-third of the soup in a blender or food processor and add to the remaining soup, then season to taste. Reheat gently. Serve hot, sprinkled with chopped bacon and garnished with parsley sprigs.

COOK'S TIP

An unusual way to use broad beans, which are often under-rated. Their flavour is delicate, and the beans are especially good when very young and tender. They are only in season from June to August, but you can substitute frozen beans or peas when the fresh vegetables are not available.

SPICED
DAL SOUP

SERVES 4-6

100 g (4 oz) channa dal	225 g (8 oz) tomatoes, skinned and roughly chopped
5 ml (1 tsp) cumin seeds	2.5 ml (½ tsp) turmeric
10 ml (2 tsp) coriander seeds	5 ml (1 tsp) treacle
5 ml (1 tsp) fenugreek seeds	5 ml (1 tsp) salt
3 dried red chillies	lemon slices and coriander sprigs, to garnish
15 ml (1 tbsp) shredded coconut	
30 ml (2 tbsp) ghee or vegetable oil	

1 Pick over the dal and remove any grit or discoloured pulses. Put into a sieve and wash thoroughly under cold running water. Drain well.

2 Place the dal in a large saucepan, cover with 600 ml (1 pint) water and bring to the boil. Cover and simmer for at least 1 hour, or until tender.

3 Finely grind the cumin, coriander, fenugreek, chillies and coconut in a small electric mill or with a pestle and mortar. Heat the ghee or oil in a heavy-based frying pan, add the spice mixture and fry, stirring, for 30 seconds. Set the spices aside.

4 Mash or purée the dal in a blender or food processor, then transfer to a large saucepan. Stir in the tomatoes, spices, treacle, salt and a further 300 ml (½ pint) water.

5 Bring to the boil, then lower the heat, cover and simmer for about 20 minutes. Taste and adjust seasoning and turn into a warmed serving dish. Garnish with lemon slices and coriander sprigs and serve immediately.

COOK'S TIP

The shredded coconut in this recipe can be fresh if you want to go to the trouble of preparing a fresh coconut, but for such a small quantity it is more practical to buy ready shredded coconut. It has larger flakes than desiccated coconut, and a fuller flavour.

MINESTRONE

SERVES 8

60 ml (4 tbsp) olive oil	100 g (4 oz) French or runner beans
1 large onion, chopped	100 g (4 oz) green cabbage
1 clove garlic, crushed	1.7 litres (3 pints) beef stock
3 sticks celery	salt and pepper
3 carrots	120 ml (8 tbsp) chopped parsley
2 large courgettes	
450 g (1 lb) tomatoes, skinned, or 400 g (14 oz) can tomatoes	400 g (14 oz) can cannellini beans
75 g (3 oz) fennel	freshly grated Parmesan cheese, to serve

1 Heat the oil in a large flameproof casserole or saucepan. Add the onion and garlic and cook until soft and beginning to turn a golden colour.
2 Finely chop the remaining vegetables, adding them to the saucepan as they are chopped; stir well to mix. The first vegetables will begin to soften as the remainder are being prepared.
3 Add the stock, seasoning and parsley. Bring to the boil, cover and simmer very gently for about 45 minutes, or until all the vegetables are nearly tender.
4 Stir in the drained cannellini beans and simmer for 15 minutes. Season. Serve sprinkled with grated Parmesan.

SCOTCH BROTH

SERVES 4

700 g (1½ lb) shin of beef	1 medium onion, diced
salt and pepper	2 leeks, thinly sliced
1 carrot, chopped	45 ml (3 tbsp) pot barley
1 turnip, chopped	15 ml (1 tbsp) chopped parsley, to garnish

1 Remove any fat from the meat and cut the meat into bite-sized pieces. Put the meat in a saucepan, cover with 2.3 litres (4 pints) water, then add salt and pepper to taste. Bring slowly to the boil, cover and simmer for 1½ hours.
2 Add the vegetables and the barley. Cover and simmer for a further 1 hour or until the vegetables and barley are soft.
3 Remove any fat that has formed on the surface with a spoon or absorbent kitchen paper.
4 Serve hot, garnished with parsley. Traditionally the meat is served with a little of the broth as a main course.

COOK'S TIP

If possible, make the soup the day before required. Allow to cool, then chill. The fat will solidify on the surface and can be removed easily.

CHICKEN WATERZOOI

SERVES 6

1.4 kg (3 lb) chicken, with giblets	salt and pepper
½ lemon	½ bottle dry white wine
2 celery sticks, chopped	2 egg yolks
2 leeks, chopped	90 ml (6 tbsp) single cream
1 medium onion, chopped	30 ml (2 tbsp) chopped parsley
2 carrots, sliced	parsley sprigs, to garnish
1 bouquet garni	

1 Prick the chicken all over with a skewer, then rub with the cut lemon, squeezing the fruit as you do so, to release the juice.

2 Put the chicken in a large saucepan with the giblets, vegetables, bouquet garni and salt and pepper to taste. Pour in the wine, then add enough water to just cover the chicken.

3 Bring the liquid to the boil, then lower the heat and half cover with a lid. Simmer for 1½ hours, or until the meat is tender and beginning to fall away from the bones.

4 Remove the chicken from the liquid. Discard the bouquet garni and the giblets. Cut the chicken flesh into bite-sized pieces, discarding all skin and bones, then return to the liquid.

5 Mix together the egg yolks and cream in a heatproof bowl. Stir in a few ladlefuls of the hot cooking liquid. Return this mixture to the pan. Simmer until thickened, stirring constantly, then add the parsley and taste and adjust seasoning. Serve hot, garnished with parsley.

SERVING SUGGESTION

A soup for a special occasion, made substantial with pieces of chicken and vegetables. Serve with wholemeal bread.

COCK-A-LEEKIE SOUP

SERVES 6

15 g (½ oz) butter or polyunsaturated margarine	1.1 litres (2 pints) chicken stock
275-350 g (10-12 oz) chicken (1 large or 2 small chicken portions)	1 bouquet garni
	salt and pepper
350 g (12 oz) leeks	6 prunes, stoned
	parsley sprigs, to garnish

1 Melt the butter or margarine in a large saucepan and fry the chicken quickly until golden on all sides.

2 Cut the white part of the leeks into four lengthways and chop into 2.5 cm (1 inch) pieces; reserving the green parts. Add the white parts to the pan and fry for 5 minutes until soft.

3 Add the stock, bouquet garni and salt and pepper to taste. Bring to the boil and simmer for 30 minutes or until the chicken is tender.

4 Shred the reserved green parts of the leeks, then add to the pan with the prunes. Simmer for a further 30 minutes.

5 To serve, remove the chicken, then cut the meat into large pieces, discarding the skin and bones. Place the meat in a warmed soup tureen and pour over the soup. Serve hot, garnished with parsley sprigs.

CHICKEN
AND PASTA BROTH

SERVES 4-6

two 275 g (10 oz) chicken portions	1 bouquet garni
1-2 small leeks, sliced	salt and pepper
2 carrots, thinly sliced	50 g (2 oz) small pasta shapes
900 ml (1½ pints) chicken stock	60 ml (4 tbsp) chopped parsley, to garnish

1 Put the chicken portions in a large pan. Add the leeks and carrots, then pour in the stock and 900 ml (1½ pints) water. Bring to the boil.
2 Add the bouquet garni and salt and pepper to taste, then lower the heat, cover the pan and simmer for 30 minutes until the chicken is tender. Remove the chicken from the liquid and leave until cool enough to handle.
3 Meanwhile add the pasta to the pan, bring back to the boil and simmer for 15 minutes, stirring occasionally, until tender.
4 Remove the chicken from the bones and cut the flesh into bite-sized pieces, discarding all skin. Return to the pan and heat through. Discard the bouquet garni. Serve hot in warmed soup bowls, sprinkled with parsley.

FISH AND
CORN CHOWDER

SERVES 4-6

25-50 g (1-2 oz) butter or polyunsaturated margarine	salt and pepper
450 g (1 lb) old potatoes, peeled and cut into 1 cm (½ inch) dice	225 g (8 oz) fresh haddock fillets
2 medium onions, thinly sliced	225 g (8 oz) smoked haddock fillets
2.5 ml (½ tsp) chilli powder	298 g (10½ oz) can cream-style sweetcorn
600 ml (1 pint) fish or vegetable stock	100 g (4 oz) cooked peeled prawns
600 ml (1 pint) semi-skimmed milk	chopped parsley, to garnish

1 Melt the butter or margarine in a large saucepan. Add the vegetables and the chilli powder and stir over a moderate heat for 2-3 minutes.
2 Pour in the stock and milk and season to taste. Bring to the boil, cover and simmer for 10 minutes.
3 Meanwhile, skin the fresh and smoked haddock fillets and divide the flesh into bite-sized pieces, discarding all the bones.
4 Add the haddock to the pan with the corn. Bring back to the boil, cover and simmer until the potatoes are tender and the fish begins to flake apart. Skim the surface of the soup.
5 Stir in the prawns with plenty of parsley. Adjust the seasoning and serve.

CULLEN SKINK

SERVES 4

1 Finnan haddock, weighing about 350 g (12 oz), skinned	700 g (1½ lb) potatoes
1 medium onion, chopped	knob of butter or margarine
600 ml (1 pint) semi-skimmed milk	salt and pepper
	chopped parsley, to garnish

1 Put the haddock into a medium saucepan, just cover it with 900 ml (1½ pints) boiling water and bring to the boil again. Add the onion, cover and simmer for 10-15 minutes, until the haddock is tender. Drain off the liquid and reserve.
2 Remove the bones from the haddock and flake the flesh, then set aside. Return the bones and strained stock to the pan with the milk. Cover and simmer gently for a further hour.
3 Meanwhile, peel and roughly chop the potatoes, then cook in boiling salted water until tender. Drain well, then mash.
4 Strain the liquid from the bones and return it to the pan with the flaked fish. Add the mashed potato and butter or margarine and stir well to give a thick creamy consistency. Adjust the seasoning and garnish with parsley. Serve with crusty bread.

COOK'S TIP

This classic fish and potato soup is good and filling. The word 'skink' means stock or broth but the strong flavour of the fish means that water and milk can be used for the liquor; there is no need to go to the trouble of making fish stock. For a smoother but less traditional texture you can whizz the soup in a food processor or blender.

CHINESE HOT AND SOUR SOUP

SERVES 4

225 g (8 oz) button mushrooms	225 g (8 oz) cooked chicken or pork
100 ml (4 fl oz) medium dry sherry	125 g (4 oz) spring onions
75 ml (5 tbsp) soy sauce	125 g (4 oz) baby corn cobs
30 ml (2 tbsp) chopped coriander	75 ml (5 tbsp) white wine vinegar
	freshly ground pepper

1 Slice the mushrooms thinly. Place in a large saucepan with the sherry, soy sauce, coriander and 1.1 litres (2 pints) water. Bring to the boil. Simmer, uncovered for 15 minutes.
2 Thinly shred the chicken or finely dice the pork and spring onions. Thinly slice the sweetcorn.
3 Stir the prepared meat and vegetables into the mushroom mixture, with the wine vinegar and season to taste with pepper. Simmer for a further 5 minutes. Serve hot.

VARIATION

Sprinkle the soup liberally with roughly torn coriander leaves just before serving.

CHINESE CABBAGE AND PRAWN SOUP

SERVES 4

30 ml (2 tbsp) polyunsaturated oil	30 ml (2 tbsp) soy sauce (preferably naturally fermented shoyu)
50 g (2 oz) French beans, trimmed and cut into 5 cm (2 inch) lengths	1.25 ml (¼ tsp) sweet chilli sauce
1 large carrot, cut into matchstick strips	30 ml (2 tbsp) medium dry sherry
1 small turnip, cut into matchstick strips	15 ml (1 tbsp) light muscovado sugar
1.1 litres (2 pints) chicken stock	175 g (6 oz) Chinese leaves, finely shredded
	75 g (3 oz) cooked peeled prawns

1   Heat the oil in a saucepan and gently cook the beans, carrot and turnip for 5 minutes.
2   Add the stock, soy sauce, chilli sauce, sherry and sugar. Simmer for 15 minutes or until the vegetables are just tender.
3   Add the Chinese leaves and prawns and cook for 2-3 minutes until the leaves are tender but still crisp. Serve immediately.

COOK'S TIP

This is a clear soup full of vegetable goodness. The pale Chinese cabbage, also known as Chinese leaves, keeps very well in the bottom of the refrigerator.

CARIBBEAN SPINACH AND CRAB SOUP

SERVES 6

450 g (1 lb) fresh spinach	5 ml (1 tsp) cayenne pepper
25 g (1 oz) polyunsaturated margarine	1.2 litres (2 pints) fish or vegetable stock
4 spring onions, trimmed and chopped	salt and pepper
2 large garlic cloves, crushed	170 g (6 oz) can white crab meat
30 ml (2 tbsp) plain flour	few drops of Tabasco sauce (optional)
30 ml (2 tbsp) desiccated coconut	

1   Trim and wash the spinach and chop the leaves roughly, discarding any thick or tough stalks.
2   Melt the margarine in a large heavy-based saucepan, add the spring onions and garlic and fry gently for 5 minutes or until soft but not coloured.
3   Add the spinach and cook gently for 2-3 minutes, then stir in the flour, coconut and cayenne. Pour in the stock and bring to the boil, stirring, then add salt and pepper to taste. Lower the heat, cover and simmer for 20 minutes, stirring occasionally.
4   Add the crab meat to the soup and heat through for at least 5 minutes, stirring gently. Taste and adjust the seasoning and add a dash of Tabasco if a more pronounced 'peppery' flavour is preferred. Serve hot.

SERVING SUGGESTION

This soup is spicily hot and very tasty. Serve it as an unusual starter for a dinner party, then follow with a Caribbean-style main course of grilled chicken. Bananas simmered in orange juice with a pinch of ground allspice would complete the West Indian theme of the meal.

STARTERS

Slim, healthy starters should be light, refreshing and attractively presented – so that they stimulate the appetite rather than take the edge off it. Keep proportions fairly small, unless you are serving these recipes as nutritious light meals in themselves – they needn't be limited to first courses.

MELON AND PARMA HAM

SERVES 4

900 g (2 lb) Cantaloupe melon, chilled	juice of 1 lemon
8 thin slices Parma ham	pepper

1 Cut the melon in half lengthways and scoop out the seeds. Cut each half into four wedges.
2 With a sharp knife and a sawing action, separate the flesh from the skin, keeping it in position on the skin.
3 Cut the flesh across into bite-sized slices, then push each in opposite directions to make an attractive pattern.
4 Roll up each slice of ham into a cigar shape. Place on serving dishes with the melon wedges and sprinkle with lemon juice and pepper to serve.

VARIATION

Replace the melon with a selection of exotic fruits such as sliced mango, paw paw and kiwi fruit.

MELON AND PRAWN SALAD

SERVES 8

1 small honeydew melon	225 g (8 oz) cucumber, diced
30 ml (2 tbsp) tomato juice	15 ml (1 tbsp) chopped tarragon
30 ml (2 tbsp) cider vinegar	salt and pepper
30 ml (2 tbsp) clear honey	tarragon sprigs and cooked whole king prawns, to garnish
1 egg yolk	
450 g (1 lb) cooked peeled prawns	

1 Cut the melon in half and scrape out the pips from the centre with a teaspoon.
2 Scoop out the melon flesh with a melon baller. Divide the melon balls equally between 8 individual serving dishes.
3 To make the tomato dressing, put the tomato juice, vinegar, honey and egg yolk in a blender or food processor and blend together until evenly mixed.
4 Toss the prawns, cucumber and tarragon in the tomato dressing. Add salt and pepper to taste. Spoon on top of the melon balls and chill in the refrigerator for at least 1 hour. Garnish with sprigs of tarragon and whole prawns before serving.

ARTICHOKE HEARTS A LA GRECQUE

SERVES 6

75 ml (5 tbsp) olive oil	salt and pepper
15 ml (1 tbsp) white wine vinegar	175 g (6 oz) button onions, skinned
10 ml (2 tsp) tomato purée	5 ml (1 tsp) caster sugar
1 large garlic clove, crushed	225 g (8 oz) small button mushrooms
7.5 ml (1½ tsp) chopped thyme or basil	two 400 g (14 oz) cans artichoke hearts

1 To make the dressing, place 45 ml (3 tbsp) oil, the vinegar, tomato purée, garlic, thyme and seasoning in a bowl and whisk together.
2 Blanch the onions in boiling water for 5 minutes; drain well. Heat the remaining oil in a heavy-based pan, add the onions and the sugar and cook for 2 minutes.
3 Add the mushrooms and toss over a high heat for a few seconds. Tip the contents of the pan into dressing. Drain the artichoke hearts, rinse and drain thoroughly. Add them to the dressing and toss together. Cover and chill for at least 30 minutes before serving.

LEEKS A LA VINAIGRETTE

SERVES 4-6

12 small leeks	10 ml (2 tsp) tomato purée
salt and pepper	10 ml (2 tsp) coriander seeds, lightly crushed
90 ml (3 fl oz) olive oil	pinch of sugar
45 ml (3 tbsp) red wine vinegar	coriander sprigs, to garnish

1 Trim the leeks and slit each leek lengthways in two or three places. Rinse thoroughly under cold running water.
2 Cook the leeks in boiling salted water for 6-8 minutes until just tender. Drain, refresh under cold running water, then leave to drain and dry on absorbent kitchen paper.
3 Make the dressing. Put the oil and vinegar in a bowl with the tomato purée, coriander seeds, sugar and salt and pepper to taste. Whisk vigorously with a fork until thick.
4 Arrange the cold leeks in a shallow serving dish and pour the dressing over them. Chill in the refrigerator for at least 30 minutes before serving. Garnish with sprigs of coriander and serve with hot garlic bread.

MARINATED MUSHROOMS

SERVES 4

450 g (1 lb) small button mushrooms	pinch of mustard powder
30 ml (2 tbsp) wine vinegar	pinch of muscovado sugar
90 ml (6 tbsp) sunflower oil	salt and pepper
	chopped parsley, to garnish

1 Leave small mushrooms whole and cut larger ones in quarters.

2 Put the vinegar, oil, mustard and sugar in a bowl with seasoning to taste. Whisk together with a fork until well blended.

3 Add the mushrooms and stir to coat in the marinade. Cover and leave to marinate in the refrigerator for 6-8 hours, stirring occasionally.

4 Taste and adjust the seasoning, then divide the mushrooms equally between 4 individual shallow serving dishes. Sprinkle with chopped parsley and serve immediately.

SERVING SUGGESTION

Marinated mushrooms make a refreshingly light start to a substantial main course. Serve with a little crusty wholemeal bread to mop up the juices.

TOMATO ICE WITH VEGETABLE JULIENNE

SERVES 4-6

8 very ripe tomatoes	30 ml (2 tbsp) chopped basil
10 ml (2 tsp) gelatine	2 small leeks
30 ml (2 tbsp) tomato purée	2 medium carrots
30 ml (2 tbsp) lemon juice	2 medium courgettes
few drops of Tabasco	120 ml (4 fl oz) low-calorie vinaigrette
salt and pepper	basil leaves, to garnish

1 Put the tomatoes in a blender or food processor and work until smooth. Press the tomato pulp through a sieve into a bowl to remove the seeds and skin.

2 Disslove the gelatine in 45 ml (3 tbsp) water.

3 Add the tomato purée to the tomato pulp with the lemon juice, Tabasco, salt and pepper to taste. Mix well.

4 Stir in the gelatine and chopped basil leaves. Pour into a chilled shallow freezer container and freeze for about 2 hours until mushy.

5 Remove from the freezer and beat the mixture with a fork to break down any ice crystals. Return to the freezer and freeze for a further 4 hours.

6 Meanwhile, wash the leeks thoroughly and cut into fine julienne strips of equal length. Cut the carrots and courgettes into julienne strips of the same size.

7 Bring a large pan of water to the boil and blanch the leeks for 1 minute, then remove with a slotted spoon and drain on absorbent kitchen paper. Blanch the carrots in the same water for about 4 minutes; drain well. Similarly, blanch the courgettes for 2 minutes and drain well.

8 Put the julienne of vegetables in a bowl, add the vinaigrette and salt and pepper to taste and toss gently to mix. Cover and chill in the refrigerator until required.

9 To serve, allow the tomato ice to soften in the refrigerator for 30 minutes. Arrange small scoops of tomato ice on chilled individual side plates with a 'nest' of julienne vegetables. Garnish with basil sprigs.

CHILLED RATATOUILLE

SERVES 6

1 large aubergine, weighing about 350 g (12 oz)	60 ml (4 tbsp) polyunsaturated oil
salt and pepper	125 g (4 oz) button mushrooms
450 g (1 lb) courgettes	150 ml (¼ pint) chicken stock
225 g (8 oz) trimmed leeks	30 ml (2 tbsp) tomato purée
450 g (1 lb) tomatoes	15 ml (1 tbsp) chopped rosemary or parsley
1 green pepper	

1 Cut the aubergine into 2 cm (¾ inch) pieces.

2 Put the aubergine pieces in a colander, sprinkling each layer lightly with salt. Cover with a plate, weight down, then leave to drain for 30 minutes. Rinse under cold running water and pat dry with absorbent kitchen paper.

3 Slice the courgettes diagonally into 5 mm (¼ inch) pieces. Cut the leeks across into similar sized pieces, discarding the root ends and any tough dark leaves. Wash, pushing the slices apart, and drain well.

4 Skin and quarter the tomatoes; push out the pips into a nylon sieve placed over a bowl; reserve the tomato juice. Halve each tomato quarter lengthwise. Slice the pepper into narrow strips, discarding core and seeds.

5 Heat the oil in a large sauté or frying pan. Add the aubergine and courgettes and fry over high heat for 2-3 minutes, turning frequently. Stir in the remaining vegetables, with the chicken stock, tomato purée, reserved tomato juice, rosemary and salt and pepper to taste.

6 Bring the contents of the pan to the boil, cover and simmer for 8-10 minutes. The vegetables should be just tender with a hint of crispness, not mushy. Adjust the seasoning and pour out into a bowl to cool for 30 minutes. Chill well in the refrigerator for at least 4 hours.

7 To serve, turn into a large serving bowl or individual dishes. Serve with French bread, preferably wholemeal.

TURKISH STUFFED AUBERGINES

SERVES 6

6 long, small aubergines	60 ml (4 tbsp) chopped parsley
salt and pepper	3.75 ml (¾ tsp) ground allspice
200 ml (7 fl oz) olive oil	
450 g (1 lb) onions, finely sliced	5 ml (1 tsp) sugar
3 garlic cloves, crushed	30 ml (2 tbsp) lemon juice
397 g (14 oz) can tomatoes, drained or 450 g (1 lb) tomatoes, skinned, seeded and chopped	chopped parsley, to garnish

1 Halve the aubergines lengthways. Scoop out the flesh and reserve; leaving a substantial shell so they do not disintegrate.

2 Sprinkle the insides of the aubergine shells with salt and invert on a plate for 30 minutes to drain off any bitter juices.

3 Heat 45 ml (3 tbsp) olive oil in a saucepan, add the onions and garlic and fry gently for about 15 minutes until soft but not coloured. Add the tomatoes, reserved aubergine flesh, parsley, allspice and salt and pepper to taste. Simmer gently for about 20 minutes until the mixture has reduced and thickened.

4 Rinse the aubergines and pat dry with absorbent kitchen paper. Spoon the filling into each half and place them side by side in a shallow ovenproof dish. They should fit quite closely together.

5 Mix the remaining oil with 150 ml (¼ pint) water, the sugar, lemon juice and salt and pepper to taste. Pour around the aubergines, cover and bake in the oven at 150°C (300°F) mark 2 for at least 1 hour until completely tender.

6 When cooked, remove from the oven, uncover and leave to cool for 1 hour. Chill in the refrigerator for at least 2 hours before serving, garnished with lots of chopped parsley.

ROASTED PEPPERS WITH PISTACHIO NUTS

SERVES 8

8 large sweet peppers	few salad leaves
60 ml (4 tbsp) virgin olive oil	300 ml (½ pint) Greek-style yogurt
salt and pepper	125 g (4 oz) shelled pistachio nuts, roughly chopped
60 ml (4 tbsp) chopped marjoram or oregano	fresh herb sprigs, to garnish

1 Place the peppers in a grill pan and cook under a hot grill until the skin is blackened. Turn the peppers over and cook until the other side is blackened. This will take at least 10-15 minutes.
2 Cover with a damp cloth and leave until cool enough to handle. Carefully peel off the skins. Cut the peppers into chunky strips and place in a shallow dish. Pour over the olive oil and season generously with salt and pepper. Sprinkle with the marjoram. Leave to marinate until ready to serve.
3 To serve, arrange the peppers on individual serving plates with a few salad leaves. Place a large spoonful of yogurt on each plate and sprinkle with the pistachio nuts. Generously grind black pepper over the top and garnish with herb sprigs.

COOK'S TIP

If making the pepper and yogurt starter a long time in advance keep it covered in the refrigerator. Remove from the refrigerator at least 1 hour before serving. It should be served at room temperature, not chilled.

GRILLED CHICORY WITH PEARS AND HAZELNUTS

SERVES 8

4 large or 8 small heads of chicory, halved and cored	15 ml (1 tbsp) chopped fresh thyme or 5 ml (1 tsp) dried
olive oil, for basting	freshly ground pepper
2 ripe pears, halved, cored and sliced	50 g (2 oz) hazelnuts, toasted and chopped
45 ml (3 tbsp) hazelnut oil	thyme sprigs, to garnish

1 Brush the chicory all over with olive oil. Place in a grill pan cut side up, and cook under a really hot grill, as near to the heat as possible, for about 3-4 minutes; 2-3 minutes for smaller heads; or until just beginning to char and soften. Turn, baste with more oil and cook for a further 2-3 minutes; 1-2 minutes for smaller heads.
2 Carefully turn the chicory again and top with slices of pear. Brush with hazelnut oil, sprinkle on the thyme, season with pepper and grill for 5-6 minutes, 4-5 minutes for smaller heads. The chicory will be very soft, so carefully transfer it to warmed plates.
3 Scatter with the hazelnuts, garnish with extra sprigs of thyme and drizzle with remaining hazelnut oil. Serve with crusty Italian bread.

COOK'S TIP

Grilling the chicory transforms it by caramelising the juices. Pears brushed with hazelnut oil cut any bitterness associated with the vegetable.

BAKED TOMATOES WITH ANCHOVIES

SERVES 6

3 firm large Marmande tomatoes	50 g (2 oz) can anchovy fillets, drained and chopped
1.25 ml (¼ tsp) sugar	20 ml (4 tsp) chopped fresh basil or 10 ml (2 tsp) dried
freshly ground pepper	
30 ml (2 tbsp) olive oil	25 g (1 oz) freshly grated Parmesan cheese
1 small onion, finely chopped	
1-2 garlic cloves, crushed	anchovy fillets, to garnish

1 Cut the tomatoes in half crossways. Stand them in an oiled baking dish, levelling the bottoms if necessary so that they will stand upright. Sprinkle with the sugar and pepper. Leave to stand.
2 Heat the oil in a heavy-based pan, add the onion and garlic and fry gently for 5 minutes until soft but not coloured.
3 Add the anchovies and cook for a few minutes more, pressing them with a wooden spoon to break them up.
4 Remove from the heat and stir in the basil, with pepper to taste. (Do not add salt because the anchovies are salty enough.)
5 Spoon the mixture on top of the tomato halves, dividing it equally between them, then sprinkle with the Parmesan.
6 Bake the tomatoes in the oven at 220°C (425°F) mark 7 for 10-15 minutes or until just tender and sizzling. Serve hot, garnished with strips of anchovies.

SERVING SUGGESTION

Serve as a tasty starter, with wholemeal bread, or as a vegetable accompaniment to plain roast or grilled meat.

COURGETTES STUFFED WITH RICOTTA

SERVES 4

8 even-sized medium courgettes	175 g (6 oz) ricotta cheese
salt and pepper	20 ml (4 tsp) chopped fresh basil or 10 ml (2 tsp) dried
30 ml (2 tbsp) olive oil	1 quantity homemade tomato sauce (see page 53)
1 medium onion, finely chopped	45 ml (3 tbsp) dried wholemeal breadcrumbs
1 garlic clove, crushed	basil sprigs, to garnish

1 Score the courgettes lengthways with the prongs of a fork, then cut them in half lengthways.
2 Scoop out the flesh from the courgette halves with a sharp-edged teaspoon. Leave a thin margin of flesh next to the skin and make sure not to scoop out all the flesh from the bottoms or the skin may break. Chop the flesh.
3 Blanch the courgette shells in boiling salted water for 10 minutes. Drain, then stand skin side up on absorbent kitchen paper.
4 Heat the oil in a frying pan, add the onion, garlic and scooped-out flesh from the courgettes. Fry gently for about 5 minutes until soft and lightly coloured, then turn into a bowl and add the ricotta, basil and salt and pepper to taste. Stir well.
5 Spoon the ricotta filling into the drained courgette shells, dividing it equally between them.
6 Pour the tomato sauce into the bottom of a shallow ovenproof dish which is large enough to hold the courgettes in a single layer. Place the filled courgettes in the dish side by side. Sprinkle with the breadcrumbs.
7 Bake in the oven at 200°C (400°F) mark 6 for 20 minutes. Serve hot, garnished with basil sprigs.

PIQUANT
MUSHROOMS

SERVES 4

25 g (1 oz) butter or polyunsaturated margarine	10 ml (2 tsp) chopped fresh tarragon or 2. 5 ml (½ tsp) dried
450 g (1 lb) button mushrooms	45 ml (3 tbsp) soured cream or smetana
15 ml (1 tbsp) plain flour	radicchio and lettuce, to serve
150 ml (¼ pint) semi-skimmed milk	tarragon leaves, to garnish
10 ml (2 tsp) wholegrain mustard	

1 Melt the butter or margarine in a medium saucepan, add the mushrooms and fry for 2 minutes.
2 Stir in the flour, then gradually stir in the milk. Heat, stirring continuously until the sauce thickens, boils and is smooth. Simmer for 1-2 minutes.
3 Stir in the mustard, tarragon and soured cream or smetana.
4 Serve hot on a nest of chicory and lettuce leaves, garnished with tarragon.

COOK'S TIP

Choose button mushrooms for their delicate flavour. There's no need to wash or peel them - a wipe with a damp cloth is all that's needed. Tarragon is very distinctive and marries well with mushrooms. Soured cream or smetana gives a hint of piquancy.

CAULIFLOWER
SOUFFLES

SERVES 8

225 g (8 oz) small cauliflower florets	15 ml (1 tbsp) wholegrain mustard
salt and pepper	100 g (4 oz) mature Farmhouse Cheddar cheese, grated
40 g (1½ oz) butter or polyunsaturated margarine	4 eggs, separated
45 ml (3 tbsp) plain flour	
200 ml (7 fl oz) semi-skimmed milk	

1 Grease eight individual ramekin dishes.
2 Put the cauliflower in a saucepan and just cover with boiling salted water. Cover and simmer until tender, then drain.
3 Meanwhile, prepare a white sauce. Put the butter, flour and milk in a saucepan and heat, whisking continuously, until the sauce thickens, boils and is smooth. Simmer for 1-2 minutes. Add the mustard and season to taste.
4 Turn the sauce into a blender or food processor. Add the cauliflower and work to an almost smooth purée.
5 Turn into a large bowl and leave to cool slightly. Stir in the cheese with the egg yolks.
6 Whisk the egg whites until stiff but not dry and fold into the sauce mixture. Spoon into the ramekin dishes.
7 Bake in the oven at 180°C (350°F) mark 4 for 25 minutes or until browned and firm to the touch. Serve at once.

COOK'S TIP

The distinctive flavour of cauliflower lends itself to soufflés. This dish, like all soufflés, can be started ahead and finished off just before baking. If the sauce base is allowed to cool, allow about 10 minutes extra cooking time. Ensure people are ready to eat the soufflé as soon as it is done.

TAPENADE

SERVES 6

175 g (6 oz) stoned black olives	15 ml (1 tbsp) lemon juice
50 g (1¾ oz) can anchovy fillets, drained	15 ml (1 tbsp) drained capers
1 small garlic clove, crushed	5 ml (1 tsp) mustard powder
	pepper
99 g (3½ oz) can tuna in brine, drained	30 ml (2 tbsp) low-fat natural yogurt

1 Purée all the ingredients in a blender or food processor until smooth. Transfer to a small bowl.
2 Store in the refrigerator, covered, for up to 1 week. Serve with French bread.

SERVING SUGGESTION

This is a delicious, pungent mixture from Provence. In France, it is served like a pâté, spread on slices of fresh or toasted French bread, with salad. It can also be accompanied with halved, hard-boiled eggs. Cook the eggs while preparing the Tapenade.

BUTTER BEAN PATE

SERVES 6-8

225 g (8 oz) dried butter beans, soaked in cold water overnight	30 ml (2 tbsp) chopped coriander
60 ml (4 tbsp) olive oil	salt and pepper
juice of 2 lemons	coriander sprigs and lemon wedges, to garnish
2 garlic cloves, crushed	

1 Drain the butter beans in a sieve and rinse thoroughly under cold running water. Put in a saucepan, cover with cold water and bring to the boil.
2 With a slotted spoon, skim off any scum that rises to the surface. Half cover the pan with a lid and simmer for 1½-2 hours until the beans are very tender.
3 Drain the beans and rinse under cold running water. Put half of the beans in a blender or food processor with half of the oil, lemon juice, garlic and coriander. Blend to a smooth purée, then transfer to a bowl. Repeat with the remaining beans, oil, lemon juice, garlic and coriander.
4 Beat the 2 batches of purée together until well mixed, then add seasoning to taste.
5 Turn the pâté into a serving bowl and rough up the surface with the prongs of a fork. Chill in the refrigerator until required.
6 Garnish this creamy dip with coriander and lemon wedges. Serve with fingers of hot wholemeal pitta bread or granary toast.

VARIATION

If you want to make this dip really quickly, use two 396 g (14 oz) cans butter beans and start the recipe from the beginning of step 3.

AUBERGINE DIP

SERVES 4-6

2 large aubergines	150 ml (¼ pint) tahini paste
salt	about 100 ml (4 fl oz) lemon juice
2-3 garlic cloves, roughly chopped	thin tomato slices, to garnish
10 ml (2 tsp) cumin seeds	crudités, to serve (see right)
90 ml (3 fl oz) olive oil	

1 Slice the aubergines, then place in a colander, sprinkling each layer with salt. Cover with a plate, weight down and leave to dégorge for 30 minutes.
2 Meanwhile, crush the garlic and cumin seeds with a pestle and mortar. Add 5 ml (1 tsp) salt and mix well.
3 Rinse the aubergines under cold running water, then pat dry with absorbent kitchen paper. Heat the oil in a large, heavy-based frying pan until very hot. Add the aubergine slices in batches and fry until golden on both sides, turning once. Remove from the pan with a slotted spoon and drain again on kitchen paper.
4 Put the aubergine slices in a blender or food processor with the garlic mixture, the tahini paste and about two-thirds of the lemon juice. Work to a smooth purée, then taste and add more lemon juice and salt if liked.
5 Turn into a serving bowl, cover and chill in the refrigerator until required. Garnish with tomato slices and serve with crudités.

AVOCADO AND GARLIC DIP WITH CRUDITES

SERVES 4-6

	CRUDITES
2 ripe avocados	4 carrots
juice of 1 lemon	4 celery sticks
225 g (8 oz) low-fat soft cheese	1 head chicory
2 large garlic cloves, crushed	100 g (4 oz) button mushrooms
dash of Tabasco sauce, to taste	8 cherry tomatoes or large radishes
salt and pepper	
celery leaves, to garnish	

1 Cut the avocados in half, then twist the halves in opposite directions to separate them. Remove the stones.
2 With a teaspoon, scoop the avocado flesh from the shells into a bowl.
3 Mash the avocado flesh with a fork, adding half of the lemon juice to prevent discoloration.
4 Whisk in the cheese and garlic until evenly mixed, then add Tabasco and seasoning to taste.
5 Transfer the dip to a serving bowl. Cover tightly then chill in the refrigerator until serving time (but no longer than 2 hours).
6 Before serving, prepare the crudités. Scrape the carrots and cut them into thin sticks. Trim the celery and cut into thin sticks. Separate the chicory into leaves. Toss the mushrooms in the remaining lemon juice.
7 To serve, uncover the dip, place the bowl in the centre of a large serving platter and garnish with celery leaves. Surround with the prepared crudités. Serve immediately, or the avocado in the dip may discolour.

HUMMUS

225 g (8 oz) dried chick peas, soaked in cold water overnight, or two 400 g (14 oz) cans chick peas	60 ml (4 tbsp) olive oil
	1-2 garlic cloves, crushed
juice of 2 large lemons	salt and pepper
150 ml (¼ pint) tahini paste	black olives and chopped parsley, to garnish

1   If using dried chick peas, drain, place in a saucepan and cover with cold water. Bring to the boil and simmer gently for 2 hours or until tender.

2   Drain the cooked or canned chick peas, reserving a little of the liquid. Put them in a blender or food processor, reserving a few for garnish, and gradually add the reserved liquid and the lemon juice, blending well after each addition in order to form a smooth purée.

3   Add the tahini paste, all but 10 ml (2 tsp) oil and the garlic. Season with salt and pepper to taste. Blend again until smooth.

4   Spoon into a serving dish and sprinkle with the reserved oil, chick peas, and the olives and chopped parsley. Serve with warm pitta bread.

SERVING SUGGESTION

Hummus – or as it is more correctly called – hummus bi tahina – is a traditional dip from the Middle East, where it is served as part of the mezze.

The mezze course is similar to the French hors d'oeuvre, a collection of savoury titbits designed to titilate the appetite before the main meal is served. In this country you can serve hummus on its own as a starter.

TARAMASALATA

225 g (8 oz) smoked cod's roe	finely grated rind and juice of 1 lemon
1 garlic clove	
50 g (2 oz) fresh wholemeal breadcrumbs	150 ml (¼ pint) olive oil
	pepper
1 small onion, finely chopped	lemon wedges, to garnish

1   Skin the smoked cod's roe and break it up into pieces. Place in a blender or food processor with the garlic, breadcrumbs, onion, lemon rind and juice and blend to form a purée.

2   Gradually add the oil and blend well after each addition until smooth. Blend in 90 ml (6 tbsp) hot water with pepper to taste.

3   Spoon into a serving dish and chill in the refrigerator for at least 1 hour. Garnish with lemon slices and serve with warm pitta bread or toast, preferably wholemeal.

COOK'S TIP

Homemade taramasalata tastes very much better than commercial varieties, and it is simple and quick to make.

GUACAMOLE DIP WITH CRUDITES

SERVES 8

1 small onion	10 ml (2 tsp) ground coriander
2-3 garlic cloves	
2.5 cm (1 inch) piece fresh root ginger, peeled	10 ml (2 tsp) ground cumin
	5 ml (1 tsp) chilli powder
4 large ripe avocados	2 ripe tomatoes, seeded and roughly chopped
finely grated rind and juice of 2 small limes	
	salt and pepper
60 ml (4 tbsp) chopped fresh coriander	coriander sprigs, to garnish

1 Using a food processor or blender and with the machine running, drop the onion, garlic and ginger through the funnel. Process until finely chopped.

2 Peel and stone the avocados, then put in the food processor or blender with all the remaining ingredients, except the tomato. Process until almost smooth. Stir in the tomato, taste and adjust seasoning as necessary.

3 Transfer to a serving bowl and chill for 30 minutes to let the flavours develop. Garnish with coriander and serve with crudités.

COOK'S TIP

If you don't own a food processor, finely chop the onion, garlic, ginger and tomato then mash the avocado before mixing with the remaining ingredients.

CRUDITÉS

Serve an assortment of crudités chosen and prepared to appeal to the eye as well as the taste buds. Baby vegetables such as carrots, baby corn, cherry tomatoes and button mushrooms can be served whole. Traditionally, crudités are cut into neat strips, all about the same size and arranged in tidy rows of colour. You may prefer to simply clean and trim vegetables to a manageable size retaining their original shape. Sliced fresh fruit such as apples, pears, nectarines, grapes, mangoes, star fruit and fresh dates make good crudités.

CRUNCHY BAKED POTATO SKINS

SERVES 4

4 medium baking potatoes	300 ml (½ pint) low-fat natural yogurt
60 ml (4 tbsp) oil	
salt and pepper	30 ml (2 tbsp) snipped chives
	salad leaves to garnish

1 Pierce the potatoes all over with a skewer, then place directly on the oven shelf. Bake in the oven at 200°C (400°F) mark 6 for 1¼ hours until tender.

2 Cut each potato in half lengthways and scoop out most of the flesh with a sharp-edged teaspoon, taking care not to split the skins.

3 Stand the potato skins on a lightly oiled baking sheet. Brush them inside and out with the oil and sprinkle with plenty of salt and pepper.

4 Increase the oven temperature to 220°C (425°F) mark 7 and bake for 10 minutes until crisp.

5 Meanwhile, whisk the yogurt and chives together with seasoning to taste. Spoon into a serving bowl.

6 Serve the potato skins piping hot, with the yogurt dressing. Garnish with salad leaves.

SERVING SUGGESTION

Crunchy baked potato skins are an American idea. Put a spoonful or two of dressing in each potato skin and either eat with the fingers as the Americans do, or with a knife and fork if you prefer. They are equally good served as a starter or as a quick and easy snack.

SMOKED MACKEREL WITH APPLE

SERVES 8

100 g (4 oz) celery, trimmed	150 ml (¼ pint) soured cream or smetana
100 g (4 oz) cucumber, skinned	30 ml (2 tbsp) lemon juice
100 g (4 oz) red eating apple, cored	paprika
350 g (12 oz) smoked mackerel	1 small crisp lettuce
	lemon wedges, to serve (optional)

1 Finely chop the celery, cucumber and apple.
2 Skin the fish, then flake the flesh roughly with a fork. Discard the bones.
3 Combine the celery, cucumber, apple and mackerel in a bowl. Stir in the soured cream or smetana, lemon juice and paprika to taste.
4 Shred the lettuce and place a little in the bases of 8 stemmed glasses. Divide the mackerel equally between them.
5 Garnish each glass with a lemon wedge if liked, and sprinkle with paprika. Serve at room temperature.

COOK'S TIP

There are two kinds of smoked mackerel available: hot-smoked and cold-smoked. Hot-smoked mackerel is the one most widely available, and it does not need cooking before eating, whereas cold-smoked mackerel does. When buying mackerel for this recipe, check with the fishmonger or packet instructions.

KIPPER MOUSSE

SERVES 4

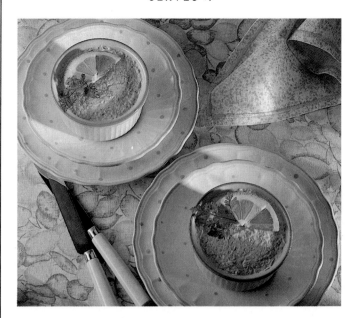

350 g (12 oz) kipper fillets	150 ml (¼ pint) low-fat natural yogurt
juice of 1 orange	1 small garlic clove, crushed
15 ml (1 tbsp) lemon juice	1.25 ml (¼ tsp) ground mace
5 ml (1 tsp) gelatine	pepper
100 g (4 oz) cottage or curd cheese	lemon or orange slices and herb sprigs, to garnish

1 Pour boiling water over the kippers and leave to stand for 1 minute. Drain, pat dry and remove the skin. Flake the flesh, discarding any bones, and put into a blender or food processor.
2 In a small heatproof bowl, mix the orange and lemon juices together. Sprinkle on the gelatine and leave to stand for a few minutes until spongy.
3 Meanwhile add the cottage cheese, yogurt, garlic and mace to the blender or food processor and blend until smooth.
4 Place the bowl of gelatine in a saucepan of hot water and heat gently until dissolved. Add to the kipper mixture and blend until evenly mixed. Season with pepper to taste.
5 Divide the kipper mousse equally between 6 oiled individual ramekin dishes. Chill in the refrigerator for at least 1 hour before serving. Garnish with lemon or orange slices and herb sprigs and serve with wholemeal toast.

COOK'S TIP

Kippers are herrings which have been cold-smoked, that is they need to be cooked before eating – standing them in boiling water for a minute or so is the traditional and the best method. When buying kippers, check for plump flesh and an oily skin – these are signs of quality. A dark-brown colour does not necessarily mean a good kipper, as this is probably an artificial dye. Some of the best kippers are the undyed Manx variety – available from good fishmongers.

SMOKED TROUT WITH TOMATOES

SERVES 8

700 g (1½ lb) smoked trout	30 ml (2 tbsp) lemon juice
225 g (8 oz) cucumber, skinned	60 ml (4 tbsp) low-fat natural yogurt
salt and pepper	4 very large Marmande tomatoes, about 350 g (12 oz) each
175 g (6 oz) mushrooms	
45 ml (3 tbsp) creamed horseradish	spring onion tops, to garnish

1 Flake the trout flesh, discarding the skin and bones.
2 Finely chop the cucumber, sprinkle with salt and leave for 30 minutes to dégorge. Rinse and drain well, then dry thoroughly with absorbent kitchen paper.
3 Finely chop the mushrooms, combine with the cucumber, horseradish, lemon juice and yogurt. Fold in the trout, then add salt and pepper to taste.
4 To skin the tomatoes, put them in a bowl, pour over boiling water and leave for 2 minutes. Drain, then plunge into a bowl of cold water. Remove the tomatoes one at a time and peel off the skin with your fingers.
5 Slice the tomatoes thickly, then sandwich in pairs with the trout mixture.
6 Arrange the tomato 'sandwiches' in a shallow serving dish. Garnish with snipped spring onion tops and chill in the refrigerator until ready to serve.

SMOKED TROUT AND LENTIL SALAD

SERVES 8

FOR THE DRESSING	FOR THE SALAD
150 ml (¼ pint) olive oil	2 medium onions
90 ml (6 tbsp) white wine vinegar	350 g (12 oz) green lentils
5 ml (1 tsp) ground coriander	700 g (1½ lb) smoked trout fillets
2.5 ml (½ tsp) caster sugar	1 bunch watercress, trimmed
10 ml (2 tsp) Dijon mustard	
salt and pepper	

1 Whisk together all the dressing ingredients and set aside. Cut the onions into wafer-thin rings.
2 Pick over the lentils and rinse well. Place in a saucepan, cover with cold water and add 5 ml (1 tsp) salt. Bring to the boil, cover and simmer for 15-20 minutes or until the lentils are tender but still al dente. Drain well, turn into a non-metallic bowl and stir in the dressing and onion rings. Cover and leave in a cool place overnight.
3 To serve, roughly flake the smoked trout. Spoon a small mound of lentils onto eight individual serving plates. Top with pieces of smoked trout. Garnish with watercress sprigs to serve.

VARIATION

Peppered smoked mackerel or smoked mussels can be used instead of smoked trout with the lentil salad.

SMOKED TROUT WITH YOGURT DRESSING

SERVES 4

4 small smoked trout	5 ml (1 tsp) creamed horseradish
finely grated rind and juice of 1 orange	salt and pepper
150 ml (¼ pint) low-fat natural yogurt	finely shredded lettuce or chicory leaves, to serve
	orange segments, to garnish

1 Carefully remove the skin from the trout, then divide each fish into 2 fillets without breaking them. Discard the bones. Cover the fillets and chill in the refrigerator for 30 minutes.
2 Meanwhile mix the orange rind, juice, yogurt and horseradish together. Season with salt and pepper to taste. Chill in the refrigerator for at least 30 minutes, with the smoked trout.
3 Cover 4 small serving plates with shredded lettuce or chicory leaves. Carefully lay 2 trout fillets on each plate and spoon over the dressing. Garnish with orange segments and serve immediately.

TUNA FISH WITH BEANS

SERVES 4

175 g (6 oz) dried white haricot or cannellini beans, soaked in cold water overnight	1 small onion, skinned and finely sliced
45 ml (3 tbsp) olive oil	200 g (7 oz) can tuna fish in brine, drained and flaked into large chunks
15 ml (1 tbsp) wine vinegar	chopped parsley, to garnish
salt and pepper	

1 Drain the beans, rinse under cold running water, then tip into a large saucepan and cover with fresh cold water. Bring to the boil, then lower the heat and simmer gently for 1½ -2 hours or until they are tender. Drain.
2 Whisk together the oil, vinegar, salt and pepper to taste and mix with the hot beans. Cool for 15 minutes.
3 Mix in the onion, then the tuna fish, being careful not to break it up too much.
4 To serve, transfer to a serving dish and sprinkle liberally with chopped parsley.

SERVING SUGGESTION

Serve as a substantial starter, or as a light lunch with a crisp leafy salad and wholemeal bread.

BAKED
CRAB RAMEKINS

SERVES 6

30 ml (2 tbsp) polyunsaturated oil	150 ml (¼ pint) low-fat natural yogurt
1 small onion, finely chopped	45 ml (3 tbsp) semi-skimmed milk
225 g (8 oz) cooked white crab meat, or white and brown mixed	cayenne pepper
	salt
50 g (2 oz) fresh wholemeal breadcrumbs	about 40 g (1½ oz) Cheddar cheese
10 ml (2 tsp) French mustard	lime slices and parsley sprigs, to garnish

1 Heat the oil in a saucepan and fry the onion gently until golden brown.
2 Flake the crab meat, taking care to remove any membranes or shell particles. Mix it into the cooked onion and add the breadcrumbs. Mix well together. Stir in the mustard, yogurt and milk. Sprinkle with cayenne, then add salt to taste.
3 Spoon the mixture into 6 individual ramekins or soufflé dishes. Grate the cheese thinly over the surface of each dish. Stand the dishes on a baking sheet. Bake in the oven at 170°C (325°F) mark 3 for 25-30 minutes, or until really hot. Serve immediately, garnished with lime slices and parsley sprigs.

STEAMED MUSSELS
IN PEPPER BROTH

SERVES 6

2 kg (4½ lb) mussels	1 garlic clove, crushed
15 ml (1 tbsp) olive oil	450 g (1 lb) tomatoes, chopped
1 medium onion, finely chopped	salt and pepper
2 large red peppers, seeded and finely chopped	45 ml (3 tbsp) chopped dill
2 bay leaves	dill sprigs, to garnish

1 Discard any cracked mussels and any that remain open when tapped sharply on the shell. Scrub the mussels thoroughly under running cold water, discarding the coarse beards from the sides of the shells.
2 Heat the oil in a medium, heavy-based saucepan. Add the onion, most of the red pepper (reserving some for garnish), 1 bay leaf and the garlic. Sauté for about 5 minutes or until beginning to soften. Add the tomatoes and cook, stirring, for 1-2 minutes before adding 600 ml (1 pint) water. Bring to the boil, cover and simmer for about 15 minutes. Leave the mixture to cool slightly, then purée in a blender or food processor. Sieve into a clean saucepan and add salt and pepper to taste.
3 Place the mussels in a large saucepan. Add 150 ml (¼ pint) water and the remaining bay leaf. Cover the pan tightly and place over a high heat. Steam the mussels, shaking the pan occasionally, for 3-5 minutes. After cooking, discard any mussels that have not opened.
4 Strain the cooking liquid from the mussels into the pepper broth. Stir in the chopped dill and bring to the boil. Adjust the seasoning. Divide the mussels among six individual serving bowls and pour over the pepper broth. Garnish with the reserved diced red pepper and dill sprigs.

GRILLED PRAWNS WITH GARLIC

SERVES 6

24 frozen raw Pacific prawns or frozen Dublin Bay prawn tails, thawed	15 ml (1 tbsp) chopped fresh oregano or 5 ml (1 tsp) dried
18 bay leaves	45 ml (3 tbsp) lemon juice
75 g (3 oz) low-fat spread	salt and pepper
3 large garlic cloves, crushed	60 ml (4 tbsp) chopped parsley, to garnish

1 If using Pacific prawns, remove the legs and with a sharp knife, make a slit down the centre of the back and remove the intestinal vein. Wash well. If using Dublin Bay prawn tails, make a slit through the shell on either side of the underside. Wash well.

2 Thread the prawns and bay leaves on to six skewers and place in a single layer on a well-oiled grill pan.

3 Melt the low-fat spread in a saucepan, add the garlic and fry gently until golden. Remove from the heat and stir in the oregano, lemon juice and salt and pepper to taste.

4 Pour the garlic mixture over the prawns, turning them to coat well. Cook under a preheated grill for 5-8 minutes or until the prawns turn pink. Arrange on a warmed serving platter, pour over the pan juices and sprinkle with chopped parsley. Serve hot, with a leafy salad.

COOK'S TIP

For this recipe it is absolutely essential to buy giant prawns, which are only usually available at good supermarket fish counters and fishmongers.

BAKED MUSHROOM CROUTES

SERVES 6

225 g (8 oz) button mushrooms	30 ml (2 tbsp) olive oil
225 g (8 oz) wild mushrooms, such as chanterelles, ceps, etc	salt and pepper
	6 thin slices of French bread
30 ml (2 tbsp) roughly chopped coriander	1 garlic clove, halved
	25 g (1 oz) low-fat spread
30 ml (2 tbsp) lemon juice	roughly chopped coriander, to garnish

1 Thinly slice the button mushrooms and any large wild ones. Place in an ovenproof dish and sprinkle over half the coriander, the lemon juice and the olive oil. Season to taste with salt and pepper.

2 Cover the dish with foil and bake in the oven at 200°C (400°F) mark 6 for about 40 minutes. Stir the mixture once, halfway through the cooking time.

3 Rub the bread slices with the halved garlic clove. Thinly spread one side of each slice with low-fat spread. Arrange the slices, fat-side uppermost, in an ovenproof dish and bake in the oven for 10 minutes.

4 Spoon the hot mushrooms and juices over the six bread slices. Return to the oven for 15 minutes. Serve garnished with coriander.

COOK'S TIP

Wild mushrooms give the best flavour, but if they are unavailable use a mixture of button mushrooms and either the large flat mushrooms or chestnut mushrooms.

LUNCHES, SUPPERS & SNACKS

In this chapter you will find plenty of imaginative recipes for delicious healthy snack meals to tempt you away from convenience foods and 'take-aways'. Ideas range from quick pasta dishes, tasty flans and pizzas to stuffed vegetables and spicy kebabs.

SALAMAGUNDI

SERVES 8

1 roasted duckling	120 ml (4 fl oz) reduced-calorie vinaigrette
1 roasted chicken	450 g (1 lb) peas, cooked
450 g (1 lb) carrots, cut into strips	1 cucumber, sliced
salt and pepper	225 g (8 oz) tomatoes, thinly sliced
450 g (1 lb) potatoes, peeled	4 celery sticks, thinly sliced

1 Remove and discard the skin from the duckling and chicken, then carefully remove the flesh and cut into thin strips, about 5 cm (2 inches) long.
2 Cook the carrots in boiling salted water until just tender; drain. Cook the potatoes in boiling salted water until tender. Drain and leave to cool, then dice finely.
3 Place the potatoes and peas in the bottom of a large oval platter to give a flat base. Arrange a layer of cucumber on top, following the oval shape of the platter.
4 Pour over a little dressing. Next, arrange a layer of carrot, slightly inside the first layer. Top with more layers of chicken meat, tomato slices, celery and duck meat. Sprinkle each one with dressing. Continue layering until all the ingredients are used.

CROSTINI

SERVES 4

225 g (8 oz) chicken livers	10 ml (2 tsp) tomato purée
30 ml (2 tbsp) olive oil	10 ml (2 tsp) chopped sage or parsley
1 small onion, finely chopped	salt and pepper
1 garlic clove, crushed	about 60 ml (4 tbsp) dry white wine
2 celery sticks, finely chopped	sage leaves, to garnish

1 Trim the chicken livers and cut into small bite-sized pieces.
2 Heat the oil in a frying pan, add the chicken livers and fry over brisk heat until just changing in colour, stirring constantly. Remove with a slotted spoon and set aside.
3 Add the onion, garlic and celery to the pan and fry gently for 7-10 minutes until softened.
4 Stir in the tomato purée, sage and salt and pepper. Return the chicken livers to the pan and add enough wine to moisten. Cook gently for about 5 minutes, stirring frequently, until just tender.
5 Pile on to hot toasted French bread to serve and garnish with sage.

45

OPEN SANDWICHES

PRAWNS WITH LEMON AND CORIANDER

Mix 10 ml (2 tsp) low-fat mayonnaise with a little chopped coriander and spread on crustless toast or dark rye bread. Cover with 50 g (2 oz) prawns. Season to taste. Garnish with lemon and coriander.

LUMPFISH ROE WITH EGGS

Lightly spread brown bread with polyunsaturated margarine and arrange a small bundle of watercress at one end. Fill the remainder with 5 ml (1 tsp) lumpfish roe topped with slices of hard-boiled egg.

BLUE BRIE, BACON AND LAMB'S LETTUCE

Lightly spread pumpernickel bread with polyunsaturated margarine. Arrange lamb's lettuce leaves along one long edge. Cover the bread with very thin slices of blue Brie cheese, overlapping them on the lettuce. Top with 1 slice of crisp, grilled back bacon.

SMOKED SALMON ON PUMPERNICKEL

Spread pumpernickel bread with low-fat soft cheese mixed with horseradish sauce to taste. Cover with sliced smoked salmon, dill sprigs or celery leaves and lemon wedges.

SMOKED MACKEREL AND COTTAGE CHEESE

Lightly spread pumpernickel bread with low-fat cottage cheese. Top with chunks of peppered smoked mackerel.

HUMMUS WITH SESAME

Spread crispbreads with hummus. Sprinkle liberally with toasted sesame seeds. Garnish with olives and parsley.

SMOKED CHICKEN WITH ORANGE

Stamp out rounds of light rye bread. Mix together equal quantities of low-fat natural yogurt and a low-fat soft cheese with herbs; spread thinly on the bread rounds. Top with thin slices of smoked chicken, orange segments and shreds of spring onion.

CHILLI PIZZA FINGERS

225 g (8 oz) lean minced beef	225 g (8 oz) plain wholemeal flour
2.5 ml (½ tsp) chilli powder	50 g (2 oz) medium oatmeal
1 garlic clove, crushed	15 ml (1 tbsp) baking powder
1 medium onion, chopped	salt and pepper
1 small green pepper, seeded and chopped	50 g (2 oz) butter or polyunsaturated margarine
100 g (4 oz) mushrooms, sliced	1 egg, beaten
225 g (8 oz) tomatoes, skinned and chopped	60 ml (4 tbsp) semi-skimmed milk
213 g (7.5 oz) can red kidney beans, drained	15 ml (1 tbsp) tomato purée
150 ml (¼ pint) beef stock	175 g (6 oz) Mozzarella cheese, thinly sliced
	basil sprigs, to garnish

1 First prepare the topping. Put the minced beef, chilli powder and garlic in a non-stick saucepan and dry fry for 3-4 minutes, stirring occasionally. Add the onion, green pepper and mushrooms and fry for a further 1-2 minutes. Stir in the tomatoes, kidney beans and stock. Bring to the boil and simmer for about 15 minutes, stirring occasionally.
2 Meanwhile combine the flour, oatmeal, baking powder and a pinch of salt in a bowl.
3 Rub in the butter or margarine until the mixture resembles fine breadcrumbs. Bind to a soft dough with the egg and milk, then turn out on to a floured surface and knead lightly until smooth.
4 Roll out the dough to a 25 x 18 cm (10 x 7 inch) rectangle. Lift on to a baking sheet, then spread carefully with tomato purée. Pile the chilli mixture on top and cover with Mozzarella cheese.
5 Bake in the oven at 200°C (400°F) mark 6 for about 30 minutes until golden and bubbling. Cut into fingers for serving, garnished with basil sprigs.

FETTUCCINE
WITH CLAM SAUCE

SERVES 4

15 ml (1 tbsp) olive oil	two 200 g (7 oz) cans or jars baby clams in brine, drained
1 medium onion, finely chopped	30 ml (2 tbsp) chopped parsley
2-3 garlic cloves, crushed	salt and pepper
700 g (1½ lb) tomatoes, skinned and roughly chopped, or a 397 g (14 oz) and a 225 g (8 oz) can tomatoes	400 g (14 oz) fettuccine or other long thin pasta, preferably wholewheat

1 To make the sauce, heat the oil in a saucepan, add the onion and garlic and fry gently for 5 minutes until soft but not coloured.
2 Stir in the tomatoes and their juice, bring to the boil and cook for 15-20 minutes until slightly reduced.
3 Stir the drained clams into the sauce with half of the parsley and salt and pepper to taste. Remove from the heat.
4 Cook the fettuccine in a large pan of boiling salted water for 8-10 minutes or until just tender.
5 Reheat the sauce just before the pasta is cooked. Drain the fettuccine well, tip into a warmed serving dish and pour over the clam sauce. Sprinkle with the remaining chopped parsley to garnish.

VARIATION

Replace the clams with canned mussels, or mussels in jars.

TAGLIATELLE IN CURD
CHEESE AND HERBS

SERVES 2

15 g (½ oz) butter or polyunsaturated margarine	salt
1 garlic clove, crushed	100 g (4 oz) tagliatelle, preferably wholewheat
50 g (2 oz) mushrooms, sliced	50 g (2 oz) low-fat curd cheese
5 ml (1 tsp) chopped sage	sage leaves, to garnish
50 g (2 oz) cooked ham, diced	

1 Melt the butter or margarine in a frying pan and fry the garlic, mushrooms and sage for 2 minutes, then stir in the ham.
2 Cook the tagliatelle in a large pan of boiling salted water for 10 minutes until just tender. Drain well and keep warm.
3 Gently heat the cheese with the mushroom mixture until melted, then stir in the noodles. Serve immediately, garnished with sage leaves.

SPAGHETTI WITH RATATOUILLE SAUCE

SERVES 4

1 aubergine	3 medium courgettes, cut into thin strips
salt and pepper	350 g (12 oz) tomatoes, skinned and finely chopped
1 garlic clove, crushed	
1 onion, finely chopped	10 ml (2 tsp) chopped basil
1 green pepper, seeded and cut into thin strips	400 g (14 oz) wholewheat spaghetti
1 red pepper, seeded and cut into thin strips	freshly grated Parmesan cheese, to serve

1 Dice the aubergine, then spread out on a plate and sprinkle with salt. Leave for 30 minutes to dégorge.
2 Tip the diced aubergine into a sieve and rinse under cold running water. Put into a large, heavy-based saucepan with the garlic, vegetables and basil. Season to taste, cover and cook over a moderate heat for 30 minutes. Shake the pan and stir the vegetables frequently during this time, to encourage the juices to flow.
3 Meanwhile, cook the spaghetti in a large saucepan of boiling salted water for 12 minutes or according to packet instructions, until al dente (tender but firm to the bite).
4 Drain the spaghetti thoroughly and turn into a warmed serving dish. Taste and adjust the seasoning of the ratatouille sauce, then pour over the spaghetti. Serve immediately, with the Parmesan cheese.

TAGLIATELLE WITH CHEESE AND WALNUTS

SERVES 4

400 g (14 oz) wholewheat or green (spinach) tagliatelle	100 g (4 oz) walnuts, chopped
salt and pepper	5 ml (1 tsp) chopped sage
100 g (4 oz) Gorgonzola cheese	75 ml (5 tbsp) olive oil
	15 ml (1 tbsp) chopped parsley, to garnish

1 Cook the tagliatelle in a large saucepan of boiling salted water for 10 minutes or according to packet instructions, until al dente (tender but firm to the bite).
2 Meanwhile, crumble the cheese into a blender or food processor. Add two-thirds of the walnuts and the sage. Blend to combine the ingredients.
3 Add the oil gradually through the funnel (as when making mayonnaise) and blend until the sauce is evenly incorporated.
4 Drain the tagliatelle well and return to the pan. Add the nut sauce and fold in gently to mix. Add seasoning to taste.
5 Transfer the pasta and sauce to a warmed serving bowl and sprinkle with the remaining walnuts. Serve immediately, garnished with chopped parsley.

SERVING SUGGESTION

Quick to make at the last-minute, this nutritious dish makes an unusual lunch or supper. Serve with a crisp green salad.

PASTA
WITH TUNA SAUCE

SERVES 4

225 g (8 oz) pasta spirals or shells	25 g (1 oz) butter or polyunsaturated margarine
salt and pepper	120 ml (4 fl oz) soured cream or smetana
5 ml (1 tsp) polyunsaturated oil	5 ml (1 tsp) anchovy essence
198 g (7 oz) can tuna, drained	30 ml (2 tbsp) wine vinegar
2 eggs, hard-boiled and shelled	60 ml (4 tbsp) chopped parsley

1 Cook the pasta in plenty of boiling salted water to which the oil has been added, for about 15 minutes until al denté (tender but firm to the bite). Drain well.
2 Meanwhile, flake the tuna fish with 2 forks. Chop the hard-boiled eggs finely.
3 Melt the butter or margarine in a deep frying pan and toss in the pasta. Stir in the soured cream or smetana, anchovy essence and vinegar.
4 Add the tuna and egg to the pan with the parsley. Season well and warm through over low heat, stirring occasionally. Serve immediately.

COOK'S TIP

The type of pasta you use for this dish is really a matter of personal taste, but remember wholewheat pasta contains more fibre than ordinary pasta.
As long as the shapes are small (pasta corta), the sauce will cling to them and not slide off – Italians serve short cut pasta with sauces like this one which have chunks of fish or meat in them. Italian pasta in the shape of shells are called conchiglie, and there are many different sizes to choose from. Farfalle are shaped like small bow-ties; fusilli are spirals, so too are spirale ricciolo; rotelle are shaped like wheels. There are also many different types of short pasta shaped like macaroni – penne are hollow and shaped like quills with angled ends, rigatoni have ridges.

MACARONI
AND BROCCOLI CHEESE

SERVES 2

75 g (3 oz) wholewheat macaroni	300 ml (½ pint) semi-skimmed milk
salt and pepper	75 g (3 oz) Red Leicester cheese, grated
25 g (1 oz) butter or polyunsaturated margarine	100 g (4 oz) broccoli florets
25 g (1 oz) wholemeal plain flour	15 ml (1 tbsp) wholemeal breadcrumbs

1 Cook the macaroni in plenty of boiling salted water for 15 minutes or until just tender. Drain.
2 Put the butter or margarine, flour and milk in a saucepan. Heat, whisking continuously, until the sauce boils, thickens and is smooth. Simmer for 1-2 minutes.
3 Remove pan from the heat, add most of the cheese and stir until melted. Season to taste.
4 Blanch the broccoli in boiling water for 7 minutes or until tender. Drain well.
5 Put the broccoli in the base of a 900 ml (1½ pint) flameproof serving dish. Cover with the macaroni and cheese sauce. Sprinkle with remaining cheese and breadcrumbs. Brown under a hot grill.

COOK'S TIP

This version of ever-popular macaroni cheese uses Red Leicester cheese, wholewheat pasta, and broccoli. If you have never used wholewheat pasta before you will find the flavour is stronger and nuttier than the plain kind.

WHOLEWHEAT MACARONI BAKE

SERVES 4-6

175 g (6 oz) wholewheat macaroni	5 ml (1 tsp) dried oregano
salt and pepper	30 ml (2 tbsp) plain wholemeal flour
30 ml (2 tbsp) polyunsaturated oil	300 ml (½ pint) semi-skimmed milk
1 onion, chopped	100 g (4 oz) low-fat soft cheese
225 g (8 oz) button mushrooms	1 egg, beaten
350 g (12 oz) tomatoes, skinned and roughly chopped	5 ml (1 tsp) English mustard powder
300 ml (½ pint) vegetable stock	30 ml (2 tbsp) wholemeal breadcrumbs
15 ml (1 tbsp) tomato purée	30 ml (2 tbsp) freshly grated Parmesan cheese
5 ml (1 tsp) dried mixed herbs	

1 Cook the macaroni in plenty of boiling salted water for 10 minutes; drain. Heat the oil in a saucepan and fry the onion for 5 minutes.

2 Cut the small mushrooms in half and slice the larger ones. Add to the pan and cook with the onion for 1-2 minutes.

3 Add the tomatoes and stock and bring to the boil, stirring constantly. Lower the heat, add the tomato purée and herbs and season to taste. Simmer for 10 minutes.

4 Put the flour and milk in a blender and blend for 1 minute. Transfer to a pan and simmer, stirring constantly, for 5 minutes or until thick. Remove from the heat and beat in the cheese, egg and mustard. Season.

5 Mix the macaroni with the mushroom and tomato sauce, then pour into a baking dish. Pour over the cheese sauce and sprinkle with breadcrumbs and Parmesan.

6 Bake in the oven at 190°C (375°F) mark 5 for 20 minutes or until golden brown and bubbling. Serve hot.

MUSHROOM FLAN

SERVES 4

100 g (4 oz) wholemeal breadcrumbs	175 g (6 oz) mushrooms, sliced
300 ml (½ pint) low-fat natural yogurt	4 spring onions, trimmed and chopped
salt and pepper	75 g (3 oz) Cheddar cheese, grated
4 eggs	watercress sprigs, to garnish
150 ml (¼ pint) semi-skimmed milk	

1 Mix the breadcrumbs and 150 ml (¼ pint) of the yogurt to a paste. Add salt and pepper to taste.

2 Use the mixture to line a 23 cm (9 inch) flan dish or tin, pressing the paste into shape with the fingers. Set aside.

3 Whisk the eggs and milk together with the remaining yogurt and salt and pepper to taste.

4 Arrange the mushrooms, spring onions and half the cheese on the base of the flan. Pour the egg mixture over the top and then sprinkle with the remaining cheese.

5 Bake the flan in the oven at 180°C (350°F) mark 4 for about 30 minutes or until brown and set. Serve warm, garnished with watercress.

COOK'S TIP

The unusual base for this flan is made simply from wholemeal breadcrumbs and yogurt – less fattening than a conventional shortcrust pastry base – and with healthier ingredients. If you prefer to use a pastry base follow the recipe given in Red Onion Tart (see right).

RED ONION TART

SERVES 8

175 g (6 oz) plain flour	4 red onions, thinly sliced
75 g (3 oz) polyunsaturated margarine or butter	75 ml (5 tbsp) semi-skimmed milk
15 ml (1 tbsp) polyunsaturated oil	3 eggs
	2.5 ml (½ tsp) cayenne pepper

1 Put the flour into a mixing bowl and rub in the margarine or butter until the mixture resembles fine breadcrumbs. Mix to a firm but pliable dough with about 30 ml (2 tbsp) cold water. Knead on a lightly floured surface.
2 Roll out the dough and use to line a 20 cm (8 inch) loose-based flan tin. Chill for 30 minutes.
3 Place a sheet of greaseproof paper in the base of the flan case, cover with baking beans and bake blind in a preheated oven at 200°C (400°F) mark 6 for 15 minutes. Remove the beans and paper, then bake for a further 5 minutes.
4 Meanwhile, heat the oil in a heavy-based saucepan, add the onions, cover and cook for 6-8 minutes or until transparent. Drain off the oil, then place the onions in the partially baked flan case.
5 Beat the milk with the eggs and cayenne. Pour into the partially baked flan case and bake in the oven at 180°C (350°F) mark 4 for 25-30 minutes or until the filling is set and golden. Serve immediately.

COOK'S TIP

Red onions are slightly oval shaped and smaller than globe onions. They have a mild, somewhat sweet flavour.
As an alternative, use wholemeal pastry for the flan. Simply replace half of the plain flour with wholemeal flour.

COURGETTE PASTICCIO

SERVES 2

400 g (14 oz) courgettes, trimmed and coarsely grated	4 egg whites, size 2
100 g (4 oz) low-fat Cheddar cheese, grated	225 g (8 oz) can chopped tomatoes
60 ml (4 tbsp) plain wholemeal flour	10 ml (2 tsp) tomato purée
5 ml (1 tsp) chopped fresh basil or 2.5 ml (½ tsp) dried	50 g (2 oz) button mushrooms, sliced
pepper, to taste	2.5 ml (½ tsp) dried oregano
	parsley sprigs, to garnish

1 Combine the courgettes, 75 g (3 oz) of the cheese, the flour, basil and pepper in a large bowl. Whisk the egg whites until frothy but not stiff, then fold into the courgette mixture.
2 Place the mixture in a 23 cm (9 inch) loose-bottomed sandwich cake tin and smooth the surface. Bake in the oven at 180°C (350°F) mark 4 for 25 minutes or until slightly browned.
3 Mix the tomatoes and tomato purée together and spread over the cooked base. Scatter over the mushrooms and sprinkle the remaining cheese and oregano on top. Return to the oven and cook for a further 5 minutes. Garnish with parsley. Cut into wedges and serve hot.

COOK'S TIP

A pasticcio is rather similar to a pizza. The grated courgettes are included in the pasticcio base. This recipe serves 2 hungry people or can be stretched to serve 4.

PERSIAN OMELETTE

SERVES 4

450 g (1 lb) fresh spinach or 226 g (8 oz) packet frozen spinach	1 medium onion, chopped
	4 eggs, beaten
225 g (8 oz) potatoes, peeled	salt and pepper
45 ml (3 tbsp) polyunsaturated oil	grated rind of ½ lemon
	juice of 1 lemon

1 If using fresh spinach, wash, and while still wet, place in a saucepan. Cover and cook gently for 5 minutes until tender.

2 Drain well and chop finely. If using frozen spinach, place in a saucepan and cook for 7-10 minutes to drive off as much liquid as possible.

3 Cut the potato into small dice. Heat 30 ml (2 tbsp) of the oil in a 20 cm (8 inch) non-stick frying pan, add the potato and fry gently for 5 minutes until just turning brown. Add the onion and cook for about 10 minutes until golden. The potato should be almost tender. Remove from the heat and set aside.

4 In a large bowl, mix the spinach with the eggs, seasoning, lemon rind and juice. Add the potato and onion and mix well.

5 Heat the remaining oil in the same frying pan, pour in the egg mixture, spreading it evenly over the bottom of the pan. Cover with a lid or foil and cook gently for 15 minutes until just set.

6 Remove the lid or foil and brown under a hot grill before serving warm.

COOK'S TIP

All this substantial omelette needs as an accompaniment is crusty wholemeal bread and a green salad.

BRUSSELS SPROUT SOUFFLE

SERVES 4

700 g (1½ lb) Brussels sprouts, trimmed weight	300 ml (½ pint) semi-skimmed milk
salt and pepper	pinch of freshly grated nutmeg
50 g (2 oz) butter or polyunsaturated margarine	3 eggs, separated
40 g (1½ oz) plain wholemeal flour	

1 Grease a 1.3 litre (2¼ pint) soufflé dish. Preheat the oven to 200°C (400°F) mark 6.

2 Cook the Brussels sprouts in boiling salted water for 10-15 minutes until tender. Drain well.

3 Melt the butter or margarine in a saucepan, add the flour and cook gently, stirring, for 1-2 minutes. Remove from the heat and gradually blend in the milk. Bring to the boil, stirring constantly, then simmer for 3 minutes until thick and smooth. Add the nutmeg and remove from the heat.

4 Chop half of the sprouts. Work the remaining sprouts in a blender or food processor to a purée with the egg yolks and a little of the sauce. Fold into the rest of the sauce with the chopped sprouts. Season with salt and pepper to taste.

5 Whisk the egg whites until stiff. Gently fold into the sprouts mixture. Turn into the soufflé dish. Bake in the oven for 30-35 minutes until risen. Serve immediately.

COOK'S TIP

A hot soufflé is the true soufflé. The tiny bubbles of air trapped within the egg whites expand as they are heated, puffing up the base mixture to which they were added, by as much as two thirds of its original size. When making hot soufflés, it is important to follow the recipe precisely; do not try to cut corners.

WHOLEWHEAT SPINACH PANCAKES

SERVES 4

175 g (6 oz) fresh spinach, washed	about 45 ml (3 tbsp) polyunsaturated oil, for frying
100 g (4 oz) wholemeal flour	225 g (8 oz) cottage cheese with prawns
salt and pepper	2.5 ml (½ tsp) paprika
150 ml (¼ pint) milk	cooked whole prawns and herb sprigs, to garnish
150 ml (¼ pint) water	
1 egg, beaten	

1 Cut away the thick midribs and stalks from the spinach and put the leaves in a saucepan with only the water that clings to them. Cover and cook gently for 5 minutes until tender.

2 Drain the spinach in a colander, pressing to extract as much water as possible from the leaves. Turn the spinach on to a board and chop very finely.

3 Put the flour in a bowl with a pinch of salt. Make a well in the centre, add half of the milk and water and the egg. Beat vigorously with a whisk, gradually incorporating the flour into the centre. Whisk in the remaining liquid and the spinach.

4 Heat a little oil in a pancake pan or heavy-based 18 cm (7 inch) frying pan. Pour one-eighth of the batter into the pan and tip and tilt the pan so that the batter runs all over the base. Cook over moderate heat for about 30 seconds until the underside is golden, then turn the pancake over and cook the other side.

5 Slide the pancake out on to a sheet of greaseproof paper placed over a plate and keep warm while cooking the remaining 7 pancakes. (As each pancake is made, stack it on top of the last one, with greaseproof paper in between.)

6 Season the cottage cheese with the paprika and salt and pepper to taste. Spread a little over each pancake, then roll up or fold into parcels. Serve immediately garnished with the prawns and herbs.

FOUR-CHEESE AND TOMATO PIZZA

SERVES 6

100 g (4 oz) plain flour	5 ml (1 tsp) dried oregano
100 g (4 oz) strong plain white flour	15 ml (1 tbsp) tomato purée
5 ml (1 tsp) fast-action dried yeast	pepper
5 ml (1 tsp) salt	FOR THE CHEESE TOPPING
10 ml (2 tsp) polyunsaturated oil	100 g (4 oz) mozzarella cheese, thinly sliced
a few olives	50 g (2 oz) dolcelatte cheese, chopped
basil leaves, to garnish	100 g (4 oz) ricotta cheese, crumbled
FOR THE TOMATO SAUCE	30 ml (2 tbsp) freshly grated Parmesan cheese
400 g (14 oz) can chopped tomatoes	

1 To make the dough, mix the flours, yeast and salt in a bowl. Add 150 ml (¼ pint) warm water and the oil. Mix to a soft dough. Turn the dough on to a floured surface and knead for 5 minutes. Return the dough to the bowl and cover with a clean cloth. Leave to rise in a warm place for 30 minutes or until doubled in size.

2 Meanwhile, place all the tomato sauce ingredients in a saucepan, adding pepper to taste, and bring to the boil. Reduce the heat and simmer, uncovered, for 15-20 minutes or until the sauce is thick and pulpy. Remove from the heat and leave to cool.

3 Quickly knead the dough, then roll out to a 25 cm (10 inch) round and place on a lightly greased baking sheet. Fold up the edges slightly to form a rim.

4 Spread the tomato sauce over the dough to within 1 cm (½ inch) of the edge. Arrange the mozzarella, dolcelatte and ricotta cheeses evenly over the sauce. Finish with a topping of Parmesan cheese. Sprinkle with olives. Bake in the oven at 200°C (400°F) mark 6 for 25-30 minutes. Serve hot, garnished with basil.

STUFFED CABBAGE ROLLS

SERVES 4

8-10 large cabbage leaves, trimmed	450 ml (¾ pint) vegetable or chicken stock
30 ml (2 tbsp) polyunsaturated oil	397 g (14 oz) can tomatoes
2 medium onions, finely chopped	5 ml (1 tsp) Worcestershire sauce
100 g (4 oz) mushrooms, chopped	2.5 ml (½ tsp) dried basil
	salt and pepper
50 g (2 oz) long-grain brown rice	50 g (2 oz) hazelnuts, skinned and chopped

1 Blanch the cabbage leaves in boiling water for 3-4 minutes. Drain thoroughly.
2 Heat 15 ml (1 tbsp) of the oil in a frying pan and fry half the onions with the mushrooms for 5 minutes until browned. Add the rice and stir well.
3 Add 300 ml (½ pint) of the stock to the rice. Cover and cook for about 40 minutes until the rice is tender and the stock has been completely absorbed.
4 Meanwhile, make a tomato sauce. Heat the remaining oil in a pan and fry the remaining onion for about 5 minutes until golden. Add the tomatoes, remaining stock, Worcestershire sauce, basil and salt and pepper to taste. Bring to the boil, stirring, and simmer for 8 minutes. Purée in a blender or food processor until smooth.
5 Stir the hazelnuts into the rice with salt and pepper to taste, then remove from the heat. Divide the rice mixture between the cabbage leaves and roll up to make neat parcels.
6 Arrange the cabbage parcels in an ovenproof dish. Pour over the tomato sauce. Cover and cook in the oven at 180°C (350°F) mark 4 for about 1 hour until tender.

STUFFED PEPPERS WITH PINE NUTS

SERVES 6

3 green peppers	100 g (4 oz) mushrooms, sliced
3 red peppers	salt and pepper
50 g (2 oz) butter or polyunsaturated margarine	75 g (3 oz) pine nuts or flaked almonds, roasted and chopped
1 onion, finely chopped	10 ml (2 tsp) soy sauce
100 g (4 oz) long grain rice	30 ml (2 tbsp) polyunsaturated oil
450 ml (¾ pint) vegetable or chicken stock	
15 ml (1 tbsp) tomato purée	

1 Cut a 2.5 cm (1 inch) lid from the stem end of the peppers. Scoop out the seeds and membrane. Blanch the shells and lids in boiling water for about 2 minutes. Drain and cool.
2 Melt the butter or margarine in a saucepan and gently fry the onion for 5 minutes until softened. Stir in the rice and cook for 1-2 minutes.
3 Add the stock, tomato purée and mushrooms. Bring to the boil and simmer for 13-15 minutes until the rice is tender and all the stock absorbed.
4 Season well and stir in the nuts and soy sauce. Use this mixture to fill the peppers.
5 Replace lids, then place the peppers in a deep oven-proof dish and pour over the oil. Cover and cook in the oven at 190°C (375°F) mark 5 for 30 minutes until tender.

SERVING SUGGESTION

With their filling of rice, mushrooms and nuts, these stuffed peppers are substantial enough to serve on their own. Alternatively, serve with wholemeal or garlic bread.

LENTIL AND CELERY STUFFED PEPPERS

SERVES 2

125 g (4 oz) red lentils	1 medium onion, finely chopped
salt and pepper	75 g (3 oz) celery, finely chopped
2 green peppers, about 175 g (6 oz) each	75 g (3 oz) low-fat soft cheese
25 g (1 oz) butter or polyunsaturated margarine	1 egg

1 Cook the lentils in boiling salted water for 12-15 minutes until just tender.
2 Meanwhile, halve the peppers lengthwise and remove the cores and seeds. Place on a steamer and steam, covered, for about 15 minutes or until soft.
3 Melt the butter in a frying pan, add the onion and celery and fry gently for 2-3 minutes.
4 Drain the lentils and add to the onion and celery. Cook, stirring, for 1-2 minutes until heated through.
5 Remove the pan from the heat and beat in the cheese and egg with salt and pepper to taste.
6 Remove the peppers from the steamer and fill with the mixture. Place under a hot grill for about 5 minutes or until golden brown. Serve hot.

COOK'S TIP

Serve these stuffed peppers for a tasty supper, accompanied by warm wholemeal bread and a tomato salad.

BAKED POTATOES WITH CHICK PEAS

SERVES 4

4 baking potatoes, each weighing about 275 g (10 oz)	2.5 ml (½ tsp) ground cumin
45 ml (3 tbsp) polyunsaturated oil	400 g (14 oz) can chick peas, drained
salt and pepper	60 ml (4 tbsp) chopped parsley
1 medium onion, roughly chopped	150 ml (¼ pint) low-fat natural yogurt
2.5 ml (½ tsp) ground coriander	chopped parsley, to garnish

1 Scrub the potatoes and pat dry. Brush them with 15 ml (1 tbsp) of the oil and sprinkle lightly with salt.
2 Run thin skewers through the potatoes to help conduct the heat through them. Place them directly on the oven shelf and bake in the oven at 200°C (400°F) mark 6 for 1¼ hours or until tender.
3 Meanwhile, heat the remaining oil in a large saucepan, add the onion, coriander and cumin and fry for 4 minutes, stirring occasionally. Add the chick peas and cook for a further 1-2 minutes, stirring all the time.
4 Halve the potatoes and scoop out the flesh, keeping the shells intact. Add the potato flesh to the chick pea mixture with the parsley and yogurt. Mash until smooth; add seasoning to taste.
5 Place the potato shells on a baking sheet and fill with the potato and chick pea mixture. Return to the oven and bake for a further 10-15 minutes. Serve hot, sprinkled with chopped parsley.

SERVING SUGGESTION

Serve these jacket potatoes with a salad of shredded cabbage, celery, apple and walnuts.

LENTIL CROQUETTES

SERVES 4-8

225 g (8 oz) split red lentils	salt and pepper
2 celery sticks, finely chopped	30 ml (2 tbsp) wholemeal flour, to coat
1 onion, chopped	5 ml (1 tsp) paprika
1-2 garlic cloves, crushed	5 ml (1 tsp) ground turmeric
10 ml (2 tsp) garam masala	60 ml (4 tbsp) polyunsaturated oil
1 egg, beaten	cucumber slices, to garnish

1 Place the lentils in a large saucepan with the celery, onion, garlic, garam masala and 600 ml (1 pint) water. Bring to the boil, stirring with a wooden spoon to mix.
2 Lower the heat and simmer gently for 30 minutes or until the lentils are tender and have absorbed all the liquid. Stir frequently to prevent the lentils sticking to the bottom of the pan.
3 Remove from the heat. Leave to cool for a few minutes, then beat in the egg and seasoning to taste.
4 Turn the mixture on to a board or flat plate and spread out evenly. Leave until cold, then chill in the refrigerator for 30 minutes to firm the mixture.
5 With floured hands, form the mixture into 8 triangular croquette shapes. Coat in the flour mixed with the paprika and turmeric. Chill again for 30 minutes.
6 Heat the oil in a large frying pan, add the croquettes and fry over moderate to high heat for 10 minutes, turning once until crisp and golden on both sides.
7 Drain on absorbent kitchen paper and serve hot, garnished with cucumber slices and accompanied by low-fat yogurt.

SERVING SUGGESTION

Serve these spicy croquettes for a tasty lunch dish with a side salad of tomato, onion and fennel. Allow 1 or 2 per person depending on appetite.

BROWN RICE RISOTTO

SERVES 4

2 onions	pinch of saffron or 5 ml (1 tsp) ground turmeric
1 green pepper, seeded	600 ml (1 pint) vegetable or chicken stock
45 ml (3 tbsp) polyunsaturated oil	salt and pepper
1 garlic clove, crushed	chopped parsley, to garnish
275 g (10 oz) long grain brown rice	freshly grated Parmesan cheese, to serve

1 Slice the onions and green pepper finely. Heat the oil in a medium flameproof casserole, add the onions, pepper and garlic and fry gently for about 5 minutes until soft.
2 Put the rice in a sieve and wash it thoroughly under cold running water until the water runs clear. Drain well.
3 Add the rice with the saffron or turmeric to the pan. Fry gently, stirring, for 1-2 minutes until the rice is coated in oil.
4 Stir in the stock, then add salt and pepper to taste. Bring to the boil, then cover the casserole tightly with its lid.
5 Cook in the oven at 170°C (325°F) mark 3 for about 1 hour or until the rice is tender and the stock absorbed. Taste and adjust seasoning and garnish with plenty of parsley. Serve hot, with the grated Parmesan cheese.

COOK'S TIP

Saffron threads are the dried stigmas of the saffron crocus, and saffron is said to be the most expensive spice in the world. The threads will give this dish a subtle colour and delicate flavour. Take care if substituting turmeric; it is more pungent so use it sparingly.

PRAWN RISOTTO

SERVES 4

1 medium onion, thinly sliced	½ sachet saffron threads
1 garlic clove, crushed	salt and pepper
1 litre (1¾ pints) chicken stock	225 g (8 oz) cooked peeled prawns
225 g (8 oz) long grain brown rice	50 g (2 oz) frozen petits pois
50 g (2 oz) small button mushrooms	12 cooked whole prawns, to garnish

1 Put the onion, garlic, stock, rice, mushrooms and saffron in a large saucepan or flameproof casserole. Add salt and pepper to taste. Bring to the boil and simmer, uncovered, for 35 minutes, stirring occasionally.
2 Stir in the prawns and petits pois. Cook over high heat for about 5 minutes, stirring occasionally, until most of the liquid has been absorbed.
3 Turn into a warmed serving dish. Garnish with the whole prawns and serve immediately.

SERVING SUGGESTION

This succulent risotto made with brown rice and prawns would be perfectly offset by a tomato, onion and basil salad.

FISH CAKES WITH HERBS

SERVES 4

275 g (10 oz) haddock, skinned and boned	15 ml (1 tbsp) snipped chives
15 ml (1 tbsp) lemon juice	15 ml (1 tbsp) chopped parsley
15 ml (1 tbsp) Worcestershire sauce	350 g (12 oz) potatoes, cooked and mashed
15 ml (1 tbsp) creamed horseradish	50 g (2 oz) wholemeal breadcrumbs
100 ml (4 fl oz) semi-skimmed milk	

1 Purée the fish in a blender or food processor with the lemon juice, Worcestershire sauce and horseradish. Transfer to a bowl and stir in the milk, chives, parsley and potatoes.
2 Shape the mixture into 4 fish cakes and coat with breadcrumbs.
3 Grill under a moderate heat for 5 minutes on each side, until browned. Serve with a fresh tomato sauce and crisp leafy salad.

COOK'S TIP

Fish cakes are an economical way of making fish go further. You can, if necessary, replace some of the fish with more breadcrumbs but check the seasoning carefully to make sure the finished cakes don't taste too bland. The addition of herbs gives flavour and also produces attractive green flecks.

BEEF KEBABS
WITH HORSERADISH

SERVES 6

700 g (1½ lb) lean minced beef	salt and pepper
250 g (9 oz) grated onion	1 egg, beaten
135 ml (9 tbsp) horseradish sauce	plain flour, for coating
45 ml (3 tbsp) chopped thyme	150 ml (¼ pint) low-fat natural yogurt
250 g (9 oz) fresh white breadcrumbs	120 ml (8 tbsp) finely chopped parsley
	parsley sprigs, to garnish

1 Put the minced beef in a large bowl and mix in the onion, 90 ml (6 tbsp) of the horseradish, the thyme and breadcrumbs. Season to taste.

2 Add enough egg to bind the mixture together and, with floured hands, shape into 18 even-sized sausages. Cover and chill in the refrigerator until required.

3 Thread the kebabs lengthways on to six oiled skewers. Cook under a preheated grill for about 20 minutes, turning frequently.

4 Meanwhile, mix the yogurt with the remaining horseradish and the parsley. Spoon into a serving dish.

5 Serve the kebabs hot, garnished with parsley and accompanied by the sauce, and brown or saffron rice if desired.

MINTED LAMB BURGERS
WITH CUCUMBER

SERVES 4

450 g (1 lb) lean minced lamb	30 ml (2 tbsp) plain wholemeal flour
1 small onion, finely chopped	½ cucumber, cut into 5 cm (2 inch) long wedges
100 g (4 oz) fresh breadcrumbs	6 spring onions, cut into 1 cm (½ inch) pieces
finely grated rind of ½ lemon	200 ml (7 fl oz) lamb or chicken stock
45 ml (3 tbsp) chopped mint	15 ml (1 tbsp) dry sherry
1 egg, beaten	mint sprigs, to garnish
salt and pepper	

1 Mix the lamb, onion, breadcrumbs and lemon rind with 15 ml (1 tbsp) of the chopped mint and the egg. Season with salt and pepper.

2 Shape into 8 burgers with floured hands, then completely coat in the flour.

3 Dry fry the burgers in a large heavy-based non-stick frying pan for about 6 minutes, until lightly browned, turning once. Add the cucumber and spring onions.

4 Pour in the stock and sherry, then add the remaining mint and salt and pepper to taste. Bring to the boil, cover and simmer gently for about 20 minutes or until the meat is tender. Skim off any excess fat before serving, and taste and adjust seasoning. Garnish with mint and serve with boiled new potatoes.

COOK'S TIP

Lamb and mint were made for each other, and the flavours marry perfectly in these quick burgers. When buying cucumbers, feel the stalk end and only buy if it is firm. Don't peel the cucumber, as both appearance and flavour are improved if the skin is left on.

SEEKH KEBABS

SERVES 6-8

900 g (2 lb) lean minced beef or lamb	olive oil, for brushing
2 medium onions, grated	paprika
30 ml (2 tbsp) ground cumin	3 spring onions, chopped
15 ml (1 tbsp) coarsely ground coriander	300 ml (½ pint) low-fat natural yogurt
60 ml (4 tbsp) finely chopped parsley	15 ml (1 tbsp) chopped mint
salt and pepper	mint sprigs, onion rings and lemon wedges, to garnish

1 Ask your butcher to mince the meat very finely, or chop it in a food processor until very fine. Knead the meat with the grated onion, cumin, coriander, parsley and seasoning to make smooth paste.

2 Take about 15-30 ml (1-2 tbsp) of the mixture and press a flat sausage shape on to the ends of wooden skewers. Brush them lightly with oil and sprinkle with a little paprika.

3 Grill about half at a time under a high heat for about 5 minutes. Turn, sprinkle with more paprika and grill the second side until well browned all over. (Keep the exposed wooden sticks away from the flame.) Keep the kebabs warm, loosely covered, until the remainder are cooked.

4 Meanwhile to make the sauce, mix the spring onions, reserving a few dark green shreds for garnish, with the yogurt and mint.

5 Serve the kebabs garnished with mint sprigs, lemon wedges, onion rings and reserved spring onion, with the sauce handed separately.

COOK'S TIP

Every region in the Middle East boasts a traditional 'kofta' recipe of minced lamb or beef minced to a soft paste with spices and fresh herbs.

SESAME CHICKEN PITTAS

SERVES 4

30 ml (2 tbsp) sesame oil	225 g (8 oz) cooked chicken breast, sliced into thin strips
1 onion, sliced	100 g (4 oz) beansprouts
100 g (4 oz) broccoli, cut into tiny florets	15ml (1 tbsp) dark soy sauce
1 red pepper, seeded and diced	30 ml (2 tbsp) toasted sesame seeds
	4 large pitta breads

1 Heat the oil in a large frying pan and stir-fry the onion for 2 minutes. Add the broccoli and pepper and cook for 3-4 minutes, stirring frequently.

2 Add the chicken strips to the pan, stir well, then add the beansprouts and soy sauce. Continue to cook for 2-3 minutes. Sprinkle over the sesame seeds and stir to combine. Remove from the heat, keeping the pan covered to keep warm.

3 Cut through a long side of each pitta bread and open the cavity to form a pocket. Place the pitta breads on a baking sheet. Bake in the oven at 200°C (400°F) mark 6 for 5-10 minutes to heat.

4 Using a slotted spoon, fill each pitta pocket with the chicken mixture.

VARIATION

Replace the chicken with lean roast beef or lamb.

CHICKEN LIVER SKEWERS

SERVES 4

2 small oranges	1 green pepper, about 175 g (6 oz), seeded and roughly chopped
200 ml (7 fl oz) unsweetened orange juice	1 medium onion, roughly chopped
5 ml (1 tsp) chopped tarragon	275 g (10 oz) beansprouts
450 g (1 lb) whole chicken livers	1 small bunch of chives, snipped
2 slices of wholemeal bread, crumbed	salt and pepper

1 Finely grate the rind of 1 of the oranges. Place in a saucepan with the orange juice and tarragon and simmer for 2-3 minutes until reduced by half.

2 Cut the tops and bottoms off both oranges, then remove the skin by working around the oranges in a spiral, using a sharp serrated knife and a sawing action.

3 Divide the oranges into segments by cutting through the membranes on either side of each segment with a sharp knife.

4 Cut the chicken livers in half and toss lightly in the breadcrumbs. Place in a lightly greased grill pan and grill under a moderately high heat for 2 minutes on each side or until just firm.

5 Thread the pepper and onion on to 4 oiled kebab skewers alternately with the livers.

6 Place the skewers in the grill pan and spoon over a little of the reduced orange juice. Grill for 2-3 minutes on each side, turning and basting occasionally.

7 Meanwhile put the beansprouts in a steamer over boiling water for 2-3 minutes until cooked but still slightly crisp. Warm the orange segments in a separate pan with the remaining reduced orange juice.

8 Mix the beansprouts with the chives and salt and pepper to taste and arrange on a warmed serving dish. Top with the skewers and spoon over the orange segments and juices. Serve immediately.

CHICKEN LIVERS IN SHERRY SAUCE

SERVES 2

225 g (8 oz) chicken livers, thawed if frozen	75 ml (3 fl oz) sherry
25 g (1 oz) plain flour	50 ml (2 fl oz) chicken stock
salt and pepper	50 g (2 oz) black or green seedless grapes, halved
25 g (1 oz) butter or polyunsaturated margarine	90 ml (3 fl oz) soured cream or smetana

1 Coat the livers in well-seasoned flour.

2 Melt the butter or margarine in a medium frying pan and fry the livers with any remaining flour for about 4 minutes, stirring once or twice. Gradually stir in the sherry and stock and simmer for 1-2 minutes.

3 Add the grapes and soured cream or smetana. Heat through gently and serve hot, with brown rice.

COOK'S TIP

Rich chicken livers have a very moist, crumbly texture. This quick dish is ideal served as a lunch or fast supper. If grapes are not available, substitute with 25 g (1 oz) sultanas.

VEGETARIAN MAIN MEALS

Vegetables, nuts, pulses, grains, cheese and eggs are all good sources of protein, vitamins and minerals – and they are all featured in this varied collection of recipes. Whether you are a vegetarian or simply enjoy occasional meals without meat or fish, you will find plenty of inspiration in this chapter.

SPINACH STUFFED PASTA SHELLS

SERVES 2

10 large pasta shells	freshly grated nutmeg
450 g (1 lb) fresh spinach, trimmed, or 225 g (8 oz) frozen spinach	salt and pepper
	150 ml (5 fl oz) low-fat natural yogurt
1-2 garlic cloves, crushed	15 ml (1 tbsp) tomato purée
100 g (4 oz) low-fat soft cheese	finely grated rind and juice of ½ lemon

1 Cook the pasta in a large saucepan of boiling salted water for 8-10 minutes or until just tender.

2 Meanwhile, wash the fresh spinach in several changes of water and roughly chop. Cook with just the water clinging to the leaves for 3-4 minutes or until just wilted. If using frozen spinach, cook for about 10 minutes or until thawed. Drain the spinach and finely chop.

3 Mix the spinach with the garlic and cheese and season generously with nutmeg and salt and pepper. Let cool.

4 Drain the pasta, rinse with cold water, then drain well. Stuff the pasta shells with the spinach mixture.

5 Mix the yogurt, tomato purée and lemon rind and juice together and season with salt and pepper to taste. Pour over the stuffed shells. Serve cold.

SPINACH ROULADE

SERVES 4

900 g (2 lb) fresh spinach, washed and trimmed	100 g (4 oz) low-fat curd cheese
4 eggs, size 2, separated	30 ml (2 tbsp) low-fat natural yogurt
salt and pepper	

1 Grease and line a 35 x 25 cm (14 x 10 inch) Swiss roll tin. Set aside.

2 Chop the spinach coarsely. Place in a saucepan with only the water that clings to the leaves. Simmer for 5 minutes, drain. Cool spinach slightly; beat in the egg yolks and salt and pepper to taste.

3 Whisk the egg whites until stiff, then fold into the spinach mixture, until evenly incorporated.

4 Spread the mixture in the tin. Bake in the oven at 200°C (400°F) mark 6 for 20 minutes until firm. Beat the cheese and yogurt together.

5 When the roulade is cooked, turn out on to a sheet of greaseproof paper, peel off the lining paper and spread immediately and quickly with the cheese mixture.

6 Roll up the roulade by gently lifting the greaseproof paper. Place, seam side down, on a serving platter. Serve hot or cold, cut into slices.

CHEESY STUFFED AUBERGINES

SERVES 4

2 aubergines	1 shallot, chopped
25 g (1 oz) polyunsaturated margarine	1 medium onion, chopped
4 small tomatoes, skinned and chopped	50 g (2 oz) wholemeal breadcrumbs
	salt and pepper
10 ml (2 tsp) chopped fresh marjoram or 5 ml (1 tsp) dried	50 g (2 oz) vegetarian Cheddar, grated
	parsley sprigs, to garnish

1 Cook the whole aubergines in boiling water for about 30 minutes until tender.

2 Cut the aubergines in half lengthways, scoop out the flesh and chop finely. Reserve the aubergine shells.

3 Melt the margarine in a pan, add the tomatoes, marjoram, shallot and onion and cook gently for 10 minutes. Stir in the aubergine flesh and a few breadcrumbs, then add salt and pepper to taste.

4 Stuff the aubergine shells with this mixture, sprinkle with the remaining breadcrumbs and then with the grated cheese. Place in a grill pan and grill under moderate heat until golden brown on top. Serve hot, garnished with parsley sprigs, accompanied by boiled rice if liked.

CYPRUS STUFFED PEPPERS

SERVES 4

8 medium peppers	5 ml (1 tsp) raw cane sugar
75 ml (5 tbsp) olive oil	salt and pepper
2 medium onions, chopped	45 ml (3 tbsp) chopped coriander
4 garlic cloves, crushed	
350 g (12 oz) tomatoes, skinned, seeded and chopped	225 g (8 oz) cooked long grain brown rice
15ml (1 tbsp) tomato purée	2.5 ml (½ tsp) ground cinnamon

1 Cut a slice off the top of each pepper and reserve. Remove the cores, seeds and membranes and discard. Wash the peppers and pat dry.

2 Heat 60 ml (4 tbsp) of the oil in a large frying pan, add the peppers and fry gently for 10 minutes, turning them frequently so that they soften on all sides. Remove from the pan with a slotted spoon and drain on absorbent kitchen paper.

3 To make the stuffing, drain off all but 30 ml (2 tbsp) of oil from the pan, then add the onions and garlic and fry very gently for about 15 minutes.

4 Add the tomatoes and fry gently to soften, stirring constantly. Increase the heat and cook rapidly to drive off the liquid – the mixture should be thick and pulpy.

5 Lower the heat, add the tomato purée, sugar and salt and pepper to taste and simmer gently for 5 minutes. Then remove the pan from the heat and stir in the coriander and rice. Spoon the stuffing into the peppers, dividing it equally between them.

6 Stand the peppers close together in a heavy-based pan or flameproof casserole into which they just fit. Sprinkle with the cinnamon, then the remaining 15 ml (1 tbsp) oil. Put the reserved 'lids' on top.

7 Pour 150 ml (¼ pint) of water into the base of the pan, then bring to the boil. Lower the heat, cover with a plate or saucer which just fits inside the rim of the pan, then simmer gently for 1 hour. Serve the peppers hot or cold.

ROASTED PEPPERS WITH LENTILS

SERVES 2

125 g (4 oz) split red lentils	75 g (3 oz) celery, trimmed and finely chopped
salt and pepper	75 g (3 oz) soft fresh goat's cheese or low-fat soft cheese
2 green peppers, about 175 g (6 oz) each, halved and seeded	1 egg
25 g (1 oz) butter or polyunsaturated margarine	about 8 pitted black olives, stoned and roughly chopped
1 medium onion, finely chopped	basil sprigs, to garnish

1 Cook the lentils in boiling salted water for 12-15 minutes until just tender. Drain.

2 Meanwhile, grill the peppers for 10-12 minutes, turning occasionally, until the skin is browned and the flesh softened.

3 Melt the butter in a saucepan and sauté the onion and celery for 2-3 minutes. Stir in the lentils. Off the heat, beat in the cheese, egg, olives and seasoning. Spoon the filling evenly into the pepper halves.

4 Grill the peppers under moderate heat for 2-3 minutes until golden. Garnish with basil sprigs and serve hot with a tomato and onion salad.

VEGETARIAN MEDLEY

SERVES 4

25 g (1 oz) butter or polyunsaturated margarine	15 ml (1 tbsp) chopped fresh sage or 5 ml (1 tsp) dried
2 carrots, sliced	125 g (4 oz) lentils, cooked
1 large onion, chopped	15 ml (1 tbsp) raisins
1 green pepper, seeded and sliced	30 ml (2 tbsp) unsalted peanuts
2 tomatoes, skinned and chopped	salt and pepper
1 large cooking apple, peeled and chopped	300 ml (10 fl oz) low-fat natural yogurt
1 garlic clove, crushed	25 g (1 oz) low-fat soft cheese
	sage leaves, to garnish

1 Melt the butter or margarine in a large frying pan and lightly fry the carrots, onion, green pepper, tomatoes, apple, garlic and sage for 15 minutes, until softened.

2 Add the lentils, raisins and peanuts. Season to taste.

3 Stir the yogurt into the soft cheese and mix well to blend. Stir into the vegetable mixture. Reheat gently for 5 minutes. Serve at once, garnished with sage.

CELERIAC WITH TOMATO SAUCE

SERVES 4

60 ml (4 tbsp) olive oil	5 ml (1 tsp) ground cinnamon
1 large onion, finely chopped	1 bay leaf
3 garlic cloves, crushed	salt and pepper
350 g (12 oz) ripe tomatoes, skinned and finely chopped	2 heads celeriac, total weight about 900 g (2 lb)
15 ml (1 tbsp) tomato purée	5 ml (1 tsp) lemon juice
30 ml (2 tbsp) red wine or red wine vinegar	50 g (2 oz) dried wholemeal breadcrumbs
60 ml (4 tbsp) chopped parsley	50 g (2 oz) freshly grated Parmesan cheese

1 To prepare the tomato sauce, heat the oil in a heavy-based saucepan, add the onion and garlic and fry gently for about 10 minutes until very soft and lightly coloured.
2 Add the tomatoes, tomato purée, wine, parsley, cinnamon, bay leaf and salt and pepper to taste. Add 450 ml (¾ pint) hot water and bring to the boil, stirring with a wooden spoon to break up the tomatoes.
3 Lower the heat, cover and simmer the tomato sauce, uncovered, for 30 minutes, stirring occasionally.
4 Meanwhile peel the celeriac, then cut into chunky pieces. As you prepare the celeriac, place the pieces in a bowl of water to which the lemon juice has been added, to prevent discoloration.
5 Drain the celeriac, then plunge quickly into a large pan of boiling salted water. Return to the boil and blanch for 10 minutes.
6 Drain the celeriac well, then put in an ovenproof dish. Pour over the tomato sauce, discarding the bay leaf, then sprinkle the breadcrumbs and cheese evenly over the top.
7 Bake in the oven at 190°C (375°F) mark 5 for 30 minutes, until the celeriac is tender when pierced with a skewer and the topping is golden brown. Serve hot.

RED KIDNEY BEAN HOT POT

SERVES 4-6

225 g (8 oz) dried red kidney beans, soaked in cold water overnight	600 ml (1 pint) vegetable stock
50 g (2 oz) butter or polyunsaturated margarine	salt and pepper
2 medium onions, sliced	225 g (8 oz) French beans, topped and tailed
225 g (8 oz) celery, sliced	225 g (8 oz) courgettes, sliced
225 g (8 oz) carrots, sliced	50 g (2 oz) wholemeal breadcrumbs
30 ml (2 tbsp) plain wholemeal flour	75 g (3 oz) vegetarian Cheddar, grated

1 Drain the soaked kidney beans and rinse well under cold running water. Put in a large saucepan, cover with plenty of fresh cold water and bring slowly to the boil.
2 Skim off any scum with a slotted spoon, then boil rapidly for 10 minutes. Half cover the pan with a lid and simmer for about 1½ hours, until the beans are tender.
3 Melt the butter in a large saucepan, add the onions and fry gently for about 5 minutes until softened. Add the celery and carrots. Cover and cook gently for 5 minutes.
4 Add the flour and cook gently, stirring, for 1-2 minutes. Remove from the heat and gradually blend in the stock. Bring to the boil, stirring constantly, then simmer for 5 minutes. Season with salt and pepper to taste.
5 Add the French beans and simmer for a further 5 minutes, then add the courgettes. Cook for a further 5-10 minutes, until the vegetables are tender but still with a bite.
6 Drain the kidney beans, add to the vegetables and heat through for about 5 minutes. Taste and adjust seasoning, then turn into a deep flameproof dish.
7 Mix the breadcrumbs and cheese together. Sprinkle on top of the bean mixture and brown under a preheated grill until crisp and crusty. Serve hot, with nutty brown rice or wholemeal bread, and a crisp green salad.

ROOT VEGETABLE HOT POT

SERVES 4-6

1 onion	salt and pepper
225 g (8 oz) potatoes	300 ml (½ pint) vegetable stock
225 g (8 oz) swede	30 ml (2 tbsp) chopped parsley
4 medium carrots	
2 medium leeks	100 g (4 oz) mature vegetarian Cheddar, grated
10 ml (2 tsp) yeast extract	

1 To prepare the vegetables, finely chop the onion. Peel the potatoes and swede and cut into chunks. Peel the carrots and slice thinly.
2 Trim the leeks, cut into thick rings, then rinse thoroughly under cold running water.
3 Put the prepared vegetables in a flameproof casserole with the yeast extract and seasoning to taste. Pour in the stock and bring to the boil, stirring to mix all the ingredients together.
4 Cover the casserole and simmer for 30 minutes until the vegetables are tender. Stir in the parsley, then taste and adjust the seasoning.
5 Sprinkle the cheese over the top of the vegetables, then put under a moderate grill for 5 minutes until melted and bubbling. Serve hot, straight from the casserole.

SERVING SUGGESTION

Serve with chunky slices of wholemeal bread, or on a bed of brown rice.

BUCKWHEAT AND LENTIL CASSEROLE

SERVES 4

150 g (5 oz) buckwheat	225 g (8 oz) red lentils
salt and pepper, to taste	3 bay leaves
30 ml (2 tbsp) polyunsaturated oil	30 ml (2 tbsp) lemon juice
1 red or green pepper, seeded and cut into strips	1 garlic clove, crushed
1 medium onion, finely chopped	2 rosemary sprigs
350 g (12 oz) courgettes, sliced	5 ml (1 tsp) cumin seeds
	600 ml (1 pint) vegetable stock
175 g (6 oz) mushrooms, sliced	chopped parsley, to garnish

1 Bring 450 ml (¾ pint) water to the boil in a saucepan, sprinkle in the buckwheat, add a pinch of salt and return to the boil. Boil rapidly for 1 minute. Lower the heat, cover and cook gently, without stirring, for 12 minutes or until the water has been absorbed. Transfer to a greased casserole.
2 Heat the oil in a flameproof casserole or saucepan and fry the pepper and onion for 5 minutes. Add the courgettes and mushrooms and fry for 5 minutes. Stir in the lentils, bay leaves, lemon juice, garlic, rosemary, cumin and stock. Add to the buckwheat and stir well.
3 Simmer for 45 minutes until the lentils are cooked, stirring occasionally. Adjust the seasoning and sprinkle with chopped parsley. Serve hot with boiled rice and grated cheese, if liked.

COOK'S TIP

Buckwheat consists of tiny, brown seeds. They are high in protein and contain most of the B vitamins. The grains are gluten free.

VEGETABLE KEBABS WITH TOFU SAUCE

SERVES 2-4

297 g (10½ oz) silken tofu	4 small courgettes, trimmed
30 ml (2 tbsp) olive oil	6 baby corn cobs, halved crossways
20 ml (4 tsp) soy sauce	16 button mushrooms
about 30 ml (2 tbsp) lemon juice	12 cherry tomatoes or 3 medium tomatoes, quartered
1-2 garlic cloves, crushed	
15 ml (1 tbsp) sesame oil (optional)	12 bay leaves
salt and pepper	30 ml (2 tbsp) sesame seeds

1 Put the tofu in a blender or food processor with half the oil and soy sauce, the lemon juice, garlic and sesame oil (if using). Work until evenly combined, then add salt and pepper to taste and more lemon juice, if liked. Pour into a jug and chill.
2 Cut each courgette into 3 pieces. Blanch in boiling salted water for 1 minute, then drain. Thread the vegetables and bay leaves on to oiled skewers.
3 Mix the remaining oil and soy sauce with the sesame seeds. Brush over the kebabs. Cook under a preheated grill for about 10 minutes, turning and brushing frequently. Serve hot, on a bed of boiled rice, if liked, with the tofu sauce handed separately.

COOK'S TIP

Tofu is also known as soya bean curd. It is off-white in colour and is formed into soft blocks. Tofu can be bought by weight from Chinese stores or in cartons from healthfood shops. Of the three forms, silken tofu is the softest and ideal for sauces. Firm tofu is made from heavily pressed bean curd and soft tofu has a texture between the two.
Tofu is high in protein, fairly low in carbohydrate and fat and is a good source of calcium, iron and the B vitamins, thiamin and riboflavin.

VEGETABLE LASAGNE

SERVES 4

175 g (6 oz) lasagne verde	5 ml (1 tsp) chopped fresh basil or 2.5 ml (2 tsp) dried
salt and pepper	
30 ml (2 tbsp) polyunsaturated oil	25 g (1 oz) walnut pieces, chopped
2 medium onions, thinly sliced	450 ml (¾ pint) low-fat natural yogurt
350 g (12 oz) tomatoes, skinned and thinly sliced	2 eggs
	75 g (3 oz) vegetarian Cheddar cheese, grated
350 g (12 oz) courgettes, thinly sliced	1.25 ml (¼ tsp) ground cumin
15 ml (1 tbsp) tomato purée	a little oil, for brushing

1 Cook the lasagne in a large saucepan of boiling salted water with 15 ml (1 tbsp) oil for 15 minutes. Drain.
2 Heat the remaining oil in a pan, add the onions, tomatoes and 300 g (10 oz) of the courgettes and fry gently until the tomatoes begin to break down. Stir in the tomato purée, basil and plenty of seasoning.
3 Grease a deep-sided 2 litre (3½ pint) ovenproof dish. Layer the vegetables, lasagne and nuts in the dish, ending with a layer of lasagne.
4 Beat the yogurt and eggs together, then stir in the cheese, cumin and seasoning to taste. Pour over the lasagne.
5 Arrange the remaining courgettes over the yogurt topping and brush them lightly with oil. Bake the lasagne in the oven at 200°C (400°F) mark 6 for about 40 minutes or until set. Serve hot, straight from the dish.

COOK'S TIP

The lasagne verde used in this recipe is the green, spinach-flavoured lasagne. Some varieties must be pre-boiled before layering with the other ingredients in the dish, as indicated in the method here. To save time, look for the pre-cooked lasagne which does not need to be boiled first.

CHEESY POTATO PIE

SERVES 4

900 g (2 lb) potatoes, peeled and cut into chunks	1 large red pepper, seeded and roughly chopped
45 ml (3 tbsp) semi-skimmed milk	450 g (1 lb) courgettes, thickly sliced
100 g (4 oz) vegetarian Cheddar or Cotswold cheese, grated	225 g (8 oz) button mushrooms
50 g (2 oz) butter or polyunsaturated margarine	10 ml (2 tsp) mild paprika
salt and pepper	25 g (1 oz) plain wholemeal flour
450 g (1 lb) leeks, sliced	300 ml (½ pint) vegetable stock

1 Cook the potatoes in boiling salted water for 15-20 minutes or until tender. Drain and mash with the milk, half the cheese and half the butter or margarine. Season to taste.

2 Meanwhile, heat the remaining butter in a large saucepan and fry the leeks and pepper for 4-5 minutes, until softened. Add the courgettes, mushrooms and paprika and fry for a further 2 minutes.

3 Sprinkle in the flour, then gradually add the stock and bring to the boil, stirring continuously. Cover and simmer for 5 minutes.

4 Spoon the vegetable mixture into an ovenproof serving dish and cover evenly with the cheesy potato. Sprinkle with the remaining cheese. Bake in the oven at 200°C (400°F) mark 6 for 20-25 minutes or until the top is crisp and golden brown.

COOK'S TIP

Buy maincrop potatoes rather than new ones for this recipe. Maris Piper is particularly good for mashing, or you could use Desirée, recognisable by its red skin. Cotswold cheese, a mixture of Double Gloucester cheese and chives, gives a lovely flavour to the crispy potato topping.

VEGETABLE COUSCOUS

SERVES 4

100 g (4 oz) chick peas, soaked in cold water overnight	1.25 ml (¼ tsp) chilli powder
225 g (8 oz) couscous	2 leeks, sliced
15 ml (1 tbsp) polyunsaturated oil	2 carrots, sliced
2 onions, chopped	600 ml (1 pint) vegetable stock
1 garlic clove, crushed	3 courgettes, sliced
5 ml (1 tsp) ground cumin	1 large tomato, coarsely chopped
5 ml (1 tsp) ground coriander	50 g (2 oz) raisins

1 Drain the chick peas, put in a saucepan, cover with cold water, bring to the boil and boil steadily for 10 minutes. Lower the heat and simmer for 40-50 minutes or until just tender, then drain.

2 Meanwhile, put the couscous in a bowl and add 450 ml (¾ pint) cold water. Leave to soak for 10-15 minutes or until the water is absorbed.

3 Heat the oil in a large saucepan, add the onions and cook for 5 minutes. Add the garlic and spices and cook, stirring, for 1 minute. Add the leeks, carrots and stock. Bring to the boil.

4 Line a large sieve with muslin and place over the vegetable stew. Put the couscous in the sieve. Cover the whole pan with foil to enclose the steam and simmer for 20 minutes.

5 Add the chick peas, courgettes, tomato and raisins to the stew. Replace the sieve and fluff up the couscous with a fork. Cover and simmer for 10 minutes. Spread the couscous in a large serving dish and spoon the vegetable stew on top.

CAULIFLOWER AND COURGETTE BAKE

SERVES 4

700 g (1½ lb) cauliflower	45 ml (3 tbsp) wholemeal flour
salt and pepper	150 ml (¼ pint) semi-skimmed milk
50 g (2 oz) butter or polyunsaturated margarine	3 eggs, separated
225 g (8 oz) courgettes, thinly sliced	15 ml (1 tbsp) freshly grated Parmesan cheese

1 Divide the cauliflower into small florets, trimming off thick stalks and leaves. Cook in boiling salted water for 10-12 minutes or until tender.

2 Meanwhile, in a separate pan, melt 25 g (1 oz) of the butter or margarine, add the courgettes and cook until beginning to soften. Remove from the pan with a slotted spoon and drain on absorbent kitchen paper.

3 Melt the remaining butter or margarine in the pan, stir in the flour and cook, stirring, for 1-2 minutes. Remove from the heat and add the milk, a little at a time, whisking constantly after each addition. Return to the heat and bring to the boil, stirring. Simmer until thickened.

4 Drain the cauliflower well and place in a blender or food processor with the warm sauce, egg yolks and plenty of seasoning. Blend together until evenly mixed, then turn into a large bowl.

5 Whisk the egg whites until stiff and carefully fold into the cauliflower mixture.

6 Spoon half the mixture into a 1.6 litre (2¾ pint) soufflé dish. Arrange the courgettes on top, reserving a few for garnish, then cover with the remaining cauliflower mixture. Top with the reserved courgettes.

7 Sprinkle over the Parmesan cheese and bake in the oven at 190°C (375°F) mark 5 for 35-40 minutes or until golden. Serve immediately.

CARROT AND BEAN SOUFFLES

SERVES 4

450 g (1 lb) carrots, thinly sliced	75 g (3 oz) vegetarian Cheddar or Gruyère cheese, grated
salt and pepper	3 eggs, separated
30 ml (2 tbsp) polyunsaturated oil	30 ml (2 tbsp) chopped coriander
15 ml (1 tbsp) wholemeal flour	10 ml (2 tsp) medium oatmeal or fresh brown breadcrumbs
425 g (15 oz) can butter beans, drained	

1 Cook the carrots in boiling salted water for 10-12 minutes or until very soft. Drain well, reserving 150 ml (¼ pint) cooking liquor.

2 Heat the oil in a saucepan. Add the flour and cook, stirring, for 1 minute. Add the reserved liquor and bring to the boil, stirring. Simmer for 2 minutes.

3 Place the carrots, sauce, butter beans, grated cheese and egg yolks in a food processor. Blend until smooth, then season. Turn into a bowl.

4 Whisk the egg whites until stiff, then fold into the carrot mixture with the coriander.

5 Spoon into four well greased individual soufflé dishes. Sprinkle with the oatmeal or breadcrumbs.

6 Bake in the oven at 190°C (375°F) mark 5 for 20-25 minutes or until golden and just firm to the touch. Serve with a watercress and cucumber salad.

COOK'S TIP

This recipe works best if the carrots are sliced very thinly in a food processor.

LEEK TART

SERVES 6

75 ml (5 tbsp) polyunsaturated oil	1.4 kg (3 lb) leeks, white parts only, sliced
225 g (8 oz) plain wholemeal flour, plus 30 ml (2 tbsp)	450 ml (¾ pint) semi-skimmed milk
salt and pepper	pinch of grated nutmeg
75 g (3 oz) polyunsaturated margarine	2 eggs
	75 g (3 oz) Gruyère cheese, grated

1 To make the pastry, put the oil and 30 ml (2 tbsp) cold water in a bowl. Beat well with a fork to form an emulsion.
2 Mix the 225 g (8 oz) flour and a pinch of salt together. Gradually add to the oil mixture to make a dough.
3 Roll out the dough on a floured surface or between pieces of greaseproof paper, and use to line a 23 cm (9 inch) flan tin or dish.
4 Prick the base, line with foil or greaseproof paper and baking beans and bake blind in the oven at 190°C (375°F) mark 5 for 10 minutes until set.
5 Meanwhile, melt 50 g (2 oz) of the margarine in a heavy-based saucepan, add the leeks, cover and sweat very gently, without allowing to colour, for 10 minutes. Add just enough water to stop the leeks from burning, shake the pan and cook until tender.
6 In a separate saucepan, melt the remaining margarine, stir in the 30 ml (2 tbsp) flour and cook for 1-2 minutes. Gradually stir in the milk and cooking liquid from the leeks until smooth. Add the nutmeg and seasoning to taste and simmer for a few minutes, stirring.
7 Spread the leeks evenly in the pastry case. Beat the eggs and add to the sauce with half the grated cheese. Pour over the leeks. Sprinkle with the remaining cheese.
8 Bake in the oven at 200°C (400°F) mark 6 for 25-30 minutes or until slightly risen and golden brown.

SPICY VEGETABLE PIE

SERVES 4-6

4 carrots, thinly sliced	100 g (4 oz) vegetarian Cheddar, grated
4 leeks, thickly sliced	1.25 ml (¼ tsp) ground mace
6 courgettes, thinly sliced	45 ml (3 tbsp) chopped coriander or parsley
salt and pepper	375 g (13 oz) packet wholemeal shortcrust pastry
90 ml (6 tbsp) polyunsaturated oil	beaten egg, to glaze
1 medium onion, sliced	
10 ml (2 tsp) ground cumin	10 ml (2 tsp) freshly grated Parmesan cheese
50 g (2 oz) wholemeal flour	pinch of cayenne or paprika
450 ml (¾ pint) semi-skimmed milk plus 30 ml (2 tbsp)	

1 To make the filling, blanch the carrots, leeks and courgettes in boiling salted water for 1 minute. Drain well.
2 Heat 15 ml (1 tbsp) of the oil in a heavy-based pan, add the onion and cumin and fry gently for 5 minutes until soft. Add the carrots, leeks and courgettes and fry for a further 5 minutes. Remove from the heat and set aside.
3 Heat the remaining 75 ml (5 tbsp) oil in a separate pan, sprinkle in the flour and cook for 1-2 minutes, stirring. Off the heat, whisk in 450 ml (¾ pint) milk; return to the heat and simmer for 5 minutes until thick and smooth.
4 Stir in the Cheddar cheese, mace and salt and pepper to taste. Fold into the vegetables with the chopped coriander and 30 ml (2 tbsp) milk, then turn into a 900 ml (1½ pint) ovenproof pie dish. Leave for 2 hours until cold.
5 Roll out the pastry thinly on a floured surface for the pie lid. Cut a thin strip to fit the rim of the pie dish. Moisten the rim with water; place the strip on the rim.
6 Moisten the strip of dough, then place the pastry lid on top and press to seal the edge. Decorate with leaves cut from the pastry trimmings.
7 Brush with egg and dust with Parmesan and paprika. Bake in the oven at 190°C (375°F) mark 5 for 20 minutes.

MEXICAN RE-FRIED BEANS

SERVES 4-6

30 ml (2 tbsp) polyunsaturated oil	1 green chilli, seeded and finely chopped
1 medium onion, finely chopped	450 g (1 lb) cooked red kidney or pinto beans, or two 425 g (15 oz) cans red kidney or pinto beans, drained
1 garlic clove, crushed	

1 Heat the oil in a large frying pan, add the onion and fry gently for about 5 minutes until soft and lightly coloured. Stir in the garlic and chilli and continue cooking for 1-2 minutes. Remove from the heat.

2 Mash the beans in a bowl with a potato masher or the end of a rolling pin. Add to the frying pan with 150 ml (¼ pint) water and stir well to mix.

3 Return the pan to the heat and fry for about 5 minutes, stirring constantly until the beans resemble porridge, adding more water if necessary. Take care that the beans do not catch and burn. Serve hot topped with grated Cheddar cheese, if liked.

COOK'S TIP

Re-fried beans can be re-fried again and again, with the addition of a little more water each time. The flavour improves with each frying.

SOUTHERN BAKED BEANS

SERVES 4

275 g (10 oz) dried haricot beans, soaked in cold water overnight	15 ml (1 tbsp) mustard powder
15 ml (1 tbsp) polyunsaturated oil	30 ml (2 tbsp) treacle
	300 ml (½ pint) tomato juice
2 medium onions, chopped	45 ml (3 tbsp) tomato purée
225 g (8 oz) carrots, chopped	300 ml (½ pint) beer
	salt and pepper

1 Drain the beans and place in a saucepan of water. Bring to the boil and simmer for 25 minutes, then drain.

2 Meanwhile heat the oil in a flameproof casserole and fry the onions and carrots for 5 minutes until light golden.

3 Remove from the heat, add the mustard, treacle, tomato juice and purée, beer and beans. Stir well.

4 Bring to the boil, cover and cook in the oven at 140°C (275°F) mark 1 for about 5 hours, stirring occasionally, until the beans are tender and the sauce is the consistency of syrup. Season with salt and pepper to taste.

VARIATION

Use pinto or black-eyed beans instead of haricot beans.

VEGETARIAN ROAST

SERVES 4-6

175 g (6 oz) long grain brown rice	100 g (4 oz) wholemeal breadcrumbs
15 g (½ oz) butter or polyunsaturated margarine	100 g (4 oz) almonds, finely chopped
1 medium onion, chopped	100 g (4 oz) vegetarian Cheddar cheese, grated
1 garlic clove, crushed	2 eggs
2 carrots, grated	salt and pepper
100 g (4 oz) button mushrooms, finely chopped	

1 Cook the rice in boiling salted water for 30-35 minutes or until tender. Drain well.
2 Meanwhile, heat the butter or margarine in a medium frying pan, add the onion, garlic, carrots and mushrooms and fry for 5-10 minutes or until softened, stirring frequently. Stir in the breadcrumbs, almonds, cooked rice, cheese and eggs. Season to taste and mix thoroughly together.
3 Pack the mixture into a greased 1.7 litre (3 pint) loaf tin and bake in the oven at 180°C (350°F) mark 4 for 1-1¼ hours or until firm to the touch and brown on top. Serve sliced, hot or cold.

VARIATION

Any type of chopped nuts can be used in the above recipe. Try substituting brazils or unsalted peanuts or cashews for the almonds.

SAVOURY NUT BURGERS

SERVES 4

25 g (1 oz) butter or polyunsaturated margarine	225 g (8 oz) chopped mixed nuts
1 large onion, chopped	15 ml (1 tbsp) soy sauce
15 ml (1 tbsp) chopped parsley	15 ml (1 level tbsp) tomato purée
30 ml (2 tbsp) plain wholemeal flour	175 g (6 oz) fresh wholemeal breadcrumbs
150 ml (¼ pint) semi-skimmed milk	1 egg, beaten
	pepper

1 Melt the butter or margarine in a medium saucepan and lightly fry the onion and parsley until soft. Stir in the flour and cook for 2 minutes.
2 Remove from the heat, gradually add the milk, then bring back to boil, stirring until the sauce thickens, boils and is smooth. Simmer for 1-2 minutes.
3 Add the nuts, soy sauce, tomato purée, breadcrumbs, egg and pepper to taste. Mix well.
4 Divide into 8 portions and shape into rounds. Cook under a preheated grill for 4 minutes each side, until golden and cooked through. Serve with a tomato salad.

SPICED CHICK PEAS WITH TOMATOES

SERVES 4

225 g (8 oz) dried chick peas, soaked in cold water overnight, or two 425 g (15 oz) cans chick peas, drained	15 ml (1 tbsp) ground cumin
4 garlic cloves, crushed	15 ml (1 tbsp) ground coriander
60 ml (4 tbsp) polyunsaturated oil	5 ml (1 tsp) garam masala
2 medium onions, finely chopped	4 tomatoes, roughly chopped
2 small green chillies, seeded and finely chopped	30 ml (2 tbsp) chopped coriander
5 ml (1 tsp) turmeric	15 ml (1 tbsp) chopped mint
5 ml (1 tsp) paprika	salt and pepper
	chopped mint or parsley, to garnish

1 Drain the dried chick peas if using, and place in a large saucepan with half of the garlic. Cover with plenty of water, bring to the boil, cover and simmer for 2-3 hours until tender. Drain well and set aside.

2 Heat the oil in a heavy-based saucepan or flameproof casserole, add the remaining garlic and the onions and fry gently for about 5 minutes until soft and lightly coloured. Add the chillies, turmeric, paprika, cumin, coriander and garam masala and fry, stirring, for a further 1-2 minutes.

3 Add the tomatoes, coriander and mint and cook, stirring, for 5-10 minutes until reduced to a pulp.

4 Add the cooked or canned chick peas and stir well. Simmer gently for another 5 minutes or until the chick peas are heated through. Add salt and pepper to taste, then turn into a warmed serving dish. Sprinkle with chopped mint or parsley. Serve hot.

MOONG DAL AND SPINACH

SERVES 6

225 g (8 oz) moong dal (split, washed moong beans)	1 garlic clove, crushed
900 g (2 lb) fresh spinach washed and trimmed, or 450 g (1 lb) frozen chopped spinach	10 ml (2 tsp) ground coriander
45 ml (3 tbsp) polyunsaturated oil	5 ml (1 tsp) ground turmeric
100 g (4 oz) onion, finely chopped	2.5 ml (½ tsp) chilli powder
15 g (½ oz) fresh root ginger, finely chopped	1.25 ml (¼ tsp) asafoetida (optional)
	salt and pepper
	lemon wedges and parsley sprigs, to garnish

1 Rinse the dal under cold running water. Place in a bowl, cover with cold water and leave to soak for about 2 hours, then drain.

2 Place the fresh spinach in a saucepan with only the water that clings to the leaves. Cover and cook gently for about 5 minutes or until tender. Drain well and chop roughly. If using frozen spinach, place in a saucepan and cook for 7-10 minutes to thaw and to remove as much liquid as possible.

3 Heat the oil in a large sauté pan, add the onion, ginger and garlic and fry for 2-3 minutes.

4 Stir in the coriander, turmeric, chilli powder, asafoetida (if using) and the dal. Fry, stirring, for 2-3 minutes.

5 Pour in 300 ml (½ pint) water, season to taste and bring to the boil. Cover and simmer for about 15 minutes or until the dal is almost tender. Add a little more water if necessary, but the mixture should be almost dry.

6 Stir in the spinach and cook, stirring, for 2-3 minutes or until heated through. Taste and adjust the seasoning before serving, garnished with lemon wedges and parsley.

THREE BEAN VEGETABLE CURRY

SERVES 6

125 g (4 oz) dried red kidney beans	30 ml (2 tbsp) plain wholemeal flour
125 g (4 oz) dried soya beans	10 ml (2 tsp) raw cane sugar
125 g (4 oz) dried black beans	20 ml (4 tsp) ground coriander
700 g (1½ lb) cauliflower	10 ml (2 tsp) ground cumin
1 medium onion	5 ml (1 tsp) turmeric
½ green pepper, seeded	2.5 ml (½ tsp) chilli powder
450 g (1 lb) courgettes	15 ml (1 tbsp) tomato purée
30 ml (2 tbsp) polyunsaturated oil	900 ml (1½ pints) vegetable stock
125 g (4 oz) button mushrooms	salt and pepper
1 small piece fresh root ginger, crushed	

1 Soak the beans separately in cold water overnight. Next day, drain beans and rinse well under cold running water. Put the kidney beans in a large saucepan, cover with plenty of cold water and bring slowly to the boil.

2 Skim off any scum with a slotted spoon, then boil rapidly for 10 minutes. Add the soya beans, half cover the pan with a lid and simmer for 30 minutes. Add the black beans and continue cooking for 1 hour, until tender.

3 Meanwhile, divide cauliflower into small florets. Slice onion and green pepper thinly. Slice courgettes thickly.

4 Heat the oil in a large saucepan, add the onion and pepper and fry gently for 5-10 minutes until lightly browned. Stir in the mushrooms and courgettes and cook for a further 5 minutes.

5 Stir in the ginger, flour, sugar, coriander, cumin, turmeric, chilli powder and tomato purée. Cook, stirring, for 1-2 minutes, then blend in the stock.

6 Drain beans and add to pan with the cauliflower and salt and pepper to taste. Cover and simmer for 20 minutes until the vegetables are tender. Serve hot.

VEGETABLE CURRY

SERVES 4

30 ml (2 tbsp) polyunsaturated oil	2 potatoes, roughly chopped
10 ml (2 tsp) ground coriander	2 carrots, sliced
5 ml (1 tsp) ground cumin	1 green pepper, seeded and chopped
2.5-5 ml (½-1 tsp) chilli powder	225 g (8 oz) tomatoes, roughly chopped
2.5 ml (½ tsp) turmeric	150 ml (5 fl oz) low-fat natural yogurt
2 garlic cloves, crushed	salt and pepper
1 medium onion, chopped	toasted flaked almonds, to garnish
1 small cauliflower, cut into small florets	

1 Heat the oil in a large saucepan, then add the coriander, cumin, chilli powder, turmeric, garlic and onion and fry for 2-3 minutes, stirring continuously.

2 Add the cauliflower, potatoes, carrots and green pepper and stir to coat in the spices. Stir in the tomatoes and 150 ml (¼ pint) water. Bring to the boil, cover and gently simmer for 25-30 minutes or until the vegetables are tender.

3 Remove from the heat, stir in the yogurt and season to taste. Serve garnished with toasted almonds and accompanied by rice and chutney.

COOK'S TIP

A subtle blend of spices gives this curry its flavour. Adjust the amount of chilli powder according to how much heat you like, and vary the vegetables according to what's in season.

DAL WITH AUBERGINE AND MUSHROOMS

SERVES 6-8

350 g (12 oz) masoor dal	45 ml (3 tbsp) polyunsaturated oil
5 ml (1 tsp) turmeric	5 ml (1 tsp) cumin seeds
2 garlic cloves, crushed	5 ml (1 tsp) black mustard seeds
1 aubergine	2.5 ml (½ tsp) fennel seeds
225 g (8 oz) mushrooms, halved	5 ml (1 tsp) garam masala
5-10 ml (1-2 tsp) salt	chopped coriander, to garnish
2.5 ml (½ tsp) sugar	

1 Pick over the dal and remove any grit or discoloured pulses. Put into a sieve and wash thoroughly under cold running water. Drain well.
2 Put the dal in a large saucepan with the turmeric and garlic. Cover with 1.4 litres (2½ pints) water. Bring to the boil and simmer for about 25 minutes.
3 Meanwhile, wash the aubergine and pat dry with absorbent kitchen paper. Cut into 2.5 cm (1 inch) cubes.
4 Add the aubergine and mushrooms to the dal with the salt and sugar. Continue simmering gently for 15-20 minutes until all the vegetables are tender.
5 Heat the oil in a separate small saucepan, add the remaining spices and fry for 1 minute or until the mustard seeds begin to pop.
5 Stir the spice mixture into the dal, cover pan tightly with the lid and remove from the heat. Leave to stand for 5 minutes, for the flavours to develop. Turn into a warmed serving dish and garnish with coriander. Serve hot.

COOK'S TIP

The Indian word *dal* means pulse. There are hundreds of different kinds used in Indian cookery – go to an Indian specialist store or health food shop for the best choice. They are all extremely nutritious, with a high vitamin content.

VEGETABLE BIRYANI

SERVES 4

350 g (12 oz) Basmati rice	5 ml (½ tsp) chilli powder
salt and pepper	3 medium carrots, thinly sliced
50 g (2 oz) ghee or clarified butter	225 g (8 oz) fresh or frozen green beans, cut in two lengthways
1 large onion, chopped	225 g (8 oz) cauliflower florets, divided into small sprigs
2.5 cm (1 inch) piece fresh root ginger, grated	
1-2 garlic cloves, crushed	5 ml (1 tsp) garam masala
5 ml (1 tsp) ground coriander	juice of 1 lemon
10 ml (2 tsp) ground cumin	hard-boiled egg wedges and coriander sprigs, to garnish
5 ml (1 tsp) turmeric	

1 Rinse the rice and put in a saucepan with 600 ml (1 pint) water and 5 ml (1 tsp) salt. Bring to the boil, then simmer for 10 minutes or until only just tender.
2 Meanwhile, heat the ghee or butter in a large heavy-based saucepan, add the onion, ginger and garlic and fry gently for 5 minutes or until soft but not coloured. Add the coriander, cumin, turmeric and chilli powder and fry for 2 minutes more, stirring constantly.
3 Remove the rice from the heat and drain. Add 900 ml (1½ pints) water to the onion and spice mixture and season to taste. Stir well and bring to the boil. Add the carrots and beans and simmer for 15 minutes, then add the cauliflower and simmer for a further 10 minutes. Lastly, add the rice. Fold gently to mix and simmer until reheated.
4 Stir the garam masala and lemon juice into the biryani and simmer for a few minutes more to reheat and allow the flavours to develop. Adjust the seasoning. Garnish with hard-boiled egg and coriander to serve.

FISH

Fish is highly nutritious and versatile. It is an excellent source of protein, vitamins and minerals, and can be cooked quickly in a variety of ways. With the exception of oily fish, it is also low in calories. The healthiest lowest-calorie methods of cooking fish are poaching, steaming, braising and baking.

COD IN A SPICY YOGURT CRUST

SERVES 4

30 ml (2 tbsp) chopped mint	10 ml (2 tsp) ground cumin
1 medium onion or 2 large spring onions, roughly chopped	10 ml (2 tsp) dried dill
	150 ml (5 fl oz) low-fat natural yogurt
2 garlic cloves, crushed	salt and pepper
5 ml (1 tsp) paprika	4 thick cod steaks or fillets, each about 225 g (8 oz)
30 ml (2 tbsp) coriander seeds	

1 First make the marinade mixture. Put the mint, onion, garlic, paprika, coriander, cumin, dill and yogurt in a blender or food processor and process until a thick paste is formed. Season the mixture to taste with salt and pepper.
2 Place the fish in a single layer in a shallow heatproof dish. Spread the paste all over the top of the fish and leave in a cool place to marinate for 2-3 hours.
3 Cook under a preheated hot grill, basting occasionally, until the fish is cooked and the yogurt mixture has formed a crust. Serve immediately.

VARIATION

Substitute haddock for cod in the above recipe. Steaks or fillets are equally suitable.

MARINATED COD STEAKS

SERVES 4

30 ml (2 tbsp) grapeseed oil	salt and pepper
30 ml (2 tbsp) white wine vinegar	4 cod steaks, each about 175 g (6 oz)
10 ml (2 tsp) sesame seeds	175 g (6 oz) onion, skinned and finely sliced into rings
pinch of dry mustard powder	mangetout, to garnish

1 In a jug, whisk together the oil, vinegar, sesame seeds, mustard powder and seasoning for the marinade.
2 Place the cod steaks in a shallow dish into which they just fit, add the onion rings and pour over the marinade. Cover and leave to marinate overnight in the refrigerator, turning once.
3 Line the grill pan with foil and carefully place the cod steaks and onion on it. Cook under a hot grill for about 4 minutes each side, brushing well with the marinade. Garnish with mangetout and serve immediately.

CEVICHE

700 g (1½ lb) haddock fillets, skinned	4 tomatoes, skinned and chopped
15 ml (1 tbsp) coriander seeds	1 small red pepper, seeded and thinly sliced
5 ml (1 tsp) black peppercorns	few drops of Tabasco sauce, or to taste
juice of 6 limes	45 ml (3 tbsp) chopped coriander
5 ml (1 tsp) salt	salt and pepper
1 hot chilli, seeded and chopped	lime slices and coriander sprigs, to garnish
1 bunch of spring onions, sliced	

1 Cut the fish fillets diagonally into thin, even strips and place in a bowl.
2 Crush the coriander seeds and peppercorns to a fine powder using a pestle and mortar. Mix with the lime juice, 5 ml (1 tsp) salt and the chilli, then pour over the fish. Cover and chill in the refrigerator for 24 hours, turning the fish occasionally.
3 To serve, drain the fish from the marinade, discarding the marinade. Mix the fish with the remaining ingredients, seasoning with salt and pepper to taste, if necessary. Serve chilled, garnished with lime slices and coriander leaves.

VARIATION

Arrange avocado slices around the chilled ceviche to serve.

COOK'S TIP

Ceviche is a Mexican dish of raw fish marinated in lime juice. The acid effectively 'cooks' the fish. Don't be put off by the idea of raw fish – it is delicious – but make sure you use absolutely fresh fish.

SOLE BONNE FEMME

4 sole fillets, each about 100 g (4 oz)	40 g (1½ oz) butter or polyunsaturated margarine
2 shallots, or 2-3 slices of onion, finely chopped	30 ml (2 tbsp) plain flour
100 g (4 oz) button mushrooms	about 150 ml (¼ pint) semi-skimmed milk
45 ml (3 tbsp) dry white wine	45 ml (3 tbsp) single cream or smetana
salt and pepper	parsley sprig, to garnish
1 bay leaf	

1 Trim off the fins, wash and wipe the sole fillets and fold each into three. Put the shallots or onion in the bottom of an ovenproof dish with the finely chopped stalks from the mushrooms. Cover with the fish, pour round the wine and 15 ml (1 tbsp) water, season to taste and add the bay leaf.
2 Cover with foil or a lid and bake in the oven at 180°C (350°F) mark 4 for about 15 minutes or until tender. Strain off the cooking liquid and keep the fish warm.
3 Melt half the butter or margarine in a frying pan, add the mushroom caps and fry gently until just beginning to soften, then drain well.
4 Melt the remaining butter or margarine in a saucepan, stir in the flour and cook gently for 1 minute, stirring. Remove from the heat and gradually stir in the cooking liquid from the fish, made up to 300 ml (½ pint) with milk.
5 Bring to the boil and continue to cook, stirring, until the sauce thickens, then remove from the heat and stir in the cream or smetana. Pour the sauce over the fish and serve garnished with the mushroom caps and parsley.

MONKFISH KEBABS

SERVES 4

700 g (1½ lb) monkfish fillets, skinned	2.5 ml (½ tsp) dried thyme
60 ml (4 tbsp) sunflower oil	freshly ground pepper
juice of 2 limes or 1 lemon	1 green pepper, halved and seeded
1 small onion, roughly chopped	16 whole cherry tomatoes or 4 small tomatoes, quartered
2 garlic cloves, crushed	8 bay leaves
2.5 ml (½ tsp) fennel seed	

1 Cut the monkfish into 4 cm (1½ inch) chunks. Place the oil, lime or lemon juice, onion, garlic, fennel, thyme and pepper in a blender or food processor and blend until smooth. Toss the fish in this mixture, cover and leave to marinate for at least 2 hours.
2 Meanwhile, place the green pepper in a saucepan of cold water and bring to the boil. Drain and cut into 12 pieces.
3 Thread the fish, green pepper, tomatoes and bay leaves on to 4 oiled skewers. Reserve the marinade for basting.
4 Cook the kebabs under a preheated moderate grill for about 10 minutes, basting with the marinade and turning once. Serve immediately.

COOK'S TIP

In summertime, these kebabs would be excellent cooked on the barbecue – the additional flavour of the charcoal goes well with quick-cooking fish, and they would make an unusual alternative to steaks, chicken and chops. Follow the recipe exactly as above and make sure the barbecue coals are hot before cooking – they should look grey in daylight, glowing red at night. Food, especially delicately textured fish, should never be put over coals that are flaming, so wait for all flames to die down before starting to cook. Oil the barbecue grid well before placing the kebabs over the fire.

MONKFISH WITH MUSTARD SEEDS

SERVES 6

45 ml (3 tbsp) black mustard seeds	300 ml (½ pint) low-fat natural yogurt
30 ml (2 tbsp) plain white flour	1 garlic clove, crushed
900 g (2 lb) monkish fillet, skinned	15 ml (1 tbsp) lemon juice
30 ml (2 tbsp) mustard oil or polyunsaturated oil	salt and pepper
1 medium onion, thinly sliced	cooked whole prawns and coriander sprigs, to garnish

1 Finely grind 30 ml (2 tbsp) of the mustard seeds in a small electric mill or with a pestle and mortar. Mix them with the flour.
2 Cut the monkfish into 2.5 cm (1 inch) cubes and toss in the flour and ground mustard seeds.
3 Heat the oil in a large heavy-based frying pan and fry the onion for about 5 minutes until golden.
4 Add the remaining mustard seeds to the pan with the monkfish. Fry over moderate heat for 3-4 minutes, turning very gently once or twice.
5 Gradually stir in the yogurt with the garlic, lemon juice and seasoning. Bring to the boil, lower the heat and simmer gently for 10-15 minutes or until the fish is tender.
6 Taste and adjust the seasoning. Turn into a warmed serving dish and garnish with the prawns and coriander. Serve immediately.

COOK'S TIP

The firm, white flesh of the monkfish comes from the tail end, as a third of the length of the fish is taken up by a large unattractive head.

MONKFISH WITH LIME AND PRAWNS

SERVES 4

550 g (1¼ lb) monkfish	225 g (8 oz) tomatoes, skinned and chopped
salt and pepper	150 ml (¼ pint) dry white wine
15 ml (1 tbsp) plain wholemeal flour	finely grated rind and juice of 1 lime
30 ml (2 tbsp) polyunsaturated oil	pinch of raw cane sugar
1 small onion, chopped	100 g (4 oz) cooked peeled prawns
1 garlic clove, chopped	lime slices, to garnish

1 Using a sharp knife, skin the fish, if it is present then cut the fish into 2.5 cm (1 inch) chunks and toss in seasoned flour.

2 Heat the oil in a flameproof casserole and gently fry the onion and garlic for 5 minutes. Add the fish and fry until golden.

3 Stir in the tomatoes, wine, rind and juice of the lime, sugar and salt and pepper to taste. Bring to the boil.

4 Cover and cook in the oven at 180°C (350°F) mark 4 for 15 minutes. Add the prawns and continue to cook for a further 15 minutes until the monkfish is tender. Garnish with lime slices and serve with rice, if liked.

STUFFED PLAICE FILLETS

SERVES 4

4 double plaice fillets	225 g (8 oz) button mushrooms, thinly sliced
salt and pepper	90 ml (6 tbsp) dry white wine
225 g (8 oz) cottage cheese with prawns	5 ml (1 tsp) chopped fresh dill or 2.5 ml (½ tsp) dried
1.25 ml (¼ tsp) Tabasco sauce, or to taste	8 cooked whole prawns and dill sprigs, to garnish
finely grated rind and juice of 1 lemon	

1 To skin the plaice fillets, lay them flat, skin side down, on a board or work surface. Dip your fingers in salt and grip the tail end, then separate the flesh from the skin at this point with a sharp knife. Work the knife slowly between the skin and flesh using a sawing action until the opposite end of the fillet is reached. Cut each fillet into two lengthways.

2 Drain off any liquid from the cottage cheese, then mash the cheese with half of the Tabasco sauce, the grated lemon rind and seasoning to taste.

3 Lay the plaice fillets flat, skinned side upwards. Divide the cheese filling equally between them, then roll up and secure with wooden cocktail sticks, if necessary.

4 Place the stuffed fish rolls close together in a single layer in a lightly oiled ovenproof dish. Sprinkle the mushrooms around the fish, then pour over the wine mixed with the lemon juice and remaining Tabasco. Sprinkle with seasoning to taste.

5 Cover the dish with foil and cook in the oven at 180°C (350°F) mark 4 for 20 minutes or until the fish is just tender. Remove the rolls from the liquid and discard the cocktail sticks. Arrange the fish on a warmed serving dish; keep warm.

6 Put the cooked mushrooms in a blender or food processor. Add the dill and blend until smooth. Pour into a pan and heat through. Taste and adjust seasoning. Serve the fish immediately, accompanied by the sauce.

MULLET BARBECUED IN VINE LEAVES

SERVES 8

90 ml (6 tbsp) olive oil	8 red mullet, each about 275 g (10 oz), cleaned and scaled
30 ml (2 tbsp) white wine vinegar or lemon or lime juice	8-10 vine leaves (depending on size)
salt and pepper	lime or lemon wedges and a few grapes, to garnish

1 Whisk the oil, vinegar or lemon or lime juice together and season to taste with salt and pepper.
2 Put the fish into a shallow dish and pour over the oil and vinegar. Leave in a cool place for at least 30 minutes to marinate.
3 Remove the fish from the marinade and wrap each in one or two of the vine leaves. Secure the leaves with string.
4 Place the fish in a greased barbecue rack and cook over a barbecue for about 12-15 minutes or until the fish is cooked, turning occasionally and brushing with the marinade. Alternatively cook under a preheated grill until tender.
5 Serve on a platter lined with vine leaves, decorated with lemon or lime wedges and a few grapes.

COOK'S TIP

Use fresh vine leaves when in season, or use vine leaves packed in brine – sold in vacuum packs in supermarkets and delicatessens. Canned vine leaves don't work as they tend to disintegrate.

SERVING SUGGESTION

Wafer-thin long courgette slices skewered on to bamboo skewers and grilled or barbecued with the fish make an excellent accompaniment. Use a potato peeler to finely slice, and baste the courgettes with vinaigrette during cooking.

GREY MULLET IN LEMON AND RED WINE

SERVES 4

15 g (½ oz) butter or polyunsaturated margarine	1-2 garlic cloves, crushed
450 g (1 lb) eating apples, peeled, cored and sliced	salt and pepper
6 spring onions, sliced	4 grey mullet, each about 275 g (10 oz), cleaned
juice and finely grated rind of 1 lemon	2 lemons, sliced
	300 ml (½ pint) dry red wine
	spring onions, to garnish

1 To make the stuffing, melt the butter or margarine in a medium saucepan and add the apples, spring onions, lemon rind, 30 ml (2 tbsp) of the lemon juice and the garlic. Fry lightly, then season to taste.
2 Make three slashes across both sides of each grey mullet and insert the lemon slices. Sprinkle the cavity of each fish with the remaining lemon juice and fill with the stuffing. Put into a large ovenproof dish.
3 Pour over the red wine and bake in the oven at 180°C (350°F) mark 4 for 20-30 minutes or until tender. Remove the fish and place on a serving dish. Keep hot.
4 Pour the cooking liquid into a small saucepan and reheat gently. Pour over the fish and serve immediately, garnished with spring onions.

STEAMED MULLET WITH CHILLI SAUCE

SERVES 2

550 g (1¼ lb) grey mullet, cleaned	1 small red pepper, seeded and cut into matchsticks
75 ml (5 tbsp) tomato ketchup	1 small green pepper, seeded and cut into matchsticks
15 ml (1 tbsp) soy sauce	5 ml (1 tsp) cornflour
pinch of chilli powder	15 ml (1 tbsp) chopped parsley
75 ml (5 tbsp) white wine	salt and pepper

1 Place the mullet in a shallow dish.
2 Whisk together the tomato ketchup, soy sauce, chilli powder and wine. Make three deep slashes in the side of each fish. Pour over the marinade, cover and leave for 2 hours.
3 Drain off the marinade and reserve. Place the fish on a rack over a roasting tin half full of water and cover tightly with foil. Steam the fish over a medium heat for 20-25 minutes or until the fish is cooked. (When cooked, the eyes should be white.)
4 To make the chilli sauce, place the marinade and peppers in a saucepan. Mix the cornflour to a smooth paste with 15 ml (1 tbsp) water and stir into the sauce. Bring to the boil and simmer for 4-5 minutes, stirring. Stir in the parsley and season to taste.
5 Carefully lift the steamed mullet on to a warmed serving plate. Spoon over the sauce and serve.

SALMON TROUT WITH HERB SAUCE

SERVES 4

900 g (2 lb) salmon trout, cleaned	45 ml (3 tbsp) chopped parsley
45 ml (3 tbsp) lemon juice	30 ml (2 tbsp) chopped chervil
50 g (2 oz) butter or polyunsaturated margarine	5 ml (1 tsp) chopped dill
salt and pepper	150 ml (¼ pint) reduced-calorie mayonnaise
1 bunch of watercress, roughly chopped	fresh herbs and lemon rind shapes, to garnish (optional)
100 g (4 oz) fresh spinach leaves, roughly chopped	

1 Place the fish in the centre of a large piece of foil. Add 30 ml (2 tbsp) of the lemon juice, then dot with 25 g (1 oz) of the butter or margarine. Season to taste.
2 Seal the foil, weigh the fish and place on a baking sheet. Calculate the cooking time at 15 minutes, plus 10 minutes per 450 g (1 lb). Bake in the oven at 180°C (350°F) mark 4 until tender.
3 Remove the fish from the foil, reserving the cooking liquor, then carefully remove the skin while still warm. Place the fish on a serving dish and leave to cool.
4 To make the sauce, put the cooking liquor and the remaining 25 g (1 oz) butter in a saucepan and heat gently. Add the watercress, spinach, parsley, chervil and dill, then cook for 2-3 minutes or until softened.
5 Put the sauce in a blender or food processor and blend until smooth. Transfer to a bowl, add the remaining lemon juice and season to taste. Leave to cool, then fold in the mayonnaise. Turn into a small serving jug and refrigerate until required.
6 Garnish the fish decoratively with herbs and lemon rind shapes, and serve with the herb sauce.

BASS WITH GINGER AND SPRING ONIONS

SERVES 8

STUFFED HERRINGS

SERVES 4

1.6-1.8 kg (3½-4 lb) sea bass, cleaned	**TO SERVE**
1 large bunch spring onions, trimmed	30 ml (2 tbsp) vegetable oil
2 celery sticks, trimmed	15 ml (1 tbsp) sesame oil
5 cm (2 inch) piece fresh root ginger	30 ml (2 tbsp) soy sauce
	5 ml (1 tsp) caster sugar
polyunsaturated oil for brushing	8 spring onions, trimmed and finely shredded
60 ml (4 tbsp) soy sauce	celery leaves, to garnish
60 ml (4 tbsp) dry sherry	
salt and pepper	

1 With kitchen shears or scissors, cut the fish tail into a 'V' shape. With a sharp knife, make several deep diagonal slashes on both sides of the fish.

2 Finely shred the spring onions and slice the celery and root ginger into very thin matchsticks.

3 Pour water under the rack of a fish kettle or large oval pan and place half of the spring onion, celery and ginger on the rack. Brush the outside of the fish lightly with oil, then place over the flavourings on the rack. Sprinkle the remaining spring onions, celery and ginger over the fish, then the soy sauce, sherry, and salt and pepper to taste.

4 Cover the kettle or pan with its lid, bring the water slowly to the boil, then simmer for 20 minutes or until the flesh of the fish is opaque when tested near the bone.

5 To serve, heat the oils in a wok or heavy frying pan, add the soy sauce and sugar and stir well to mix. Add the shredded spring onions and stir to coat.

6 Discard the flavourings from the top, then transfer the fish to a warmed large serving plate. Arrange the freshly cooked spring onion over the fish in a criss-cross pattern and drizzle with the cooking liquid. Serve immediately, garnished with celery leaves.

40 g (1½ oz) butter or polyunsaturated margarine	juice and finely grated rind of 1 lemon
1 medium onion, finely chopped	45 ml (3 tbsp) chopped mixed herbs (chives, parsley, rosemary, thyme)
50 g (2 oz) fresh wholemeal breadcrumbs	salt and pepper
50 g (2 oz) walnut pieces, roughly chopped	4 herrings, each about 275 g (10 oz), cleaned, boned and heads and tails removed
15 ml (1 tbsp) prepared English mustard	

1 Melt 15 g (½ oz) of the butter in a saucepan, add the onion and fry gently for about 5 minutes or until softened, stirring occasionally.

2 Meanwhile, mix together the breadcrumbs, walnuts, mustard, lemon rind, 15 ml (1 tbsp) lemon juice and the mixed herbs. Season to taste. Add the onion and mix together well.

3 Open the herring fillets and lay skin side down. Press the stuffing mixture evenly over each fillet. Fold the herring fillets back in half and slash the skin several times.

4 Melt the remaining butter or margarine in a large frying pan, add the fish and fry for about 10 minutes or until they are tender and browned on each side, turning the fish once. Serve immediately.

SALMON STEAKS WITH FENNEL

SERVES 4

4 salmon steaks, each about 175 g (6 oz)	2 parsley stalks, crushed
2 shallots, chopped	150 ml (¼ pint) dry white wine
1 small fennel bulb, finely chopped	salt and pepper
1 bay leaf	lemon juice, to taste
	fennel sprigs, to garnish

1 Place the salmon steaks in a shallow ovenproof dish. Scatter the shallots, fennel, bay leaf and parsley over the top. Pour in the wine, cover tightly and bake the oven at 180°C (350°F) mark 4 for 15 minutes or until the fish is tender.

2 Strain off 100 ml (4 fl oz) of the cooking liquor into a saucepan. Reserve 10 ml (2 tsp) of the chopped fennel. Turn off the oven, re-cover the salmon and keep warm.

3 Boil the strained liquor until reduced by about half. Add the reserved cooked fennel and season to taste, adding a little lemon juice, if desired.

4 Transfer the salmon steaks to warmed serving plates. Spoon the cooking liquor over and garnish with fennel sprigs. Serve immediately.

ITALIAN MARINATED TROUT

SERVES 4

30 ml (2 tbsp) olive oil	300 ml (½ pint) dry white wine
4 trout, each about 225 g (8 oz), cleaned	finely grated rind and juice of 1 orange
30 ml (2 tbsp) plain wholemeal flour	salt and pepper
1 small fennel bulb, finely sliced, tops reserved	orange slices and fennel tops, to garnish
1 medium onion, finely sliced	

1 Heat the olive oil in a frying pan. Dip the trout in the flour and fry gently for 4 minutes on each side. With a fish slice, transfer the fish to a shallow dish.

2 With a sharp knife, score the skin diagonally, being careful not to cut too deeply into the flesh. Set aside.

3 Add the fennel and onion to the frying pan and fry for 5 minutes. Add the wine, orange rind and juice and salt and pepper to taste. Bring to the boil. Boil rapidly for 1 minute, add the chopped fennel tops and pour immediately over the fish. Cool.

4 Marinate in the refrigerator for at least 8 hours, but no more than 2 days.

5 Serve at room temperature, garnished with orange slices and fennel tops.

COOK'S TIP

The bulb vegetable Florence fennel looks rather like a squat version of celery with feathery leaves. The flavour of fennel is like aniseed. For the most subtle taste of aniseed, buy white or pale green fennel; for a stronger flavour, choose vegetables which are dark green in colour.

TROUT POACHED IN WINE

SERVES 8

8 whole small trout, cleaned	4 carrots, very thinly sliced
salt and pepper	300 ml (½ pint) dry white wine
25 g (1 oz) low-fat spread	300 ml (½ pint) fish stock
1 large onion, sliced	bouquet garni
4 celery sticks, sliced	parsley sprigs, to garnish

1   Season the inside of the trout.
2   Melt the low-fat spread in a small saucepan. Add the onion, celery and carrots and stir well to coat with fat. Cover and sweat for 5 minutes.
3   Lay the vegetables in a large casserole and arrange the fish on top. Pour over the wine and stock and add the bouquet garni.
4   Cover tightly and cook in the oven at 180°C (350°F) mark 4 for about 25 minutes or until the trout are cooked.
5   Transfer to a warmed serving dish and keep hot.
6   Pour the cooking juices into a small pan, discarding the bouquet garni, and boil rapidly until reduced by half. Pour into a sauceboat or jug.
7   Garnish the trout with parsley and serve accompanied by the sauce.

BAKED TROUT WITH CUCUMBER SAUCE

SERVES 4

4 trout, each about 275 g (10 oz), cleaned	300 ml (10 fl oz) Greek-style natural yogurt
salt and pepper	5 ml (1 tsp) chopped tarragon
300 ml (½ pint) fish or vegetable stock	tarragon sprigs, to garnish
½ small cucumber	

1   Arrange the trout in a single layer in a shallow ovenproof dish. Season to taste. Pour over the stock.
2   Cover and bake in the oven at 180°C (350°F) mark 4 for about 25 minutes, until the trout are tender.
3   Remove the fish from the cooking liquor and carefully peel off the skin, leaving the head and tail intact. Leave to cool.
4   Just before serving, make the sauce. Coarsely grate the cucumber, then add the yogurt and tarragon. Season to taste.
5   Coat the trout in some of the sauce, leaving the head and tail exposed. Garnish with tarragon. Serve the remaining sauce separately in a bowl. Accompany with a green salad.

COOK'S TIP

This cold dish would be ideal for a summer gathering. Use freshwater trout, that is river, lake or rainbow trout. These are now increasingly easy to find at supermarkets. Shiny, slippery skins and bright eyes are the hallmarks of freshness.

TARRAGON STUFFED TROUT

SERVES 6

100 g (4 oz) cooked peeled prawns	60 ml (4 tbsp) polyunsaturated oil
25 g (1 oz) long grain brown rice	5 ml (1 tsp) chopped tarragon
salt and pepper	30ml (2 tbsp) lemon juice
225 g (8 oz) button mushrooms	6 trout, each about 225 g (8 oz), cleaned
1 medium onion	tarragon sprigs, to garnish

1 Cut up each of the peeled prawns into two or three pieces. Cook the rice in boiling salted water for about 30-40 minutes until tender, then drain.
2 Meanwhile roughly chop the mushrooms and finely chop the onion. Heat the oil in a large frying pan, add the onion and fry for 5 minutes until golden brown.
3 Add the mushrooms with the tarragon and salt and pepper to taste, then cook over high heat for 5-10 minutes until all excess moisture has evaporated. Leave to cool for about 30 minutes.
4 Mix the prawns, rice, lemon juice and mushroom mixture together.
5 Place the fish side by side in a lightly greased ovenproof dish and stuff with the mixture. Cover and cook in the oven at 180°C (350°F) mark 4 for about 30 minutes. To serve, garnish with sprigs of tarragon.

COOK'S TIP

The fat in oily fish, such as trout is distributed throughout the flesh. It has a high proportion of polyunsaturated fat and contains valuable amounts of vitamins A and D.

MACKEREL PARCELS

SERVES 4

4 mackerel, each about 175 g (6 oz), cleaned	30 ml (2 tbsp) chopped mint
about 25 g (1 oz) polyunsaturated margarine	5 ml (1 tsp) sugar
½ large cucumber, sliced	salt and pepper
60 ml (4 tbsp) white wine vinegar	low-fat natural yogurt and mint leaves, to serve

1 Cut the heads off the mackerel just below the gills with a sharp knife. Cut off the fins and tails with kitchen scissors. Extend the cut through the belly from head to tail. Wash the fish thoroughly.
2 Lay the fish flat on a board or work surface with the skin uppermost. Press firmly along the backbone with your knuckles to flatten the fish and loosen the backbone. Turn the fish over and lift out the backbone. Cut each fish lengthways into two fillets. Dry thoroughly.
3 Grease 8 squares of kitchen foil with a little margarine. Put a mackerel fillet in the centre of each square, skin side down.
4 Arrange cucumber slices down one half of the length of each fillet, then sprinkle with vinegar, mint and sugar. Season. Dot with the remaining margarine.
5 Fold the mackerel fillets over lengthways to enclose the cucumber filling, then wrap in the foil. Place the foil parcels in a single layer in an ovenproof dish. Cook in the oven at 200°C (400°F) mark 6 for 30 minutes or until tender.
6 To serve, unwrap the foil parcels and carefully place the mackerel fillets in a circle on a warmed platter. Spoon the yogurt in the centre and garnish with mint to serve.

SPICED GRILLED MACKEREL

SERVES 4

4 mackerel, each about 275 g (10 oz), cleaned	5 ml (1 tsp) ground cumin
juice of 1 lemon	5 ml (1 tsp) chilli powder
60 ml (4 tbsp) chopped coriander	salt and pepper
10 ml (2 tsp) garam masala	30 ml (2 tbsp) polyunsaturated oil
	lime wedges, to garnish

1 First bone the mackerel. With a sharp knife, cut of the heads just behind the gills. Extend the cut along the belly to both ends of the fish so that the fish can be opened out.
2 Place the fish on a board, skin side facing upwards. With the heel of your hand, press along the backbone to loosen it. Turn the fish over and lift out the backbone, using the tip of the knife if necessary to help pull the bone away from the flesh cleanly. Discard the bone.
3 Remove the tail and cut each fish in half lengthways, then wash under cold running water and pat dry. Score the skin side in several places with a knife.
4 Mix the lemon juice, half of the coriander, the garam masala, cumin, chilli powder and seasoning together.
5 Put the mackerel in a grill pan and pour over the marinade. Cover and leave at cool room temperature for 2 hours, turning once and brushing with the marinade.
6 When ready to cook, brush half the oil over the skin side of the mackerel. Cook under a preheated moderate grill for 5 minutes, then turn the fish over and brush with the remaining oil. Grill for a further 5 minutes.
7 Transfer the fish to a warmed serving platter and sprinkle with the remaining coriander. Serve immediately, garnished with lime wedges.

COOK'S TIP

Like all oily fish, mackerel are a good source of vitamins A and D. Choose ones with rigid bodies and bright eyes and gills – indications of freshness.

ITALIAN SQUID STEW

SERVES 4

1 kg (2¼ lb) small squid	2 garlic cloves, crushed
75 ml (5 tbsp) olive oil	juice of ½ lemon
salt and pepper	15 ml (1 tbsp) chopped parsley
75 ml (3 fl oz) dry white wine	

1 Wash the squid in plenty of cold water. Grip the head and tentacles firmly and pull them away from the body. The entrails will follow. Discard these and pull out the transparent quill.
2 With your hands, carefully peel the skin from the body and fins of the squid.
3 Cut the tentacles from the head and remove the skin. Reserve two ink sacs, being careful not to pierce them. Discard the rest of the head.
4 Cut the squid bodies into 5 mm (¼ inch) rings. Place in a bowl with the tentacles and spoon over 45 ml (3 tbsp) of the oil. Season well and leave for 3 hours.
5 Pour the squid and marinade into a large frying pan and cook the squid for 5 minutes, turning frequently. Add the wine and garlic and cook for a further 5 minutes. Add the ink sacs, breaking them up with a spoon.
6 Cover and cook over a low heat for about 40 minutes or until the squid is tender.
7 Add the remaining oil, the lemon juice and parsley. Stir for 3 minutes over a high heat, taste and adjust the seasoning and serve.

SERVING SUGGESTION

Serve this rich stew with slices of French bread that have been rubbed with garlic and baked in the oven until crisp. End the meal with a refreshing sorbet or fresh fruit.

BOUILLABAISSE

SERVES 6

900 g (2 lb) fillets of mixed white fish and shellfish, eg whiting, conger eel, monkfish and prawns	2 garlic cloves, crushed
	bay leaf
60 ml (4 tbsp) olive oil	2.5 ml (½ tsp) dried thyme
2-3 onions, sliced	few parsley sprigs
1 celery stick, chopped	salt and pepper
225 g (8 oz) tomatoes	pinch of saffron strands
pared rind of 1 orange	cooked whole prawns, to garnish

1 Wash the fish and pat it dry with absorbent kitchen paper. Remove any skin, then cut the fish into fairly large, thick pieces.
2 Heat the oil in a large heavy-based saucepan and lightly fry the onions and celery for 5 minutes or until soft. Skin and slice the tomatoes.
3 Finely shred the orange rind, then stir half into the onion and celery with the garlic, herbs, salt and pepper. Infuse the saffron in a little hot water.
4 Put the fish into the pan with the vegetables. Add the saffron water, then pour in just enough cold water to cover the fish. Bring to the boil and simmer, uncovered, for 8 minutes.
5 Add the prawns and cook for a further 5-8 minutes. Serve garnished with the whole prawns and remaining orange rind.

COOK'S TIP

Saffron strands are the dried stigma of the autumn flowering crocus. Although they are very expensive to buy (saffron is the most expensive spice in the world), you should always use them in recipes like this one which calls for saffron water. They impart a superb delicate flavour.

SPANISH COD AND MUSSEL STEW

SERVES 4

700 g (1½ lb) cod fillets	1 green pepper, seeded and sliced
1 litre (1¾ pints) mussels (about 450 g/1 lb)	1-2 garlic cloves, crushed
30 ml (2 tbsp) polyunsaturated oil	450 g (1 lb) tomatoes, skinned and chopped
2 onions, sliced	300 ml (½ pint) white wine
1 red pepper, seeded and sliced	2.5 ml (½ tsp) Tabasco sauce
	1 bay leaf
	salt and pepper

1 Using a sharp knife, skin the cod and cut it into chunks.
2 Scrub the mussels, discarding any which are open. Place in a pan, cover and cook over a high heat for about 8 minutes or until the mussels have opened. Discard any that do not open.
3 Shell all but four of the mussels. Heat the oil in a frying pan and cook the onions, peppers and garlic for about 5 minutes or until starting to soften. Add the tomatoes and wine, bring to the boil and simmer for 5 minutes, then add the Tabasco.
4 Using a slotted spoon, remove the vegetables from the wine sauce and layer them with the fish chunks in a casserole. Add the bay leaf and seasoning and pour over the sauce. Push the four unshelled mussels into the top layer. Cover and cook in the oven at 180°C (350°F) mark 4 for 40 minutes or until the fish is tender.

SERVING SUGGESTION

This substantial meal-in-one fish dish is ideal for a family supper. Serve with hot French bread.

ITALIAN FISH STEW

SERVES 4

good pinch of saffron strands	450 g (1 lb) tomatoes, skinned, seeded and chopped
about 900 g (2 lb) mixed fish fillets, eg red mullet, bream, bass, brill, monkfish, plaice or cod	2 canned anchovy fillets, drained
10-12 whole cooked prawns	150 ml (¼ pint) dry white wine
60 ml (4 tbsp) olive oil	2 bay leaves
1 large onion, finely chopped	45 ml (3 tbsp) chopped basil
3 garlic cloves, crushed	salt and pepper
2 slices of canned pimiento, drained and sliced	10-12 mussels, in their shells
	4 slices of hot toast, to serve

1 To prepare the saffron water, soak the saffron strands in a little boiling water for 30 minutes. Meanwhile, skin the fish and cut into bite-sized pieces. Peel the prawns.

2 Heat the oil in a large heavy-based pan, add the onion, garlic and pimiento and fry for 5 minutes or until soft.

3 Add the tomatoes and anchovies and stir with a wooden spoon to break them up. Pour in the wine and 150 ml (¼ pint) water and bring to the boil, then lower the heat and add the bay leaves and half the basil. Simmer, uncovered, for 20 minutes, stirring occasionally.

4 Add the firm fish to the tomato mixture, then strain in the saffron water and add seasoning to taste. Cook for 10 minutes, then add the delicate fish and cook for a further 5 minutes.

5 Add the prawns and mussels, re-cover and cook for 5 minutes or until the mussels open. Discard the bay leaves and any mussels that do not open.

6 To serve, put one slice of toast in each of four individual bowls. Spoon over the fish stew and sprinkle with the remaining chopped basil.

SEAFOOD PILAKI

SERVES 8

30 ml (2 tbsp) olive oil	700 g (1½ lb) monkfish fillet, trimmed and cut into chunks
2 garlic cloves, crushed	450 g (1 lb) cleaned squid, cut into rings
1 large onion, chopped	900 g (2 lb) mussels, cleaned
2 celery sticks, chopped	30-45 ml (2-3 tbsp) chopped parsley
3 large carrots, sliced	salt and pepper
finely grated rind and juice of 1 lemon	chopped celery leaves, to garnish
397 g (14 oz) can chopped tomatoes	

1 Heat the oil in a large heavy-based pan. Add the garlic, onion, celery, carrots and lemon rind and cook for about 5 minutes, stirring all the time.

2 Add the lemon juice and the tomatoes with their juice, cover and cook on a low heat for about 25 minutes or until the vegetables are very tender. Stir occasionally and add a little water if the liquid is evaporating too rapidly.

3 Add the fish and squid and a little water. Re-cover and cook for 3-5 minutes. Arrange the mussels on the top, re-cover the pan and cook for about 5 minutes or until the fish is just tender, stirring occasionally. The mussels should have opened; discard any that remain shut. Stir in plenty of parsley and season to taste with salt and pepper. Serve hot or cold, garnished with torn celery leaves.

TANDOORI FISH

SERVES 2

350 g (12 oz) thick white fish fillet, eg monkfish, cod or haddock	1.25 ml (¼ tsp) ground cumin
	1.25 ml (¼ tsp) turmeric
30 ml (2 tbsp) low-fat natural yogurt	pinch of paprika
15 ml (1 tbsp) lemon juice	few knobs of butter or polyunsaturated margarine
1 small garlic clove, crushed	coriander sprigs and lime wedges, to garnish
1.25 ml (¼ tsp) ground coriander	

1 Skin the fish fillet, and then cut into two equal portions with a sharp knife.
2 To make the tandoori marinade, put the yogurt and lemon juice in a bowl with the garlic and spices. Stir well to mix.
3 Place the fish on a sheet of foil and brush with the marinade. Leave in a cool place for 30 minutes.
4 Dot the fish with a few knobs of butter or margarine. Cook under a preheated moderate grill for about 8 minutes, turning once. Serve immediately, garnished with coriander and lime wedges.

SERVING SUGGESTION

Serve with saffron rice, accompanied by a green salad with plenty of chopped fresh coriander.

INDONESIAN FISH CURRY

SERVES 4

1 small onion, chopped	salt
1 garlic clove, chopped	700 g (1½ lb) haddock fillets, skinned and cut into bite-sized pieces
2.5 cm (1 inch) piece fresh root ginger, chopped	
5 ml (1 tsp) turmeric	225 g (8 oz) cooked peeled prawns
2. 5 ml (½ tsp) laos powder	300 ml (½ pint) coconut milk
1.25 ml (¼ tsp) chilli powder	juice of 1 lime
30 ml (2 tbsp) polyunsaturated oil	shredded coconut and lime wedges, to garnish

1 Put the onion, garlic, ginger, turmeric, laos powder, chilli powder and oil in a blender or food processor with 2.5 ml (½ tsp) salt and blend to a paste.
2 Transfer the mixture to a flameproof casserole and fry gently, stirring, for 5 minutes. Add the haddock pieces and prawns and fry for a few minutes more, tossing the fish to coat with the spice mixture.
3 Pour in the coconut milk, shake the pan and turn the fish gently in the liquid. (Take care not to break up the pieces of fish.) Bring slowly to the boil, then lower the heat, cover and simmer for 10 minutes or until tender.
4 Add the lime juice, taste and adjust the seasoning, then transfer to a warmed serving dish and sprinkle with coconut. Serve hot, garnished with lime wedges.

COOK'S TIP

Loas powder is used extensively in the cooking of South-East Asia. It comes from a root rather like ginger and has a peppery hot taste.
To make 300 ml (½ pint) coconut milk, break 100 g (4 oz) block creamed coconut into a jug and pour in 300 ml (½ pint) boiling water. Stir, then strain.

TANDOORI PRAWNS

SERVES 2

60 ml (4 tbsp) low-fat natural yogurt	seeds of 6 green cardamoms
2.5 cm (1 inch) piece fresh root ginger, chopped	1.25 ml (¼ tsp) cayenne pepper
1 large garlic clove, roughly chopped	10 ml (2 tsp) yellow natural food colouring
30 ml (2 tbsp) lime or lemon juice	5 ml (1 tsp) red natural food colouring
10 ml (2 tsp) ground cumin	8 'jumbo' Mediterranean prawns, in their shells
5 ml (1 tsp) garam masala	polyunsaturated oil, for brushing
5 ml (1 tsp) salt	

1 First make the marinade. Put the yogurt in a blender or food processor with the ginger, garlic, lime or lemon juice, cumin, garam masala, salt, cardamoms and cayenne. Work to a paste, then turn into a bowl and stir in the food colouring. (Alternatively, crush the ginger and garlic with a pestle and mortar, then turn into a bowl and stir in the yogurt and lime or lemon juice with the spices, salt and food colouring.)

2 Loosen the shell underneath the prawns, then score the exposed flesh with a fork.

3 Brush the prawns with the marinade, working it under the shells and into the scored flesh as much as possible. Place in a shallow dish or on a plate, cover and marinate in the refrigerator for about 4 hours.

4 When ready to cook, place the prawns on an oiled barbecue grid or grill rack. Sprinkle with some of the oil.

5 Cook the prawns over or under moderate heat for about 10 minutes. Turn the prawns once during cooking and sprinkle with oil. Serve hot.

MONKFISH AND MUSSEL SKEWERS

SERVES 6

12 streaky bacon rashers, halved	60 ml (4 tbsp) chopped parsley
900 g (2 lb) monkfish, skinned, boned and cut into 2.5 cm (1 inch) cubes	finely grated rind and juice of 1 large lemon
36 cooked mussels, shelled	4 garlic cloves, crushed
25 g (1 oz) butter or polyunsaturated margarine	salt and pepper
	shredded lettuce, to serve
	lemon slices, to garnish

1 Roll the bacon rashers up neatly. Thread the cubed fish, mussels and bacon alternately on to 12 oiled skewers.

2 Melt the butter or margarine in a saucepan, remove from the heat, then add the parsley, lemon rind and juice, and garlic. Season to taste; take care when adding salt as both the mussels and the bacon are naturally salty.

3 Place the skewers on an oiled grill rack. Brush with the parsley mixture, then cook under a preheated moderate grill for 15 minutes. Turn the skewers frequently during cooking and brush with the parsley mixture with each turn.

4 Arrange the hot skewers on a serving platter lined with shredded lettuce. Garnish with lemon slices and serve immediately.

COOK'S TIP

Keep the skewers well brushed while grilling to prevent the fish from drying out.

DRESSED CRAB

SERVES 2-3

1 medium cooked crab, about 900 g (2 lb)	30 ml (2 tbsp) fresh wholemeal breadcrumbs
salt and pepper	1 egg, hard-boiled
15 ml (1 tbsp) lemon juice	chopped parsley, to garnish
	lettuce or endive, to serve

1 Carefully remove the white and dark meat from the crab, discarding the feathery gills and dead man's fingers. Flake all the white meat into a bowl. Season to taste with salt and pepper and add 5 ml (1 tsp) of the lemon juice.
2 Pound the brown meat and work in the breadcrumbs with the remaining lemon juice and salt and pepper to taste.
3 Using a small spoon, put the white meat in both ends of the crab's empty shell, making sure that it is well piled up into the shell. Keep the inside edges neat.
4 Then spoon the brown meat in a neat line down the centre, between the 2 sections of white crab meat.
5 Hold a blunt knife between the white and brown crab meat and carefully spoon lines of parsley, sieved egg yolk and chopped egg white across the crab, moving the knife as you go to keep a neat edge. Serve the stuffed shell on a bed of lettuce or endive, surrounded by the small legs.

SEAFOOD STIR-FRY WITH BABY CORN

SERVES 4

2 celery sticks, trimmed	1 garlic clove, crushed
1 medium carrot, peeled	100 g (4 oz) cooked peeled prawns
350 g (12 oz) coley, haddock or cod fillet, skinned	425 g (15 oz) can whole baby corn cobs, drained
350 g (12 oz) Iceberg or Cos lettuce	salt and pepper
about 45 ml (3 tbsp) polyunsaturated oil	

1 Slice the celery and carrot into thin matchsticks, 5 cm (2 inches) long. Cut the fish into 2.5 cm (1 inch) chunks.
2 Shred the lettuce finely with a sharp knife, discarding the core and any thick ribs.
3 Heat 15 ml (1 tbsp) of the oil in a wok or large frying pan until smoking. Add the lettuce and fry for about 30 seconds until lightly cooked. Transfer to a serving dish with a slotted spoon and keep warm.
4 Heat another 30 ml (2 tbsp) of oil in the pan until smoking. Add the celery, carrot, white fish and garlic and stir-fry over high heat for 2-3 minutes, adding more oil if necessary.
5 Lower the heat and add the prawns and baby corn. Toss well together for 2-3 minutes to heat through and coat all the ingredients in the sauce; the fish will flake apart.
6 Add salt and pepper to taste, spoon on top of the lettuce and serve immediately, with boiled rice if liked.

MIXED FISH STIR-FRY

SERVES 4

225 g (8 oz) monkfish fillet	1 small yellow pepper, seeded and finely sliced
225 g (8 oz) scallops, cleaned	1 medium onion, finely sliced
5 ml (1 tsp) flour	225 g (8 oz) tomatoes, skinned and cut into eighths
10 ml (2 tsp) ground coriander	125 g (4 oz) beansprouts
10 ml (2 tsp) ground cumin	75 ml (5 tbsp) dry white wine
30 ml (2 tbsp) polyunsaturated oil	chopped coriander or parsley, to taste
1 small green pepper, seeded and finely sliced	salt and pepper

1 Slice the monkfish into thin strips and the scallops into thin rounds, removing their orange roe to cook separately. On a plate, mix the flour and spices together. Lightly coat all the fish in this mixture.

2 Heat 15 ml (1 tbsp) oil in each of two medium frying pans. Place the peppers and onion in one pan and stir-fry over a high heat until beginning to brown. Add the fish to the other pan and stir-fry for 2-3 minutes or until tender.

3 Add the tomatoes and bean sprouts to the vegetables and cook for 2-3 minutes or until the tomatoes begin to flop.

4 Stir the contents of both pans together. Mix in the wine with coriander and seasoning to taste and allow to bubble up. Serve with rice or noodles.

PRAWN AND CHICKEN GUMBO

SERVES 8-10

50 g (2 oz) streaky bacon, rinded and chopped	175 g (6 oz) long grain rice
2 garlic cloves, finely chopped	225 g (8 oz) okra
1 large onion, finely chopped	450 g (1 lb) cooked chicken meat, skinned and diced
15 ml (1 tbsp) plain flour	450 g (1 lb) cooked peeled prawns, thawed if frozen
2 tomatoes, skinned and chopped	few drops of Tabasco sauce
1 green pepper, seeded and finely sliced	few drops of Worcestershire sauce
1 bay leaf	salt and pepper
1.2 litres (2 pints) chicken stock	whole cooked crayfish, to garnish (optional)

1 In a large heavy-based saucepan, cook the bacon gently in its own fat for 2-3 minutes or until transparent. Add the garlic and onion and fry gently for about 7 minutes or until golden.

2 Sprinkle in the flour. Stir well, cook for 1-2 minutes, then remove from the heat.

3 Add the tomatoes and green pepper with the bay leaf and stock. Stir well, return to the heat and bring to the boil. Cover and simmer for 20 minutes. Add the rice and boil for a further 10 minutes.

4 Slice the okra into rings. Add to the gumbo with the chicken and prawns, then add the Tabasco and Worcestershire sauces with salt and pepper to taste.

5 Simmer for 10 minutes or until heated through. Ladle the gumbo into a warmed soup tureen and serve hot, garnishing each portion with a whole crayfish, if available.

COOK'S TIP

Gumbo is the American term for okra, which is sometimes also known as 'ladies' fingers'. Its slightly gelatinous quality when cooked is used to thicken soups and stews.

MUSSELS AND CLAMS WITH TOMATOES

SERVES 2-3

900 g (2 lb) mussels	150 ml (¼ pint) dry white wine
450 g (1 lb) small clams, such as venus clams	225 g (8 oz) ripe tomatoes, chopped
25 g (1 oz) butter or polyunsaturated margarine	finely grated rind of 1 lemon
1-2 large garlic cloves, crushed	30 ml (2 tbsp) chopped parsley
1 small onion, finely chopped	salt and pepper

1   Scrub the mussels thoroughly under cold running water, removing their 'beards'. Discard any that are cracked or open.

2   Melt the butter or margarine in a saucepan and cook the garlic and onion until soft. Add the wine, tomatoes, lemon rind and half the parsley. Bring to the boil.

3   Add the mussels and clams to the pan, cover and cook over a high heat for 3-4 minutes or until the mussels and clams are open, shaking the pan occasionally. Discard any mussels or clams that have not opened.

4   Season to taste. Transfer to large bowls or soup plates and sprinkle with the remaining parsley. Serve at once.

FISHERMAN'S PIE

SERVES 4

50 g (2 oz) low-fat spread	100 g (4 oz) button mushrooms, halved
100 g (4 oz) red pepper, seeded and thinly sliced	450 ml (¾ pint) tomato juice
100 g (4 oz) green pepper, seeded and thinly sliced	550 g (1¼ lb) cod fillet, skinned
50 g (2 oz) onion, sliced	450 g (1 lb) potatoes, peeled and very thinly sliced
salt and pepper	50 g (2 oz) Edam cheese, grated

1   Melt 25 g (1 oz) of the low-fat spread in a frying pan, add the peppers and onion and fry gently for 10 minutes or until soft but not coloured. Transfer to a 2.3 litre (4 pint) ovenproof dish. Season well with salt and pepper to taste.

2   Add the mushrooms to the frying pan and cook in the remaining fat for 3-4 minutes, stirring frequently, until evenly coloured.

3   Pour the tomato juice evenly over the pepper and onion mixture in the dish.

4   Cut the fish into large cubes. Arrange the cubes on top of the tomato juice, pressing them down gently into the juice. Top with the mushrooms. Season again with salt and pepper to taste.

5   Arrange the potato slices on top of the mushrooms. Melt the remaining low-fat spread and brush over the potatoes. Bake in the oven at 190°C (375°F) mark 5 for 25 minutes.

6   Sprinkle the grated cheese over the pie, return to the oven and bake for a further 15 minutes or until melted and bubbling. Serve hot, straight from the dish.

POULTRY & GAME

Chicken and turkey are becoming increasingly popular as healthier alternatives to red meat. They are also versatile and represent value for money. These white meats are low in fat too – especially if the skin isn't eaten – good news for slimmers!

HINDLE WAKES

SERVES 4-6

1.6 kg (3½ lb) chicken with giblets, trussed	6 carrots, thickly sliced
salt and pepper	225 g (8 oz) prunes, soaked overnight and stoned
30 ml (2 tbsp) polyunsaturated oil	25 g (1 oz) polyunsaturated margarine
450 g (1 lb) leeks, sliced	

1 Place the giblets in a saucepan with 600 ml (1 pint) water and salt to taste. Bring to the boil, then cover and simmer for 30 minutes.
2 Meanwhile heat the oil in a large flameproof casserole and fry the chicken for about 8 minutes until browned all over. Remove from the casserole.
3 Fry the leeks and carrots for 3 minutes. Return the chicken to the casserole and add the drained prunes. Strain in the giblet stock and season with pepper.
4 Cover and cook in the oven at 170°C (325°F) mark 3 for about 2-2½ hours or until tender.
5 Arrange the chicken, vegetables and prunes on a large warmed platter.

HONEY BARBECUED DRUMSTICKS

SERVES 8

60 ml (4 tbsp) clear honey	2.5 ml (½ tsp) ground coriander
grated rind and juice of 2 lemons	salt and pepper
grated rind and juice of 2 oranges	16 chicken drumsticks, skinned
90 ml (6 tbsp) soy sauce	

1 Mix together the honey, lemon rind and juice, orange rind and juice, soy sauce and coriander.
2 Score the drumsticks with a sharp knife, lay in a shallow dish, and pour over the honey marinade. Cover and marinate in the refrigerator for 1-2 hours, turning the chicken occasionally during this time.
3 Cook the drumsticks on a preheated barbecue or under a preheated moderate grill for 15-20 minutes, or until tender, turning frequently and basting with the honey marinade. Serve hot.

CHICKEN AND SPINACH BAKE

SERVES 4

4 cooked chicken portions	45 ml (3 tbsp) wholemeal flour
900 g (2 lb) fresh spinach or 450 g (1 lb) frozen leaf spinach	5 ml (1 tsp) dried tarragon
1.25 ml (¼ tsp) grated nutmeg	225 g (8 oz) button mushrooms, roughly chopped
salt and pepper	1 egg, beaten
600 ml (1 pint) semi-skimmed milk	50 g (2 oz) Gruyère cheese

1 Skin the chicken portions and then remove the meat from the bones. Cut the meat into bite-sized pieces.

2 Trim the fresh spinach, discarding any thick stalks. Wash the leaves thoroughly, then place in a saucepan with only the water that clings to them. Cover the pan and cook for about 5 minutes until tender. Drain and chop roughly. If using frozen spinach, put in a heavy-based saucepan and heat gently for 7-10 minutes until defrosted. Season the spinach with the nutmeg and plenty of salt and pepper.

3 Put the milk and flour in a blender or food processor. Blend until evenly mixed, then pour into a heavy-based saucepan. Bring slowly to boiling point, then simmer for 5 minutes, stirring frequently, until thickened.

4 Remove the sauce from the heat, reserve one third and stir the chicken, tarragon and seasoning to taste into the remaining sauce.

5 Spread one third of the spinach over the bottom of a lightly greased ovenproof dish. Arrange half of the mushrooms on top of the spinach then pour over half of the chicken sauce. Repeat these layers once more, then spread over the remaining spinach.

6 Stir the egg into the reserved sauce, then pour over the spinach. Grate the cheese over the top. Bake in the oven at 190°C (375°F) mark 5 for about 30 minutes. Serve hot.

CIRCASSIAN CHICKEN

SERVES 4-6

1.8 kg (4 lb) chicken	25 g (1 oz) butter or polyunsaturated margarine
1 medium onion, sliced	45 ml (3 tbsp) polyunsaturated oil
2 celery sticks, roughly chopped	1.25 ml (¼ tsp) ground cinnamon
1 carrot, roughly chopped	1.25 ml (¼ tsp) ground cloves
few parsley sprigs	5 ml (1 tsp) paprika
salt and pepper	parsley sprigs and onion rings, to garnish
100 g (4 oz) shelled walnuts	

1 Put the chicken in a large saucepan with the vegetables, parsley, and salt and pepper to taste. Cover the chicken with water and bring to the boil. Lower the heat, half cover the pan with a lid and simmer for 40 minutes.

2 Remove the chicken from the pan, strain the cooking liquid and set aside. Cut the chicken into serving pieces, discarding the skin.

3 Pound the walnuts with a pestle in a mortar until very fine, or grind them in an electric grinder or food processor.

4 Melt the butter or margarine with 15 ml (1 tbsp) of the oil in a large frying pan. Add the chicken pieces and fry over moderate heat for 3-4 minutes until well coloured.

5 Add 450 ml (¾ pint) of the cooking liquid, the walnuts, cinnamon and cloves. Stir well to mix, then simmer, uncovered, for about 20 minutes or until the chicken is tender and the sauce coats it thickly. Stir the chicken and sauce frequently during this time.

6 Just before serving, heat the remaining oil in a separate small pan. Sprinkle in the paprika, stirring to combine with the oil.

7 Arrange the chicken and sauce on a warmed serving platter and drizzle with the paprika oil. Garnish with parsley sprigs and onion rings. Serve at once, with saffron rice if liked.

CHICKEN KEBABS WITH PEANUT SAUCE

SERVES 4

4 large chicken pieces	1 red pepper
75 ml (5 tbsp) soy sauce	1 green pepper
30 ml (2 tbsp) sesame or vegetable oil	75 g (3 oz) creamed coconut
30 ml (2 tbsp) clear honey	75 ml (5 tbsp) dark crunchy peanut butter
juice of 1 lemon	10 ml (2 tsp) dark soft brown sugar
2.5 ml (½ tsp) chilli powder	shredded lettuce, to serve

1 Skin the chicken pieces. Cut away the flesh from the bones with a sharp, pointed knife and slice the flesh into small cubes.
2 Put 45 ml (3 tbsp) of the soy sauce in a bowl with the oil, honey, lemon juice and chilli powder. Whisk with a fork until well combined.
3 Add the cubes of chicken to the marinade, stir well to coat, then cover and leave to marinate for 24 hours, turning the chicken occasionally.
4 When ready to cook, halve the peppers, remove the cores and seeds and cut the flesh into neat squares.
5 Thread the chicken cubes and pepper squares on to 4 oiled kebab skewers, place on a rack in the grill pan and brush liberally with the marinade.
6 To make the peanut sauce, grate the creamed coconut into a heavy-based saucepan. Add 150 ml (¼ pint) boiling water and bring slowly back to the boil, stirring. Simmer, stirring, until the coconut has dissolved.
7 Add the peanut butter, remaining soy sauce and the sugar to the pan and whisk to combine. Simmer very gently over the lowest possible heat, stirring occasionally until smooth.
8 Meanwhile, grill the chicken under moderate heat for 15 minutes, turning the skewers frequently and brushing with the remaining marinade. Serve the kebabs on a bed of shredded lettuce with a little of the sauce poured over. Hand the remaining sauce separately.

BANG BANG CHICKEN

SERVES 4-6

15 ml (1 tbsp) finely chopped fresh root ginger	10 ml (2 tsp) sesame oil
1.4 kg (3 lb) chicken	30 ml (2 tbsp) sesame seeds
salt and pepper	10 ml (2 tsp) crushed dried red chillies
60 ml (4 tbsp) soy sauce	5 ml (1 tsp) soft brown sugar
3 carrots, very thinly sliced	45 ml (3 tbsp) dry sherry
75 g (3 oz) beansprouts	lettuce leaves, to serve
60 ml (4 tbsp) polyunsaturated oil	spring onion tassels, to garnish

1 Put the ginger inside the cavity of the chicken, then rub the outside of the bird with salt and pepper. Place the bird in a large saucepan and sprinkle over half of the soy sauce. Leave to stand for 30 minutes.
2 Pour enough water into the pan to just cover the chicken. Bring to the boil, then lower the heat, cover and simmer for about 1 hour until the chicken is tender. Leave to cool in the cooking liquid, then remove.
3 Separate the legs and wings from the carcass, then cut the carcass into four. Bang the pieces several times with a rolling pin to loosen the meat from the bones.
4 Cut the meat into neat slices (not too small) or strips. Discard the bones and skin. Combine the chicken with the carrots and beansprouts.
5 Heat the oils in a heavy-based pan, add the sesame seeds and chillies and fry over brisk heat for a few minutes, stirring until lightly coloured. Remove from the heat and stir in the remaining soy sauce with the sugar and sherry. Pour over the chicken and vegetables, cover and leave to marinate in the refrigerator overnight.
6 To serve, put the chicken and vegetables into a shallow serving dish, lined with lettuce leaves. Pour over any remaining marinade and garnish with spring onion tassels. Serve cold.

DEVILLED POUSSINS

SERVES 6

15 ml (1 tbsp) mustard powder	50 g (2 oz) polyunsaturated margarine, melted
15 ml (1 tbsp) paprika	three poussins, each about 700 g (1½ lb)
20 ml (4 tsp) turmeric	
20 ml (4 tsp) ground cumin	15 ml (1 tbsp) poppy seeds
60 ml (4 tbsp) no-sugar tomato ketchup	watercress sprigs and cherry tomatoes, to serve
15 ml (1 tbsp) lemon juice	

1 Place the mustard powder, paprika, turmeric and cumin in a small bowl. Add the tomato ketchup and lemon juice. Beat well to form a thick, smooth paste. Slowly pour in the melted margarine, stirring all the time.

2 Place the poussins on a chopping board, breast side down. With a small sharp knife, cut right along the backbone of each bird through skin and flesh. With scissors, cut through the backbone to open the birds up. Turn the birds over, breast side up. Continue cutting alone the breast bone which will split the birds into 2 equal halves.

3 Lie the birds, skin side uppermost, on a large edged baking sheet. Spread the paste evenly over the surface of the birds and sprinkle with the poppy seeds. Cover loosely and leave in a cool place for at least 1-2 hours.

4 Cook the poussins, uncovered on the baking sheet in the oven at 220°C (425°F) mark 7 for 15 minutes until the skin is well browned and crisp.

5 Reduce the temperature to 180°C (350°F) mark 4 and cook for a further 20 minutes or until the poussins are tender. Serve immediately, on a bed of watercress sprigs garnished with cherry tomatoes.

TANDOORI CHICKEN

SERVES 4

4 chicken quarters, skinned	5 ml (1 tsp) ground cumin
30 ml (2 tbsp) lemon juice	5 ml (1 tsp) garam masala
1 garlic clove	15 ml (1 tbsp) paprika
2.5 cm (1 inch) piece fresh root ginger, peeled and chopped	salt
	30 ml (2 tbsp) melted ghee or polyunsaturated oil
1 green chilli, seeded	shredded lettuce, lemon wedges and onion rings, to serve
60 ml (4 tbsp) low-fat natural yogurt	

1 Using a sharp knife or skewer, pierce the flesh of the chicken pieces all over.

2 Put the chicken in an ovenproof dish and add the lemon juice. Rub this into the flesh. Cover and leave for 30 minutes.

3 To make the marinade, put the garlic, ginger and green chilli, and 15 ml (1 tbsp) water in a blender or food processor and grind to a smooth paste.

4 Add the paste to the yogurt, with the ground cumin, garam masala, paprika, salt to taste and the melted ghee or oil. Mix all the ingredients together, then pour them slowly over the chicken pieces.

5 Coat the pieces liberally with the yogurt marinade. Cover and leave to marinate at room temperature for 5 hours. Turn once or twice during this time.

6 Roast the chicken pieces, uncovered, in the oven at 170°C (325°F) mark 3 for about 1 hour, basting frequently and turning once, until they are tender and most of the marinade has evaporated. Alternatively, grill the chicken or barbecue, or roast it in a chicken brick. Serve with shredded lettuce, lemon wedges and onion rings.

SPICED CHICKEN

SERVES 4

40 g (1½ oz) plain wholemeal flour	1 medium onion, chopped
5 ml (1 tsp) curry powder	450 ml (¾ pint) semi-skimmed milk
2.5 ml (½ tsp) cayenne pepper	60 ml (4 tbsp) apple chutney
350 g (12 oz) boneless chicken, skinned and diced	100 g (4 oz) sultanas
40 g (1½ oz) polyunsaturated margarine	30-45 ml (2-3 tbsp) low-fat natural yogurt
	2.5 ml (½ tsp) paprika

1 Mix together the flour, curry powder and cayenne, add the chicken and toss until coated. Reserve any excess flour.
2 Melt the margarine in a large saucepan, add the chicken and onion and fry for 5-6 minutes or until the chicken is brown and the onion is lightly coloured.
3 Stir in the remaining flour, then gradually blend in the milk. Heat gently, stirring continuously, until the sauce thickens, boils and is smooth.
4 Add the chutney and sultanas and simmer gently for 30-35 minutes or until the chicken is tender.
5 Remove the pan from the heat and drizzle with the yogurt. Sprinkle with the paprika and serve at once.

COOK'S TIP

If you are cutting down on calories, always remove the skin of poultry before cooking because it is the main source of fat.

SPICED CHICKEN WITH CASHEW NUTS

SERVES 8

8 boneless chicken breasts, each 75-100 g (3-4 oz), skinned	1 medium onion, roughly chopped
15 g (½ oz) fresh root ginger, peeled and roughly chopped	50 g (2 oz) cashew nuts
5 ml (1 tsp) coriander seeds	2.5 ml (½ tsp) chilli powder
4 cloves	10 ml (2 tsp) turmeric
10 ml (2 tsp) black peppercorns	40 g (1½ oz) ghee or polyunsaturated margarine
300 ml (½ pint) low-fat natural yogurt	salt
	toasted cashew nuts, chopped, and chopped coriander, to garnish

1 Make shallow slashes across each of the chicken breasts.
2 Put the ginger in a blender or food processor with the coriander seeds, cloves, peppercorns and yogurt and work until blended to a paste.
3 Pour the yogurt mixture over the chicken, cover and marinate for about 24 hours, turning the chicken once.
4 Put the onion in a blender or food processor with the cashew nuts, chilli powder, turmeric and 150 ml (¼ pint) water. Blend to a paste.
5 Lift the chicken out of the marinade. Heat the ghee or margarine in a large frying pan, add the chicken pieces and fry until browned on both sides.
6 Stir in the marinade with the nut mixture and bring slowly to the boil. Season with salt to taste. Cover the pan and simmer for about 20 minutes or until the chicken is tender, stirring occasionally. Garnish with cashew nuts and coriander just before serving, with boiled rice if liked.

CHICKEN KORMA

SERVES 4

50 g (2 oz) unsalted cashew nuts or blanched almonds	5 ml (1 tsp) chilli powder
2 garlic cloves, roughly chopped	5 ml (1 tsp) saffron threads
2.5 cm (1 inch) piece fresh root ginger, peeled and chopped	45 ml (3 tbsp) ghee or polyunsaturated oil
	2 onions, finely chopped
5 cm (2 inch) cinnamon stick, lightly crushed	150 ml (¼ pint) low-fat natural yogurt
2 whole cloves	8 chicken portions, skinned
seeds of 4 green cardamoms	30 ml (2 tbsp) chopped coriander or parsley
50 g (2 oz) white poppy seeds	30 ml (2 tbsp) chopped mint
10 ml (2 tsp) coriander seeds	45 ml (3 tbsp) lemon juice
5 ml (1 tsp) cumin seeds	mint sprigs, to garnish

1 Put the cashew nuts, garlic, ginger and 150 ml (¼ pint) water in a blender or food processor. Work until smooth.
2 Grind the cinnamon, cloves, cardamom, poppy, coriander and cumin seeds into a fine powder. Add to the nut mixture with the chilli powder and salt to taste.
3 Place the saffron threads in a bowl, pour over 300 ml (½ pint) of boiling water and leave to soak.
4 Heat the ghee or oil in a deep frying pan, add the chopped onions and fry gently for 10 minutes, stirring occasionally, until soft and golden brown.
5 Add the spice and nut mixture and the yogurt and continue cooking, stirring all the time, until the ghee begins to separate.
6 Add the saffron mixture and stir well. Add the chicken portions, bring to the boil, cover and simmer gently for 45 minutes, stirring occasionally.
7 Add the chopped coriander and mint. Sprinkle over the lemon juice. Re-cover and cook for 15 minutes, or until the chicken is tender and the sauce thickened.
8 Serve garnished with the mint or coriander, with rice if liked.

INDIAN SPICED ROAST CHICKEN

SERVES 4

2 kg (4 lb) oven-ready chicken, trussed	60 ml (4 tbsp) chopped mint
juice of 1 lemon	5 cm (2 inch) piece fresh root ginger, peeled and crushed
10 ml (2 tsp) coriander seeds, finely crushed	4 garlic cloves, crushed
2.5 ml (½ tsp) chilli powder	5 ml (1 tsp) paprika
300 ml (½ pint) low-fat natural yogurt	5 ml (1 tsp) turmeric
	salt to taste
60 ml (4 tbsp) chopped coriander	45 ml (3 tbsp) melted ghee or polyunsaturated oil

1 Prick the skin of the chicken all over with a fine skewer. Mix together the lemon juice, crushed coriander seeds and chilli powder and brush all over the chicken. Leave to stand for about 30 minutes.
2 Meanwhile mix together all the remaining ingredients, except the ghee or oil and the garnish.
3 Stand the chicken, breast side up, in a roasting tin. Brush with one-quarter of the yogurt mixture. Roast in the oven at 200°C (400°F) mark 6 for about 30 minutes, or until the yogurt dries on the skin of the chicken.
4 Turn the chicken over on its side and brush with another quarter of the yogurt mixture. Return to the oven for a further 30 minutes until the yogurt dries again. Continue turning the chicken and brushing with yogurt twice more, until it has been cooking for 2 hours.
5 Stand the chicken breast side up again and brush with the ghee or oil. Increase the oven temperature to 220°C (425°F) mark 7 and roast the chicken for a further 15 minutes or until the juices run clear when the thickest part of a thigh is pierced with a skewer.
6 Transfer the chicken to a warmed serving dish and remove the trussing string and skewers. Serve hot.

CHICKEN WITH SPICY YOGURT SAUCE

SERVES 4

4 large boneless chicken breasts	seeds of 3 green cardamoms, crushed
90 ml (6 tbsp) low-fat natural yogurt	salt
juice of 1 lime or lemon	30 ml (2 tbsp) ghee or polyunsaturated oil
2 garlic cloves, crushed	2.5 ml (½ tsp) garam masala
2.5 ml (½ tsp) turmeric	30 ml (2 tbsp) chopped coriander
15 ml (1 tbsp) paprika	

1 Skin the chicken breasts and cut the flesh into strips about 1 cm (½ inch) wide. Put the chicken strips into a bowl with the yogurt, lime or lemon juice, garlic, turmeric, paprika, cardamom seeds and salt to taste. Mix well to coat.
2 Cover and leave to marinate in the refrigerator for at least 2 hours.
3 Heat the ghee or oil in a heavy frying pan or wok. Add the chicken and marinade and stir-fry for 10 minutes.
4 Lower the heat and add the garam masala and coriander. Stir-fry for a further 5-10 minutes until the chicken is tender. Transfer to a warmed serving dish and serve immediately, with lime wedges. Accompany the chicken with rice if liked.

CHICKEN WITH SPICY TOMATO SAUCE

SERVES 4

15 g (½ oz) butter or polyunsaturated margarine	large pinch of chilli powder
15 ml (1 tbsp) polyunsaturated oil	8 chicken thighs
1 medium onion, chopped	397 g (14 oz) can tomatoes
1 garlic clove, crushed	15 ml (1 tbsp) tomato purée
5 ml (1 tsp) ground cumin	salt and pepper
5 ml (1 tsp) ground coriander	30 ml (2 tbsp) chopped parsley

1 Heat the butter or margarine and oil in a large frying pan, add the onion and garlic, cover and cook for 4-5 minutes or until the onion is softened. Add the cumin, coriander and chilli powder and cook for 1 minute, stirring continously.
2 Push the onions to one side of the pan, then add the chicken and brown on both sides. Stir in the tomatoes and the tomato purée and season to taste.
3 Bring to the boil, stirring continuously. Cover and simmer gently for about 30 minutes or until the chicken is tender. Stir in the parsley and serve immediately.

COOK'S TIP

Meaty little chicken thighs make a good, inexpensive midweek meal. The tasty tomato sauce is well spiced with cumin and coriander, and a pinch of chilli powder adds a pleasant heat without being fiery.

CHICKEN AND VEGETABLE RISOTTO

SERVES 4

175 g (6 oz) carrots, peeled	2 medium onions, chopped
225 g (8 oz) turnips, peeled	1 celery stick, chopped
175 g (6 oz) brown rice	50 g (2 oz) lean streaky bacon, rinded
350 ml (12 fl oz) chicken stock	salt and pepper
25 g (1 oz) butter or polyunsaturated margarine	90 ml (6 tbsp) dry white wine
4 chicken quarters, halved	chopped parsley, to garnish

1 With a small sharp knife, cut the carrots and turnips into thick, even matchstick strips.
2 In a large saucepan, combine the rice and stock. Bring to the boil, then cover the pan and simmer for 15 minutes.
3 Melt the fat in a flameproof casserole. Add the chicken portions and fry for about 10 minutes until well browned. Remove from the pan.
4 Add all the vegetables to the casserole and cook for 5 minutes until brown. Snip the bacon into the pan, and fry gently for a further 2 minutes.
5 Stir in the rice mixture and season well. Arrange the chicken portions on top of the rice and vegetables. Spoon over the white wine.
6 Cover the casserole tightly with the lid or foil, then bake in the oven at 180°C (350°F) mark 4 for about 1 hour until the chicken is tender.
7 Just before serving, fork up the rice and vegetables round the chicken. Taste and adjust seasoning, then serve immediately, garnished with chopped parsley.

CHICKEN WITH NUTS AND MUSHROOMS

SERVES 4

4 chicken breast fillets, skinned and cut into thin strips	45 ml (3 tbsp) polyunsaturated oil
5 cm (2 inch) piece fresh root ginger, peeled and thinly sliced	125 g (4 oz) mushrooms, halved
45 ml (3 tbsp) soy sauce	¼ cucumber, cut into chunks
60 ml (4 tbsp) dry sherry	75 g (3 oz) walnut pieces, roughly chopped
5 ml (1 tsp) five spice powder	pepper

1 Put the chicken in a bowl with the ginger, soy sauce, sherry and five spice powder. Stir well, cover and leave to marinate for at least 1 hour.
2 Remove the chicken from the marinade with a slotted spoon, reserving the marinade.
3 Heat the oil in a large frying pan or wok. Add the chicken and cook for 3-4 minutes, stirring continuously.
4 Add the mushrooms, cucumber and walnuts and continue to cook for 1-2 minutes, until the chicken is cooked and the vegetables are tender but still crisp.
5 Stir in the reserved marinade and cook for 1 minute, until hot. Season to taste with pepper. Serve immediately, with rice or noodles.

VARIATION

Replace the walnut pieces with cashew nuts and sprinkle with a little sesame oil before serving.

STIR-FRIED CHICKEN WITH COURGETTES

SERVES 4

30 ml (2 tbsp) polyunsaturated oil	1 red pepper, seeded and cut into thin strips
1 garlic clove, crushed	45 ml (3 tbsp) dry sherry
450 g (1 lb) chicken breast fillets, skinned and cut into thin strips	15 ml (1 tbsp) soy sauce
	60 ml (4 tbsp) low-fat natural yogurt
450 g (1 lb) courgettes, cut into thin strips	pepper

1 Heat the oil in a large frying pan or a wok and fry the garlic for 1 minute. Add the chicken and cook for 3-4 minutes, stirring continuously.

2 Add the courgettes and pepper and continue to cook for 1-2 minutes, until the chicken is cooked and the vegetables are tender but still crisp.

3 Stir in the sherry and soy sauce and cook for 1 minute, until hot. Stir in the yogurt and season to taste with pepper. Serve immediately, with boiled rice or noodles.

VARIATION

This colourful stir-fry can be varied according the vegetables in season. In winter, try substituting the courgettes with a mixture of sliced leeks and broccoli, divided into tiny florets.

STIR-FRIED CHICKEN WITH VEGETABLES

SERVES 4

4 skinned chicken breast fillets	2 carrots, grated
30 ml (2 tbsp) polyunsaturated oil	175 g (6 oz) button mushrooms, finely sliced
1 bunch of spring onions, trimmed and finely sliced	10 ml (2 tsp) cornflour
	30 ml (2 tbsp) dry sherry
3 celery sticks, finely sliced	15 ml (1 tbsp) soy sauce
1 green pepper, seeded and cut into thin strips	15 ml (1 tbsp) hoisin sauce
	5 ml (1 tsp) soft brown sugar
100 g (4 oz) cauliflower florets, divided into tiny sprigs	50 g (2 oz) cashew nuts
	salt and pepper

1 With a sharp knife, cut the chicken into bite-sized strips, about 4 cm (1½ inches) long.

2 Heat the oil in a wok or deep frying pan, add all the prepared vegetables and stir-fry over a brisk heat for 3 minutes. Remove the vegetables with a slotted spoon and set aside.

3 In a jug, mix the cornflour to a paste with the sherry, soy sauce and hoisin sauce, then add the sugar and 150 ml (¼ pint) water.

4 Add the chicken strips to the pan and stir-fry over a moderate heat until lightly coloured on all sides. Pour the cornflour mixture into the pan and bring to the boil, stirring constantly, until thickened.

5 Return the vegetables to the pan. Add the cashew nuts and salt and pepper to taste, and stir-fry for a few minutes more. Serve immediately.

TURKEY STROGANOFF

SERVES 4

450 g (1 lb) turkey fillet	salt and pepper
15 ml (1 tbsp) polyunsaturated oil	225 g (8 oz) button mushrooms, sliced
25 g (1 oz) butter or polyunsaturated margarine	1 green pepper, seeded and sliced
30 ml (2 tbsp) brandy	60 ml (4 tbsp) soured cream or smetana
1 garlic clove, crushed	

1 Slice the turkey fillet into pencil-thin strips, using a sharp knife.
2 Heat the oil and butter in a large sauté pan and brown the turkey strips. Remove from the heat. Heat the brandy in a small pan, ignite and pour over the turkey. Return to the heat, then add the garlic and seasoning.
3 Cover the pan and simmer for about 4-5 minutes or until the turkey is just tender.
4 Increase the heat, add the mushrooms and pepper and cook for 3-4 minutes, turning occasionally, until just softened.
5 Reduce the heat, stir in the soured cream or smetana, taste and adjust seasoning. Serve immediately on a bed of rice or noodles, with a crisp green salad.

TURKEY ESCALOPES EN PAPILLOTE

SERVES 4

4 boneless turkey breasts	30 ml (2 tbsp) chopped parsley
15 ml (1 tbsp) polyunsaturated oil	salt and pepper
1 small red pepper, seeded and thinly sliced	60 ml (4 tbsp) medium dry sherry
225 g (8 oz) tomatoes, skinned and sliced	40 g (1½ oz) fresh wholemeal breadcrumbs, toasted

1 Split each turkey breast in half horizontally with a sharp knife, then bat out between 2 sheets of greaseproof paper to make 8 thin escalopes.
2 Place a large sheet of foil on a baking sheet and brush lightly with the oil. Put half of the turkey escalopes side by side on the foil.
3 Blanch the pepper slices for 1 minute in boiling water, drain and refresh under cold running water. Pat dry with absorbent kitchen paper.
4 Layer the pepper and tomato slices on top of the escalopes with half of the parsley and seasoning to taste.
5 Cover with the remaining escalopes, spoon 15 ml (1 tbsp) sherry over each and close up the foil like a parcel.
6 Bake in the oven at 180°C (350°F) mark 4 for 35-40 minutes or until the meat is tender when pierced with a fork or skewer.
7 Arrange the escalopes on a warmed serving dish, cover and keep warm in the oven turned to its lowest setting. Transfer the juices to a pan and boil to reduce to 60 ml (4 tbsp), then spoon over the turkey. Sprinkle with the freshly toasted breadcrumbs and the remaining parsley and serve immediately.

MARINATED TURKEY WITH ASPARAGUS

SERVES 4-6

900 g (2 lb) turkey breast fillets	1 garlic clove, crushed
900 ml (1½ pints) chicken stock	20 ml (4 tsp) ground ginger
salt and pepper	300 ml (½ pint) reduced-calorie vinaigrette
30 ml (2 tbsp) chopped parsley	450 g (1 lb) asparagus, trimmed
50 g (2 oz) walnuts, chopped	5 ml (1 tsp) salt
	celery leaves, to garnish

1 Put the turkey fillets in a large saucepan and add enough chicken stock to cover. Season to taste. Poach for about 20 minutes or until tender. Leave to cool in the liquid.

2 Meanwhile, to make the marinade, stir the parsley, walnuts, garlic and ginger into the vinaigrette.

3 Tie the asparagus stalks into two neat bundles. Wedge upright in a large deep saucepan and cover the tips with foil.

4 Pour in enough boiling water to come three-quarters of the way up the asparagus stalks. Add salt, return to the boil and simmer gently for about 10 minutes.

5 Lift the bundles carefully out of the water, place in a dish and remove the string. Whilst still hot, pour over half the dressing. Leave the asparagus to cool.

6 Cut the turkey into 5 mm (¼ inch) wide strips. Marinate in the remaining dressing for 3-4 hours.

7 To serve, lift the turkey strips and asparagus out of the marinade, using a slotted spoon, and arrange in a serving dish. Garnish with celery leaves. Serve chilled.

TURKEY ESCALOPES WITH DAMSONS

SERVES 4

two 225 g (8 oz) turkey breast fillets, skinned and cut widthways into 5 cm (2 inch) slices	5 ml (1 tsp) chopped fresh thyme or 1.25 ml (½ tsp) dried
75 ml (5 tbsp) unsweetened apple juice	15 g (½ oz) butter or polyunsaturated margarine
45 ml (3 tbsp) soy sauce	15 ml (1 tbsp) polyunsaturated oil
45 ml (3 tbsp) dry sherry	225 g (8 oz) damsons, halved and stoned
1 small garlic clove, crushed	pepper

1 Place the turkey slices between two sheets of dampened greaseproof paper and beat out with a rolling pin or meat mallet until about 2.5 cm (1 inch) thick.

2 Place the turkey slices in a large shallow dish and pour over the apple juice, soy sauce, sherry, garlic and thyme. Cover and leave in the refrigerator to marinate for 3-4 hours or overnight.

3 Remove the turkey from the marinade, reserving the marinade. Heat the butter or margarine and oil in a frying pan, add the turkey and fry quickly until browned on both sides. Add the damsons, reserved marinade and pepper to taste.

4 Cover and simmer gently for 10-15 minutes or until tender, stirring occasionally. Serve immediately.

COOK'S TIP

If damsons are not available, substitute plums.

TURKEY IN SPICED YOGURT

SERVES 6

1.1 kg (2½ lb) turkey leg meat on the bone	30 ml (2 tbsp) lemon juice
7.5 ml (1½ tsp) ground cumin	45 ml (3 tbsp) polyunsaturated oil
7.5 ml (1½ tsp) ground coriander	2 medium onions, sliced
2.5 ml (½ tsp) turmeric	45 ml (3 tbsp) desiccated coconut
2.5 ml (½ tsp) ground ginger	30 ml (2 tbsp) plain wholemeal flour
salt and pepper	150 ml (¼ pint) chicken stock
300 ml (½ pint) low-fat natural yogurt	chopped parsley, to garnish

1 Cut the turkey meat off the bone into large fork-sized pieces, discarding the skin; there should be about 900 g (2 lb) meat.

2 To make the marinade, in a large bowl mix the spices with salt and pepper to taste, the yogurt and lemon juice. Stir well until evenly blended. Add the turkey meat and turn until coated with the yogurt mixture. Cover tightly and leave to marinate in the refrigerator overnight.

3 Heat the oil in a flameproof casserole, add the onions and fry for about 5 minutes until lightly browned. Add the coconut and flour and fry gently, stirring, for about 1 minute.

4 Remove from the heat and stir in the turkey with its marinade, and the stock. Return to the heat and bring slowly to the boil, stirring all the time to prevent sticking.

5 Cover tightly and cook in the oven at 170°C (325°F) mark 3 for 1-1¼ hours or until the turkey is tender when tested with a fork. Serve garnished with chopped parsley.

TURKEY GROUNDNUT STEW

SERVES 4-6

30 ml (2 tbsp) polyunsaturated oil	60 ml (4 tbsp) crunchy peanut butter
2 medium onions, chopped	10 ml (2 tsp) tomato purée
1 garlic clove, crushed	225 g (8 oz) tomatoes, skinned and roughly chopped, or 225 g (8 oz) can tomatoes, drained
1 large green pepper, seeded and chopped	
900 g (2 lb) boneless turkey, cut into cubes	2.5-5 ml (½-1 tsp) cayenne pepper
175 g (6 oz) shelled peanuts	few drops of Tabasco sauce
600 ml (1 pint) chicken stock	chopped green pepper, to garnish
salt and pepper	

1 Heat the oil in a flameproof casserole, add the onions, garlic and green pepper and fry gently for 5 minutes until they are soft but not coloured.

2 Add the turkey and fry for a few minutes more, turning constantly until well browned on all sides.

3 Add the peanuts, stock and salt and pepper to taste and bring slowly to boiling point. Lower the heat, cover and simmer for 45 minutes or until the turkey is tender.

4 Remove the turkey from the cooking liquid with a slotted spoon and set aside. Leave the cooking liquid to cool for about 5 minutes.

5 Work the cooking liquid and nuts in a blender or food processor, half at a time, until quite smooth. Return to the pan. Add all the remaining ingredients, with the turkey and heat through. Taste and adjust seasoning before serving, adding more cayenne if a hot flavour is preferred. Garnish with chopped green pepper to serve.

QUICK
TURKEY CURRY

SERVES 4-6

30 ml (2 tbsp) polyunsaturated oil	2.5 ml (½ tsp) chilli powder
3 bay leaves	salt and pepper
2 cardamom pods, crushed	50 g (2 oz) unsalted cashew nuts
1 cinnamon stick, broken into short lengths	700 g (1½ lb) turkey fillets, skinned and cut into bite-size pieces
1 medium onion, thinly sliced	2 medium potatoes, peeled and cut into chunks
1 green pepper, seeded and chopped (optional)	4 tomatoes, skinned and chopped, or 225 g (8 oz) can tomatoes
10 ml (2 tsp) paprika	bay leaves, to garnish
7.5 ml (1½ tsp) garam masala	
2.5 ml (½ tsp) turmeric	

1 Heat the oil in a flameproof casserole, add the bay leaves, cardamom and cinnamon and fry over moderate heat for 1-2 minutes. Add the onion and green pepper if using, with the spices and salt and pepper to taste. Pour in enough water to moisten, then cook, stirring, for 1 minute.

2 Add the cashews and turkey, cover and simmer for 20 minutes. Turn the turkey occasionally during this time to ensure even cooking.

3 Add the potatoes and tomatoes and continue cooking for a further 20 minutes until the turkey and potatoes are tender. Garnish with bay leaves. Serve with boiled rice.

TURKEY SAUTE WITH
LEMON AND WALNUTS

SERVES 4

450 g (1 lb) turkey breast fillets, skinned	30 ml (2 tbsp) lemon juice
30 ml (2 tbsp) cornflour	45 ml (3 tbsp) lemon marmalade
45 ml (3 tbsp) polyunsaturated oil	5 ml (1 tsp) white wine vinegar
1 green pepper, seeded and thinly sliced	1.25 ml (¼ tsp) soy sauce
40 g (1½ oz) walnut halves or pieces	salt and pepper
60 ml (4 tbsp) chicken stock	lemon wedges and parsley sprigs, to garnish

1 Cut the turkey flesh into 5 cm (2 inch) pencil thin strips. Add to the cornflour and toss until coated.

2 Heat half the oil in a large sauté or deep frying pan, add the pepper strips and walnuts and fry for 2-3 minutes. Remove from the pan with slotted spoon.

3 Add the remaining oil to the pan and fry the turkey strips for 10 minutes or until golden. Add the stock and lemon juice, stirring well to scrape up any sediment at the bottom of the pan. Add the lemon marmalade, vinegar and soy sauce. Season to taste.

4 Return the walnuts and green pepper to the pan. Cook gently for a further 5 minutes or until the turkey is tender. Taste and adjust the seasoning and serve immediately, garnished with lemon wedges and pasley.

VARIATION

Turkey Sauté with Orange and Pine Nuts
Substitute 30 ml (2 tbsp) orange juice and 45 ml (3 tbsp) orange marmalade for the lemon juice and marmalade in the above recipe. Replace the walnuts with pine nuts. Garnish with thin slices or wedges of orange to serve.

TURKEY
PAPRIKA WITH PASTA

SERVES 4

30 ml (2 tbsp) polyunsaturated oil	1 green pepper, seeded and sliced
75 g (3 oz) onion, sliced	100 g (4 oz) small pasta shapes
450 g (1 lb) turkey breast fillets, skinned	90 ml (3 fl oz) low-fat natural yogurt
10 ml (2 tsp) paprika	paprika and parsley sprigs, to garnish
450 ml (¾ pint) chicken stock	
salt and pepper	

1 Heat the oil in a large sauté pan and fry the onion for 5 minutes until golden brown.
2 Cut the turkey breast fillets into small finger-sized pieces.
3 Add the turkey and paprika to the pan and toss over a moderate heat for 2 minutes.
4 Stir in the stock and seasoning and bring to the boil. Add the green pepper and pasta, cover and simmer gently for 15-20 minutes until turkey and pasta are tender.
5 Stir in the yogurt and adjust the seasoning. Garnish with a little paprika and parsley. Serve with a green salad.

DUCK
WITH MANGO

SERVES 4

1 ripe, but still firm mango	2.5 ml (½ tsp) ground allspice
4 duck breasts or lean duck portions	45 ml (3 tbsp) plum jam
60 ml (4 tbsp) peanut oil	20 ml (4 tsp) wine vinegar
	salt and pepper

1 Skin and thickly slice the mango on either side of the large central stone.
2 Remove any excess fat from the duck portions. Divide each portion into three and place in a saucepan. Cover with cold water and bring to the boil. Lower the heat and simmer gently for 15-20 minutes. Drain well and pat dry with absorbent kitchen paper. Trim the bones.
3 Heat the oil in a wok or large frying pan until hot and smoking. Add the duck pieces and allspice and cook until well browned on all sides.
4 Stir in the jam and vinegar. Cook for a further 2-3 minutes, stirring constantly, until well glazed. Stir in the mango slices and season to taste. Heat through, then turn into a warmed serving dish and serve immediately.

VARIATION

Tropical Duck
Other tropical fruits could be used instead of the mango in the above recipe. Try guava, papaya or lychees.

CRISPY DUCK WITH MANGETOUT

SERVES 6

4 duck breast fillets	225 g (8 oz) mangetout, topped and tailed
salt	2 garlic cloves, crushed
25 ml (1½ tbsp) clear honey	2-3 good pinches five spice powder
45 ml (3 tbsp) polyunsaturated oil	15 ml (1 tbsp) raw cane sugar
1 bunch spring onions, trimmed and cut into 2.5 cm (1 inch) lengths	45 ml (3 tbsp) dark soy sauce
	15 ml (1 tbsp) malt vinegar
1 large green pepper, seeded and cut into thin strips	16 water chestnuts, sliced
	40 g (1½ oz) toasted cashew nuts, chopped

1 Prick the duck breast skin all over with a skewer or fork and rub well with salt to help crisp the skin. Place, skin side uppermost on a rack or trivet in a roasting tin.
2 Bake in the oven at 180°C (350°F) mark 4 for 15 minutes. Brush the skin with the honey and cook for a further 15 minutes or until cooked through. Remove from the oven and leave to cool. When cold, cut into thin strips.
3 In a wok or large frying pan, heat the oil. Add the spring onion, green pepper, mangetout, garlic and five spice powder and stir-fry for 2 minutes. Add the sugar, soy sauce, vinegar and duck strips and toss in the sauce to heat through and glaze. Add the water chestnuts and toss through lightly.
4 Serve at once, sprinkled with toasted cashew nuts and accompanied by rice.

GUINEA FOWL WITH PLUM SAUCE

SERVES 4

2 guinea fowl	salt and pepper
100 ml (4 fl oz) red wine	25 g (1 oz) butter or polyunsaturated margarine
1 shallot or 2 spring onions, trimmed and finely chopped	30 ml (2 tbsp) crushed juniper berries
30 ml (2 tbsp) thick plum or damson jam	watercress sprigs, to garnish
1.25-2.5 ml (¼-½ tsp) ground ginger, to taste	

1 Cut each guinea fowl into four joints.
2 To make the plum sauce, put the wine and shallot or onion in a small saucepan, cover and simmer for 5 minutes or until soft. Add the jam, ginger and salt and pepper to taste. Heat gently until the jam melts, then bring to the boil and simmer for a few minutes or until thickened slightly. Remove from the heat.
3 Melt the butter or margarine in a small pan with the juniper berries and salt and pepper to taste. Place the guinea fowl, skin side down, on an oiled grill and brush with half of the juniper berry mixture. Grill under a medium heat for 7 minutes, then turn the guinea fowl over and brush with the remaining mixture. Grill for a further 7 minutes until cooked through and the skin crisp.
4 Just before the guinea fowl are ready to serve, pour the cooking juices into the plum sauce and reheat. Taste and adjust the seasoning. Arrange the guinea fowl portions on a serving platter and garnish with watercress. Serve the sauce separately.

COOK'S TIP

Nowadays, guinea fowl are bred for the table, so these smallish birds are plumper than the wild guinea fowl. The tender flesh has a delicious flavour rather like gamey chicken, but it must be kept moist during cooking as it has a tendency to dry out.

PHEASANT WITH CHESTNUTS

SERVES 4-6

15 ml (1 tbsp) polyunsaturated oil	150 ml (¼ pint) dry red wine
2 oven-ready pheasants, trussed	salt and pepper
2 medium onions, sliced	grated rind and juice of ½ orange
225 g (8 oz) peeled chestnuts	10 ml (2 tsp) redcurrant jelly
45 ml (3 tbsp) plain flour	1 bouquet garni
450 ml (¾ pint) hot chicken stock	parsley sprigs, to garnish

1 Heat the oil in a large non-stick frying pan and fry the pheasant for about 5 minutes stirring until evenly browned. Remove from the pan and put into a large casserole.

2 Add the onions and chestnuts to the pan and fry in the remaining oil for a few minutes or until brown, then add to the pheasant.

3 Stir the flour into the fat remaining in the pan and cook, stirring, for 2-3 minutes. Remove from the heat and gradually stir in the stock and wine. Bring to the boil, stirring continuously, until thickened and smooth. Season with salt and pepper to taste and pour over the pheasant in the casserole. Add the orange rind and juice, redcurrant jelly and bouquet garni.

4 Cover and bake in the oven at 180°C (350°F) mark 4 for about 1 hour or until the pheasant is tender. Remove the bouquet garni before serving, garnished with parsley.

COOK'S TIP

Many supermarkets now sell oven-ready fresh or frozen pheasant during the season, which runs from 1 October to 1 February (10 December in Scotland). You may also be able to buy fresh game from your butcher, in which case ask for the bird to be plucked and drawn.

VENISON ESCALOPES WITH RED WINE

SERVES 6

6 venison escalopes, cut from the haunch (leg), each about 175 g (6 oz)	300 ml (½ pint) dry red wine
1 small onion, finely chopped	15 g (½ oz) butter or polyunsaturated margarine
1 bay leaf	15 ml (1 tbsp) polyunsaturated oil
2 parsley sprigs	30 ml (2 tbsp) redcurrant jelly
8 juniper berries	salt and pepper

1 Put the venison escalopes in a large shallow dish and sprinkle with the onion, bay leaf, parsley and juniper berries. Pour on the wine, cover and leave to marinate in the refrigerator for 3-4 hours or overnight, turning the escalopes occasionally.

2 Remove the escalopes from the marinade, reserving the marinade. Heat the butter and oil in a large frying pan and fry the escalopes for 3-4 minutes on each side. Transfer to a warmed serving dish and keep warm while making the sauce.

3 Strain the reserved marinade into the frying pan and stir to loosen any sediment. Increase the heat and boil rapidly for 3-4 minutes, until reduced. Stir in the redcurrant jelly and season the mixture to taste. Cook, stirring, for 1-2 minutes.

4 Pour the sauce over the escalopes to serve.

MEAT DISHES

For the recipes in this chapter, buy the new leaner cuts of meat – now widely available – and trim off any fat before cooking. Try one of the colourful quick stir-fries in which a little meat goes a long way, or a tasty curry or casserole – remembering to skim off any fat before serving.

MINTED LAMB GRILL

SERVES 4

4 lamb chump chops	30 ml (2 tbsp) clear honey
30 ml (2 tbsp) chopped mint	salt and pepper
20 ml (4 tsp) white wine vinegar	mint sprigs, to garnish

1 Trim any excess fat off the chump chops using a pair of sharp kitchen scissors.
2 With a knife, slash both sides of the chops to a depth of about 5 mm (¼ inch).
3 To make the marinade, mix the mint, vinegar, honey and seasonings together, stirring well.
4 Place a sheet of foil in the grill pan and turn up the edges to prevent the marinade running into the pan.
5 Place the chops side by side on the foil and spoon over the marinade. Leave in a cool place for about 1 hour, basting occasionally.
6 Grill under a moderate heat for 5-6 minutes on each side, turning once only. Baste with the marinade during the cooking time. Garnish with mint before serving.

LAMB CUTLETS WITH LEMON AND GARLIC

SERVES 4

2 lemons	1 medium onion, finely chopped
3 small garlic cloves, crushed	175 ml (6 fl oz) low-fat natural yogurt
salt and pepper	
8 lamb cutlets	150 ml (¼ pint) chicken stock
60 ml (4 tbsp) polyunsaturated oil	5 ml (1 tsp) chopped basil

1 Finely grate the rind of 1½ lemons into a bowl. Add the garlic and pepper to taste and blend thoroughly.
2 Place the cutlets on a board and spread the lemon rind and garlic evenly over them. Leave for 15 minutes.
3 Heat the oil in a pan, add the cutlets and fry for about 3 minutes on each side or until tender. Drain and keep warm on a serving dish.
4 Pour off all but 30 ml (2 tbsp) fat from the pan, add the onion and fry gently for 5 minutes until soft but not coloured. Stir in the yogurt and stock with the squeezed juice of the 1½ lemons and the basil. Bring to the boil and simmer for 2-3 minutes. Add salt and pepper to taste.
5 Spoon the juices over the meat and garnish with the remaining ½ lemon, cut into wedges, if liked. Serve at once.

LAMB
WITH CHERRIES

SERVES 6

225 g (8 oz) streaky bacon rashers, chopped	1 celery stick, sliced
15 g (½ oz) butter or polyunsaturated margarine	1 garlic clove, sliced
	600 ml (1 pint) dry red wine
1.4 kg (3 lb) boneless leg or shoulder of lamb, cut into 4 cm (1½ inch) cubes	bouquet garni
	pinch of grated nutmeg
	salt and pepper
1 medium onion, sliced	450 g (1 lb) fresh red cherries, stoned
1 medium carrot, sliced	

1 In a large frying pan, fry the bacon in its own fat until browned. Add the butter or margarine to the pan and fry the lamb, a little at a time, until browned. Remove from the pan with the bacon and put in an ovenproof casserole.
2 Add the onion, carrot, celery and garlic to the fat remaining in the pan and fry for about 5 minutes or until lightly browned. Add the vegetables to the casserole.
3 Pour over the wine and add the bouquet garni and nutmeg. Season to taste, cover and cook in the oven at 150°C (300°F) mark 2 for about 2½ hours or until tender.
4 Thirty minutes before the end of the cooking time, stir the cherries into the casserole and continue to cook until the meat is tender and the cherries soft. Serve hot.

COOK'S TIP

Look for red-skinned sour cherries for this dish. Dark skinned Morellos are also a good choice.

MINTED
LAMB MEATBALLS

SERVES 4

225 g (8 oz) crisp cabbage, finely chopped	397 g (14 oz) can tomato juice
450 g (1 lb) lean minced lamb	1 bay leaf
100 g (4 oz) onion, finely chopped	10 ml (2 tsp) chopped fresh mint or 5 ml (1 tsp) dried
2.5 ml (½ tsp) ground allspice	15 ml (1 tbsp) chopped parsley
salt and pepper	mint sprigs, to garnish

1 Steam the cabbage for 2-3 minutes or cook in boiling salted water until softened. Drain thoroughly.
2 Place the lamb and cabbage in a bowl with the onion, allspice and seasoning to taste. Beat well to combine all the ingredients.
3 With your hands, shape the mixture into 16-20 small balls. Place the meatballs in a shallow large ovenproof dish.
4 Mix the tomato juice with the bay leaf, mint and parsley. Pour over the meatballs. Cover the dish tightly and bake in the oven at 180°C (350°F) mark 4 for about 1 hour until the meatballs are cooked.
5 Skim any fat off the tomato sauce before serving, and taste and adjust seasoning. Serve hot, garnished with mint.

LAMB FILLET WITH REDCURRANT SAUCE

SERVES 3

450 g (1 lb) lamb fillet	salt and pepper
1 garlic clove, crushed	30 ml (2 tbsp) dry red wine
5 ml (1 tsp) wholegrain mustard	30 ml (2 tbsp) redcurrant jelly

1 Put the lamb fillet in a roasting tin and rub with the garlic, mustard and seasoning, all over. Roast in the oven at 180°C (350°F) mark 4 for 30 minutes or until tender and cooked to your liking. Transfer the lamb to a warmed serving dish and keep warm.
2 Add the wine to the roasting tin, stirring in any sediment from the bottom of the tin. Stir in the redcurrant jelly. Bring to the boil and boil for 1-2 minutes or until thickened slightly.
3 Slice the lamb and serve with the sauce spooned over.

SERVING SUGGESTION

If possible buy the new season's spring lamb for this dish and serve with new potatoes and steamed courgettes or mangetout.

LAMB KEBABS IN SPICY YOGURT DRESSING

SERVES 4

1 large corn-on-the-cob	15 ml (1 tbsp) coriander seeds
8 shallots	700 g (1½ lb) boned leg of lamb, cut into 2. 5 cm (1 inch) cubes
salt and pepper	
150 ml (5 fl oz) low-fat natural yogurt	225 g (8 oz) courgettes, cut into 5 mm (¼ inch) slices
1 garlic clove, crushed	4 tomatoes, halved
2 bay leaves, crumbled	lemon wedges, to garnish
15 ml (1 tbsp) lemon juice	
5 ml (1 tsp) ground allspice	

1 Blanch the corn in boiling water for 1 minute, drain well, then cut into eight pieces and set aside. Blanch the shallots in boiling salted water for 1 minute, skin and set aside.
2 To make the marinade, pour the yogurt into a shallow dish and stir in the garlic, bay leaves, lemon juice, allspice, coriander seeds and salt and pepper to taste.
3 Thread the lamb cubes on to eight skewers with the courgettes, tomatoes, corn and shallots. Place in the dish, spoon over the marinade, cover and leave for 2-3 hours, turning occasionally to ensure even coating.
4 Cook the kebabs under a preheated grill for 15-20 minutes, turning and brushing with the marinade occasionally.
5 Serve on a bed of rice. Spoon the remaining marinade over the kebabs and garnish with lemon wedges.

SPICED LEG OF LAMB

SERVES 6

2 medium onions, roughly chopped	15 ml (1 tbsp) ground coriander
6 garlic cloves, roughly chopped	2.5 ml (½ tsp) freshly grated nutmeg
5 cm (2 inch) piece fresh root ginger, peeled and chopped	10 ml (2 tsp) turmeric
75 g (3 oz) whole blanched almonds	10 ml (2 tsp) chilli powder
5 cm (2 inch) cinnamon stick	salt
10 green cardamoms	30 ml (2 tbsp) lemon or lime juice
4 whole cloves	600 ml (1 pint) low-fat natural yogurt
5 ml (1 tsp) aniseed	2.3 kg (5 lb) leg of lamb
30 ml (2 tbsp) cumin seed	slivered almonds and mint sprigs, to garnish

1 Place all the ingredients, except the lamb, in a blender or food processor and work until smooth.

2 Remove all the fat and white membrane from the lamb. With a sharp knife, make deep slashes all over the meat through to the bone.

3 Rub one third of the yogurt mixture well into the lamb and place in an ovenproof baking dish or casserole. Pour the remaining yogurt mixture over the top of the meat and around the sides. Cover and leave to marinate in the refrigerator for 12 hours.

4 Allow the dish to come to room temperature, then cover tightly with the lid or foil. Bake in the oven at 180°C (350°F) mark 4 for 1¼ hours, then uncover and bake for a further 45 minutes, or until the lamb is completely tender, basting occasionally.

5 Transfer the lamb to a warmed serving dish and garnish with the almonds and mint sprigs. Serve hot with the sauce handed separately.

SPICED LAMB AND LENTIL BAKE

SERVES 4

8 middle neck lamb chops, total weight about 1.1 kg (2½ lb)	5 ml (1 tsp) ground cinnamon
45 ml (3 tbsp) polyunsaturated oil	75 g (3 oz) red lentils
2 medium onions, thinly sliced	salt and pepper
15 ml (1 tbsp) turmeric	450 g (1 lb) potatoes, peeled and thinly sliced
5 ml (1 tsp) paprika	450 g (1 lb) swede, thinly sliced
	300 ml (½ pint) lamb or chicken stock

1 Trim the fat from the chops. Heat the oil in a large sauté or frying pan, add the chops and brown well on both sides. Remove from the pan with a slotted spoon.

2 Add the onions to the pan with the turmeric, paprika, cinnamon and lentils. Fry for 2-3 minutes. Add salt and pepper to taste and spoon into a shallow 2 litre (3½ pint) ovenproof dish.

3 Place the chops on top of the onion and lentil mixture. Arrange the vegetable slices on top of the chops, then sprinkle with salt and pepper to taste and pour over the stock.

4 Cover the dish tightly and cook in the oven at 180°C (350°F) mark 4 for about 1½ hours, or until the chops are tender. Uncover and cook for a further 30 minutes, or until lightly browned on top.

5 Serve hot, straight from the dish.

COOK'S TIP

There are many different types of lentil available. The red lentils used in this recipe are the most common kind, sometimes also described as 'split red lentils' or even 'Egyptian lentils'. They do not need soaking and are quick-cooking, but they tend to lose their shape.

LAMB KORMA

SERVES 4

2 medium onions, chopped	5 ml (1 tsp) ground coriander
2.5 cm (1 inch) piece fresh root ginger, peeled	1.25 ml (¼ tsp) cayenne pepper
40 g (1½ oz) blanched almonds	900 g (2 lb) boned lean shoulder or leg of lamb
2 garlic cloves	45 ml (3 tbsp) polyunsaturated oil or ghee
5 ml (1 tsp) ground cardamom	300 ml (½ pint) low-fat natural yogurt
5 ml (1 tsp) ground cloves	salt and pepper
5 ml (1 tsp) ground cinnamon	parsley sprigs and lime slices, to garnish
5 ml (1 tsp) ground cumin	

1 Put the onions, ginger, almonds and garlic in a blender or food processor with 90 ml (6 tbsp) water and blend to a smooth paste. Add the spices and mix well.
2 Cut the lamb into cubes, trimming off excess fat. Heat the oil or ghee in a heavy-based saucepan and fry the lamb for 5 minutes until browned on all sides.
3 Add the paste mixture and fry for about 10 minutes, stirring, until the mixture is lightly browned. Stir in the yogurt 15 ml (1 tbsp) at a time, reserving a little for garnish, and season with salt and pepper to taste.
4 Cover with a tight-fitting lid, reduce the heat and simmer for 1¼ -1½ hours or until the meat is really tender.
5 Transfer to a warmed serving dish and top with the reserved yogurt. Garnish with parsley and lime slices. Serve with boiled rice.

PORK FILLET IN WINE AND CORIANDER

SERVES 4

700 g (1½ lb) pork fillet or tenderloin, trimmed and cut into 1 cm (½ inch) slices	15 g (½ oz) plain flour
15 g (½ oz) butter or polyunsaturated margarine	15 ml (1 tbsp) coriander seeds, ground
15 ml (1 tbsp) polyunsaturated oil	150 ml (¼ pint) chicken stock
1 small green pepper, seeded and sliced into rings	150 ml (¼ pint) dry white wine
1 medium onion, chopped	salt and pepper
	coriander sprigs, to garnish

1 Place the pork between 2 sheets of greaseproof paper and flatten with a mallet or rolling pin until thin.
2 Heat the butter or margarine and oil in a large saucepan, add the pork and brown on both sides. Add the pepper and onion and lightly cook for 8-10 minutes, until softened.
3 Stir in the flour and coriander and cook for 1 minute. Gradually add the stock and wine, stirring until the sauce thickens, boils and is smooth. Season to taste. Simmer gently for 5-10 minutes, until the pork is tender and cooked through.
4 Serve garnished with coriander sprigs.

COOK'S TIP

Coriander seeds quickly lose their mild, orangy flavour when ground, so try to buy whole seeds to crush yourself.

STIR-FRIED PORK AND VEGETABLES

SERVES 4

450 g (1 lb) pork fillet or tenderloin, trimmed	1 bunch of spring onions, trimmed and finely chopped
60 ml (4 tbsp) dry sherry	1-2 garlic cloves, crushed
45 ml (3 tbsp) soy sauce	30 ml (2 tbsp) cornflour
10 ml (2 tsp) ground ginger	300 ml (½ pint) chicken stock
salt and pepper	175 g (6 oz) beansprouts
1 medium cucumber	spring onion tassels, to garnish
30 ml (2 tbsp) polyunsaturated oil	

1 Cut the pork into thin strips and place in a bowl. Add the sherry, soy sauce, ginger and salt and pepper to taste, then stir well.

2 Cut the cucumber into strips, about 2.5 cm (1 inch) long, discarding the seeds.

3 Heat the oil in a wok or large, heavy-based frying pan, add the spring onions and garlic and fry gently for about 5 minutes until softened, then remove from the pan with a slotted spoon and set aside.

4 Add the pork to the pan, increase the heat and stir-fry for 2-3 minutes until lightly coloured.

5 Mix the cornflour with a little of the cold chicken stock and set aside.

6 Add the cucumber, spring onions and beansprouts to the pork, with the cornflour and stock. Stir-fry until the juices thicken and the ingredients are well combined. Taste and adjust the seasoning, then turn into a warmed serving dish. Garnish with spring onion tassels and serve immediately, with rice.

COOK'S TIP

Spring Onion Tassels

Trim the spring onions, discarding the dark ends, to 7.5 cm (3 inch) lengths. With a sharp knife, shred each end leaving about 2 cm (¾ inch) intact in the middle. Leave in a bowl of iced water to open out.

APPLE BAKED CHOPS

SERVES 4

225 g (8 oz) eating apples	4 lean pork loin chops, each about 175 g (6 oz)
1 medium onion	3 or 4 green cardamoms, lightly crushed
50 g (2 oz) raisins	30 ml (2 tbsp) dry white wine or cider
200 ml (7 fl oz) unsweetened apple juice	basil or parsley sprigs, to garnish
45 ml (3 tbsp) chopped parsley	
salt and pepper	

1 Core and finely chop the apples. Finely chop the onion. Place in a saucepan with the raisins and apple juice. Simmer gently, uncovered, for 3-4 minutes until the apple begins to soften slightly.

2 Remove from the heat, drain off the juices and reserve. Stir the parsley into the apple mixture with salt and pepper to taste, then leave to cool.

3 Meanwhile trim the rind and fat from the chops then make a horizontal cut through the flesh, almost to the bone. Open out to form a pocket for the apple.

4 Spoon a little of the apple mixture into the pocket of each chop. Place in a shallow flameproof dish. Sprinkle any remaining stuffing around the chops, with the crushed cardamoms. Mix the reserved juices with the wine or cider and pour over the chops.

5 Cover with foil and bake in the oven at 190°C (375°F) mark 5 for about 45 minutes until tender.

6 Remove the chops from the dish and place in a grill pan. Grill until browned.

7 Meanwhile pour the cooking juices from the chops into a pan and boil rapidly until reduced by half. Arrange the chops on a dish and pour over the reduced juices. Garnish with basil or parsley to serve.

PORK
IN PLUM SAUCE

SERVES 4

450 g (1 lb) plums	25 g (1 oz) butter or polyunsaturated margarine
300 ml (½ pint) rosé wine	1 large onion, chopped
salt and pepper	175 g (6 oz) white cabbage, shredded
25 g (1 oz) plain wholemeal flour	30 ml (2 tbsp) low-fat natural yogurt
700 g (1½ lb) pork fillet (tenderloin), cubed	

1 Put the plums and wine in a saucepan and simmer for 5 minutes or until tender. Strain, reserving the juice. Remove the stones from the plums and purée half in a blender or food processor.
2 Season the flour, add the pork and toss until coated.
3 Melt the butter or margarine in a large saucepan or flameproof casserole and lightly fry the onion and cabbage for 3 minutes. Add the meat and fry until brown on all sides.
4 Pour in the reserved plum juice and puréed plums, then simmer, uncovered, for 10-15 minutes or until tender. Add the remaining plums and yogurt and reheat gently. Serve immediately.

COOK'S TIP

There are many varieties of plum and one type or another should be available from late July through to October. Monarch, a large black cooking plum in season from mid September would be a good choice, or the widely grown Victoria, which comes into the shops a little earlier, could be used instead. And damsons, if you happen to find them, can also be substituted.

BACON CHOPS WITH
GOOSEBERRY SAUCE

SERVES 4

15 ml (1 tbsp) muscovado sugar	15 g (½ oz) butter or polyunsaturated margarine
5 ml (1 tsp) mustard powder	1 large onion, chopped
pepper	150 ml (¼ pint) vegetable stock
4 bacon chops, each 175 g (6 oz)	100 g (4 oz) gooseberries, topped and tailed

1 Mix together the brown sugar, mustard and pepper and rub into both sides of the bacon chops.
2 Melt the butter or margarine in a large frying pan or flameproof casserole and cook the onion for 2 minutes, then add the bacon chops, half the stock and the gooseberries. Simmer gently for 15 minutes.
3 Remove the chops from the pan. Purée the onions and gooseberries in a blender or food processor until smooth.
4 Return the chops and purée to the pan with the remaining stock. Simmer gently for 10 minutes, until the chops are tender and cooked through. Serve at once with boiled sliced red cabbage.

COOK'S TIP

At the start of the season gooseberries are too acid and hard to be eaten raw, but are perfect for cooking. Look for thick prime back bacon chops, good for gentle braising.

CHILLI CON CARNI

SERVES 6

900 g (2 lb) lean chuck steak	2.5 ml (½ tsp) dried oregano or marjoram
225 g (8 oz) dried red kidney beans, soaked in cold water overnight	2.5 ml (½ tsp) cayenne pepper
30 ml (2 tbsp) polyunsaturated oil	1.25 ml (¼ tsp) sesame seeds
2 medium onions, chopped	salt and pepper
1 large garlic clove, crushed	30-45 ml (2-3 tbsp) chilli seasoning or 2.5 ml (½ tsp) chilli powder
1 bay leaf	30 ml (2 tbsp) tomato purée
1 green chilli, seeded and chopped	793 g (28 oz) can tomatoes
5 cm (2 inch) cinnamon stick	pinch of raw cane sugar
4 whole cloves	5 ml (1 tsp) malt vinegar
	2 coriander sprigs
	coriander sprigs, to garnish

1 Trim the meat of fat and cut into cubes.
2 Drain the beans and place in a saucepan of cold water. Bring to the boil, boil fast for 10 minutes, then drain.
3 Meanwhile heat the oil in a flameproof casserole and fry the onions for 5 minutes until softened. Add the meat and cook, turning, for about 8 minutes until browned.
4 Add the next 10 ingredients to the meat and continue to fry for 2 minutes stirring constantly. Add the tomato purée, tomatoes with their juice, sugar, vinegar, coriander and the boiled and drained beans.
5 Bring to the boil, cover and cook in the oven at 170°C (325°F) mark 3 for 2¼ hours or until the meat and beans are tender. Garnish with coriander and serve with rice.

SLIMMERS' MOUSSAKA

SERVES 4

2 medium aubergines	15 ml (1 tbsp) chopped parsley
salt and pepper	300 ml (½ pint) low-fat natural yogurt
450 g (1 lb) lean minced beef	2 eggs, beaten
2 medium onions, sliced	pinch of freshly grated nutmeg
1 garlic clove, finely chopped	15 ml (1 tbsp) freshly grated Parmesan cheese
397 g (14 oz) can tomatoes	
30 ml (2 tbsp) tomato purée	

1 Thinly slice the aubergines and place in a colander, sprinkling each layer with salt. Cover with a plate, weight down and leave to stand for about 30 minutes.
2 Drain the aubergine slices, then rinse and pat dry.
3 Dry fry the aubergine slices on both sides in a non-stick frying pan over high heat until brown, pressing them with the back of a spatula to release the moisture. Remove from the pan; set aside.
4 In the same pan, cook the meat for 5 minutes until browned, stirring and pressing with a wooden spoon to break up any lumps. Stir in the onions and cook for a further 5 minutes until lightly browned.
5 Add the garlic, tomatoes with their juice, the tomato purée, parsley and salt and pepper to taste. Bring to the boil, stirring, then lower the heat and simmer for 20 minutes until the meat is cooked.
6 Arrange a layer of aubergines in the bottom of an ovenproof dish. Spoon over the meat mixture, then finish with a layer of the remaining aubergines.
7 Beat the yogurt and eggs together with the nutmeg and salt and pepper to taste. Pour over the dish and sprinkle with the grated Parmesan cheese.
8 Bake in the oven at 180°C (350°F) mark 4 for about 45 minutes until golden. Serve hot, straight from the dish, accompanied by crusty granary bread and a green salad.

BOILED
BEEF AND CARROTS

SERVES 6

1.6 kg (3½ lb) lean salted silverside or brisket of beef	8 cloves
bouquet garni	2 small turnips, quartered
6 black peppercorns, lightly crushed	2 celery sticks, chopped
	1 leek, chopped
2 small onions, quartered	18 small carrots

1 If necessary, soak the meat in cold water for several hours or overnight, then rinse. Tie up into a neat joint.
2 Place the beef in a large saucepan, add just enough water to cover and bring slowly to the boil. Skim the surface, then add the bouquet garni, peppercorns, onions (each quarter stuck with a clove), turnips, celery and leek. Lower the heat and simmer very gently for about 2 hours.
3 Add the small carrots and simmer gently for a further 20-30 minutes or until the carrots are tender.
4 Carefully transfer the beef and small carrots to a warmed serving plate and keep warm.
5 Skim the fat from the surface of the cooking liquor, then strain. Boil the liquid to reduce slightly, then pour into a warmed sauceboat or jug.
6 Serve the beef surrounded by the carrots, with the sauce served separately.

COOK'S TIP

The length of time the meat is soaked depends on how salty it is; check with the butcher. The greyish colour turns an appetising pink when cooked.

BURGUNDY
BEEF

SERVES 4

10 ml (2 tsp) olive oil	150 ml (¼ pint) red wine, ie Burgundy
550 g (1¼ lb) beef topside, trimmed and cubed	150 ml (¼ pint) hot beef stock (optional)
15 g (½ oz) plain flour	225 g (8 oz) shallots or pickling onions
30 ml (2 tbsp) brandy	
1 onion, chopped	225 g (8 oz) button mushrooms
2 carrots, sliced	lemon juice
1 garlic clove, crushed	chopped parsley, to garnish
pepper	
1 bouquet garni	

1 Brush a heavy-based frying pan with 5 ml (1 tsp) of the oil and heat. Toss the beef in the flour, add to the pan and cook over a medium heat for about 1 minute to seal.
2 Remove the pan from the heat, pour the brandy over and, holding the pan at a safe distance, ignite. When the flame dies down, add the chopped onion, carrots, garlic, pepper to taste and the bouquet garni. Stir for 1 minute, add the wine and heat gradually. When the mixture begins to bubble, pour into an ovenproof casserole with a tight-fitting lid. The meat and vegetables should be covered by the liquid, so add the stock if necessary.
3 Cover and cook in the oven at 150°C (300°F) mark 2 for 1½ hours.
4 Brush the frying pan with the remaining oil, add the shallots or pickling onions and cook over a high heat until browned. Add to the casserole and cook for a further 30 minutes. Add the mushrooms and cook for a further 15 minutes. Add lemon juice to taste. Remove bouquet garni and serve piping hot, garnished with parsley.

COOK'S TIP

Be sure to trim all visible fat from the beef to keep the calorie content of this beef casserole as low as possible.

PAPRIKA BEEF

SERVES 4

450 g (1 lb) lean shin of beef	225 g (8 oz) carrots, sliced
15 ml (1 tbsp) plain wholemeal flour	200 ml (7 fl oz) beef stock
7.5 ml (1½ tsp) paprika	15 ml (1 tbsp) tomato purée
1.25 ml (¼ tsp) caraway seeds	1 garlic clove, crushed
1.25 ml (¼ tsp) dried marjoram	1 whole clove
salt and pepper	100 g (4 oz) button mushrooms, sliced
2 medium onions, sliced	chopped parsley, to garnish

1 Cut the meat into chunky cubes, trimming off all fat. Mix together the flour, paprika, caraway seeds, marjoram and salt and pepper to taste. Toss the beef in the seasoned flour.
2 Layer the meat, onions and carrots in a 2 litre (3½ pint) flameproof casserole.
3 Whisk together the stock, tomato purée, crushed garlic and clove. Pour into the casserole. Bring to the boil and simmer, uncovered, for 3-4 minutes.
4 Cover the casserole and cook in the oven at 180°C (350°F) mark 4 for about 1½ hours, stirring occasionally.
5 Remove the casserole from the oven and stir in the mushrooms. Cover again and return to the oven for a further 15 minutes or until the meat is tender. Garnish with chopped parsley to serve.

KOFTA CURRY

SERVES 4

450 g (1 lb) lean minced beef	1 green chilli, seeded and chopped
5 ml (1 tsp) garam masala	3 green cardamoms
5 ml (1 tsp) ground cumin	4 whole cloves
15 ml (1 tbsp) finely chopped coriander	6 black peppercorns
30 ml (2 tbsp) ghee or polyunsaturated oil	5 cm (2 inch) cinnamon stick
3 medium onions, chopped	1 bay leaf
1 garlic clove, chopped	10 ml (2 tsp) ground coriander
2.5 cm (1 inch) piece fresh root ginger, peeled and chopped	2.5 ml (½ tsp) turmeric
	300 ml (½ pint) low-fat natural yogurt

1 Mix together the beef, garam masala, cumin, fresh coriander and salt and pepper to taste. Set aside.
2 To make the sauce, heat the ghee or oil in a large saucepan and fry the onions, garlic, ginger and chilli for 10 minutes until golden.
3 Add the cardamoms, cloves, peppercorns, cinnamon and bay leaf and fry over a high heat for 3 minutes. Add the ground coriander, turmeric and salt to taste. Fry for 3 minutes.
4 Gradually add the yogurt, a tablespoon at a time, stirring thoroughly after each addition, then 150 ml (¼ pint) water. Simmer for 10 minutes or until thickening.
5 Meanwhile shape the meat mixture into 16 small balls. Lower the meatballs into the sauce so that they are completely covered. Cover and simmer gently for 30 minutes or until cooked.
6 Skim off any fat, then transfer to a warmed serving dish and serve with rice.

PEPPERED BEEF SAUTE

SERVES 2-3

350 g (12 oz) sirloin steaks	90 ml (6 tbsp) smetana or natural low-fat yogurt
10 ml (2 tsp) green peppercorns in brine, drained	15 ml (1 tbsp) lemon juice
30 ml (2 tbsp) olive oil	salt
175 g (6 oz) red onion, thinly sliced	lemon slices, to garnish

1 Cut the steaks into fine, thin strips. Finely chop the peppercorns.
2 Heat the oil in a medium-sized sauté pan. Add the onion and fry until just beginning to soften.
3 Stir in the beef and peppercorns and cook over a high heat for about 2-3 minutes or until the meat is tender, stirring frequently.
4 Lower the heat and stir in the smetana or yogurt and lemon juice with salt to taste. To serve, garnish with lemon slices and accompany with noodles.

CHILLI BEEF WITH NOODLES

SERVES 4

450 g (1 lb) rump steak	10 ml (2 level tsp) dried oregano or dried mixed herbs
225 g (8 oz) red pepper, halved and seeded	50 g (2 oz) dried tagliarini (thin pasta noodles)
225 g (8 oz) broccoli	30 ml (2 tbsp) sherry or medium white wine
30 ml (2 tbsp) polyunsaturated oil	300 ml (½ pint) beef stock
1 medium onion, roughly chopped	5 ml (1 tbsp) soy sauce
2.5 ml (½ level tsp) chilli powder or few drops of Tabasco sauce	pepper

1 Trim the steak of any excess fat. Cut into bite-sized pieces. Cut the pepper into similar-sized pieces. Thinly slice the broccoli stalks, and divide the remainder into small florets.
2 Heat the oil in a large sauté pan and brown the beef well on all sides for about 2-3 minutes. Remove with a slotted spoon. Add the vegetables, chilli powder and oregano. Sauté, stirring, for 1-2 minutes.
3 Mix in the tagliarini, sherry, stock and soy sauce. Cover and simmer for 5 minutes or until the noodles and broccoli are tender.
4 Return the beef to the pan. Bring to the boil and simmer for 1 minute to heat through. Adjust seasoning, adding pepper as necessary.

SZECHUAN
SHREDDED BEEF

SERVES 4

350 g (12 oz) rump steak	2 garlic cloves, crushed
75 ml (5 tbsp) hoisin sauce	2 medium red peppers, seeded and chopped
60 ml (4 tbsp) dry sherry	
30 ml (2 tbsp) polyunsaturated oil	2.5 cm (1 inch) piece fresh root ginger, peeled and shredded
2 red or green chillis, seeded and finely chopped	225 g (8 oz) can bamboo shoots, drained and sliced
1 large onion, thinly sliced	15 ml (1 tbsp) sesame oil

1 Put the steak in the freezer for at least 20 minutes, to make it easier to slice thinly.
2 Cut the steak into thin slices, then cut lengthways into thin matchstick strips. Put in a bowl, add the hoisin sauce and sherry and stir well. Leave to marinate while cooking the vegetables.
3 Heat the oil in a wok. Add the chillies, onion and garlic and stir-fry over moderate heat for 3-4 minutes until softened. Remove with a slotted spoon and set aside. Add the red peppers, increase the heat and stir-fry for a few seconds. Remove with a slotted spoon and set aside with the chillies.
4 Add the steak and marinade to the wok in batches. Stir-fry each batch over high heat for about 2 minutes, removing each batch with a slotted spoon.
5 Return the vegetables to the wok. Add the ginger and bamboo shoots, then the meat and stir-fry for a further minute to heat through.
6 Turn the mixture into a warmed serving dish, sprinkle with the sesame oil and serve immediately.

JAPANESE
SKEWERED BEEF

SERVES 4

700 g (1½ lb) fillet steak, trimmed	60 ml (4 tbsp) soy sauce
5 cm (2 inch) piece fresh root ginger, crushed	30 ml (2 tbsp) sesame or vegetable oil
2 garlic cloves, crushed	5 ml (1 tsp) muscovado sugar
100 ml (4 fl oz) sake or dry sherry	carrot and cucumber slices, to garnish

1 Cut the steak across the grain into slices about 1 cm (2 inch) thick, using a very sharp knife.
2 Put the crushed ginger and garlic in a bowl with the sake, soy sauce, oil and sugar. Whisk with a fork until well combined, then add the sliced steak and turn to coat in the marinade. Cover and leave to marinate for at least 8 hours, turning occasionally.
3 When ready to cook, thread the slices of steak on to oiled metal kebab skewers, or wooden skewers that have been soaked for 30 minutes in water. Grill under moderate heat for 5 minutes only, turning frequently to ensure even cooking and basting with the marinade.
4 Serve immediately, garnished with carrot and cucumber slices.

SERVING SUGGESTION

Eat these beef kebabs in Japanese style on their own, followed by a stir-fried dish of egg noodles, beansprouts, mushrooms and grated carrot.

VEAL WITH COURGETTES AND GRAPEFRUIT

SERVES 4

450 g (1 lb) veal fillet, in one piece, trimmed of all fat	450 g (1 lb) courgettes, thinly sliced
2 grapefruit	few saffron strands
30 ml (2 tbsp) olive oil	salt and pepper

1 Cut the veal into wafer-thin slices. Place between two sheets of dampened greaseproof paper and bat out with a rolling pin or meat mallet.

2 With a potato peeler, pare the rind from one grapefruit. Cut into thin julienne strips. Squeeze the juice from the grapefruit and reserve.

3 With a serrated knife, peel the remaining grapefruit as you would an apple, removing all skin and pith. Make sure none of the pith remains. Slice the flesh thinly and set aside.

4 Heat half the oil in a large non-stick frying pan. Add a few of the veal slices and sauté for about 2-3 minutes or until well browned on both sides. Transfer to a warmed serving dish, cover and keep warm in the oven while sautéeing the remainder.

5 Heat the remaining oil in the pan, add the courgettes and sauté for 2-3 minutes or until beginning to brown. Add the julienne strips of grapefruit, the saffron strands and 90 ml (6 tbsp) of the reserved grapefruit juice.

6 Bring to the boil, then lower the heat and simmer for 4-5 minutes or until the liquid is well reduced. Stir in the thinly sliced grapefruit and heat through. Add salt and pepper to taste, pour over the veal and serve.

SERVING SUGGESTION

This dish has its own vegetable and therefore needs no accompaniment other than plain boiled rice or pasta, such as tagliatelle.

VEAL ESCALOPES IN MUSHROOM SAUCE

SERVES 4

4 veal escalopes, each 175 g (6 oz)	1 small onion, chopped
2 slices cooked ham, halved	100 g (4 oz) button mushrooms, sliced
40 g (1½ oz) butter or polyunsaturated margarine	30 ml (2 tbsp) wholemeal plain flour
1 celery stick, chopped	150 ml (¼ pint) semi-skimmed milk
1 eating apple, peeled and chopped	salt and pepper
25 g (1 oz) Cheddar cheese, grated	30 ml (2 tbsp) fromage frais
	celery leaves, to garnish

1 Put each escalope between a sheet of greaseproof paper and beat until thin with a meat mallet or rolling pin.

2 Place a ham slice on each escalope.

3 Melt 15 g (½ oz) of the butter or margarine in a large frying pan and lightly fry the celery and apple for 3-4 minutes. Stir in the cheese.

4 Place some of the stuffing on each escalope and roll up, securing with wooden cocktail sticks or fine string or strong cotton.

5 Melt the remaining butter or margarine in the pan. Add the veal rolls, brown on all sides and cook for 10 minutes. Remove from the pan, place on a warmed serving plate and keep hot.

6 Add the onion and mushrooms to the pan and cook for about 5 minutes, until softened. Stir in the flour and cook for 2 minutes, then gradually add the milk, stirring continuously, until the sauce thickens, boils and is smooth. Simmer for 1-2 minutes. Season to taste.

7 Stir in the fromage frais. Pour the sauce over the escalopes and garnish with celery leaves. Serve at once.

COOK'S TIP

As an alternative to veal, slices of turkey or pork fillet can be used. Fromage frais adds smoothness to the sauce.

KIDNEYS PROVENCAL

SERVES 4

12-16 lamb's kidneys	100 ml (4 fl oz) red wine or stock
30 ml (2 tbsp) olive oil	10 ml (2 tsp) chopped fresh basil or 5 ml (1 tsp) dried
1 large onion, chopped	
1-2 garlic cloves, crushed	salt and pepper
3 medium courgettes, sliced	12 black olives
4 large tomatoes, skinned and roughly chopped	parsley sprigs, to garnish

1 Skin the kidneys, then cut each one in half. Snip out the cores with kitchen scissors. Cut each half into two.
2 Heat the oil in a large heavy-based frying pan, add the onion and garlic to the pan and fry gently for 5 minutes until soft but not coloured.
3 Add the kidneys and fry over low heat for 3 minutes until they change colour. Shake the pan and toss the kidneys frequently during frying.
4 Add the courgettes, tomatoes and wine or stock and bring to the boil, stirring constantly. Lower the heat and add half the basil with seasoning to taste. Simmer gently for 8 minutes until the kidneys are tender.
5 Add the olives to the pan and heat through for 1-2 minutes. Taste and adjust the seasoning. Sprinkle with the remaining basil. Serve immediately, garnished with parsley.

SERVING SUGGESTION

This strong flavoured dish needs a plain accompaniment such as boiled rice. Follow with a simple green salad and fresh fruit for a complete, well-balanced meal.

SAUTEED KIDNEYS WITH TOMATOES

SERVES 3-4

12 lamb's kidneys	100 g (4 oz) mushrooms, sliced
45 ml (3 tbsp) plain wholemeal flour	397 g (14 oz) can tomatoes
60 ml (4 tbsp) polyunsaturated oil	10 ml (2 tsp) French mustard
	salt and pepper
1 large onion, sliced	chopped parsley, to garnish

1 Skin the kidneys, cut them in half lengthways and using scissors, remove the cores. Toss the kidneys in the flour.
2 Heat the oil in a large flameproof casserole or frying pan, add the onion and fry for about 5 minutes until golden brown.
3 Add the kidneys to the pan with any remaining flour and cook for 3-4 minutes, stirring occasionally, until lightly browned. Add the mushrooms and cook for a further 2-3 minutes.
4 Stir in the tomatoes with their juice, mustard and salt and pepper to taste. Bring to the boil, stirring all the time, then cover and simmer for 15 minutes until tender. Serve hot, garnished with chopped parsley.

COOK'S TIP

Compared with other cuts of meat, offal is lower in fat, higher in protein and contains more vitamins and minerals.

LAMB'S LIVER AND MUSHROOMS

SERVES 3

15 g (½ oz) butter or polyunsaturated margarine	150 ml (¼ pint) beef stock
1 medium onion, sliced	4 tomatoes, skinned and roughly chopped
450 g (1 lb) lamb's liver, sliced	30 ml (2 tbsp) Worcestershire sauce
15 ml (1 tbsp) plain flour	salt and pepper
100 g (4 oz) button mushrooms	90 ml (3 fl oz) low-fat natural yogurt

1   Melt the butter or margarine in a large frying pan and gently fry the onion for 5 minutes or until soft.
2   Cut the liver into thin strips, add to the flour and toss until coated. Add to the pan with the mushrooms. Fry for 5 minutes, stirring well, then add the stock and bring to the boil.
3   Stir in the tomatoes and Worcestershire sauce. Season to taste, then simmer for 3-4 minutes. Stir in the yogurt and reheat without boiling. Serve hot.

CALF'S LIVER WITH GRAPES AND MADEIRA

SERVES 4

50 g (2 oz) butter or polyunsaturated margarine	24 large green grapes, peeled, halved and seeded
50 g (2 oz) onion or shallot, finely chopped	4 slices of calf's liver, each about 75-100 g (3-4 oz), trimmed
175 ml (6 fl oz) chicken stock	4 sage leaves, thinly sliced
100 ml (4 fl oz) Madeira	4 sage sprigs, to garnish
salt and pepper	

1   Melt half the butter or margarine in a frying pan and fry the onion until golden. Add the stock and Madeira, season and bring to the boil. Boil rapidly for 4-5 minutes or until reduced and of a slightly syrupy consistency. Add the grape halves and warm through gently. Taste and adjust the seasoning.
2   Melt the remaining butter or margarine in a large frying pan. Season the liver, and fry with the sliced sage leaves for 3-5 minutes, turning once.
3   Remove the liver from the pan and serve at once with the Madeira sauce. Garnish with sprigs of fresh sage.

SERVING SUGGESTION

Seasoned with sage and served with a slightly sweet sauce, calf's liver is a delicious, light main course. Serve with rice and courgettes or broccoli.

LIVER STROGANOFF

SERVES 4

4 thin slices of lamb's liver, total weight 350 g (12 oz)	15 ml (1 tbsp) tomato purée
25 g (1 oz) butter or polyunsaturated margarine	10 ml (2 tsp) Dijon-style mustard
1 medium onion, thinly sliced	30 ml (2 tbsp) brandy
	salt and pepper
225 g (8 oz) button mushrooms, thinly sliced	150 ml (¼ pint) low-fat natural yogurt
	chopped parsley, to garnish

1 Slice the liver into thin strips. Melt the butter or margarine in a large, heavy-based frying pan, add the liver and fry over moderate heat for about 5 minutes, stirring constantly so that the strips become evenly and lightly coloured. Remove with a slotted spoon and set aside.

2 Add the sliced onion to the pan and fry over a moderate heat for about 5 minutes until soft but not coloured. Remove the onion with a slotted spoon and add to the liver.

3 Add the mushrooms to the pan, increase the heat and toss until the juices run. Remove and add to the liver and onions.

4 Stir the tomato purée and mustard into the pan juices, then the brandy. Stir over high heat, scraping up the sediment from the base of the pan.

5 Return the liver, onion and mushrooms to the pan and stir to combine with the juices. Add salt and pepper to taste, then remove from the heat.

6 Stir about half of the yogurt into the stroganoff. Turn the stroganoff into a warmed serving dish and drizzle with the remaining yogurt. Sprinkle with chopped parsley, and serve with noodles.

LIVER GOUJONS WITH ORANGE SAUCE

SERVES 4

350 g (12 oz) lamb's liver, sliced	1 medium onion, sliced
75 ml (5 tbsp) plain wholemeal flour	300 ml (½ pint) lamb or beef stock
salt and pepper	finely grated rind and juice of 1 medium orange
1 egg, beaten	5 ml (1 tsp) dried sage
125 g (4 oz) medium oatmeal	dash of gravy browning
75 ml (5 tbsp) polyunsaturated oil	

1 Cut the liver into 5 cm (2 inch) pencil-thin strips. Coat in 45 ml (3 tbsp) of the flour, seasoned with salt and pepper.

2 Dip the liver in the beaten egg, then roll in the oatmeal to coat. Chill in the refrigerator while preparing the sauce.

3 Heat 30 ml (2 tbsp) of the oil in a saucepan, add the onion and fry gently until golden brown. Add the remaining flour and cook gently, stirring, for 1-2 minutes.

4 Gradually blend in the stock, orange rind and juice, sage and salt and pepper to taste. Bring to the boil, stirring constantly, then simmer for 10-15 minutes. Add the gravy browning and taste and adjust seasoning.

5 Heat the remaining oil in a non-stick frying pan, add the liver goujons and fry gently for 1-2 minutes until tender.

6 Arrange the goujons on a warmed serving platter and pour over a little of the sauce. Hand the remaining sauce separately.

COOK'S TIP

Nutritious liver is an excellent source of iron, protein and B vitamins. Never overcook liver as it will harden.

SALADS

All kinds of mouth-watering salads are featured in this extensive collection, from tasty shellfish salads to protein-packed bean mixtures and crisp colourful leafy salads. Many are substantial enough to serve as a meal in themselves, with wholemeal bread. Remember to use a low-calorie dressing – and in moderation!

CRAB SALAD

SERVES 2

15 ml (1 tbsp) lemon juice	2 tomatoes, skinned and cubed
15 ml (1 tbsp) reduced-calorie mayonnaise	50 g (2 oz) pasta shells, cooked
15 ml (1 tbsp) low-fat natural yogurt	pepper
225 g (8 oz) cooked crab meat, thawed if frozen	TO SERVE
½ cucumber, diced	shredded lettuce
	lemon slices, to garnish

1 Mix together the lemon juice, mayonnaise and yogurt. Combine the crab meat with the dressing.
2 Mix the remaining ingredients together and spoon on to serving plates. Top with shredded lettuce and arrange the crab salad in the centre. Garnish with cucumber and lemon slices.

COOK'S TIP

You can buy fresh or frozen cooked crab meat (if the latter, thaw thoroughly before use) in a mixture of dark and light meat. If buying freshly cooked crabs in their shells you'll need one large crab to produce about the weight specified. If you have them, garnish the dish with crab claws.

PRAWN AND CUCUMBER SALAD

SERVES 4

1 cucumber, thinly sliced	225 g (8 oz) peeled cooked prawns, thawed if frozen
salt and pepper	30 ml (2 tbsp) chopped dill
45 ml (3 tbsp) white wine vinegar	15 ml (1 tbsp) snipped chives (optional)
15 ml (1 tbsp) sugar	150 ml (5 fl oz) low-fat natural yogurt

1 Put the cucumber slices in a colander, sprinkling each layer with salt. Cover with a plate and weigh down. Leave to drain for 30 minutes.
2 Meanwhile, put the vinegar, 45 ml (3 tbsp) water and sugar in a small pan and heat gently until sugar dissolves. Boil for 1 minute, then remove from heat and let cool.
3 Rinse the cucumber under cold running water and pat dry. Place in a bowl with the prawns and half of the dill. Pour over the cold vinegar mixture. Cover and chill for at least 30 minutes or overnight.
4 Just before serving, mix remaining dill and the chives with the yogurt and seasoning. Spoon the salad on to four plates and top each with a spoonful of the flavoured yogurt. Serve with crusty granary bread.

PASTA, PRAWN AND APPLE SALAD

SERVES 6

175 g (6 oz) wholewheat pasta shells	225 g (8 oz) cooked peeled prawns
salt and pepper	225 g (8 oz) crisp eating apples
150 ml (¼ pint) unsweetened apple juice	lettuce leaves, to serve
5 ml (1 tsp) chopped mint	paprika, to garnish
5 ml (1 tsp) white wine vinegar	

1 Cook the pasta in boiling salted water until just tender. Drain well, rinse in cold running water and drain again.

2 Meanwhile make the dressing. Whisk together the apple juice, mint, vinegar and salt and pepper to taste.

3 Dry the prawns with absorbent kitchen paper. Quarter, core and roughly chop the apples. Stir the prawns, apples and cooked pasta into the dressing until well mixed. Cover and refrigerate for 2- 3 hours.

4 Place a few lettuce leaves in each of 6 individual dishes. Spoon the prawn salad on top and dust with paprika to serve.

SALAD NICOISE

SERVES 4

175 g (6 oz) small new potatoes, scrubbed and halved	50 g (2 oz) black olives, stoned
salt and pepper	½ small cucumber, thinly sliced
90 ml (6 tbsp) olive oil	225 g (8 oz) cooked French beans
30 ml (2 tbsp) white wine vinegar	2 hard-boiled eggs, shelled and quartered
15 ml (1 tbsp) lemon juice	½ iceberg lettuce, cut into chunks
15 ml (1 tbsp) mild wholegrain mustard	30 ml (2 tbsp) chopped parsley
large pinch of sugar	8 anchovy fillets, drained and halved
198 g (7 oz) can tuna fish, drained	
225 g (8 oz) tomatoes, quartered	

1 Cook the potatoes in boiling salted water until tender. Meanwhile, make the dressing by whisking together the oil, vinegar, lemon juice, mustard and sugar. Season generously with salt and pepper.

2 Drain the potatoes and toss in the dressing. Leave to cool, stirring occasionally.

3 Flake the tuna into large chunks. Arrange in a bowl with the tomatoes, olives, cucumber, beans, eggs, lettuce and cold potatoes. Sprinkle with parsley and anchovies. Serve with French bread.

SMOKED CHICKEN AND AVOCADO SALAD

SERVES 4-6

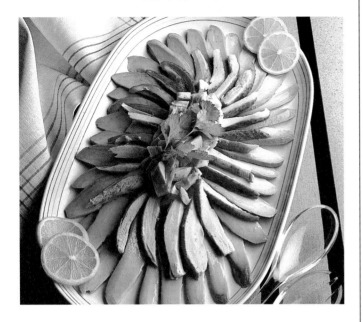

1 kg (2 lb) smoked chicken	2.5 ml (½ tsp) green peppercorn mustard
90 ml (6 tbsp) olive oil	2 ripe avocados
juice of 1 lemon	salt and pepper
5 ml (1 tsp) bottled grated horseradish	coriander sprigs and lemon slices, to garnish

1 Remove all the meat from the chicken carcass, taking care to cut thin, even slices which will look attractive in the finished dish.
2 To make the dressing, whisk together the oil, lemon juice, horseradish and mustard. Add the chicken and coat in the dressing. Cover and leave for 30 minutes to 1 hour.
3 Halve the avocados and remove the stones. Peel off the skin, then cut the flesh lengthways into thin, even slices.
4 Arrange the chicken and avocado slices alternately on a flat oval plate, overlapping them.
5 Chop any remaining oddly-shaped pieces of chicken and avocado and toss them together. Pile this mixture into the centre of the plate.
6 Season the dressing remaining in the bowl and brush over the avocado slices to prevent discoloration.
7 Garnish the salad with coriander and lemon slices, and serve immediately with the dressing.

DEVILLED DUCKLING SALAD

SERVES 6

two 1.4 kg (3 lb) oven-ready ducklings	15 ml (1 tbsp) mild curry paste
salt	salt and pepper
90 ml (3 fl oz) low-fat natural yogurt	50 g (2 oz) cashew nuts
90 ml (6 tbsp) reduced-calorie mayonnaise	350 g (12 oz) fresh apricots, stoned and thickly sliced
15 ml (1 tbsp) clear honey	curly endive leaves, to serve

1 Cut away any surplus fat from the ducklings, then wipe them with a damp cloth. Pat dry.
2 Prick the birds all over with a sharp fork or skewer and sprinkle generously with salt. Place the ducklings, breast side down, side by side, on a wire rack or trivet in a large roasting tin.
3 Roast in the oven at 180°C (350°F) mark 4 for about 1¾ hours or until the birds are really tender, basting occasionally. Half-way through the cooking time, turn the birds over so they are standing breast-side up.
4 Meanwhile, prepare the dressing. In a large bowl, mix together the yogurt, mayonnaise, honey and curry paste. Season and stir in the cashew nuts and apricots.
5 While the ducklings are still warm, strip off the crisp breast skin and reserve. Remove the meat from the bones.
6 Coarsely shred the meat, discarding all the remaining skin, fat and bones. Fold the shredded duckling meat into the dressing, cover and chill for 2-3 hours.
7 Using a pair of kitchen scissors, cut the reserved duckling skin into strips and quickly crisp it further under a hot grill.
8 To serve, spoon the duckling salad down the centre of a large flat platter, then arrange the crisp duck skin over the top. Surround with curly endive leaves.

TURKEY, PINEAPPLE AND PASTA SALAD

SERVES 6

700 g (1½ lb) cooked turkey meat	1 small pineapple
45 ml (3 tbsp) olive or polyunsaturated oil	150 ml (¼ pint) low-fat natural yogurt or smetana
30 ml (2 tbsp) lemon juice	15 ml (1 tbsp) horseradish sauce
paprika	5 ml (1 tsp) tomato purée
salt and pepper	225 g (8 oz) celery, trimmed and finely sliced
225 g (8 oz) wholewheat pasta shapes	25 g (1 oz) salted peanuts

1 Cut the turkey into bite-sized pieces. In a large bowl, mix together the oil, lemon juice, 2.5 ml (½ tsp) paprika and salt and pepper to taste. Stir in the turkey, cover and leave in a cool place for about 1 hour.
2 Meanwhile, cook the pasta in boiling salted water until just tender; drain and rinse well under cold water.
3 To prepare the pineapple, with a sharp knife, cut off the leafy top and discard. Cut the pineapple into 1 cm (½ inch) slices. Cut off the skin and dig out the 'eyes' with the tip of the knife. Cut out the core from each slice with an apple corer or small biscuit cutter. Cut the flesh into chunks.
4 Put the yogurt or smetana in a large bowl, add the horseradish and tomato purée and stir well to mix. Fold in the pasta, celery and pineapple, with salt and pepper to taste.
5 Stir the turkey into the pasta mixture, cover and chill in the refrigerator for at least 1 hour. Taste and adjust seasoning. Transfer to a serving dish and sprinkle with the peanuts and paprika. Serve chilled.

BEEF AND OLIVE SALAD

SERVES 4

450 g (1 lb) rolled lean brisket	12 black olives
1 bay leaf	450 g (1 lb) French beans
6 peppercorns	salt and pepper
1 large bunch of spring onions	45 ml (3 tbsp) soy sauce
	20 ml (4 tsp) lemon juice

1 Put the beef, bay leaf and peppercorns in a small saucepan. Add enough water to cover. Bring to the boil, cover and simmer gently for about 1 hour or until the meat is tender. Leave to cool in the cooking liquid for about 2 hours.
2 Slice the spring onions diagonally into thick pieces. Quarter and stone the olives. Trim and halve the French beans. Cook the beans in boiling salted water for 5-10 minutes until just tender. Drain well, rinse under cold water and drain again thoroughly.
3 Drain the beef and trim off the fat. Slice thinly and cut into 4 cm (1½ inch) long shreds.
4 Put the beef in a bowl, add the spring onions, olives, beans, soy sauce and lemon juice. Toss well together, then season with pepper. (The soy sauce should provide sufficient salt.) Cover and chill in the refrigerator for about 30 minutes before serving.

VARIATION

Slice the cooked beef into about 12 thin slices. Finely chop 20 stoned black olives and mix with 1 crushed garlic clove and 45 ml (3 tbsp) olive oil. Spread the olive mixture thinly and evenly over both sides of each slice of beef. Roll up each slice loosely from the shortest end and arrange on a flat serving dish. Cover and chill in the refrigerator. Trim and thinly slice a large bunch of radishes; skin and thinly slice 1 small onion. Mix in a bowl with 15 ml (1 tbsp) olive oil. Spoon the radish and onion mixture around the beef rolls.

PORK AND MUSHROOM SALAD

SERVES 6

2 pork fillets or tenderloins, each about 350 g (12 oz), well trimmed	10 green olives, stoned and chopped
30 ml (2 tbsp) polyunsaturated oil	120 ml (4 fl oz) low-fat natural yogurt or smetana
225 g (8 oz) small button mushrooms	1.25 ml (¼ tsp) mustard powder
juice of ½ lemon	salt and pepper
1 small onion, finely sliced	5 ml (1 tsp) chopped marjoram or mint
1 small green pepper, seeded and finely shredded	lemon wedges, to garnish

1 Cut the pork into 1 cm (½ inch) slices on the diagonal, then cut each slice into neat strips, about 5 cm x 5 mm (2 x ¼ inch).

2 Heat the oil in a large frying pan, add half the pork and fry quickly to seal the meat. Repeat with the remaining meat, then return all to the pan. Lower the heat and slowly cook for about 10-15 minutes, until very tender. Using a slotted spoon lift the meat out of the pan and leave to cool.

3 Add the mushrooms to the pan with 50 ml (2 fl oz) water and the lemon juice. Cook, stirring, for 1-2 minutes. Using a slotted spoon remove from the pan and leave to cool.

4 Put the onion and green pepper in a pan of cold water, bring to the boil and simmer for 1-2 minutes. Drain and cool under running cold water. Stir into the pork with the cooled mushrooms and olives.

5 Mix the yogurt or smetana with the mustard, season to taste and stir into the pork mixture. Cover and chill for at least 3 hours.

6 Stir the salad well before serving, sprinkled with marjoram or mint and garnished with lemon wedges.

WHOLEWHEAT BRAZIL SALAD

SERVES 4-6

75 g (3 oz) dried black-eyed beans, soaked in cold water overnight	salt and pepper
100 g (4 oz) wholewheat grain, soaked in cold water overnight	½ cucumber, diced
90 ml (6 tbsp) low-fat natural yogurt	225 g (8 oz) tomatoes, skinned and roughly chopped
30 ml (2 tbsp) olive oil	100 g (4 oz) Cheddar cheese, grated
45 ml (3 tbsp) lemon juice	100 g (4 oz) Brazil nuts, roughly chopped
45 ml (3 tbsp) chopped mint	lettuce leaves, to serve
	mint sprigs, to garnish

1 Drain the beans and place in a saucepan of water. Bring to the boil and simmer gently for 1½ hours or until tender.

2 Meanwhile, drain the wholewheat and place in a saucepan of water. Bring to the boil and simmer gently for 20-25 minutes or until tender. Drain, rinse well with cold water and cool for 30 minutes. When the beans are cooked, drain and cool for 30 minutes.

3 Whisk the yogurt and olive oil together with the lemon juice, mint and seasoning to taste.

4 Put the wholewheat, beans, cucumber, tomatoes, cheese and Brazil nuts in a bowl. Pour over the dressing and mix well.

5 Line a salad bowl with lettuce leaves and pile the wholewheat salad on top. Garnish with mint and chill before serving.

CHEESE, BEANSPROUT AND PINEAPPLE SALAD

SERVES 4

225 g (8 oz) carrots, peeled	275 g (10 oz) beansprouts
225 g (8 oz) Edam cheese	10 ml (2 tsp) wine vinegar
227 g (8 oz) can pineapple slices in natural juice	salt and pepper

1 Cut the carrots into 2.5 cm (1 inch) matchstick thin strips. Coarsely grate the cheese.
2 Drain the pineapple, reserving the juice. Cut the pineapple into thin strips.
3 In a large bowl, mix together the beansprouts, carrot, cheese and pineapple. Cover and chill in the refrigerator until required.
4 To make the dressing, whisk the pineapple juice and vinegar together with seasoning to taste.
5 Just before serving, pour the dressing over the salad and toss well to mix. Serve at room temperature.

VARIATION

Replace the cheese with the same quantity of tofu – cut into cubes. Tofu is available from the chilled cabinet of health food stores and large supermarkets.

COLESLAW WITH CHEESE AND BRAZIL NUTS

SERVES 6

225 g (8 oz) hard white cabbage	60 ml (4 tbsp) reduced-calorie mayonnaise
175 g (6 oz) shelled Brazil nuts	juice of 1 lemon
225 g (8 oz) Edam or Gouda cheese, grated	30 ml (2 tbsp) polyunsaturated oil
2 large carrots, peeled and grated	30 ml (2 tbsp) chopped parsley
60 ml (4 tbsp) low-fat natural yogurt	2.5-5 ml (½-1 tsp) caraway seeds, according to taste
	salt and pepper

1 Shred the cabbage finely with a sharp knife or grater. Place in a bowl. Chop the nuts roughly. Add the nuts to the cabbage, reserving 30 ml (2 tbsp) for the garnish. Add two thirds of the cheese to the bowl with the carrots.
2 In a separate bowl, mix the yogurt with the mayonnaise, lemon juice, oil, parsley and caraway seeds. Add salt and pepper to taste.
3 Pour the dressing over the salad ingredients, then toss well to mix. Sprinkle with the reserved nuts and the remaining cheese. Cover and chill in the refrigerator for 30 minutes. Taste and adjust seasoning before serving.

BEAN, CHEESE AND AVOCADO SALAD

SERVES 4

225 g (8 oz) dried red kidney beans, soaked in cold water overnight	175 g (6 oz) Edam cheese, rinded and diced
90 ml (6 tbsp) olive oil	1 small onion, finely chopped
finely grated rind and juice of 1 lemon	2 celery sticks, finely chopped
1.25 ml (¼ tsp) Tabasco sauce	2 tomatoes, skinned and chopped
salt and pepper	1 ripe avocado
	celery leaves, to garnish

1 Drain the kidney beans and rinse under cold running water. Put in a saucepan, cover with fresh cold water and bring to the boil. Boil rapidly for 10 minutes, then simmer for 1-1½ hours until tender.

2 Drain the beans and put in a bowl. Add the oil, lemon rind and juice, Tabasco and seasoning. Toss well, then leave until cold.

3 Add the cheese, onion, celery and tomatoes to the beans and toss again to mix the ingredients together. Cover and chill in the refrigerator until serving time.

4 When ready to serve, peel the avocado, cut in half and remove the stone. Chop the flesh into chunky pieces. Fold the avocado pieces gently into the bean salad and taste and adjust seasoning. Garnish with celery leaves and serve.

VEGETABLE SALAMAGUNDY

SERVES 8

50 g (2 oz) green lentils	½ small head of celery, trimmed and sliced
1 bay leaf	50 g (2 oz) lamb's lettuce, trimmed
salt and pepper	
225 g (8 oz) French beans, trimmed	1 small onion, thinly sliced
225 g (8 oz) mangetout, trimmed	2 Cox's apples, sliced
	black olives
225 g (8 oz) beef tomatoes, sliced	120 ml (4 fl oz) low-calorie vinaigrette
225 g (8 oz) cherry tomatoes	fresh herbs, to garnish
1 yellow pepper, seeded and cut into strips	

1 Cook the lentils in boiling salted water with the bay leaf, until just tender. Drain and leave to cool. Blanch the beans and mangetout in boiling salted water for 2 minutes. Drain, rinse under cold running water and drain.

2 Arrange all the ingredients on one or two large platters in a symmetrical pattern. Sprinkle with the dressing and garnish with the fresh herbs.

COOK'S TIP

Salamagundy is an old English supper dish which dates back to the eighteenth century. It originally contained a varied mixture of meats. Here we make the most of fresh colourful vegetables. Use others in season if you prefer. Add hard-boiled quail's eggs, or nuts, if liked.

GREEK SALAD

SERVES 4

½ large cucumber	100 g (4 oz) Feta cheese, cut into cubes
salt and pepper	60 ml (4 tbsp) olive oil
450 g (1 lb) firm ripe tomatoes	15 ml (1 tbsp) lemon juice
1 medium red onion	good pinch of dried oregano
18 black olives	

1 Peel the cucumber and slice thinly. Put into a colander or sieve, sprinkle with a little salt and leave to stand for about 15 minutes.

2 Slice the tomatoes thinly. Slice the onion into thin rings. Rinse the cucumber under cold running water, drain and pat dry with absorbent kitchen paper.

3 Arrange the cucumber, tomatoes and onion in a serving dish. Scatter the olives and cubed cheese over the top.

4 In a bowl, whisk together the oil, lemon juice, oregano and salt and pepper to taste. Spoon the dressing over the salad, cover and chill in the refrigerator for 2-3 hours or overnight. Allow to come to room temperature for 30 minutes before serving, with warm pitta bread.

CRUNCHY WINTER SALAD

SERVES 4

2 eating apples	1 small onion, finely sliced
finely grated rind and juice of ½ lemon	2 celery sticks, sliced
45 ml (3 tbsp) polyunsaturated oil	100 g (4 oz) Cheddar cheese, diced
150 ml (¼ pint) low-fat natural yogurt	100 g (4 oz) natural unsalted peanuts
salt and pepper	grapefruit segments and celery leaves, to garnish
225 g (8 oz) red cabbage, finely sliced	

1 Quarter and core the apples, then cut into chunks. Toss in 30 ml (2 tbsp) of the lemon juice.

2 To make the dressing, in a bowl, whisk the remaining lemon juice with the rind, oil, yogurt and salt and pepper to taste until well emulsified.

3 Put the cabbage, onion, celery, apple, cheese and peanuts in a large bowl, pour over the dressing and toss well. Garnish with grapefruit segments and celery leaves.

MIXED BEAN SALAD

SERVES 4

450 g (1 lb) broad beans, shelled	15 ml (1 tbsp) mild wholegrain mustard
salt and pepper	15 ml (1 tbsp) lemon juice
225 g (8 oz) French beans, trimmed	397 g (14 oz) can red kidney beans, drained and rinsed
15 ml (1 tbsp) polyunsaturated oil	125 g (4 oz) Charnwood or Applewood cheese, cubed
150 ml (5 fl oz) low-fat natural yogurt	chopped parsley, to garnish

1 Cook the broad beans in boiling salted water for 10 minutes. Add the French beans and continue to cook for 5-10 minutes, until both are tender.
2 Meanwhile, mix together the oil, yogurt, mustard, lemon juice and salt and pepper until well blended.
3 Drain the cooked beans and while still hot, combine with the drained kidney beans and dressing. Leave to cool.
4 Toss in the cubes of cheese and garnish with chopped parsley just before serving.

COOK'S TIP

Charnwood, or Applewood, cheese is a mature Cheddar variation, smoked and coated with paprika. Cubed, it adds colour and bite to this summertime salad, which mixes fresh French and broad beans with canned kidney beans.

CHICORY AND CELERY SALAD

SERVES 4-6

1 eating apple, cored and chopped	2.5 ml (½ tsp) prepared English mustard
1 head of celery, trimmed and sliced	2.5 ml (½ tsp) sugar
1 cooked beetroot, peeled and sliced	60 ml (4 tbsp) low-fat natural yogurt or smetana
2 heads of chicory, sliced	10 ml (2 tsp) white wine vinegar
1 punnet of mustard and cress, trimmed	salt and pepper
	3 eggs, hard-boiled and cut into wedges

1 Lightly mix the apple, celery, beetroot and chicory together with the cress in a large salad bowl.
2 To make the dressing, whisk the mustard, sugar, yogurt or smetana and vinegar together. Season to taste. Pour over the salad and toss together so that everything is coated in the dressing. Add the eggs, then serve at once.

COOK'S TIP

Smetana is a type of soured cream, made from skimmed milk and single cream. It contains less calories than ordinary soured cream.

CELERIAC AND BEAN SALAD

SERVES 4-6

225 g (8 oz) dried flageolet beans, soaked in cold water overnight	15 ml (1 tbsp) wholegrain mustard
1 large green pepper	1 garlic clove, crushed
finely grated rind and juice of 1 lemon	45 ml (3 tbsp) chopped parsley
60 ml (4 tbsp) polyunsaturated oil	salt and pepper
	225 g (8 oz) celeriac

1 Drain the soaked beans and rinse well under cold running water. Put the beans in a large saucepan and cover with plenty of fresh cold water. Bring slowly to the boil, then skim off any scum with a slotted spoon. Half cover the pan with a lid and simmer gently for about 1 hour, or until the beans are just tender.

2 Meanwhile, halve the pepper and remove the core and seeds. Cut the flesh into cubes.

3 In a bowl, whisk together the grated lemon rind, about 30 ml (2 tbsp) lemon juice, the oil, mustard, garlic, parsley and salt and pepper to taste.

4 Just before the beans are ready, peel the celeriac and chop roughly into 2.5 cm (1 inch) cubes. Blanch in boiling salted water for 5 minutes. Drain well.

5 Drain the beans well and place in a bowl. Add the celeriac and toss all the salad ingredients together while the beans and celeriac are still hot. Leave to cool for 20 minutes, then cover and chill in the refrigerator for at least 1 hour before serving.

WINTER CABBAGE AND CAULIFLOWER SALAD

SERVES 4

225 g (8 oz) hard white cabbage	90 ml (6 tbsp) reduced-calorie mayonnaise
225 g (8 oz) cauliflower florets	90 ml (6 tbsp) low-fat natural yogurt
2 large carrots, peeled	10 ml (2 tsp) French mustard
75 g (3 oz) mixed shelled nuts, roughly chopped	30 ml (2 tbsp) polyunsaturated oil
50 g (2 oz) raisins	juice of ½ lemon
60 ml (4 tbsp) chopped parsley or coriander	salt and pepper
	3 red-skinned eating apples

1 Shred the cabbage finely with a sharp knife and place in a large bowl. Divide the cauliflower florets into small sprigs and add to the cabbage. Mix the vegetables gently with your hands.

2 Grate the carrots into the bowl, then add the nuts, raisins and parsley. Mix the vegetables together again until evenly combined.

3 Put the remaining ingredients except the apples in a jug. Whisk well to combine, then pour over the vegetables in the bowl and toss well.

4 Core and chop the apples, but do not peel them. Add to the salad and toss again to combine with the other ingredients. Cover the bowl and chill the salad in the refrigerator for about 1 hour before serving.

SERVING SUGGESTION

This crunchy, colourful salad can be served as an accompaniment to a selection of cold meats for a quick and nutritious lunch. With extra nuts, for vegetarians, it would make a meal in itself, served with cheese and wholemeal or granary bread.

INDONESIAN SALAD

SERVES 4

1 small pineapple	30 ml (2 tbsp) crunchy peanut butter
½ cucumber	20 ml (4 tsp) soy sauce
175 g (6 oz) young carrots, peeled	60 ml (4 tbsp) olive oil
1 crisp green eating apple	juice of ½ lemon
100 g (4 oz) beansprouts	salt and pepper

1 Cut the top and bottom off the pineapple. Stand the fruit upright on a board. Using a large, sharp knife, slice downwards in sections to remove the skin and 'eyes' of the fruit. Slice off the pineapple flesh, leaving the core, then discard the core.

2 Cut the pineapple flesh into small cubes, then cut the cucumber and carrots lengthways into thin matchstick shapes. Quarter and core the apple (but do not peel), then chop roughly. Combine all the fruit and vegetables together in a bowl with the beansprouts.

3 To make the dressing, put the peanut butter in a bowl, then gradually whisk in the remaining ingredients with a fork. Season.

4 Pour the dressing over the salad and toss well to mix. Cover and leave to stand for 30 minutes before serving.

RED CABBAGE AND APPLE SALAD

SERVES 8

½ red cabbage, about 900 g (2 lb), finely shredded	120 ml (4 fl oz) polyunsaturated oil
3 dessert apples, peeled, cored and sliced	60 ml (4 tbsp) cider vinegar
1 small garlic clove, crushed	60 ml (4 tbsp) low-fat natural yogurt
	salt and pepper

1 Blanch the cabbage for 2-3 minutes in boiling salted water; do not over-blanch as it will lose its crisp texture. Drain and cool.

2 Combine the apples with the cabbage in a bowl. Put the rest of the ingredients in a screw-top jar; shake well. Pour at once over the cabbage and toss to mix.

3 Cover the salad and refrigerate overnight. Toss again to mix well before serving.

VARIATION

Add 50 g (2 oz) crumbled Danish Blue cheese to the salad with the dressing.

WHOLEWHEAT, APRICOT AND NUT SALAD

SERVES 6-8

225 g (8 oz) wholewheat grain, soaked in cold water overnight	50 g (2 oz) unsalted peanuts
3 celery sticks	60 ml (4 tbsp) olive oil
125 g (4 oz) dried apricots	30 ml (2 tbsp) lemon juice
125 g (4 oz) Brazil nuts, roughly chopped	salt and pepper
	coriander and cucumber slices, to garnish

1 Drain the wholewheat grain, then tip into a large saucepan of boiling water. Simmer gently for 25 minutes or until the grains are cooked but have a little bite left.
2 Drain the wholewheat in a colander and rinse under cold running water. Tip into a large serving bowl and set aside.
3 Cut the celery into small diagonal pieces with a sharp knife. Stir into the wholewheat.
4 Using kitchen scissors, snip the apricots into small pieces over the wholewheat. Add the nuts and stir well to mix.
5 Mix the oil and lemon juice together with salt and pepper to taste. Pour over the salad and toss well. Chill in the refrigerator for 2 hours. Toss again just before serving, garnished with coriander and cucumber.

COOK'S TIP

You can buy the wholewheat grain for this recipe in any good health food shop. Sometimes it is referred to as 'kibbled' wheat, because the grains are cracked in a machine called a 'kibbler', which breaks the grain into little pieces. Do not confuse wholewheat grain with cracked wheat (sometimes also called bulghar or burghul), which is cooked wheat which has been dried and cracked, used extensively in the cooking of the Middle East. Although different, the two kinds of wheat can be used interchangeably in most recipes.

LEMONY BEAN SALAD

SERVES 4

100 g (4 oz) dried flageolet beans, soaked in cold water overnight	50 g (2 oz) black olives
90 ml (6 tbsp) olive oil	30 ml (2 tbsp) chopped mixed fresh herbs, eg basil, marjoram, lemon balm, chives
finely grated rind and juice of 1 lemon	4 large firm tomatoes
1-2 garlic cloves, crushed	about 1.25 ml (¼ tsp) raw cane sugar
salt and pepper	lemon slices, to garnish

1 Drain and rinse the beans, then place in a saucepan with plenty of water. Bring to the boil, then lower the heat, half cover with a lid and simmer for about 1 hour until tender.
2 Drain the beans, transfer to a bowl and immediately add the oil, lemon rind and juice, garlic and salt and pepper to taste. Stir well to mix, then cover and leave for at least 4 hours to allow the dressing to flavour the beans.
3 Stone the olives, then chop roughly. Add to the salad with the herbs.
4 To skin the tomatoes, put them in a bowl, pour over boiling water and leave for 2 minutes. Drain, then plunge into a bowl of cold water. Remove the tomatoes one at a time and peel off the skin with your fingers.
5 Slice the tomatoes thinly, then arrange on 4 serving plates. Sprinkle with the sugar and salt and pepper to taste. Pile the bean salad on top of each plate. Serve chilled, garnished with lemon slices.

THREE BEAN SALAD

SERVES 4-6

75 g (3 oz) dried red kidney beans, soaked in cold water overnight	100 ml (4 fl oz) reduced-calorie vinaigrette
75 g (3 oz) dried black-eyed beans, soaked in cold water overnight	15 ml (1 tbsp) chopped coriander
	1 small onion, sliced into rings
75 g (3 oz) dried pinto or borlotti beans, soaked in cold water overnight	salt and pepper
	coriander sprig, to garnish

1 Drain the beans and put in a saucepan of water. Bring to the boil and boil rapidly for 10 minutes, then boil gently for 1½ hours until tender.
2 Drain the cooked beans thoroughly and place them in a large salad bowl.
3 Combine the French dressing and coriander, and pour over the beans while they are still warm.
4 Toss thoroughly and leave to cool for 30 minutes. Mix the onion into the beans, add salt and pepper to taste and chill for 2-3 hours before serving, garnished with fresh coriander.

ORIENTAL SALAD

SERVES 8

1 large cucumber	30 ml (2 tbsp) soy sauce
salt and pepper	15 ml (1 tbsp) peanut butter
1 small head Chinese leaves	30 ml (2 tbsp) sesame oil
1 red pepper	30 ml (2 tbsp) rice or wine vinegar
125 g (4 oz) button mushrooms	50 g (2 oz) shelled unsalted peanuts
225 g (8 oz) beansprouts	

1 Cut the cucumber in half lengthways and scoop out the seeds. Cut the halves into 5 cm (2 inch) sticks, leaving the skin on.
2 Shred the Chinese leaves. Halve the red pepper and remove the core and seeds; cut the flesh into thin strips. Wipe and slice the mushrooms. Trim the beansprouts.
3 Just before serving, mix the soy sauce in a large bowl with the peanut butter, oil, vinegar and salt and pepper to taste. Add the salad ingredients and the peanuts and toss together. Transfer to a serving bowl.

COOK'S TIP

Chinese leaves are an extremely versatile vegetable and can be lightly braised, steamed or served raw in salads. Look for Chinese leaves also under the name of Chinese cabbage or Chinese celery cabbage; it has long white stems and should not be confused with a similar-looking vegetable called 'bok choy', which has dark green stems.

MOZZARELLA, AVOCADO AND TOMATO SALAD

SERVES 4

2 ripe avocados	4 medium tomatoes, thinly sliced
120 ml (8 tbsp) reduced-calorie vinaigrette	chopped parsley and mint sprigs, to garnish
175 g (6 oz) mozzarella cheese, thinly sliced	

1 Halve the avocados lengthways and carefully remove the stones. Then peel and cut the avocados into slices.
2 Pour the dressing over the avocado slices. Stir to coat the slices thoroughly and prevent discoloration.
3 Arrange slices of mozzarella, tomato and avocado on 4 individual serving plates. Spoon over the dressing and garnish with chopped parsley and a sprig of mint.

COOK'S TIP

Mozzarella is an Italian curd cheese, pale-coloured and egg-shaped. When fresh it is very soft and dripping with whey. Traditionally made from water buffalo's milk, mozzarella is now also made from cow's milk. It should be eaten fresh, as the cheese ripens quickly and is past its best in a few days. Mozzarella is now readily available from delicatessens and supermarkets and can be used in salads, pizzas etc.

SALAD ELONA

SERVES 4

½ medium cucumber	45 ml (3 tbsp) polyunsaturated oil
salt	15 ml (1 tbsp) Balsamic or wine vinegar
225 g (8 oz) ripe strawberries	a few lettuce leaves, to serve
10 ml (2 tsp) green peppercorns in brine	

1 Score the skin of the cucumber lengthways with a canelle knife or the prongs of a fork. Slice the cucumber very thinly, then place on a plate and sprinkle with salt. Leave to stand for about 30 minutes to draw out the excess moisture.
2 Meanwhile, prepare the strawberries. Reserve a few small ones for garnish. Hull the remaining strawberries, and slice in half lengthways.
3 Drain the peppercorns and pat dry with absorbent kitchen paper. Crush them with the back of a metal spoon in a small bowl. Add the oil and vinegar and whisk with a fork until well combined.
4 Drain the cucumber and pat dry with absorbent kitchen paper. Shred the lettuce, then arrange on serving plates. Arrange the cucumber slices and halved straw-berries on the lettuce, alternating rings of each. Sprinkle over the dressing, then garnish the centre with the reserved whole strawberries. Serve as soon as possible.

COOK'S TIP

The combination of sweet and sour in this salad is unusual, but most refreshing. Do not use malt vinegar as it is too strong. Wine vinegar can be used, but if you are able to buy balsamic vinegar or aceto balsamico from a good delicatessen, it is perfect. It is also excellent in dressings for green salads, and for sprinkling over roast and barbecued meat just before serving.

MANGETOUT AND MUSHROOM SALAD

SERVES 4

225 g (8 oz) mangetout, trimmed	90 ml (3 fl oz) reduced-calorie mayonnaise
salt and pepper	30 ml (2 tbsp) low-fat natural yogurt
175 g (6 oz) button mushrooms, wiped and sliced	60 ml (4 tbsp) chopped parsley
	30 ml (2 tbsp) chopped chives

1 Cut the mangetout into diamond slices. Blanch in boiling salted water for 1 minute, drain and rinse under cold running water. Mix with the mushrooms.
2 Beat together the mayonnaise, yogurt, parsley and half the chives in a bowl. Season with salt and pepper to taste. If you have time, leave to stand for a while to allow the flavours to infuse.
3 Arrange the mangetout and mushrooms on individual plates. Top with the dressing and sprinkle with the remaining chives.

COOK'S TIP

If you are cutting down on calories, always buy reduced-fat mayonnaise instead of the full-fat version and don't use more than you really need.

CAULIFLOWER, BROCCOLI AND PEPPER SALAD

SERVES 6

225 g (8 oz) broccoli, cut into florets	1 garlic clove, crushed
225 g (8 oz) cauliflower, cut into florets	60 ml (4 tbsp) tahini
1 small yellow pepper, seeded and thinly sliced	90 ml (6 tbsp) lemon juice
	salt and pepper
1 small red pepper, seeded and thinly sliced	sesame seeds, to garnish

1 Blanch the broccoli and cauliflower in a saucepan of boiling water for 3 minutes, then drain and leave to cool. Place the broccoli, cauliflower and peppers in a salad bowl.
2 To make the dressing, whisk the garlic, tahini, 60 ml (4 tbsp) water, lemon juice and seasoning together in a small bowl.
3 Pour the dressing over the salad and toss gently to coat. Cover and chill. Sprinkle with sesame seeds just before serving.

COOK'S TIP

Tahini is a thick creamy paste made from ground sesame seeds and sesame oil, which has long been popular in the Middle East. Light and dark varieties are available, the dark being made with unhusked sesame seeds and having a stronger, slightly bitter flavour. Some brands are thicker than others. Always stir the contents of the jar thoroughly before using, as the oil tends to separate. If yours is very thick, thin it with a little vegetable oil.

FLAGEOLET
AND TOMATO SALAD

SERVES 4

90 ml (6 tbsp) olive oil	4 tomatoes, skinned and chopped
30 ml (2 tbsp) lemon juice	1 small onion, finely chopped
30 ml (2 tbsp) reduced-calorie mayonnaise	2 garlic cloves, finely chopped
45 ml (3 tbsp) chopped mixed fresh herbs, eg parsley, chervil, chives, marjoram, basil	TO SERVE
	lettuce leaves
salt and pepper	snipped chives and lemon twists, to garnish
397 g (14 oz) can flageolet beans	

1 Put the olive oil, lemon juice, mayonnaise, herbs and seasoning in a bowl and whisk until thick.
2 Rinse the beans under cold running water. Drain and add to the dressing with the tomatoes, onion and garlic.
3 Toss well, cover and chill for 30 minutes. Serve on individual plates lined with lettuce leaves. Garnish with chives and lemon twists.

WALDORF
SALAD

SERVES 4

450 g (1 lb) eating apples	½ head celery, trimmed and sliced
juice of 1 lemon	50 g (2 oz) walnut halves
2.5 ml (½ tsp) raw cane sugar	lettuce leaves, to serve
90 ml (3 fl oz) reduced-calorie mayonnaise	

1 Core the apples, but do not peel. Slice one and dice the rest. Dip the slices in some of the lemon juice to prevent discoloration.
2 In a large bowl, toss the diced apples in 30 ml (2 tbsp) lemon juice, the sugar and 15 ml (1 tbsp) mayonnaise. Leave to stand for about 30 minutes.
3 Just before serving, add the sliced celery, chopped walnuts and the remaining mayonnaise, and toss together.
4 Serve the salad in a bowl lined with lettuce leaves and garnish with the apple slices.

AUBERGINE AND PEPPER SALAD

SERVES 4

3 small aubergines, about 700 g (1½ lb) total weight	90 ml (6 tbsp) olive oil
1 red pepper, about 225 g (8 oz)	30 ml (2 tbsp) red wine vinegar
1 green pepper, about 225 g (8 oz)	salt and pepper
175 g (6 oz) slice white bread	60 ml (4 tbsp) chopped fresh oregano or 20 ml (4 tsp) dried

1 Make 2 or 3 long slits in the skin of each aubergine. Place under a hot grill with the peppers and grill until the skins begin to blacken and peel away. Leave the aubergines under the grill for 15-20 minutes; they must feel very soft.
2 Cool slightly before peeling away the skins. Cube the aubergines and peppers and arrange on a flat serving dish.
3 Lightly toast the bread, cut into cubes and scatter over the salad.
4 Mix together the oil, vinegar, seasoning and oregano. Drizzle over the salad. Serve warm or cold.

FRENCH BEAN, OLIVE AND CUCUMBER SALAD

SERVES 8

900 g (2 lb) French beans, topped and tailed	60 ml (2 fl oz) white wine vinegar
salt and pepper	7.5 ml (1½ tsp) Dijon mustard
2 small heads Florence fennel	2 avocados
1 large cucumber	about 20 black olives
150 ml (¼ pint) olive oil	

1 Halve the French beans and cook in boiling salted water until just tender. Drain, refresh under cold water and drain well. Remove the feathery fennel tops, finely chop and reserve. Thinly slice the fennel; blanch in boiling water for 1 minute. Drain and refresh. Peel, halve and thickly slice the cucumber.
2 Whisk together the oil, vinegar, mustard and reserved fennel tops. Season to taste. Peel, halve and stone the avocado, then thickly slice into the dressing.
3 Toss together all the prepared vegetables, olives, avocado and dressing. Serve immediately.

COOK'S TIP

The French beans, cucumber and fennel can be prepared ahead as in stage 1, then kept in the refrigerator.

FENNEL
AND CUCUMBER SALAD

SERVES 4

½ or 1 small cucumber	15 ml (1 tbsp) chopped mint
2 small fennel bulbs	pinch of raw cane sugar
90 ml (6 tbsp) olive oil	salt and pepper
30 ml (2 tbsp) lemon juice	sliced large radishes or tomatoes, to serve
1 garlic clove, crushed	

1 Peel the cucumber and halve lengthways. Scoop out the seeds and discard. Dice the flesh.
2 Trim the fennel, reserving a few feathery tops for the garnish. Grate the fennel into a bowl, add the diced cucumber and mix together.
3 Whisk together the oil, lemon juice, garlic, mint, sugar and salt and pepper to taste. Pour over the fennel and cucumber and toss lightly.
4 Line a shallow serving dish with radish or tomato slices then pile the salad in the centre. Garnish with the reserved fennel tops.

VARIATION

Add 1 bunch of watercress, trimmed and divided into sprigs.

FENNEL
AND TOMATO SALAD

SERVES 6

90 ml (6 tbsp) polyunsaturated oil, or half polyunsaturated oil and half walnut oil	salt and pepper
	12 black olives, halved and stoned
45 ml (3 tbsp) lemon juice	450 g (1 lb) Florence fennel
	450 g (1 lb) ripe tomatoes

1 In a bowl, whisk together the oil(s), lemon juice and salt and pepper to taste. Add the olives to the dressing.
2 Snip off the feathery ends of the fennel and refrigerate them in a polythene bag until required.
3 Halve each bulb of fennel lengthways, then slice thinly crossways, discarding the roots. Blanch in boiling water for 2-3 minutes, then drain. While still warm, stir into the dressing.
4 Leave to cool, cover and refrigerate until required. Meanwhile skin and slice the tomatoes and refrigerate, covered.
5 Just before serving, arrange the tomatoes and fennel mixture on individual serving plates and snip the fennel tops over them.

VARIATION

To make a simple tomato salad, thinly slice really ripe tomatoes. Arrange in a large shallow dish, sprinkle with olive oil and a little raspberry or white wine vinegar, salt, pepper and chopped basil, chervil or tarragon.

CHERRY TOMATO AND BEAN SALAD

SERVES 8

225 g (8 oz) broad beans (shelled weight)	30 ml (2 tbsp) lemon juice
salt and pepper	45 ml (3 tbsp) chopped basil
225 g (8 oz) French beans, topped and tailed	125 g (4 oz) mozzarella cheese, diced
150 ml (¼ pint) olive oil	700 g (1½ lb) cherry tomatoes, halved
1 garlic clove, crushed	basil leaves, to garnish
30 ml (2 tbsp) dry white wine	

1 Cook the broad beans in boiling salted water for about 3 minutes. Drain, skin, if wished. Cook the French beans in boiling water for 7-10 minutes. Drain.
2 Place the oil, garlic, wine and lemon juice in a food processor and blend to an emulsion; alternatively shake in a screw-topped jar to mix. Stir in the chopped basil and seasoning.
3 Mix together the beans, mozzarella and tomatoes. Pour over the dressing and stir to coat completely. Cover and leave to marinate for at least 1 hour. Garnish with basil leaves, to serve.

COOK'S TIP

Broad beans are better if skinned. You could use frozen broad beans or a 440 g (14 oz) can of lima beans, if preferred.

MANGETOUT AND GREEN PEPPER SALAD

SERVES 8

350 g (12 oz) mangetout, trimmed	grated rind and juice of 1 lemon
2 bunches spring onions, finely shredded	small pinch of caster sugar
4 medium green peppers, seeded and finely shredded	90 ml (3 fl oz) olive oil
	salt and coarsely ground pepper

1 Cook the mangetout in boiling salted water for 2-3 minutes or until just tender. Drain and refresh under cold water. Toss with the onions and peppers in a bowl.
2 Whisk together the grated rind and strained lemon juice, the sugar, olive oil and seasoning. Stir into the salad before serving.

COOK'S TIP

It's worth taking the time to shred the onions and peppers finely; use a very sharp knife to make it easier.

VARIATION

Replace the mangetout with fine asparagus spears.

SPINACH AND MUSHROOM SALAD

SERVES 6

225 g (8 oz) fresh spinach, washed and trimmed	1 garlic clove, crushed (optional)
2 large slices of wholemeal bread	90 ml (6 tbsp) sunflower oil
2 oranges	30 ml (2 tbsp) lemon juice
10 ml (2 tsp) wholegrain mustard	salt and pepper
	2 avocados
	225 g (8 oz) button mushrooms, sliced

1   Tear the spinach leaves into small pieces and place in a bowl. Set aside.
2   To make the 'croûtons', cut the crusts off the slices of bread, then cut the bread into 5 mm (¼ inch) cubes or into shapes with a small cutter. Toast until evenly browned.
3   Peel the oranges using a serrated knife, cutting away all the skin and pith. Cut the oranges into segments, removing the membrane. Discard any pips.
4   Whisk together the mustard, garlic, sunflower oil, lemon juice and seasoning to taste until well emulsified.
5   Halve the avocados and remove the stones. Peel the avocados and chop the flesh into even-sized chunks.
6   Place the oranges, avocados and mushrooms on top of the spinach and pour over the dressing. Mix carefully and sprinkle with the croûtons. Serve immediately.

SUMMER HERB SALAD

SERVES 8

few large handfuls of mixed herb leaves, eg Good King Henry, rocket, sorrel, lamb's lettuce, dandelion, salad burnet	15 ml (1 tbsp) dry mustard
	10 ml (2 tsp) clear honey
	60 ml (4 tbsp) lemon juice
handful of chervil sprigs	2.5 ml (½ tsp) paprika
handful of parsley sprigs	60 ml (4 tbsp) sunflower oil
few herb flowers – sweet violet, marigold (if available)	30 ml (2 tbsp) walnut oil
	salt and pepper

1   Wash and dry the leaves carefully. Shred them roughly with the hands and place them in a bowl with the chervil and parsley sprigs. Sprinkle the herb flowers over the top.
2   Blend the mustard powder with the honey until smooth. Add the lemon juice, paprika, sunflower and walnut oils and seasoning, and mix well.
3   Dress the salad about 10 minutes before serving.

COOK'S TIP

Fresh herbs will last for several days provided they're kept cool, wrapped in a polythene bag. If they're really sad, stand the stems in a jug of water, tie a polythene bag over the whole thing and leave for an hour or two; most herbs will revive their spirits. Don't leave herbs standing in water for more than a few hours, though, or you'll find that they begin to discolour.

ENDIVE, AVOCADO AND PEANUT SALAD

SERVES 4

½ small head curly endive, separated into sprigs	45 ml (3 tbsp) orange juice
2 oranges, peeled and segmented	15 ml (1 tbsp) olive oil
	salt and pepper
30 ml (2 tbsp) natural roasted peanuts	1 garlic clove, crushed
	15 ml (1 tbsp) chopped mint
¼ cucumber, halved, seeded and chopped	1 ripe avocado

1 Put the endive into a serving bowl and add the orange segments, peanuts and cucumber.
2 To make the dressing, mix the orange juice, olive oil, seasoning, garlic and mint together in another bowl.
3 Halve the avocado and remove the stone, peel and cut into thin slices. Toss gently in the dressing, then add with the dressing to the salad. Toss lightly together and serve.

COOK'S TIP

The peanuts and avocado provide a range of amino acids, making this salad a good source of protein.

ENDIVE, ORANGE AND HAZELNUT SALAD

SERVES 4-6

4 large oranges	1 small red pepper, seeded and cut into thin strips
1 head of curly endive, torn into small pieces	150 ml (5 fl oz) low-fat natural yogurt
1 bunch of watercress, stalks removed and torn into sprigs	salt and pepper
	25 g (1 oz) hazelnuts

1 Remove all of the peel and the white pith from three of the oranges, then segment them. Mix the orange segments with the endive, watercress and pepper in a large salad bowl.
2 To make the dressing, finely grate the rind from the remaining orange into a small bowl, then squeeze in the juice. Whisk in the yogurt and season to taste with salt and pepper.
3 Spread the hazelnuts out on a baking sheet and toast lightly under a hot grill. Turn the nuts on to a clean tea-towel and rub off the loose skins. Roughly chop the nuts.
4 Just before serving, drizzle the dressing over the salad and sprinkle with the nuts. Serve at once while the nuts are still crunchy.

COOK'S TIP

Curly endive is rather like a lettuce with very crinkly leaves, ranging through shades of green to yellow. It is called 'frisée'. Endive wilts quickly, so buy it fresh when needed and don't store for more than a couple of days.

MIXED LEAF
AND PINE NUT SALAD

SERVES 4

1 small head radicchio	45 ml (3 tbsp) grapeseed oil
1 small bunch lamb's lettuce	30 ml (2 tbsp) white wine vinegar
½ head oak leaf lettuce	10 ml (2 tsp) clear honey
½ head curly endive	salt and pepper
25-50 g (1-2 oz) alfalfa sprouts	25 g (1 oz) pine nuts, toasted

1   Wash the salad leaves and shred roughly. Rinse the alfalfa sprouts in a sieve or colander. Pat the salad leaves and the alfalfa sprouts dry with absorbent kitchen paper.
2   To make the dressing, whisk together the grapeseed oil, white wine vinegar and honey. Season.
3   Toss the salad leaves, alfalfa sprouts, pine nuts and dressing together in a large salad bowl. Serve immediately.

COOK'S TIP

For the crispest salad, remember to toss the leaves and dressing together at the very last minute.

WILD RICE
AND THYME SALAD

SERVES 8

150 g (5 oz) French beans, trimmed and halved	50 g (2 oz) small button mushrooms, halved
150 g (5 oz) broad beans	30 ml (2 tbsp) chopped thyme
salt and pepper	15 ml (1 tbsp) walnut oil
50 g (2 oz) wild rice	30 ml (2 tbsp) white wine vinegar
175 g (6 oz) long-grain brown rice	15 ml (1 tbsp) Dijon mustard
30 ml (2 tbsp) grapeseed oil	

1   Cook the French beans in a saucepan of boiling water for 10-12 minutes until just tender. Drain and refresh under cold running water and set aside to cool completely.
2   Cook the broad beans in a pan of boiling salted water for 5-7 minutes. Drain and refresh under cold running water, slipping off their outer skins if wished, and set aside to cool completely.
3   Place the wild rice in a large pan of boiling, salted water. Boil for 10 minutes before adding the brown rice. Boil together for a further 25-30 minutes or until both are just tender. Drain and refresh the rice under cold running water.
4   Stir together the French beans, broad beans and rice in a large bowl.
5   Heat the grapeseed oil in a small frying pan and fry the mushrooms with the thyme for 2-3 minutes. Remove from the heat, stir in the walnut oil, vinegar, mustard and seasoning. Add to the rice mixture and stir well. Adjust the seasoning. Cool, cover and refrigerate until required.

COOK'S TIP

Expensive wild rice is not actually rice at all, but is the seed from a wild grass.

VEGETABLE ACCOMPANIMENTS

Here you will find plenty of inspiring ideas to turn vegetables into tasty accompaniments which can be enjoyed in their own right. Fresh vegetables add low-calorie bulk, nutrients and colour to meals, and these recipes will enable you to liven up any plain meat or fish dish.

GLAZED CARROTS WITH CUMIN

SERVES 4-6

700 g (1½ lb) baby carrots, scrubbed and trimmed	5 ml (1 tsp) cumin seeds
15 g (½ oz) butter or polyunsaturated margarine	salt and pepper
10 ml (2 tsp) demerara sugar	young carrot tops or parsley sprigs, to garnish

1 Place the carrots in a large saucepan of boiling water. Simmer for about 10 minutes or until just tender. Drain.
2 Melt the butter or margarine in the saucepan with the sugar. Add the cumin seeds and cook, stirring, for 1 minute.
3 Toss the carrots into the pan and stir until coated. Add 30 ml (2 tbsp) water and cook for 4-5 minutes, or until the liquid has evaporated to leave a glaze, stirring frequently. Season with salt and pepper to taste. Garnish with carrot tops or parsley sprigs.

BROCCOLI WITH ALMONDS

SERVES 4

700 g (1½ lb) broccoli florets, trimmed	25 g (1 oz) butter or polyunsaturated margarine
salt and pepper	50 g (2 oz) flaked almonds
	juice of ½ lemon

1 Cook the broccoli in boiling salted water for about 10 minutes, until just tender.
2 Meanwhile, melt the butter or margarine in a small saucepan and cook the almonds over a gentle heat until golden brown. Stir in the lemon juice and season with pepper to taste.
3 Drain the broccoli well, then toss with the almonds. Serve at once.

COOK'S TIP

The delicious crunch of almonds makes broccoli into something quite special. Broccoli does not keep well, so buy it as fresh as possible, without any signs of yellowing. Beware of overcooking it – some crispness should be retained.

CREAMED BROCCOLI BAKE

SERVES 6

700 g (1½ lb) broccoli	60 ml (4 tbsp) plain flour
450 ml (¾ pint) semi-skimmed milk	1.25 ml (¼ tsp) grated nutmeg
salt and pepper	2 eggs, separated
50 g (2 oz) butter or polyunsaturated margarine	25 g (1 oz) white breadcrumbs

1   Divide the broccoli florets into small pieces. Place in a medium saucepan with the milk and seasoning and bring to the boil. Cover the pan tightly and simmer gently for 10-15 minutes.
2   Strain off the milk and reserve; finely chop the cooked broccoli. Rinse out and dry the saucepan, then melt the butter or margarine and stir in the flour. Cook for 1-2 minutes. Gradually stir in the reserved milk, there should be about 300 ml (½ pint). Season well and bring to the boil, then simmer for 2 minutes, stirring.
3   Remove from the heat, beat in the chopped broccoli, nutmeg and egg yolks. Adjust the seasoning according to taste.
4   Whisk the egg whites until stiff, and fold into the sauce. Spoon into a well greased 1.4 litre (2½ pint) shallow ovenproof dish.
5   Scatter the breadcrumbs over the top, and bake in the oven at 170°C (325°F) mark 3 for about 50 minutes or until the topping has just set. Serve immediately.

COURGETTES WITH MUSHROOMS

SERVES 8

1.1 kg (2½ lb) courgettes	225 g (8 oz) button mushrooms
50 g (2 oz) butter or polyunsaturated margarine	90 ml (3 fl oz) soured cream or smetana
salt and pepper	basil sprig, to garnish

1   Cut the courgettes into 5 mm (¼ inch) slices.
2   Melt the butter or margarine in a roasting tin, add the courgettes and turn to coat; season well with salt and pepper.
3   Bake the courgette slices in the oven at 200°C (400°F) mark 6 for about 15 minutes.
4   Meanwhile, slice the mushrooms. Stir into the courgettes and return to the oven for a further 10-15 minutes.
5   Stir the soured cream or smetana into the vegetables and heat through on top of the stove; make sure that the cream does not boil or it might curdle. To serve, adjust the seasoning and spoon the vegetables into a serving dish. Garnish with the basil.

VARIATION

French beans or young broccoli or cauliflower florets can be used instead of the courgettes.

BAKED CHERRY TOMATOES

SERVES 8

32 cherry tomatoes, about 700 g (1½ lb) total weight	30 ml (2 tbsp) chopped parsley
50 g (2 oz) butter or polyunsaturated margarine	salt and pepper
	parsley sprigs, to garnish

1 Make a small slash in the skin of each tomato. Place in a large bowl and pour over enough boiling water to cover. Leave for 1 minute, drain and refresh under cold running water.
2 Peel each tomato and place in a large ovenproof dish.
3 Melt the butter or polyunsaturated margarine and stir in the parsley. Brush over the tomatoes and season well.
4 Bake at 220°C (425°F) mark 7 for about 10 minutes or until hot and just beginning to soften. Garnish with parsley, to serve.

COOK'S TIP

It's not absolutely essential to peel the tomatoes but it does give a better finish.

SAUTEED AUBERGINES AND COURGETTES

SERVES 8

4 small aubergines	15 ml (1 tbsp) toasted sesame seeds
salt and pepper	
450 g (1 lb) small courgettes	oregano or marjoram sprigs, to garnish
45 ml (3 tbsp) olive oil	

1 Cut the aubergines lengthways into 2.5 cm (1 inch) slices. Cut the slices across into 1 cm (½ inch) wide fingers. Put the aubergines in a colander and sprinkle generously with salt. Leave to dégorge for at least 30 minutes.
2 Rinse the aubergines and dry thoroughly. Trim the courgettes and cut into pieces about the same size as the aubergine.
3 Heat the oil in a large heavy-based frying pan and sauté the aubergines for 3 minutes. Add the courgettes and continue cooking for 3-4 minutes or until just tender but not soggy. Season with salt and pepper. Sprinkle with the sesame seeds and garnish with oregano or marjoram.

COOK'S TIP

Aubergines can contain bitter juices, especially when mature. Salting and draining before cooking helps to remove these juices and also reduces the aubergine's tendency to absorb large quantities of oil during cooking. This process is known by the French term dégorger. Courgettes and cucumber may also be treated in this way. Choose small aubergines in preference to the larger plump variety, as they are less bitter.

BRAISED CELERY

SERVES 4

1 small onion, finely chopped	1 garlic clove, crushed
50 g (2 oz) carrot, finely chopped	4 small celery hearts
25 g (1 oz) butter or polyunsaturated margarine	150 ml (¼ pint) chicken stock
	chopped parsley, to garnish

1 Sauté the onion and carrot in half the butter or margarine for 5 minutes. Add the garlic and transfer to an ovenproof casserole.
2 Evenly brown the celery hearts in the remaining butter or margarine and put on top of the vegetables. Spoon over the stock and season well.
3 Cover tightly and bake in the oven at 180°C (350°F) mark 4 for about 1½ hours. Turn the celery hearts in the juices to glaze. Serve hot, scattered with chopped parsley.

COOK'S TIP

Celery is an extremely versatile vegetable, full of flavour and just as good raw or cooked. For a tasty way of serving celery hot, try this savoury dish in which celery hearts are browned, then braised slowly in chicken stock.

BAKED FENNEL

SERVES 4-6

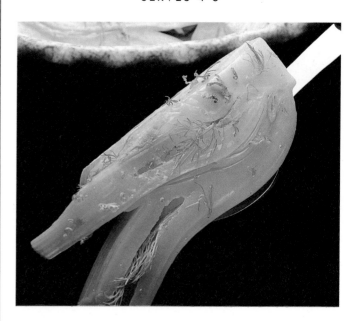

700 g (1½ lb) Florence fennel	finely grated rind of 1 large thin-skinned lemon and 30 ml (2 tbsp) lemon juice
salt and pepper	
40 g (1½ oz) butter or polyunsaturated margarine	

1 Trim the base and top stems of the fennel, reserving some of the feathery green tops. Quarter each head lengthwise. Blanch in boiling salted water for 5 minutes.
2 Melt the butter or margarine in a shallow flameproof casserole. Remove from the heat, then add the lemon rind together with the lemon juice. Season.
3 Arrange the fennel in the casserole in a single layer and turn in the butter or margarine. Cover tightly with a lid or foil and bake in the oven at 150°C (300°F) mark 2 for about 1¼ hours. Garnish with snipped fennel tops. Serve hot.

COOK'S TIP

Prized for its unusual aniseed flavour, fennel is called Florence fennel after the Italian city of that name – the Italians are very fond of this vegetable, which grows prolifically all over the Mediterranean. It is the bulb of the vegetable which is used in this recipe, although the leaves of the fennel herb and its seeds are also widely used in cooking, particularly with fish.

CABBAGE WITH JUNIPER BERRIES

SERVES 4

25 g (1 oz) butter or polyunsaturated margarine	6 juniper berries, crushed
1 medium onion, chopped	450 g (1 lb) cabbage, shredded
1 garlic clove, crushed	salt and pepper

1 Melt the butter or margarine in a large saucepan. Add the onion, garlic and juniper berries and lightly cook for 5 minutes, until the onion is soft.
2 Add the cabbage and stir well. Season to taste. Cover and cook the cabbage in its own juice for 10 minutes, stirring occasionally; the cabbage should still be slightly crunchy and not soft. Serve hot.

COOK'S TIP

You can use any type of cabbage that happens to be in season for this delicious recipe. Juniper berries are wrinkled and black and, when crushed, release their delightful aroma. The flavour is reminiscent of gin, since juniper is a basic ingredient of the spirit. As a faint background hint, married with garlic, it adds a very special touch to cabbage.

BAKED BEETROOT

SERVES 4

4 raw beetroot, each about 225 g (8 oz)	low-fat natural yogurt or fromage frais, to serve
	salt and pepper

1 Wash the beetroot, but do not trim. Wrap them in greased foil or place in a greased ovenproof dish.
2 Cover tightly and bake in the oven at 180°C (350°F) mark 4 for 2-3 hours. When the beetroot are cooked the skin will slide off easily. Serve with a slice cut off the top, but not skinned, topped with the yogurt or fromage frais and seasoned to taste.

COOK'S TIP

Beetroot is usually served cold in salads, but it is also delicious served hot. Be careful when preparing the beetroot for cooking in a conventional oven – if the skin is damaged the colour will 'bleed' during baking. For the same reason, do not prod them with a fork to see if they are done, but instead test whether the skin slides off easily.

MARROW WITH TOMATO AND ONION

SERVES 4-6

25 g (1 oz) butter or polyunsaturated margarine	6 large tomatoes, skinned and chopped
2 medium onions, chopped	30 ml (2 tbsp) tomato purée
1 garlic clove, crushed	30 ml (2 tbsp) chopped fresh mixed herbs or 10 ml (2 tsp) dried mixed herbs
1 medium marrow, peeled, seeded and cubed	salt and pepper

1 Melt the butter or margarine in a large saucepan and gently fry the onions and garlic for 5 minutes, until soft. Add the marrow and cook for a further 5 minutes.
2 Stir in the remaining ingredients, cover and simmer for 30 minutes, until the vegetables are tender. Season to taste. Serve at once.

COOK'S TIP

Make this accompaniment in the autumn when marrows are plentiful. Choose one with a shiny skin which yields slightly when pressed gently with the thumb.

FRENCH BEANS WITH PAPRIKA

SERVES 4

700 g (1½ lb) French beans	salt and pepper
25 g (1 oz) butter or polyunsaturated margarine	150 ml (¼ pint) chicken stock
1 small onion, chopped	90 ml (3 fl oz) soured cream or smetana
5 ml (1 tsp) paprika	

1 Top and tail the French beans and cut them into 2.5 cm (1 inch) lengths. Melt the butter or margarine in a pan, add the onion and cook gently for 5 minutes until soft and golden, but do not brown.
2 Stir in 2.5 ml (½ tsp) paprika, the beans, seasoning and stock. Bring to the boil, cover and simmer for 5-10 minutes until the French beans are tender.
3 Stir the cream or smetana into the pan and reheat without boiling. Turn into a heated serving dish and dust the top with the remaining paprika.

RUNNER BEANS WITH TOMATOES

SERVES 4-6

700 g (1½ lb) young runner beans, topped and tailed	1 garlic clove, crushed
15 g (½ oz) butter or polyunsaturated margarine	397 g (14 oz) can chopped tomatoes
1 medium onion, chopped	15 ml (1 tbsp) chopped basil
	salt and pepper

1 Cut the runner beans into 1 cm (½ inch) lengths.

2 Melt the butter or margarine in a large saucepan and cook the onion and garlic gently for 3-5 minutes, until softened but not browned. Add the tomatoes with their juice, bring to the boil and simmer for 10-15 minutes, until reduced.

3 Stir the beans into the sauce with the dried basil, if using, cover tightly and cook for 10-15 minutes, until the beans are tender but still crisp. Stir in the fresh basil, if using, and season to taste. Serve hot or cold.

VARIATION

Replace the French beans with thickly sliced courgettes.

CAULIFLOWER AND POTATO BAKE

SERVES 4

450 g (1 lb) new potatoes, thinly sliced	pinch of freshly grated nutmeg
salt and pepper	150 ml (5 fl oz) semi-skimmed milk
1 small cauliflower, broken into florets	50 g (2 oz) Cheddar cheese, grated
1 garlic clove, crushed	

1 Cook the potatoes in boiling salted water for 5 minutes. Drain well.

2 Layer the potatoes and cauliflower in a lightly oiled 1.1 litre (2 pint) ovenproof serving dish. Stir the garlic and nutmeg into the milk and pour over the potatoes and cauliflower.

3 Sprinkle with the cheese, cover and bake in the oven at 180°C (350°F) mark 4 for 45-50 minutes, until the vegetables are tender. Uncover and place under a medium grill until lightly browned. Serve at once.

COOK'S TIP

Cauliflower is available all year round and is often eaten with a sauce, as in this recipe. Freshly grated nutmeg and garlic add flavour to the sauce, which is soaked up deliciously by the potatoes.

PARSNIP CROQUETTES

SERVES 4

700 g (1½ lb) parsnips, peeled and cut into large chunks	1 egg, plus 1 egg yolk
salt and pepper	100 g (4 oz) dry breadcrumbs
50 g (2 oz) low-fat soft cheese	watercress sprigs, to garnish

1　Cook the parsnips in boiling salted water until tender. Drain well, then return to the pan and cook over a high heat, stirring, until all of the water has evaporated.
2　Mash or sieve the parsnips, then beat in the cheese and egg yolk. Allow to cool.
3　With floured hands, shape the mixture into dumpy logs, about 6 cm (2½ inches) in length. Place on a baking sheet and chill for about 15 minutes or until firm.
4　Coat the croquettes in lightly beaten egg, then breadcrumbs, and chill for a further 15 minutes.
5　Place the baking sheet of croquettes under a hot grill and cook for about 7 minutes, turning frequently. Serve garnished with watercress.

COOK'S TIP

Croquettes usually absorb quite a lot of oil during frying. Grilling them instead dispenses with the need for oil. These tasty croquettes are ideal served with casseroles and stews.

PEPERONATA

SERVES 6

60 ml (4 tbsp) olive oil	700 g (1½ lb) ripe tomatoes, skinned and roughly chopped
1 large onion, finely sliced	15 ml (1 tbsp) chopped parsley
6 red peppers, seeded and sliced into strips	salt and pepper
2 garlic cloves, crushed	parsley sprigs, to garnish

1　Heat the oil in a frying pan, add the onion and fry gently for 5 minutes until soft but not coloured.
2　Add the peppers and garlic to the pan, cook gently for 2-3 minutes, then add the tomatoes, parsley and salt and pepper to taste.
3　Cover and cook gently for 30 minutes until the mixture is quite dry. If necessary, remove the lid about 10 minutes before the end of cooking to allow the liquid to evaporate. Taste and adjust the seasoning.
4　Garnish with parsley sprigs before serving, either hot or cold.

BRAISED MIXED VEGETABLES

SERVES 8

10 dried Chinese mushrooms	16 baby corn cobs
45 ml (3 tbsp) peanut oil	225 g (8 oz) broccoli, cut into very small florets
1 garlic clove, crushed	2.5 cm (1 inch) piece fresh root ginger, peeled and grated
1 Chinese cabbage, cut crossways into 2.5 cm (1 inch) strips	175 ml (6 fl oz) chicken stock
2 onions, cut into eighths and separated into layers	15 ml (1 tbsp) cornflour
2 carrots, peeled and thinly sliced	30 ml (2 tbsp) light soy sauce
	5 ml (1 tsp) caster sugar

1 Soak the mushrooms in hot water for 20 minutes. Squeeze out as much water as possible. Discard the stalks and thinly slice the caps.
2 Heat the oil in a wok or large frying pan. Add the garlic, cabbage, onions, carrots, baby corn, broccoli and ginger and stir-fry for 2 minutes. Stir in the stock, cover and cook for 2-3 minutes.
3 Blend the cornflour with the soy sauce to a smooth paste. Remove the vegetables from the wok or pan, using a slotted spoon and keep on one side. Stir the cornflour mixture into the wok and bring to the boil, stirring all the time. Boil for 1 minute. Add the sugar.
4 Return the vegetables to the pan and toss lightly to heat through. Serve at once.

CHINESE VEGETABLE STIR-FRY

SERVES 4

30 ml (2 tbsp) polyunsaturated oil	2 large red peppers, seeded and sliced
15 ml (1 tbsp) sesame oil (optional)	225 g (8 oz) can water chestnuts, drained and shredded
1 bunch of spring onions, shredded	30 ml (2 tbsp) dry sherry
5 cm (2 inch) piece of fresh root ginger, shredded	30 ml (2 tbsp) soy sauce
1-2 garlic cloves, crushed	10 ml (2 tsp) honey or soft brown sugar
350 g (12 oz) mangetout, topped and tailed	10 ml (2 tsp) tomato purée
	salt and pepper

1 Heat the oils in a wok or deep heavy-based frying pan. Add the spring onions, ginger and garlic and stir-fry for 2-3 minutes. Add the mangetout, peppers and water chestnuts, and stir-fry briefly.
2 In a bowl or jug, mix together the remaining ingredients, with salt and pepper to taste. Pour over the vegetables, moisten with about 60 ml (4 tbsp) water and mix well. Cook for about 5 minutes, stirring constantly, until the mangetout and red peppers are tender but still crunchy.
3 Transfer to a warmed serving bowl and serve immediately.

SERVING SUGGESTION

Serve this colourful stir-fried dish with pork, beef or duck, or with steamed or fried fish. Chinese egg noodles can be stir-fried with the vegetables, or served separately.

ROASTED
OATMEAL VEGETABLES

SERVES 6

450 g (1 lb) carrots	175 g (6 oz) coarse oatmeal
450 g (1 lb) parsnips	5 ml (1 tsp) paprika
450 g (1 lb) medium onions	salt and pepper
120 g (8 tbsp) polyunsaturated oil	

1 Peel the carrots and parsnips and cut into large chunks; quarter the onions, keeping the root end intact.
2 Put the carrots and parsnips in a saucepan of water, bring to the boil and cook for 2 minutes. Drain well.
3 Put 30 ml (2 tbsp) of the oil in the saucepan and add the carrots and parsnips. Add the onions, oatmeal, paprika and salt and pepper to taste. Stir gently to coat the vegetables.
4 Put the remaining oil in a large roasting tin and heat in the oven at 200°C (400°F) mark 6. When very hot, add the vegetables and any remaining oatmeal and baste to coat.
5 Roast in the oven for about 1 hour, or until the vegetables are just tender and golden brown, basting occasionally during cooking. Spoon into a warmed serving dish and sprinkle over any oatmeal 'crumbs'. Serve hot.

VARIATION

Replace the carrots and parsnips with swede and turnips.

CREAMED
BUTTER BEANS

SERVES 6

350 g (12 oz) dried butter beans, soaked in cold water overnight or three 425 g (15 oz) cans butter beans	50 g (2 oz) butter or polyunsaturated margarine
	salt and pepper
	chopped parsley, to garnish

1 Drain the soaked beans and place in a saucepan of water. Bring to the boil, cover and simmer for 1½-1¾ until the beans are quite tender. If using canned butter beans, reheat as directed on the can.
2 Drain, then return to the pan and mash until smooth with a potato masher.
3 Push the purée to one side of the pan, melt the butter or margarine in the other side, then stir into the purée with seasoning. Stir over a low heat until thoroughly hot.
4 Spoon into a serving dish and scatter generously with parsley to serve.

COOK'S TIP

A tasty savoury purée is one of the classic French ways of making simple vegetables into something special. Use plenty of chopped fresh parsley to give these delicious creamed butter beans their extra appeal.

DESSERTS & BAKING

This tempting collection of lower-calorie desserts will enable you to make the most of fresh fruits in season. Serve them with yogurt or fromage frais, rather than cream or custard. Turn to the end of the chapter for a selection of light gâteaux, moist fruity teabreads and traybakes.

THREE FRUIT SALAD

SERVES 8

50 g (2 oz) raw cane sugar	1 pineapple, weighing about 1.1 kg (2½ lb)
15 ml (1 tbsp) lemon juice	225 g (8 oz) black grapes
15 ml (1 tbsp) kirsch	4 kiwi fruit

1 Put the sugar in a heavy-based saucepan with 150 ml (¼ pint) water. Heat gently until the sugar has dissolved, then bring to the boil and bubble for 2 minutes. Remove from the heat, stir in the lemon juice and kirsch, then set aside to cool.
2 Prepare the pineapple. With a sharp knife, cut off the leafy top and discard. Cut the pineapple into 1 cm (½ inch) pieces. Cut off the skin and dig out the 'eyes' with the tip of the knife. Cut out the core from each slice with an apple corer or small biscuit cutter. Cut the flesh into chunks.
3 Wash and dry the grapes, then halve. Remove the pips by flicking them out with the point of a sharp knife.
4 Peel the kiwi fruit using a potato peeler or sharp knife, then slice the flesh thinly.
5 Stir the prepared fruits into the syrup, cover and chill well in the refrigerator before serving.

FRAGRANT FRUIT SALAD

SERVES 8

50 g (2 oz) raw cane sugar	700 g (1½ lb) lychees
grated rind and juice of 1 lemon	3 ripe mangoes, peeled
2 stem ginger (from a jar of ginger in syrup), finely chopped	450 g (1 lb) fresh or canned pineapple in natural juice
	4 ripe kiwi fruit, peeled
60 ml (4 tbsp) ginger wine	50 g (2 oz) Cape gooseberries, to decorate (optional)

1 Put the sugar in a pan with 150 ml (¼ pint) water and the lemon rind and juice. Heat gently until the sugar dissolves. Bring to the boil and simmer for 1 minute. Remove from the heat and stir in the chopped ginger and wine. Leave to cool.
2 Peel the lychees, cut in half and remove the shiny stones. Halve the mango, stone and cut the flesh into cubes.
3 If using fresh pineapple, peel, slice and remove the tough centre from each slice. Cut the pineapple slices into cubes. Thinly slice the kiwi fruit and halve the slices.
4 Mix together the fruit and syrup. Cover and refrigerate for several hours to allow the flavours to develop. If using Cape gooseberries, peel back each calyx to form a 'flower'. Arrange on the fruit salad to serve.

SPICED DRIED FRUIT COMPOTE

SERVES 4

15 ml (1 tbsp) jasmine tea	100 g (4 oz) dried apple rings
2.5 ml (½ tsp) ground cinnamon	150 ml (¼ pint) dry white wine
1.25 ml (¼ tsp) ground cloves	50 g (2 oz) raw cane sugar
100 g (4 oz) dried apricots, soaked overnight, drained	toasted flaked almonds, to decorate
100 g (4 oz) dried prunes, soaked overnight, drained and stoned	

1   Put the tea, cinnamon and cloves in a bowl and pour in 300 ml (½ pint) boiling water. Leave for 20 minutes.
2   Put the dried fruit in a saucepan, then strain in the tea and spice liquid. Add the wine and sugar and heat gently until the sugar has dissolved.
3   Simmer for 20 minutes until tender, then cover and leave for 1-2 hours until cold.
4   Turn the compote into a serving bowl and chill for at least 2 hours. Sprinkle with almonds just before serving.

COOK'S TIP

Dried fruits are full of concentrated goodness. All dried fruits are an excellent source of dietary fibre and have a high mineral content.

If possible, when buying dried fruits, choose the duller, stickier kinds that are usually sold in healthfood shops. The shiny fruits in sealed plastic packs sold by supermarkets are coated in a mineral oil. Should you buy this type of fruit, wash it well before using.

GINGER FRUIT SALAD

SERVES 4

2 apricots	50 g (2 oz) green grapes
2 dessert apples	2 bananas
1 orange	30 ml (2 tbsp) lemon juice
241 ml (8½ fl oz) bottle low-calorie ginger ale	

1   Prepare the fruits to be macerated. Plunge the apricots into a bowl of boiling water for 30 seconds. Drain and peel off the skin with your fingers.
2   Halve the apricots, remove the stones and dice the flesh. Core and dice the apples, but do not peel them. Peel the orange and divide into segments, discarding all white pith.
3   Put the prepared fruits in a serving bowl with the ginger ale. Stir lightly, then cover and leave to macerate for 1 hour.
4   Cut the grapes in half, then remove the seeds by flicking them out with the point of a knife.
5   Peel and slice the bananas and mix them with the lemon juice to prevent discoloration.
6   Add the grapes and bananas to the macerated fruits. Serve in individual glasses, topped with a spoonful of natural yogurt, if desired.

WHISKY MARINATED GRAPES

SERVES 6

350 g (12 oz) black grapes	45 ml (3 tbsp) clear honey
350 g (12 oz) green grapes	5 ml (1 tsp) lemon juice
30 ml (2 tbsp) whisky	

1 Wash the grapes, drain well and dry with absorbent kitchen paper.
2 Cut the grapes carefully in half lengthways, then ease out the pips with the point of a knife.
3 In a large mixing bowl, stir together the whisky, honey and lemon juice. Add the grapes and stir well. Cover and leave in a cool place (not the refrigerator) to marinate for at least 4 hours, preferably overnight.
4 Spoon into a serving dish and chill in the refrigerator for 30 minutes before serving. Serve with yogurt.

COOK'S TIP

When choosing grapes for eating, avoid fruit which is shiny; fresh grapes should have a powdery whitish bloom on their skin. For this recipe, try to buy the seedless green grapes, which will save you time on preparation.

PEARS IN RED WINE

SERVES 4

4 large firm Comice pears	50 g (2 oz) raw cane sugar
25 g (1 oz) blanched almonds, split in half	300 ml (½ pint) red wine
	2 cloves

1 Peel the pears, leaving the stalks on. Spike the pears with the almond halves.
2 Put the sugar, wine and cloves in a saucepan just large enough to hold the pears and heat gently until the sugar has dissolved. Add the pears, standing them upright in the pan. Cover and simmer gently for about 15 minutes until the pears are just tender. Baste them from time to time with the liquid.
3 Using a slotted spoon, transfer the pears to a serving dish. Boil the syrup in the pan until the liquid is reduced by half.
4 Pour the wine syrup over the pears. Serve hot or cold with natural yogurt or smetana.

VARIATION

Use medium dry cider in place of the red wine.

PEARS IN HONEY AND CINNAMON

SERVES 4-6

60 ml (4 tbsp) white wine, vermouth or sherry	75 g (3 oz) wholemeal breadcrumbs (made from a day-old loaf)
60 ml (4 tbsp) clear honey	40 g (1½ oz) demerara sugar
5 ml (1 tsp) ground cinnamon	4 ripe dessert pears
40 g (1½ oz) polyunsaturated margarine	

1 In a jug, mix together the wine, honey and half of the cinnamon. Set aside.
2 Melt the margarine in a small pan, add the breadcrumbs, sugar and remaining cinnamon and stir together until evenly mixed. Set aside.
3 Peel and halve the pears. Remove the cores. Arrange the pear halves, cut side down, in a greased ovenproof dish and pour over the white wine mixture.
4 Sprinkle the pears evenly with the breadcrumb mixture and bake in the oven at 190°C (375°F) mark 5 for 40 minutes. Serve hot.

COOK'S TIP

Accompany with yogurt flavoured with grated orange rind.

STRAWBERRIES WITH RASPBERRY SAUCE

SERVES 6

900 g (2 lb) small strawberries	artificial sweetener (optional)
450 g (1 lb) raspberries	

1 Hull the strawberries and place them in individual serving dishes.
2 Purée the raspberries in a blender or food processor until just smooth, then work through a nylon sieve into a bowl to remove the pips.
3 Sweeten the raspberry purée with a little artificial sweetener if desired, then pour over the strawberries. Chill in the refrigerator for at least 30 min-utes before serving.

COOK'S TIP

Freshly picked raspberries freeze successfully (unlike strawberries which tend to lose texture and shape due to their high water content). If you have raspberries which are slightly overripe or misshapen, the best way to freeze them is as a purée; this takes up less space in the freezer and is immensely useful for making quick desserts and sauces at the last minute. For this recipe, for example, you can freeze the purée up to 12 months in advance, then it will only take minutes to assemble the dessert after thawing the purée.

STRAWBERRY CREAM

SERVES 6

100 g (4 oz) cottage cheese	a little clear honey, to taste
150 ml (¼ pint) low-fat natural yogurt	700 g (1½ lb) strawberries

1 Work the cottage cheese in a blender or food processor until smooth. Alternatively, work through a fine wire sieve by pushing with the back of a metal spoon.
2 In a bowl, beat the cheese and yogurt together with honey to taste. Set aside.
3 Hull the strawberries and slice finely, reserving 6 whole ones to decorate.
4 Divide the sliced strawberries equally between 6 individual glasses or glass serving dishes.
5 Pour the cheese mixture over the strawberries and chill in the refrigerator for about 1 hour. Serve chilled, decorated with the reserved whole strawberries.

SERVING SUGGESTION

Strawberry Cream is rich and creamy in flavour yet surprisingly low in calories. Serve as a special summertime dessert, with langues de chat or wholemeal shortbread biscuits.

APPLE MINT MERINGUES

SERVES 8

FOR THE MERINGUE	15 ml (1 tbsp) granulated artificial sweetener
2 egg whites	
125 g (4 oz) caster sugar	4 mint sprigs
FOR THE FILLING	150 ml (5 fl oz) Greek-style yogurt, or fromage frais
450 g (1 lb) sweet eating apples, peeled, cored and thinly sliced	15 ml (1 tbsp) icing sugar
	mint sprigs and apples slices, to decorate

1 Whisk the egg whites until stiff but not dry. Add half of the sugar and whisk until stiff and shiny. Fold in the remaining sugar.
2 Mark sixteen 7.5 cm (3 inch) rounds on a sheet of non-stick baking parchment. Place on a baking sheet, pencil side down. Divide the meringue mixture between the rounds and spread with a round bladed knife to fill. Alternatively, using a 5 mm (¼ inch) plain nozzle, pipe the mixture into the rounds. Bake at 140°C (275°F) mark 1 for about 1 hour or until completely dried out and crisp. Leave to cool on a wire rack.
3 Place the apple in a saucepan with the sweetener, mint and 30 ml (2 tbsp) water. Cover and cook very gently for about 10 minutes or until the apple has softened. Cool, cover and chill for at least 1 hour.
4 To serve, spoon a little apple onto 8 meringue rounds. Top with the yogurt and the remaining meringues. Dust lightly with icing sugar and decorate with the sprigs of fresh mint and apple slices to serve.

COOK'S TIP

The egg whites must be whisked until they are very stiff and will hold an unwavering peak on the end of the whisk. The sugar can be added in two halves or whisked in a little at a time. This type of meringue is known as meringue Suisse.

ORANGE GRANITA

SERVES 6

175 g (6 oz) sugar	10 large oranges
450 ml (¾ pint) water	1½ lemons

1 To make the sugar syrup, place the sugar and water in a medium saucepan. Heat gently until the sugar dissolves, then boil gently for 10 minutes without stirring.
2 Meanwhile, using a potato peeler, thinly pare the rind from four oranges and the lemons. Add the orange and lemon rind to the sugar syrup and leave until cold.
3 Squeeze the juice from the four oranges and the lemons. Strain into a measuring jug – there should be 450 ml (¾ pint).
4 Strain the cold syrup into a shallow freezer container and stir in the fruit juices. Mix well. Cover and freeze for about 4 hours until mushy in texture.
5 Remove from the freezer and turn the frozen mixture into a bowl. Beat well with a fork to break down the ice crystals. Return to the freezer container and freeze for at least 4 hours or until firm.
6 Meanwhile, using a serrated knife, cut away the peel and pith from the remaining oranges.
7 Slice the oranges down into thin rings, ease out and discard any pips. Place the oranges in a serving bowl, cover tightly and refrigerate until serving time.
8 Place the water ice in the refrigerator for 45 minutes to soften before serving. Serve with the fresh orange slices.

VARIATIONS

Lemon Water Ice
With 6-8 lemons as a basis, follow the recipe using the pared rind of four lemons and enough juice to give 450 ml (¾ pint).

Coffee Granita
Put 30 ml (2 tbsp) sugar and 50 g (2 oz) finely ground Italian coffee in a jug. Pour over 600 ml (1 pint) boiling water and leave to stand for 1 hour. Strain the coffee through a filter paper or muslin, then freeze as in steps 4-5.

GERANIUM GRAPE SORBET

SERVES 6

100 g (4 oz) sugar	90 ml (6 tbsp) dry white vermouth
300 ml (½ pint) water	2 egg whites
15 ml (½ tbsp) chopped rose- or lemon-scented geranium leaves	rose- or lemon-scented geranium leaves, to decorate
700 g (1½ lb) seedless green grapes	

1 To make the sugar syrup, dissolve the sugar in the water over a low heat. Bring to the boil and boil gently for 10 minutes without stirring. Add the geranium leaves, cover and leave to cool.
2 Purée the grapes in a blender or food processor and then work through a sieve. There should be 600 ml (1 pint) purée. Add the vermouth and the strained sugar syrup, mix well and pour this mixture into a shallow freezer container. Freeze for about 1 hour until half frozen and mushy.
3 Turn the half frozen mixture into a large bowl and break up with a fork.
4 Whisk the egg whites until stiff and fold into the grape mixture. Return to the container and freeze for about 2-3 hours until firm. Serve straight from the freezer, decorated with geranium leaves.

COOK'S TIP

A sorbetière or ice cream machine will freeze a sorbet and churn it at the same time, to give a smooth, even textured result. When making sorbet, any egg white should be lightly whisked with a fork and added at the start of the churning process. Freezing time is usually about 20-30 minutes. The sorbet should then be transferred to the freezer and frozen for 1-2 hours to allow the flavours to develop. Soften slightly at room temperature before serving.

TEA CREAM WITH FRUITS

SERVES 6

300 ml (½ pint) semi-skimmed milk	450 g (1 lb) mixed red fruits, such as cherries, redcurrants, boysenberries, blueberries and raspberries
4 Earl Grey tea bags	
2 eggs	300 ml (½ pint) unsweetened apple juice
15 ml (1 tbsp) sugar	
15 g (½ oz) powdered gelatine	artificial sweetener
150 ml (5 fl oz) whipping cream, lightly whipped	30 ml (2 tbsp) crème de cassis
	mint sprigs, to decorate
150 ml (5 fl oz) low-fat natural yogurt	

1 Heat the milk to just below boiling point. Pour over the tea bags, cover and leave to infuse for 15-20 minutes. Squeeze the tea bags and discard.

2 Separate 1 egg, reserving the white. Beat the yolk with the remaining whole egg and the sugar. Add to the milk, beating well. Strain into a heavy-based pan. Cook over a gentle heat, stirring, until the custard thickens and coats the back of a wooden spoon; do not allow to boil. Remove from the heat and cool.

3 Sprinkle the gelatine over 45 ml (3 tbsp) cold water in a heatproof bowl and let soak for 1 minute. Place over a pan of simmering water and stir until gelatine is dissolved. Leave to cool slightly, then stir into the custard.

4 When just beginning to set, stir in the cream, then the yogurt. Whisk the reserved egg white until stiff and fold into the mixture. Pour into a dampened 900 ml (1½ pint) mould and chill for 2-3 hours or until set.

5 To make the fruit sauce, prepare the fruit, removing stones, as necessary. Put in a saucepan with the apple juice and sweetener to taste. Simmer gently until softened but still retaining some shape. Cool, then stir in the cassis.

6 Unmould the tea cream by dipping quickly into hot water and inverting on to a serving dish. Surround with the poached fruits and serve at once, decorated with mint.

STRAWBERRY YOGURT MOULD

SERVES 6

3 eggs	20 ml (4 tsp) powdered gelatine
50 g (2 oz) caster sugar	
finely grated rind and juice of 1 lemon	150 ml (5 fl oz) low-fat natural yogurt
450 g (1 lb) strawberries	150 ml (5 fl oz) low-fat strawberry yogurt

1 Put the eggs, sugar and lemon rind in a large bowl. Using an electric mixer, whisk together until the mixture is pale, thick and creamy and leaves a trail when the whisk is lifted from the bowl.

2 Hull half of the strawberries and place in a blender or food processor with half of the lemon juice. Purée until smooth.

3 Gradually whisk the purée into the mousse mixture, whisking well to keep the bulk.

4 Sprinkle the gelatine over the remaining lemon juice in a small bowl and leave to soak for 5 minutes. Place the bowl over a saucepan of simmering water and stir until dissolved. Leave until lukewarm, then gradually add to the mousse mixture with the natural and strawberry yogurts. Stir carefully but thoroughly to mix. Pour into a greased 1.7 litre (3 pint) ring mould and chill for 4-5 hours or until set.

5 To serve, dip the mould briefly in hot water, then invert on to a serving plate. Hull most of the remaining strawberries, but leave a few of the green hulls on for decoration. Fill the centre of the ring with the fruit. Serve with extra natural yogurt, if liked.

CAPPUCCINO CREAMS

SERVES 8

550 g (1¼ lb) fromage frais	175 g (6 oz) dark or bitter chocolate
15-30 ml (1-2 tbsp) finely ground espresso coffee	chocolate curls, to decorate
15 ml (1 tbsp) icing sugar (optional)	

1 Mix the fromage frais with the coffee and icing sugar, if liked.
2 Pulverise the chocolate in an electric blender or liquidiser until very fine. Alternatively grate finely.
3 Spoon half the fromage frais into eight individual ramekins or glass dishes. Sprinkle over most of the chocolate mixture. Top with the remaining fromage frais and sprinkle with the remaining chocolate mixture. Decorate with chocolate curls.

COOK'S TIP

These little desserts are light but creamy and can be made with low-fat fromage frais if preferred. Use a good dark chocolate – the flavour is so much better.

BANANA WHIPS

SERVES 4

2 egg whites	30 ml (2 tbsp) muscovado sugar
300 ml (½ pint) low-fat natural set yogurt	2 medium bananas
finely grated rind and juice of ½ orange	50 g (2 oz) crunchy breakfast cereal

1 Whisk the egg whites until standing in stiff peaks. Put the yogurt in a bowl and stir until smooth. Fold in the egg whites until evenly incorporated.
2 In a separate bowl, mix together the orange rind and juice and the sugar. Peel the bananas and slice thinly into the juice mixture. Fold gently to mix.
3 Put a layer of the yogurt mixture in the bottom of 4 individual glasses. Cover with a layer of cereal, then with a layer of the banana mixture. Repeat these 3 layers once more. Serve immediately.

COOK'S TIP

A quickly made dessert that appeals particularly to children of all ages.

KHEER

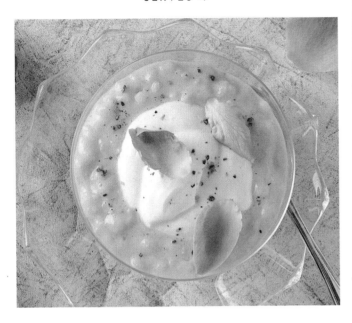

75 g (3 oz) pudding rice	2.5-5 ml (½-1 tsp) rose water
seeds of 6 cardamoms, crushed	60 ml (4 tbsp) Greek strained yogurt
1.1 litres (2 pints) semi-skimmed milk	rose petals, to decorate (optional)
60 ml (4 tbsp) clear honey	

1 Put the rice and crushed cardamom seeds in a heavy-based non-stick saucepan. Pour in the milk, then add the honey and bring to the boil, stirring continuously.
2 Lower the heat and simmer for about 1¼ hours or until the rice is tender and the milk has reduced to a thick, creamy consistency. Stir frequently to prevent the milk and rice catching on the bottom of the pan.
3 Leave the kheer to cool, then cover the surface closely and chill overnight.
4 Stir in the rose water, then divide the kheer equally between 4 stemmed glasses. Very lightly spoon the yogurt on top of each serving, then place rose petals on top, if liked. Serve well chilled.

COOK'S TIP

These rice creams are a simple adaptation of a traditional Indian pudding. In the original recipe, full-cream milk and a great deal of sugar are used; this version is lighter and less sweet. If you like, whipping cream can be substituted for the Greek strained yogurt, although this will raise the fat content of the dessert.

COEURS A LA CREME

225 g (8 oz) curd or ricotta cheese	few drops of vanilla essence
300 ml (½ pint) crème fraîche	25 g (1 oz) caster sugar
	2 egg whites

1 Line four small heart-shaped perforated moulds with muslin.
2 Press the cheese through a nylon sieve into a bowl. Lightly whip the cream, vanilla essence and sugar together. Mix into the cheese.
3 Whisk the egg whites until stiff, then fold into the cheese mixture.
4 Turn the mixture into the prepared moulds. Leave to drain overnight in the refrigerator. Turn out and serve with strawberries.

COOK'S TIP

Light, delicate and refreshing, these are best eaten with soft summer fruit, ideally, tiny wild strawberries. This dessert takes its name from the small heart-shaped white porcelain colanders in which it is made.

FLOATING SPICE ISLANDS

SERVES 6-8

FOR THE SAUCE	FOR THE MERINGUE
350 g (12 oz) blackcurrants, stalks removed	2 egg whites
30 ml (2 tbsp) crème de cassis	50 g (2 oz) caster sugar
artificial sweetener	freshly grated nutmeg
	pinch of salt

1 To make the sauce, place the blackcurrants, and 60 ml (4 tbsp) water in a small saucepan. Cover tightly and cook gently until the fruit softens. Rub through a nylon sieve, then leave to cool. Stir in the liqueur and sweetener to taste. Cover and chill.
2 Meanwhile to make the meringue, whisk the egg whites in a bowl until stiff, but not dry. Gradually whisk in the caster sugar, keeping the mixture stiff. Fold in 1.25 ml (¼ tsp) grated nutmeg.
3 Pour 2 cm (¾ inch) water into a large frying pan and bring to a gentle simmer. Add the salt.
4 Shape the meringue into small egg shapes, using two spoons as moulds. Slide about six or eight at a time into the liquid and poach gently for 2-3 minutes. The meringue will pull up then shrink back a little. When cooked, it will be firm if lightly touched. Remove with a fish slice and drain on absorbent kitchen paper. Poach the remaining mixture. Store in a cool place for not more than 2 hours.
5 To serve, spoon a little blackcurrant sauce on to individual serving dishes. Float a few 'islands' on top and sprinkle with nutmeg.

MINTED STRAWBERRY CUSTARDS

SERVES 6

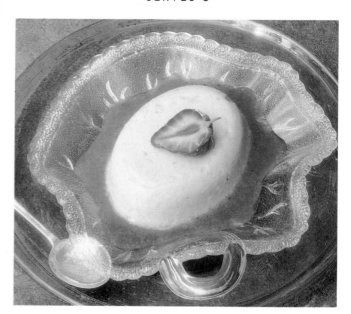

450 ml (¾ pint) semi-skimmed milk	20 ml (4 tsp) powdered gelatine
4 large mint sprigs	700 g (1½ lb) strawberries, hulled
1 egg	artificial sweetener (optional)
2 egg yolks	strawberries, to decorate
45 ml (3 tbsp) caster sugar	

1 Oil six 150 ml (¼ pint) ramekin dishes.
2 Place the milk and mint sprigs in a saucepan. Bring slowly to the boil, remove from the heat, cover and leave to infuse for about 30 minutes.
3 Whisk the egg and egg yolks with the caster sugar in a bowl. Strain over the milk. Return to the pan and cook gently, stirring, until the custard just coats the back of a wooden spoon. Do not boil. Leave to cool.
4 Sprinkle the gelatine over 45 ml (3 tbsp) water in a small heatproof bowl and leave to soak for 2-3 minutes. Place the bowl over a pan of simmering water and stir until dissolved. Stir the gelatine into the custard.
5 Purée and sieve the strawberries. Whisk about two-thirds into the cold, but not set, custard. Pour the custard into the prepared dishes and chill for about 3 hours or until set.
6 Meanwhile, sweeten the remaining strawberry purée to taste with artificial sweetener, if desired. Chill.
7 To serve, turn out the custards. Surround with strawberry sauce, then decorate with strawberries.

VARIATION

Replace the mint with a few lemon geranium leaves, if available, to produce a subtle and refreshing lemon flavour.

ORANGE SEMOLINA SOUFFLES

SERVES 6

5 large juicy oranges	3 eggs, separated
25 g (1 oz) granulated sugar	icing sugar, for dusting
25 g (1 oz) semolina	orange slices, to decorate

1   Finely grate the rind and squeeze the juice from 2 of the oranges into a measuring jug. You will need 300 ml (½ pint) juice. Make up with juice from one of the remaining oranges if there is not enough.

2   Halve the remaining oranges. Scoop out any loose flesh still attached to the skins and eat separately or use in another recipe. You need six clean orange halves to serve the soufflés in. Cut a thin slice from the bottom of each so that they stand flat.

3   Place the orange juice and rind, sugar and semolina in a pan and simmer until thickened, stirring all the time.

4   Cool slightly, then stir in the egg yolks. Whisk the egg whites until stiff and fold into the mixture. Spoon into the reserved orange shells and stand on a baking sheet.

5   Bake in the oven at 200°C (400°F) mark 6 for 15-20 minutes or until risen and golden brown. Dust with icing sugar and serve immediately, surrounded by orange slices.

ALMOND BAKED APPLES

SERVES 4

75 g (3 oz) dried figs, rinsed and chopped	50 g (2 oz) ground almonds
grated rind of 1 lime or ½ lemon	15 ml (1 tbsp) light muscovado sugar
4 cooking apples, each about 225 g (8 oz)	15 ml (1 tbsp) melted polyunsaturated margarine

1   Put the figs in a bowl, cover with boiling water and leave to soak for 5 minutes. Drain, then mix in the grated lime or lemon rind. Peel the cooking apples and remove the cores, using an apple corer. Fill the centre of the apples with the figs, packing down firmly.

2   Mix the ground almonds and sugar together in a bowl. Brush each apple with the melted margarine, then roll the apples in the ground almond mixture. Place in a shallow 1.1 litre (2 pint) ovenproof dish.

3   Bake in the oven at 180°C (350°F) mark 4 for about 45-50 minutes or until the apples are cooked through and tender when pricked with a skewer. Serve hot.

SUMMER PUDDING

SERVES 4-6

700 g (1½ lb) mixed summer fruit, such as redcurrants, blackcurrants, raspberries, prepared about 25 g (1 oz) muscovado sugar	8-10 thin slices of day-old bread, crusts removed fruit and mint sprigs, to decorate

1 Stew the fruit gently with 60-90 ml (4-6 tbsp) water and the sugar until soft but still retaining their shape. The exact amounts of water and sugar depend on the ripeness and sweetness of the fruit.

2 Meanwhile, cut a round from one slice of bread to neatly fit the bottom of a 1.1 litre (2 pint) pudding basin and cut 6-8 slices of the bread into fingers about 5 cm (2 inches) wide. Put the round at the bottom of the basin and arrange the fingers around the sides, overlapping them so there are no spaces.

3 When the fruit is cooked, and still hot, pour it gently into the basin, being careful not to disturb the bread framework. Reserve about 45 ml (3 tbsp) of the juice. When the basin is full, cut the remaining bread and use to cover the fruit so a lid is formed.

4 Cover with a plate or saucer which fits just inside the bowl and put a weight on top. Leave the pudding until cold, then put into the refrigerator and chill overnight.

5 To serve, run a knife carefully round the edge to loosen, then invert the pudding on to a serving dish. Pour the reserved juice over the top. Decorate with fruit and mint sprigs. Serve cold, with yogurt or fromage frais.

VARIATION

Autumn Pudding

Replace the summer fruits with a selection of autumn fruits, such as apples or pears, blackberries and plums.

SUGAR-FREE CHRISTMAS PUDDING

SERVES 6

225 g (8 oz) mixed dried fruit juice of 2 oranges 150 ml (¼ pint) brandy 1 large carrot, grated 1 large apple, grated 50 g (2 oz) plain wholemeal flour	50 g (2 oz) fresh wholemeal breadcrumbs 25 g (1 oz) blanched almonds, chopped 5 ml (1 tsp) grated nutmeg 5 ml (1 tsp) ground cinnamon 2 eggs, beaten

1 Put the mixed dried fruit in a large bowl. Stir in the orange juice and the brandy. Cover and leave overnight. Add all the remaining ingredients and mix well together.

2 Grease a 900 ml (1½ pint) pudding basin and fill with the mixture. Cover with a piece of pleated greaseproof paper and then foil. Secure tightly with string, making a handle for easy lifting in and out of pan.

3 Place the basin in a steamer or in a saucepan containing enough boiling water to come halfway up the sides of the basin. Steam over boiling water for about 4 hours, topping up with boiling water as necessary.

4 When cooked, remove the pudding from the pan and leave to cool for at least 2 hours. Unwrap, then rewrap in fresh greaseproof paper and foil.

5 Store in a cool, dry place to mature for at least 1 month. To serve, steam for a further 2 hours. Turn out on to a warmed plate and decorate with holly.

COOK'S TIP

The combination of grated carrot and fruit in this recipe is quite sweet enough without additional sugar, and the absence of suet also helps to make it a 'healthy' recipe.

BLACKBERRY UPSIDE DOWN PUDDING

SERVES 8

FOR THE TOPPING	5 ml (1 tsp) baking powder
90 ml (6 tbsp) reduced-sugar raspberry jam	large pinch of salt
	1 egg
350 g (12 oz) blackberries	finely grated rind and juice of 1 large orange
1 large eating apple, peeled, cored and roughly chopped	
	30 ml (2 tbsp) semi-skimmed milk
FOR THE CAKE	
75 g (3 oz) self-raising flour	75 g (3 oz) polyunsaturated margarine
75 g (3 oz) self-raising wholemeal flour	75 g (3 oz) caster sugar

1 Grease a 23 cm (9 inch) round spring-release cake tin.
2 To make the topping, gently heat the jam in a small saucepan and pour into the prepared cake tin. Arrange the blackberries and apple evenly over the base of the cake tin.
3 To make the cake, put all the ingredients into a large bowl and beat until smooth and glossy. Carefully spread over the fruit and level the surface.
4 Bake in the oven at 190°C (375°F) mark 5 for about 1 hour or until well risen and firm to the touch. Cover the top with a double sheet of greaseproof paper after 40 minutes to prevent overbrowning.
5 Leave the pudding to cool in the tin for 5 minutes, then turn out and serve.

CHOCOLATE AND RASPBERRY ROULADE

SERVES 8

FOR THE ROULADE	FOR THE FILLING
50 g (2 oz) plain chocolate	175 g (6 oz) natural fromage frais
30 ml (2 tbsp) cocoa powder	225 g (8 oz) raspberries
30 ml (2 tbsp) semi-skimmed milk	FOR THE DECORATION
3 eggs, separated	5 ml (1 tsp) icing sugar
75 g (3 oz) plus 10 ml (2 tsp) caster sugar	few raspberries
	geranium or mint leaves

1 Grease a 23 x 33 cm (9 x 13 inch) Swiss roll tin, line with greaseproof paper and grease the paper.
2 To make the roulade, break the chocolate into small pieces. Place in a heatproof bowl standing over a pan of simmering water and heat gently until the chocolate has melted. Stir in the cocoa powder and milk.
3 Whisk the egg yolks and 75 g (3 oz) sugar together in a bowl until very thick and pale in colour. Beat in the chocolate mixture. Whisk the egg whites until stiff, then fold carefully into the mixture. Pour into the prepared tin and spread out evenly.
4 Bake in the oven at 180°C (350°F) mark 4 for 20-25 minutes or until well risen and firm to the touch.
5 While the roulade is cooking, lay a piece of greaseproof paper on a flat work surface and sprinkle with the remaining caster sugar. When the roulade is cooked, turn it out on to the paper. Carefully peel off the lining paper. Cover the roulade with a warm, damp tea-towel and leave to cool.
6 To make the filling, spread the fromage frais over the roulade. Sprinkle with the raspberries, then crush them slightly with a fork. Starting from one of the narrow ends, carefully roll up the roulade, using the greaseproof paper to help. Transfer the roulade to a serving plate and dust with the icing sugar. Decorate with raspberries and geranium or mint leaves.

RHUBARB BROWN BETTY

SERVES 6

450 g (1 lb) rhubarb	2.5 ml (½ tsp) ground ginger
225 g (8 oz) fresh wholemeal breadcrumbs	50 ml (2 fl oz) fresh orange juice
50 g (2 oz) muscovado sugar	

1 Trim the rhubarb and cut the stalks into short lengths. Put in a greased 900 ml (1½ pint) ovenproof dish.

2 Mix the breadcrumbs, sugar and ground ginger together and sprinkle over the fruit. Spoon the orange juice over the crumbs.

3 Bake in the oven at 170°C (325°F) mark 3 for 40 minutes or until the fruit is soft and the topping browned. Serve hot or cold, with natural yogurt.

COOK'S TIP

Rhubarb Brown Betty is equally good served hot or cold, with natural yogurt. Any leftover will also reheat well.

LEMON MUESLI CHEESECAKE

SERVES 6

175 g (6 oz) sugar-free muesli	225 g (8 oz) low-fat soft cheese
75 g (3 oz) butter or polyunsaturated margarine, melted	150 ml (5 fl oz) low-fat natural yogurt
3 lemons	60 ml (4 tbsp) clear honey
15 ml (3 tsp) gelatine	2 egg whites

1 Mix the muesli and melted butter or margarine together. With the back of a metal spoon, press the mixture over the base of a greased 20 cm (8 inch) springform cake tin. Chill in the refrigerator to set while making the filling.

2 Finely grate the rind of two of the lemons. Set aside. Squeeze the juice from the 2 lemons and make up to 150 ml (¼ pint) with water. Pour into a heatproof bowl.

3 Sprinkle the gelatine over the lemon juice and leave to stand for 5 minutes until spongy. Stand the bowl in a pan of hot water and heat gently, stirring occasionally, until dissolved. Remove the bowl from the water and set aside to cool slightly.

4 Whisk the cheese, yogurt and honey together in a separate bowl. Stir in the grated lemon rind and cooled gelatine until evenly incorporated.

5 Whisk the egg whites until stiff. Fold into the cheesecake mixture until evenly incorporated.

6 Spoon the mixture into the springform tin and level the surface. Chill in the refrigerator for at least 4 hours until set.

7 To serve, remove the cheesecake from the tin and place on a serving plate. Slice the remaining lemon thinly and arrange on top of the cheesecake. Serve chilled.

LEMON CAKE

SERVES 8

25 g (1 oz) butter or polyunsaturated margarine	5 ml (1 tsp) baking powder
30 ml (2 tbsp) semi-skimmed milk	finely grated rind of 1 lemon
3 eggs	FOR THE FILLING
75 g (3 oz) raw cane sugar	75 g (3 oz) quark or low-fat soft cheese
50 g (2 oz) plain wholemeal flour	10 ml (2 tsp) lemon juice
25 g (1 oz) bran	15 ml (1 tbsp) clear honey
	lemon slices, to decorate

1 Grease and base-line two 18 cm (7 inch) sandwich tins. Grease the lining papers.
2 Put the butter or margarine and milk in a small saucepan. Warm gently until the fat melts. Cool slightly.
3 Put the eggs and sugar in a large bowl. Using an electric whisk, beat the mixture until very thick and light.
4 Fold in the flour, bran, baking powder and lemon rind. Gently stir in the fat until evenly incorporated.
5 Divide the mixture between the prepared tins. Bake in the oven at 190°C (375°F) mark 5 for about 25 minutes until firm to the touch. Leave to cool for a few minutes in the tins then turn out on to a wire rack. Remove the lining paper and leave to cool for about 1 hour.
6 Put the quark, lemon juice and honey in a bowl and beat together until evenly mixed. Use to sandwich the cakes together. Keep in a cool place until serving time. Decorate with lemon slices.

RED FRUIT GATEAU

SERVES 8-10

3 eggs	FOR THE FILLING AND TOPPING
75 g (3 oz) soft brown sugar	100 g (4 oz) natural fromage frais
75 g (3 oz) plain flour	450 g (1 lb) mixed summer fruit, such as raspberries, strawberries, redcurrants, loganberries and figs
finely grated rind of 1 lemon	

1 Grease and base-line two 18 cm (7 inch) sandwich tins. Grease the paper. Put the eggs and sugar in a large bowl. Using an electric whisk, beat the mixture until very thick and pale.
2 Carefully fold in the flour and lemon rind. Divide the mixture between the prepared tins. Bake in the oven at 190°C (375°F) mark 5 for about 25 minutes. When cooked, the cake will look evenly brown, spring back when lightly pressed, and will have shrunk slightly from the sides of the tins. Cool in the tins for 5 minutes, then turn out on to a wire rack and leave to cool completely.
3 To assemble the gâteau, sandwich the cakes together with the fromage frais and most of the fruit. Use the remaining fruit to decorate the cake.

WHOLEMEAL DATE AND BANANA BREAD

225 g (8 oz) stoned dates, roughly chopped	100 g (4 oz) polyunsaturated margarine
5 ml (1 tsp) bicarbonate of soda	75 g (3 oz) shelled hazelnuts, chopped
300 ml (½ pint) semi-skimmed milk	2 medium ripe bananas
275 g (10 oz) self-raising wholemeal flour	1 egg, beaten
	30 ml (2 tbsp) clear honey

1 Grease a 1.3 litre (2¼ pint) loaf tin and line with greaseproof paper.
2 Put the dates in a pan with the soda and milk. Bring slowly to boiling point, stirring, then remove from the heat and leave until cold.
3 Put the flour in a large bowl and rub in the margarine. Stir in the hazelnuts, reserving 30 ml (2 tbsp) for the decoration.
4 Peel and mash the bananas, then add to the flour mixture with the dates and the egg. Beat well to mix.
5 Spoon the mixture into the prepared tin and bake in the oven at 180°C (350°F) mark 4 for 1-1¼ hours until a skewer inserted in the centre comes out clean.
6 Leave the loaf to cool in the tin for about 5 minutes. Turn out, peel off the lining paper and place on a wire rack.
7 Heat the honey gently, then brush over the top of the loaf. Sprinkle with the reserved hazelnuts and leave until cold.

COOK'S TIP

It may seem unusual to have a cake made entirely without sugar, but this is because of the high proportion of dates used in this recipe. Dates have the highest natural sugar content of all dried fruit and if used in cakes such as this one there is no need to add extra sugar.

PRUNE AND NUT LOAF

275 g (10 oz) self-raising flour	1 egg
pinch of salt	100 ml (4 fl oz) semi-skimmed milk
7.5 ml (1½ tsp) ground cinnamon	50 g (2 oz) shelled walnuts, chopped
75 g (3 oz) polyunsaturated margarine	100 g (4 oz) no-soak prunes, chopped
75 g (3 oz) muscovado sugar	15 ml (1 tbsp) clear honey

1 Grease a 2 litre (3½ pint) loaf tin, line with greaseproof paper and grease the paper.
2 Sift the flour and salt into a bowl and add the cinnamon. Rub in the margarine until the mixture resembles fine breadcrumbs.
3 Stir in the sugar, and make a well in the centre. Add the egg and milk and gradually draw in the dry ingredients to form a smooth dough.
4 Using floured hands shape the mixture into sixteen even-sized rounds. Place eight in the base of the tin. Sprinkle over half of the nuts and all of the prunes.
5 Arrange the remaining dough rounds on top and sprinkle over the remaining chopped walnuts.
6 Bake in the oven at 190°C (375°F) mark 5 for about 50 minutes or until firm to the touch. Check near the end of the cooking time and cover with greaseproof paper if it is overbrowning.
7 Turn out on to a wire rack and leave to cool for 1 hour. When cold brush with the honey to glaze. Wrap and store for 1-2 days in an airtight tin before slicing.

COOK'S TIP

This fruity teabread improves as it matures, the flavour and moisture from the fruit penetrating the cake and mellowing it over a number of days.

PRUNE
AND CINNAMON BUNS

MAKES 12

225 g (8 oz) strong plain white flour	about 175 ml (6 fl oz) tepid semi-skimmed milk
2.5 ml (½ tsp) easy-blend dried yeast	175 g (6 oz) stoned prunes, roughly chopped
2.5 ml (½ tsp) salt	finely grated rind of 1 lemon
15 ml (1 tbsp) ground cinnamon	50 g (2 oz) soft light brown sugar
15 g (½ oz) polyunsaturated margarine	15 ml (1 tbsp) clear honey
	15 ml (1 tbsp) lemon juice

1 Lightly grease and base-line an 18 cm (7 inch) square shallow cake tin.

2 Mix together the flour, dried yeast, salt and cinnamon. Rub in the margarine, then beat in enough milk to mix to a soft dough.

3 Turn the dough on to a lightly floured surface and knead for about 5 minutes or until smooth. Place in a bowl, cover with a clean cloth and leave to rise in a warm place for about 1 hour or until doubled in size.

4 Knock back the dough and roll out to a 30 x 23 cm (12 x 9 inch) rectangle. Cover with the prunes and sprinkle over the lemon rind and sugar.

5 Roll up the dough from the longest edge like a Swiss roll and press down well to seal the edge. Cut into six thick slices and halve each slice diagonally. Place the slices, cut-side uppermost, in the prepared tin. Cover lightly with a clean cloth and leave to rise in a warm place for about 30 minutes or until the dough feels springy.

6 Bake in the oven at 190°C (375°F) mark 5 for about 30 minutes or until well risen and golden. Turn out of the tin on to a wire rack placed over a baking sheet. Gently remove the lining paper.

7 Mix the honey with the lemon juice and brush over the buns while still warm. Serve warm or cool. Wrap in foil and store in an airtight container for up to 2 days.

APRICOT
OAT CRUNCHIES

MAKES 12

75 g (3 oz) plain wholemeal flour	100 g (4 oz) polyunsaturated margarine
75 g (3 oz) rolled (porridge) oats	100 g (4 oz) dried apricots, soaked in cold water overnight
75 g (3 oz) raw cane demerara sugar	

1 Lightly grease a shallow oblong tin measuring 28 x 18 x 3.5 cm (11 x 7 x 1½ inches).

2 Mix together the flour, oats and sugar in a bowl. Rub in the margarine until the mixture resembles breadcrumbs.

3 Spread half the mixture over the base of the prepared tin, pressing it down evenly.

4 Drain and chop the apricots. Spread them over the oat mixture in the tin.

5 Sprinkle over the remaining crumb mixture and press down well. Bake in the oven at 180°C (350°F) mark 4 for 25 minutes until golden brown. Leave in the tin for about 1 hour until cold. Cut into bars to serve. Wrap in foil and keep in an airtight tin for 3-4 days if wished.

INDEX